NO DREAM IMPOSSIBLE

by
Nigel May

Grosvenor House
Publishing Limited

The right of Nigel May to be identified as the author
of this work has been asserted in accordance with Section 78
of the Copyright, Designs and Patents Act 1988

The book cover is copyright to Nigel May
Cover design by Brian Jones

This book is published by
Grosvenor House Publishing Ltd
Link House
140 The Broadway, Tolworth, Surrey, KT6 7HT.
www.grosvenorhousepublishing.co.uk

This book is a work of fiction. Any resemblance to
people or events, past or present, is purely coincidental.

A CIP record for this book
is available from the British Library

Paperback ISBN 978-1-83615-324-5
eBook ISBN 978-1-83615-325-2

To every person who feels total euphoria about a certain song contest.

This book is dedicated to you.

ACKNOWLEDGEMENTS

Douze points go to Alan for saving his kisses for me. To Andy Downs for shining a light on my dreams and making my mind up. To Viva La Lever for silver-sequinned euphoria. Hallelujah to Lottie for always A-Ba-Ni-Being the best of friends. To every single Euro star who has made my heart go ding-a-dong. And to the legendary Sandra Kim for serving a tune back in 1986 that still thrills me to this day. J'aime la vie! I love you all.

ABOUT THE AUTHOR

Hello there. Or I'm guessing I should say bonjour, hola or hallå seeing as I'm diving headfirst into the wonderful world of the *Eurovision Song Contest*. Welcome to *No Dream Impossible* by me, Nigel (Come What) May – my name is Nigel May but I had to add the 'Come What' as it would be rude not too seeing as it fits perfectly into my douze-points *Eurovision* loving existence.

This book is based at the totally fictional *Eurowide Song Contest*. It's not set at *Eurovision* and has nothing to do with *Eurovision* other than the fact that a lot of the characters in it are obsessed, like me, with the greatest show on earth – the glittery, boom-bang-a-banging world of *Eurovision*. I have been a fan of *Eurovision* ever since I first saw it on TV back in 1974 when ABBA romped to victory in Brighton (a town I now live in – I still get goosebumps every time I go to the Brighton Dome thinking, *Agnetha and the gang were on that stage!*). I loved the costumes, the strange and wondrous variety of songs and the clunky joyousness of the voting. Plus, I think a five-year-old me thought host Katie Boyle was the most glamourous of deities. I was hooked and have watched pretty much every year since. For me, *Eurovision* has been an obsession of many many decades. These days it's become an annual pilgrimage to *Eurovision* week if possible. To the host city and the euphoria and drama of the arena.

The drama that happens at *Eurowide* could never happen at *Eurovision*, it wouldn't be allowed, hence why the madness of *Eurowide* was born! This is my homage to my favourite song contest, a tale I could decorate with a gazillion *Eurovision* references and see if lifelong fans notice. Jemma La Vie is kind of me in another body. Her knowledge is my knowledge. Her love is my love. And her excitement about 1986 Eurovision winner Sandra Kim (a true legend) is my excitement. *No Dream Impossible* is a fun, camp and murderously saucy whodunnit story with enough celebrities and classic *Eurovision* mentions to keep even the most obsessive of songfest aficionados squealing. It's a glittery tongue-in-cheek world of dazzling divas, dodgy dance routines and deathly dealings. With added Russian grannies and hamster wheel too, of course... some things will never change, no matter what the contest. But it's nothing to do with *Eurovision*, okay! Let's all come together and enjoy the ride.

And that concludes the vote of my own personal jury. Love, Nigel x

Set in a time before Europe blasted into Space, Man...

PROLOGUE

How it began…

THE DIARY OF TONYA BABBIDGE, AGE 13

Oh my God, diary. I swear I have just found the coolest thing. At least I think it's cool. My mate, Char, does too so I guess I'm not the only weird one. I found this really ace song on an old CD that I bought at the car boot at Peterborough dog track. Like really flipping ace. I only went down there as I wanted to see if me and Char could find some second-hand roller skates as Mum says I can't have a new pair as according to her my feet are still growing. I think she's just being tight as she doesn't want to spend too much cash as she's saving up for a weekend at some holiday camp in Skegness. Plus, if my feet get any bigger, they'll need flippers not roller skates. They're already bigger than some of the boys in my class at school. I get them from Mum I guess, as Dad is always saying she has feet like a clown's. She has got whoppers. At least ours don't smell. Dad's give off a right whiff when he takes his slippers off. Any anyway, can't you make roller skates bigger and smaller?

So, this CD was 20p (BARGAIN!) and called Euro Energy *or something and I only bought it cos Char and me thought the man on the front cover was hot and he* had his top off showing all his big muscles. So I'm playing it, most of it was total rubbish, lots of noise and hardly any words, but then all of a sudden this bloody fabulous song comes on. It was a really fun, bouncy kind of tune. It was in a foreign language that I totally didn't understand. French apparently but it's nothing like the words I've learnt at school. So I listened to it three million times and fell in love. Well, I played it on repeat for about half an hour, so maybe not three million. I think I pissed off Mum playing it over and over but she's in my bad books until I get my skates so she can just do one.

If it was in English, the title of the song would be 'I Love Life' apparently. I read that when I looked it up on YouTube. The girl who sings it is like my age and from Belgium. That's near France, I think. I never concentrate in geography as it's too dull. Mr Ryder tried to teach us about some place called Hetty Pegler's Tump last week. I mean what the actual heck is a tump? A hole in the ground apparently. I wrote the name down as it's so weird. And they wonder why I lose interest. Like... duh.

But I am proper in love with this song. And the singer. Her outfit when she sings it is like something one of the dodgy market stalls in town sells – massive shoulder pads and a bow tie. I'd wear stuff like that if I could, but Char says we might not look that cool. I think I would. Sandra's her name, she was wearing it on stage to sing in front of hundreds of people and looked really great in a weird kinda way. It must be the fashion in Belgium. Or it was when Sandra was my age. She's much older now apparently. Well, she would be,

YouTube said the song was from the 1980s. Apparently she was in this competition where different countries send different songs to try and beat each other. What a daft idea. Well, that's what I thought at first. But then I started watching more and more videos online about this competition. It's called the Eurovision Song Contest *and it happens every year. It's been around since Grandad was a small boy. Yep, that long! Who knew? Lots of people apparently, just not me or Char. Until now.*

Char and I watched loads of it online. And she thinks it's cool too now. She likes Sandra as well but not as much as me, as she doesn't think she'd suit her shoulder pads. I must have watched hours of it today. Loads of different songs too. Some in languages that I had never even heard of. It was amazing. So many different styles. I've never seen anything like it before. Some were really good. Some were pants. None as good as Sandra though. She won the contest. Too right. I think it's the best song I've ever heard. Better than a lot of the rubbish people at school listen to. Even if I don't understand it. I'm gonna learn French and sing it at school. That'll impress my French teacher, Madame Zarra. That's not her real name, I heard one of the other teachers call her Nicola and she's not really French but it's what she calls herself in class to bring, what she says is 'a true flavour of France'. Snails and garlic apparently according to Char. It's pretty neat that Madame Zarra is changing her name though to be cool. I'd love to do that. Tonya Babbidge is not a cool and funky name in any way. One of the girls in our class is called Sasha. That's a cool name. I'd love to change mine.

I'm thinking that if I learn all about singer Sandra's home country, Belgium, then maybe I'll get a better mark in geography too. I could learn about all of the countries in Eurovision. I think I'm a Eurovision fan now. In fact I know I am. I keep watching. And I was smiling all the time when I was watching it. I spoke to Mum and she said I can watch the next one when it's on TV live, as long as it doesn't clash with something she likes. She also told me that most of the songs are 'shite'. Her words not mine. What does she know?

I am obsessed with Sandra. Her full name is Sandra Kim. She's my new thing. I want to sing her song and learn a dance routine and perform it. I'd do it on roller skates if I could. How cool would that be? If only Mum wasn't so bloody tight.

I thought I wanted to be dental nurse when I grow older as you can have free toothpaste and check-ups, but now I think I want to win a song contest when I'm grown up. I'm a tiny bit older than Sandra was when she won already so I had better get cracking. I'm going to be 14 next birthday. Maybe I can sing the song at my birthday party. If Mum lets me have one. She'll say she's still saving for Skegness knowing her. Tightwad.

Bye, diary! Loving life, or as Sandra Kim would say, J'Aime La Vie. Love Tonya (yep, might change that one day) x.

How it continued... Several years later in the same person's diary...

Oh my God, diary, guess what's happened! There's a new song contest being launched and the industry experts are looking for fresh young talent to represent the UK. I'm young-ish... and I'm usually fresh, unless I've managed to tread in something icky which I did this morning on the way to Zumba. Size of a giant Toblerone it was and it stank big-time. How I missed it on the pavement in the first place I don't know. Must have come from a dog the size of a donkey. That stinker and my awks jiggling at Zumba left me far from fresh afterwards, I can tell you. But a long soak in the tub with my unicorn pouf bath bomb left me fresh as anything. And a little stained in places by the pouf's dayglo colouring. That'll teach me to buy cheap ones from the back of the pub. Some of my bits are a right funny colour now.

I trod in that heap of doggy-doo because I had my head buried in my music magazine. That's where I saw the announcement. NEW EUROPEAN SONG CONTEST LAUNCHED. If ever there was a headline to grab my attention then that is it. Apparently because Eurovision *has been such a massive hit – why wouldn't it be? It's the best thing like evah – somebody is now launching the* Eurowide Song Contest. *It's so even more songs can be heard and other countries can enter too. The first one is gonna be held next year. They're looking for people to put songs forward and fresh young talent. Not established names. Well it hardly worked for Bonnie and Engelbert did it? Fresh young talent. That's me. This is my chance. Young... although I won't see 18 again... and fresh. I'm gonna write a song, see what I can do. I just need to try and scrub some of that pouf off first. My big toe is pink and one of my boobs is looking a bit yellow. I'm off to scrub my bits now. Laters.*

Chapter 1

How it's going now...

"...look at me, I'm a beautiful creature..."

'Please don't let me say anything ridiculous, swear like a trooper, or let rip with a nervous fart,' smiled Jemma La Vie. She scanned her eyes proudly across the width of wall-to-wall tables before her and simultaneously attempted to yank out her piano-wire thong from being eaten by her somewhat ample backside underneath her dress as she did so. A camera flash popped behind her. 'Shit,' she grumbled to herself, 'that'll be the front page of some rag tomorrow. I can see the headline now: "UK'S JEMMA FINDS ANOTHER BUM NOTE AT EUROWIDE".'

Jemma should have known better by now. She did know this kind of song contest inside out after all. It had been her passion for as long as she could remember. And now her lifelong dreams were coming true as the first UK hopeful for the newly launched *Eurowide Song Contest*. Ever since she'd been plucked from obscurity by a 'talented' TV jury of two mahogany-hued glamour models, a porn-actor-turned-reality-TV-star and a himbo of a celebrity chef to be this year's UK's entry for the glitter-dipped debut songfest that was *Eurowide* her formerly normal existence had been turned upside down. Nothing was private anymore. That was the payoff for capturing the jury's vote (although what any of them knew about music and song contests was beyond Jemma) and more importantly the adoration of a million-plus fans (mostly gay men to be fair) across the UK with her self-penned, oh-so-catchy mind-worm of a song, 'Beep the World (Hear my Horn)'. She could barely adjust her underwiring these days without somebody taking a photo, which was unfortunate as she tended to do it a lot. The woes of a fuller top rack and a wince-inducing ill-fitting bra, she guessed.

It had always been Jemma's fantasy to one day represent her country in a song contest, just like the one that she'd watched religiously on telly every year since the life-altering moment she'd discovered it after buying a CD with a *Euro* song on it at a car boot sale. She was and always had been obsessed ever since. Her knowledge of *Euro* hits was now encyclopaedic. She struggled to really remember a time when she wasn't dancing around her bedroom with the front room window nets wrapped around her waist pretending to be Celine Dion or telling her dad that it was okay to nip to the local Co-op in her bare feet because that's how Sandie Shaw did things three million years ago. Although she was pretty sure Sandie never ended up with glutinous lumps of dog poop between her toes like Jemma did. Jemma hadn't been born or even thought about for most of *Eurovision's* long and lustrous life, but it was her thing. And it always would be. Some people bird-watched, she *Euro*-watched.

There was a bit of Jemma that actually thought that *Euro* glitter was in her DNA. In her mind, had she been able to and had she known about it, she'd have probably been tapping her toes and *diggy-loo-diggy-leying* inside her mum Shirley's womb, but she couldn't remember that far back. Shame really, she'd read in a book that babies can apparently dream when they're in the womb. If that was true then her wombly (was that a word? Jemma didn't think so, but hey...) dreams would have been of taking centre stage and belting out a frothy *Euro*-hit for the entire planet to feast on. Key changes, sequins, sparkle... and more than *ooh-ah, just a little bit* of glamour of course.

But even for a mega fan like Jemma, nothing had prepared her for the constant inconvenient press invasion into her life. If she'd seen one sweaty-pitted or camel-hoofed photo of herself in *Reveal* or *New!* magazine or online on every *Euro*-obsessed fan's vlog or TikTok feed then she'd seen at least a cringe-making few dozen. *Why me*, she asked herself. You never saw Beyoncé or Ariana Grande flaunting a knicker-escaping ass-crack or a face redder and rounder than beetroot when they were working out and hanging with their honeys in Hollywood, did you?

But then, in fairness, Beyoncé or Ari weren't likely to be swinging a kettlebell or reworking a Joe Wicks workout in the middle of a playing field in Jemma's Fenland hometown, Whittlesey. Nor would pop royalty be trying to avoid smashed beer bottles and the puddles of yet another East Anglian downpour as she did so. Trying to shift a few pounds in La La Land seemed a lot more glamorous – a full-face of make-up and a pearly-white "I'm-dead-famous-don'tcha-know" smile were obviously given out with gym memberships in Tinseltown. In certain quarters of Whittlesey, sometimes teeth themselves were beyond sparse, which is why Jemma had not exactly been expert at coping with her "overnight success".

Her rise to fame had been meteoric to say the least. It was all because of that *Eurowide* advert in her music magazine. One minute she'd been serving battered cod to battered punters being turfed out of The Pig and Pickle pub and falling into the Chips Ahoy Fish Bar (apparently "bar" made it sound better than your run-of-the-mill, greasy-floored, peely-wallpapered fish 'n' chip shop) on a Saturday night. The next... here she was walking into the press room of the inaugural *Eurowide Song Contest* in a purpose-built scout hut in Ermpit, the beyond-dull 60-shades-of-grey city in the most easterly tip of Rottimoldovia, the host nation for the songfest.

Sending her demo tape and a song she'd written into the producers of TV's *Euro Starburst* as instructed by the ad was the smartest move she'd ever made. She was shortlisted as one of six finalists and before she knew it the "BIG GIRL WITH THE BIG VOICE" (they must have deliberated for days at *The Sun* over that headline after seeing her size 18 figure) was sharing the chat show sofa with Graham Norton, talking the joys of pickled eggs on *Saturday Kitchen* and waving more Union Jacks than *Last Night Of The Proms*. And now here she was in a city that 219 Tripadvisor reviews professed was one of the most boring places in Europe. But to Jemma, it didn't matter. She could have been on Pluto for all she cared. As long as she was on Planet *Eurowide*, then she was sure to be dizzy with glee and enjoying every minute.

And what made the entire experience even better was that she had her best mate and backing singer, Charlene

Grills, by her side for company. Charlene, or Char, for short, which made her Char Grills, a fact she loved as she always told potential boyfriends that she was "cheap to run and would heat up at the push of a button" (causing Brian Blessed-style belly laughs from her and Jemma, but strangely no one else), had four main things in common with Jemma – they both hailed from Whittlesey, they both shared a deep-seated love of song contests, they both had pairs of lungs that could challenge any wannabe Mariah or Whitney (they both still blubbed belting out 'I Will Always Love You' on a karaoke night out) and they both had backsides that were more akin to The Weather Girls. If it wasn't Jemma winkle-picking her knickers from her own ample butt cheeks, then you could guarantee that Char would be doing hers. But as lead vocalist on 'Beep the World' and the one who was carrying the hopes of the UK on her shoulders for the contest, any shameful magazine photo of a shifty tit-scratch or a satisfying nostril-excavation was always of Jemma and not of her backing-singing best buddy. A fact that Char loved. Being the backing singer meant that she had the fun and fame, but not the shame.

'So what are we here for, exactly?' quizzed Char, oblivious to the camera flash that had just perfectly captured her best mate's backside.

'It's meet-the-press day. And you're here to keep me company and keep me sane, while I paint on a smile and answer questions from a gazillion different journalists. Doubtless it will be the same questions but in loads of different accents. Hopefully I can come up with enough interesting quotes to make me front page news in every newspaper from Ermpit to Reykjavik or, as Scooch would say, *all the way from Paris to Tallinn, Helsinki onto Prague, don't matter where we are... yeah yeah ye-ah...'*

Char grinned widely and started humming. 'Gotta love a slice of classic Scooch. Although sadly one of the few tunes that even you and I couldn't persuade arsey DJ Dirk to play for us at FagButts. Grumpy sod.'

Ah FagButts, the girls' favourite nightclub for a debauched night out back home. It was really called Fabrics but the girls had renamed it as they spent most of their time freezing their barely covered bodies off whilst trying to impress the gangs of lads outside whilst enjoying a crafty ciggie.

'But Dirk does give us queen Loreen and a Katrina dance remix on rotation when we flirt, so he's not all bad. And he's a great snogger,' smirked Jemma.

Jemma whistled with buoyant anticipation at the mass of press tables in front of her. 'Right, I've got to make a good job of this. We haven't properly won this kind of contest since T-Rexes roamed the earth so it's about time we did, don't you think?'

'If anyone can bring it home, you can, Jemma. Shouldn't cute little press officer, Daniel, be here with you for this, Jem? Or at least one of the many fussy delegation people that seem to follow us around constantly,' asked Char. 'Daniel will make sure you say the right thing. Not that you don't know what to say. How many times did we play make believe, back in your bedroom after school, that one of us had won a contest like this and that the other one was the ever-smiley host asking how magical we felt. At least a hundred.'

'I hope I say the right thing. But if my mouth is open, you know me, I can normally put my size eights sole-deep in it, eh? As for Daniel, well he would have been here except for the fact that he's been *throwing up his hoop* all morning – his words, not mine. He's as sick as a dog. Poor boy. Apparently the tequila cocktails and the local fish eye canapés at last night's welcome party were not a good mix for our Ryan Gosling lookalike record company PR. He phoned me at the hotel this morning. He's trying to keep his sickness secret from the rest of the delegation as it would be frowned upon. It was Daniel who suggested you come along to keep me on the straight and narrow as the others in the delegation are doing urgent telly stuff to introduce the contest to everyone. This was Daniel's bag. But... straight and narrow? Fat chance, eh!'

Both girls collapsed into a fit of giggles. They often did.

'He's going to meet us afterwards. He must be so delicate. Personally, I loved the canapés. They were like really strong crabsticks. Right tasty and a real treat. Mind you, my guts have known about it this morning.' She wafted one hand up and down in front of her face and held her nose with the other.

'D'you know my mum still won't have crab in the house ever since falling in love with Mr Krabs on *Spongebob*. She thinks it's inhumane to serve something that cute. It's a sodding cartoon for heaven's sake, Mother.'

For the next three hours, Jemma and Char sat at the table set aside for the UK entrant and answered a succession of *Euro*-based questions. Well, at least Jemma did. Char sat and silently scored the journalists out of 12, marking them for looks, fashion flare and accent comedy value. By the 20th interview, Jemma knew every question by heart. *How has life changed since winning back in the UK? How does it feel to have the whole of the UK behind you for Eurowide? What did she think of Ermpit? Had she had a chance to discover more about Rottimoldovia?*

Jemma's answers were becoming equally uniform. *Life has changed greatly – I love it* (truth). *I intend to win for the good people of the UK for putting their faith in me* (despite certain quarters still banging on about a predictable political voting system as ever, but also 100% true). *Ermpit seemed a wonderful city full of colour and vibrancy* (far from true unless deathly drab was deemed to be the new vibrant). *Rottimoldovia was a place that she longed to visit again* (big fat lie – she'd rather spend a fortnight's stay in Wentworth Prison getting picked on by The Freak than actually come back, unless it was for *Eurowide* of course, but for holiday destinations she was much more a Benidorm or Magaluf kinda girl).

The last interview of the session was with a weasely journalist from the hosting country. He sported a sleeve of demonic tattoos and those big hula-hoop things in his ears that stretched his ears lobes to the size of Wagon Wheels.

'Nul points,' mused Char. There was definitely an air of grubby menace about his appearance and the frosty, glazed expression on his face suggested that he was as bored of asking questions as Jemma now was of answering them. His direct and somewhat offbeat form of probing took Jemma totally by surprise. After of series of reporters with clown-sized smiles and an abundance of kids' telly presenter cheeriness he was at complete odds with his predecessors.

He dived straight in without introduction. 'Ze UK never vin zis kinda competition. You are famed for coming near ze bottom most years at zee things, yes.'

If it hadn't been for a nameplate stating his nation attached to his grimy T-shirt (did they not have wash tabs in this country?) the girls would have been none the wiser as to where his highly rich and gigglesome accent (*douze points for that*, thought Char) came from.

'Well I intend to be the first to bring the *Eurowide* crown home. We have had mixed fortunes over the years in the other contest but there have been many great wins,' started Jemma. 'Look at the joyous Bucks Fizz back in the 80s for a start...'

'But not for ze longest period,' he snapped, cutting her off in mid flow. 'What about zis song you wrote and sing... it is, vot is ze vord? Stoopid.'

'Prick,' coughed Char, hoping Jemma would hear her.

She did. A knowing smile curled across her lips. 'I'm proud of the song, I wrote it myself,' said Jemma. 'I think it's very *Euro*. My country seems to like it. In fact—' She was going to tell him that it was currently sitting at number 14 in the UK charts but he cut her short.

'Many ozzer vomen here, zey are much healzier than you. You are big voman. Zey zing about love. You find it hard, yes? Finding ze love?'

Char let out a hiss of incredulous disgust from between her teeth. The journalist had shot from quirkily annoying to downright rude quicker than you could say "Lulu".

A little piece of Jemma wished that press officer Daniel had been sitting alongside her. Or someone from the UK delegation. Someone would have advised her what to do and how to handle the question. A much more substantial, minxier piece of her was glad that Daniel was not. She was already way beyond stopping. Like a spaceship ready to blow, she launched.

'I am more than happy with the way I look, thank you. There are lots of ladies here skinnier than me and good luck to them. Ladies come in all different shapes and sizes but we all have one thing in common. We have a brain. Brains are awesome, I wish everyone had one, but obviously you don't. Is that common in your country? If you're a prime example of the pathetic specimens around here, then I'm pretty sure it is. I like my body. In fact, I intend to maintain my fat beautiful ass for as long as possible so that way more people can kiss it! Yourself included…'

As Jemma kicked back her chair as forcefully as she could to convey her anger but without enough oomph to draw attention from other tables, she turned on her heels and slapped herself on the backside to emphasise her point. As she did so, she accidentally let out a small yet very audible fart. She cringed. Char let out a deep laugh and marched off after her best mate out of the press room. The snidey reporter was still trying to work out what Jemma had said and done as the odour of her departing gift hit his nostrils.

Was that fish eye he could smell?

Chapter 2

"...pounding away, pounding away,
won't you be mine..."

Record company PR Daniel Spirit lay in his hotel bed and stared at the ceiling above him. Despite the fact that it was painted in the dullest shade a decorator could lay hands on – a dirty nicotine yellow was how Daniel would describe it – it seemed a better option than to stare at the man alongside him in his bed. How the hell had he let that one crawl between the sheets with him?

Daniel could only blame the cocktails at last night's *Eurowide* Teal Carpet welcome reception. They'd given him more than a generous eye when it came to scouting for trade... a lot more. The heady mix of Rottimoldovian gin and some red viscous treacle of a mixer had obviously gone straight to the 30-year-old's head and sent his sexual libido through the roof while plummeting his ability to distinguish a good-looking fella so far south it could possibly warm itself in the fires of Hell.

What had he been thinking? He was supposed to be working, not acting like he was on a mission-to-pull night out at his local gay bar. The man alongside him was what the gay world referred to as a prawn. He had an amazingly tasty body – meaty and delicious to feast upon – but you'd really want to pull the head off before doing anything with it. Why hadn't Daniel stayed professional? How had he let this happen? As the press officer for the first *Eurowide* UK entry he was supposed to part of the team guiding Jemma and chaperoning her to keep her out of trouble. As it was, he'd been the one who had sailed into troubled waters faster than an erogenous-zone-seeking-torpedo – blitzing his morals, his professionalism, and his usual sense of only hooking up with red-hot-model-fit stunners to complete buggery at the same time. He'd already been reprimanded by the head of the UK delegation for getting more than merry at one of the pre-show parties across Europe. He guessed his latest absence, if he got caught out, would go down like a lead balloon.

He'd had to lie to Jemma about feeling sick to get out of the press conference. Not that he felt particularly perky. His skull felt like someone was circling a Wall of Death around it and his legs felt thick with fatigue. Jemma would be fine though, what harm could happen? She knew what to say after all. She may have been a bit rough around the edges on occasion, but she was hugely endearing. At least that was what his brain was telling him, even if deep down he didn't believe it.

No, he'd have to bite the bullet and attempt to shift the snoring carcass alongside him as soon as possible. There was a whole day of interviews, rehearsals, performances and photo opps ahead for Jemma and he needed to be there for her. It was his bloody job after all – and it was one he intended to keep.

Finally tearing his eyes away from the ceiling, he slipped himself out from under the bed sheet and walked around to the other side of the bed. He was naked apart from a torn open condom packet that seemed to have stuck itself like a sneering souvenir to his hips. If he'd had his legs in the air all night that would explain the dull ache in his thighs. He brushed the packet off, trying to erase the memories of what he knew had occurred, despite knowing full well he had loved every moment of it. A few drinks and the glimpse of a heaving pectoral muscle and Daniel's legs would have been in the air faster than a jump jet. The soundtrack to Daniel's sex life wouldn't be "Rock Bottom", it would be "Total Bottom".

'Er… hello… it's time to get up.'

Daniel stabbed at the man's body with an urgent finger. The snoring stopped momentarily and the man, who'd been sleeping on his side, rolled onto his back. His body was carved to perfection. Daniel was an avid gym bunny and was proud of his own toned appearance, but this guy was like RoboGay. Two exquisitely chiselled pecs, his skin a deep shade of olive, sat on top of not just a six-pack but what was more like a ten-pack. Daniel had seen more fat on display at London Fashion Week. He possessed a sizable centrepiece too, not that Daniel was a size queen. Well not much. Not that he'd admit anyway. Maybe a bit. Maybe 100 per cent.

But then there was his face. It was interesting to say the least. Interesting in the same way you'd look at a toddler's painting and think, *oh bless, they tried their best but the end result is a bit messy and I'm not quite sure what it's supposed to be*. To say that he'd not been at the front of the line when good looks were dished out would be akin to saying that Conchita Wurst was rather partial to the odd sequin. There was the pock-marked skin, slightly droopy eye, hairline scar across the cheek, crooked nose. The list went on. Daniel liked a face with character, but this was a fissog with more shady characters than *EastEnders*.

And Daniel had slept with him. This had to stay hidden. Had anyone seen him leave the party with him? He prayed to God Jemma hadn't, or Char. They'd never let him live it down. And as for any of the delegation, they'd crucify him. Daniel dreamt of promotion, not humiliation. Surely Jemma and Char had put out before just because a bloke had a fit body, even if his face was fit-inducing. He'd just deny it, whatever they said. Ignorance would be bliss. Even if he couldn't stop mulling over the fact that the sex had been blissful. Better than any model catwalk trade he'd copped off with lately.

The man in the bed finally stirred, his eyes opening. Daniel smiled awkwardly, unsure how to react.

He smiled up at Daniel and said, 'Morning, sexy boy,' his accent rich and layered with more than a hint of exotic. English was obviously not his first language. He checked his watch as he spoke. 'Shit, I must leave, Latreena will kill me, I should have been with her hours ago. She wants me. She will not forgive me despite our years together. I see you later, yes, that is good. Thank you for much fun.' He leapt from the bed, retrieved his clothes that lay in a pile on the floor and ran towards the door. Before opening it, he turned back and grabbed Daniel with his huge tree trunk arms, planted a kiss on his lips and hugged him. It was actually more of a squeeze and winded Daniel somewhat. 'You nice, I like...' said the man.

Still naked he ran towards the door, opened it and disappeared out of sight. Two seconds later he reappeared.

'That's the bathroom...' offered Daniel.

'Thank you, goodbye, handsome.' Again he ran towards another door. He opened it and just stopped himself in time from running full pelt into an ironing board and a stack of spare toilet rolls.

'Er... that's the storage cupboard,' said Daniel. 'I suggest you try...' He pointed towards the third and final door leading from his hotel room.

'Thank you,' said the slab of muscle. And again he ran towards the door, flustered by his own ignorance. He yanked it open and ran off, still naked and carrying his clothes in his arms.

A shrill female scream sounded from the corridor outside Daniel's room. Followed by a guttural belly laugh. *I guess somebody just saw that rather impressive appendage*, mused Daniel, glad that the risk of morning after small talk was gone. The man had an awesome body, indeed from the neck down he was off the scale, but he obviously had a girlfriend – was that who he mentioned, Daniel hadn't been concentrating – and was playing away behind her back. Daniel would tick it off as drunken pre-contest revelry and fun and hopefully their paths wouldn't cross again. That face wasn't easily forgotten (how could it be given its *quirky* nature?) but the body and the sex were on another level! Onwards. He needed to get back to work.

He continued with his thoughts. *Three attempts to leave a hotel room and still you do it bollock-naked. How stupid can you be? Christ, sometimes I look at people and think, really, that's the sperm that won?* he could have just asked. *Obviously in a hurry to get back to lady LaToya, or Lucrezia, or whatever the girlfriend is called,* he said to himself.

As he walked towards the bathroom, he felt a squidge beneath his bare foot. It was cold and wet. He looked down.

'Okay, so that's where the condom got to.'

Chapter 3

"…like a queen in all her glory… viva le diva…"

'So, you slagged off every male in the host nation the minute my back is turned? This is not a cool move, Jemma!' Daniel was more than a little incensed. Not only with worry about his own lack of professionalism, but by Jemma's recount of what had happened at the press conference. 'You are going to have to do some serious grovelling and licking ass to make up for this. I'll try and stop anything too harsh hitting the papers before the contest, but I can't promise.'

'The man was a total prick. A complete fattist. He'll die of constipation he was so full of shit!' countered Jemma, annoyed at Daniel's annoyance.

'Totes,' concurred Char, sitting behind Daniel and her best friend in the second row of Ermpit's specially erected Johnny Logan Coliseum, which would be the site for the contest in just a few days' time. At the moment it seemed to be still in the early stages of completion and was buzzing with bemused tattooed, sweaty-pitted workmen trying to fathom out just how a stage, enough light bulbs to put Las Vegas to shame, and seating for 12,000 eager *Eurowide* fans would miraculously come together for a week of live shows. Even Eurovision winner Johnny Logan, strangely still an entertainment deity in Rottimoldovia despite having only set foot in the country twice in his entire career, had remarked that things "didn't even look half-finished" at the venue ribbon-cutting ceremony the day before. Not that he'd lose sleep about it after pocketing a sizable lump of the local currency for his time and Irish charm.

Jemma let out a harrumph of vexation at Daniel. 'Well, if you hadn't been shacking up with Uncle Fester, we'd have been fine, wouldn't we? We all saw you leave with him last night. Quite the pairing...'

'Tale as old as time... *Beauty and the Beast*...' sing-songed Char, sniggering as she did so.

'For God's sake...' stated Daniel, his cheeks turning the colour of a rich Merlot. 'Never let me drink again...' His mind was still on the sex though. That was something he didn't want to forget.

'And never leave me alone to answer questions from hideous journalists again please,' volleyed Jemma.

'Done,' said Daniel.

'Anyway, you do know who Sister Steroid is, don't you?' asked Jemma.

The blank look and raised eyebrow from Daniel showed that he didn't.

'His name is Igor. How perfect is that. His name couldn't be more meat-head if he tried. He's the bodyguard of that cow of a Swiss entry, Latreena. This year's diva. Bombshell looks but with a time-bomb attitude. She has a death stare that could sour even the sweetest Swiss chocolate. I've been so nice and polite to everyone this week, weasely journalist excepted, as this is the pinnacle of our dreams to be here, but when I went up to tell her that I loved her song she literally blanked me. Like full on "talk to the hand, the Botoxed face ain't listening". How blinking rude is that. Mind you, I would kill for that gown of hers. It's like H-to-T bling... head to toe.'

Daniel didn't need to ask which gown as he let his eye line follow the direction in which Jemma was pointing. The shafts of TRON-like light he encountered almost hurt his pupils. Wafting into the auditorium in a dress that literally lit up like the Blackpool Illuminations was a vision of total glamour. The hair thick, dark and shinily lustrous. The dress a retina-singeing collection of tiny crystals. The make-up a masterclass of rouged cheeks and deep red lips. Even if the skin it rested on was more than a little taught and wrinkle-free for a woman approaching 40. Her hands fly-swatted non-existent people out the way as she moved towards the stage. Not entirely necessary, seeing as Igor was indeed by her side, a mountainous mass of muscle protecting her from any unwanted approaches. Doubtless he would be useful had they been in some heaving Geneva nightspot and were working their way through to VIP but amongst a group of workmen who didn't give a stuff and a host of fellow contestants it hardly seemed necessary. But once a diva, always a diva... and a diva always needs to make an entrance.

'That's daywear?' questioned Daniel, looking at his watch. It was a little after one in the afternoon. 'There's less bling on a Kardashian sister photoshoot. And yep... there's Igor... just peachy. So that was the woman he was talking about. How did I not know this? How had I not spotted him at one of the pre-contest parties around Europe?' His tone was steeped in confusion, even if his eyes were immediately drawn to the bodyguard's monumental chest and legs the size of rolls of loft insulation. Maybe he was a new arrival to Latreena's team.

'Rumour has it that diva Latreena has insisted with contest bosses that she sings first in today's soundchecks and rehearsals. Apparently, *Madame Le Mutton* waits for no one,' said Jemma. She and Char had nicknames for everyone. 'Hence why everyone else here is sat twiddling their *Euro*-thumbs.'

It was true, a quick scan at the seats behind them revealed the smorgasbord of contestants due to rehearse today dotted around them in various states of smiley numbness through to snarly impatience.

There was the German entry, the heavy rock band, Die Bolzen (literal translation, The Bolts, although they said it meant "The Studs" because of, A; the copious ones on their leather jackets and, B; telling people that they had a combined sexual libido the size of the Berlin Tower). Indeed, their *Eurowide* hotel room had already been nicknamed "Checkpoint Charlie" by contest groupies due to the amount of sex, drugs and rock 'n' roll that happened behind its doors. Enveloped in leather and always easy to locate due to the fact that each of the four long-haired members seemed to be competing with each other as to who could have the worst body odour, they all sat either air-guitaring with their fingers or devil-horning them at any passing female. Their lack of personal hygiene was ironic seeing as their song, apparently a guitar-smothered tale of bringing Europe together through the joy of peace, unity and shouty lyrics, was called "The Sweet Smell Of Europe". It was actually one of the favourites to win the contest even if its lyrical content was somewhat dodgy in parts.

Sitting mercifully away from Die Bolzen, given their BO-woes, was the Swedish entry, Bjorn Bjork. A six-foot-three tower of lean, mean smiling machine. Teeth whiter than icecaps and eyes bluer than the Swedish archipelago, 20-year-old Bjorn looked more Swedish than Ikea, ABBA and meatballs all wrapped together in a Swedish flag with a sign saying "Property of Sweden" hanging above it. With his trademark blue and yellow neckerchief-come-cravat wrapped around his neck and his spray-on sateen-trousered legs crossed Bjorn casually blew his college-kid fringe away from his eyes and waited patiently for his turn to sing. He was a vision of wholesome, blond, butter-wouldn't-melt-in-your-mouth goodness in platform heels. If only people knew…

Sitting just behind Jemma, Char and Daniel were the Turkish contestants, Baran and Meli, a married couple now in their late 40s who had been solidly working their way through the Turkish sardines-in-a-basket low-rent cabaret market, singing their folky, jokey songs at every sticky-floored dive from Ankara to Istanbul and beyond for the past two decades. They were giving their country a welcome return to song contests after many years of absence. The reason was purely that their country's newly elected president was a power-crazed mega *Euro* fan and insisted his country enter the new contest due to the escalating costs of doing the other one and nobody else actually being that bothered.

Their names translated into English as "Rain" and "Honey", which was more than apt considering she found him incredibly wet and unlikable and she was quite thick and made him feel sick. They had been on the point of divorcing and going their separate ways when they'd been spotted by a Turkish TV exec who was looking for people to star on his new telly show featuring people at home reviewing that week's TV programmes. Their sulky, snippy way with each other made them an overnight success and before they could even contemplate putting pen to divorce papers they were asked to represent their country at *Eurowide*, singing the beyond lyrically-banal, but highly traditional, "La Goes Up, La Goes Down, La in Every Euro Town". It made The Cheeky Girls look like Coldplay. But with added belly dance of course.

Baran And Meli were now obliged to smile happily and sing melodiously for three minutes of hip-swaying nonsense to keep their president happy but as soon as the last note sounded it was back to black moods and put-downs a shade-throwing drag queen would be proud of. And their stern, disinterested faces as they waited for their turn to sing showed it.

'Those two from Turkey look as miserable as a wet weekend in Cromer,' commented Char, scanning across at Baran and Meli as they scowled venomously at each other like cats fighting over a hapless rodent. 'Don't you think, Jem? Mind you, she's definitely had some work done.'

Char let her eyes drift across the other contestants at today's sound check – the Pavarotti-sized Dane with Viking beard, the slick Italian crooner with a rather too-penetrating gaze that he would use on any passing female, the excitable Latvian boy band, the aloof French torch singer, the Maltese child star desperate to win with the painted-on smile, the confrontational Bosnian female trio.

'They're an eclectic weird bunch, aren't they?' she mused.

Her words fell on deaf ears as both Jemma and Daniel were too busy watching Latreena as she sashayed hypnotically towards the stage, Igor by her side.

'I sing now?' she snapped. It was definitely more of a demand than a question. 'Is my disco ball ready? It is in position is it not?'

The disco ball in question was a massive one, virtually the size of the Matterhorn, hanging above the two *Eurowide* hosts positioned on the Rottimoldovian stage. It was very much part of the dazzling production for Latreena's song and would rotate in sparkly perfection above her as she sang.

The two hosts were busy running through their opening lines on the stage. This year's presenters were Szymon Rybak, a former *Eurovision* song contest entrant who had been placed 23rd five years before and Weronika Seksi who had reigned supreme on *Rottimoldovia's Got Talent* the previous year with her body-grinding ways and Lopez-esque vocals but had been overlooked for *Eurowide* host nation contestant duties in favour of her already successful singing twin sister, Wiktoria Seksi.

Not that Weronika was bitter… much. At least she'd bagged presentation duties, not that she was particularly skilled in her delivery. It was the dashingly debonair Szymon who was definitely carrying her.

Any chance of the two hosts carrying on with a much-needed practise of their chirpy *Euro* banter disappeared once diva Latreena marched onto the stage and dismissed both Szymon and Weronika with the nonchalant flick of a manicured finger. Nobody crossed the chanteuse, not even the show hosts.

Seething within, but with professional *Euro*-wide smiles emblazoned across their faces, Szymon and Weronika scuttled off the stage.

Having placed herself centre stage Latreena dismissed buff bodyguard Igor to go and sit in front of the stage to watch her – something he was highly joyful about as it allowed him to park himself down next to Daniel, much to Jemma's amusement. Was that a wonky-eyed wink Igor gave as he sat down next to a blushing Daniel? She did believe it was.

Not sure what to do with himself and where to look, Daniel smiled feebly and turned to Jemma. 'When are you on?' He knew the answer but needed to do something to take his mind off Glad the Impaler breathing rather excitedly and mucky-phone-call-like alongside him.

'We're on after the wailing girl trio from Bosnia Hurtzmyvagina,' said Jemma.

'That's Herzegovina,' deadpanned Daniel. Was that Igor's fingers he could feel tracing their way along his outer thigh? His voice wavered slightly as he spoke.

'You say it your way, I'll say it mine,' laughed Jemma. 'Now, a bit of hush please, I want to hear Latreena. The bookies are pushing this up the odds and saying she's a strong contender to win. "Crush Me With Your Love" has already been a massive hit in Switzerland. It's a classic ballsy ballad. Ticks every box when it comes to heartfelt angst, massively long notes and key changes.' She smiled at Daniel, whose face appeared to be turning more puce by the second. 'You just carry on with your GrindR hook-up.'

'Not funny in any way, shape or form,' sneered Daniel, as the lights around him dimmed as a sole spotlight searched out Latreena on the main stage.

Twinkles of glittery light danced off both the massive disco ball and her dress as it found her luminous presence. A hushed expectancy blanketed those gathered in the arena. The initial rousing orchestral notes of "Crush Me With Your Love" filled the air. Latreena raised her arms aloft, flamboyant to a fault and began to sing.

It was pure Bond theme tune eleganza.

'I wanted you, you wanted me,

There was a thing we couldn't see…

That you would crush me with your love.'

Latreena sang for all her might, her vocals drenching those looking on with their power.

'Gotta say it again, honey, she sure does have a fine set of pipes,' whispered Char, leaning forward to convey her opinion to Jemma. 'She is slaying those notes.'

'Shhhh.'

Jemma was lost in the song. So deep not even the most industrious of Boy Scouts would've found her. For the next two and a half minutes, Jemma, just like everyone else listening immersed herself into the honey-rich crystal-noted world of Latreena's song. She may have been famous for her bounty of bitching but her pitching was perfect. The diva was a definite threat come the final if she made it through her semi and Jemma couldn't see that there would be any doubting that. She was evidently a highly sexy threat too, judging by the way two members of Die Bolzen were blatantly grabbing their denim-clad crotches.

Char was obviously not so enraptured, her interest not managing to last for the full song. She tapped Jemma on the shoulder again during the penultimate verse. 'How many thousands of euros do you think she spent on that dress, Jem? I bet I could get it knocked up for under a tenner by that dodgy woman at Whittlesey market who can run up anything with a needle and a length of fabric. I might see if I can find a stretch of something sparkly on eBay.'

'Will you shut it, Char!' snipped Jemma only semi-jokingly. 'I want to see if she can hold the end note. It's orgasmic.' She let out a short breath. 'Here it comes…'

As Latreena reached the climax of her vocals, she drew breath before launching into the final words. 'And now I know that you will crush me with your love… crush me!'

As she sang the words "crush me" her voice grew louder and stronger, elongating the note, raising her hands in euphoric delight. 'Meeeeeeee!'

And then it happened, as quick as anything you've ever witnessed. The huge disco ball overhead came crashing down and with an all-shattering, all flattening force, landed directly on Latreena and rocked from side to side. She didn't finish the note. She couldn't. Her breath had gone. For good.

Cries of, 'Mein Gott!' sounded from Die Bolzen, two of them still fondling their own personal *bratwursts*, a high-pitched squeal came from Bjorn Bjork, his hand shooting up to his neckerchief in horror, and both Baran and Meli leapt to their feet in shock as the lights went back on around the auditorium and people rushed to the stage. A Maltese child star began crying. Both Jemma and Char were catching flies with their mouths wide open at what they both just witnessed.

As all gathered stared at the boulder-sized disco ball, it continued to move and then rolled away towards the side of the stage, as if trying to escape the horror.

It revealed a gooey mass of limbs, sequins and blood. Enough blood to know that Latreena was way beyond just needing a plaster or a couple of paracetamols.

'Fuck a duck, Daniel, she's dead!' cried Jemma. 'Crushed by her own disco ball!'

Daniel could only muster a winded gasp as Igor wrapped his arms around him and bear hugged him to within an inch of his life. Tears running down his face, poor Igor was doing some crushing of his own.

Chapter 4

"…once I'm reborn, I rise up to the sky…"

Eurowide pandemonium had kicked in. Unsurprisingly, the sound checks and rehearsals were put on hold after Latreena's flatter than flat final performance. With the pressing matter of a few hundred dislodged crystals and a couple of pints of blood to mop away from the stage, all other acts were dismissed and Jemma returned to her hotel room, suddenly at a shocking loss for things to do. She prayed that the contest would still go ahead despite the terrible accident. What would the head of the EWU – the Eurowide Union, the people organising the contest, have to say? This was hardly good publicity for your first attempt at a song contest. She would sit and wait for Daniel to call with instructions. That's if he ever managed to extract himself from the constrictor-like clutches of an inconsolable Igor. Who knew a Muscle Mary could produce so many tears?

Jemma felt unusually glum. This wasn't supposed to happen at the contest of her dreams. It was supposed to be all la la la and halle-flipping-lujah. She was in shock for Latreena. What a way to die. Crushed by a ginormous disco ball. Here today, gone tomorrow, smashed to bits under a tonne of sparkle. Mind you, death by an avalanche of sequins – how very showbizzy and ultra-glam.

News of the diva's death was being kept hush-hush until the *Eurowide* press office, and the EWU head honcho had decided on a course of action for dealing with the reporters and fans who would doubtless go wild with grief when news of Latreena's last performance became public knowledge. Maybe the show would be binned out of respect. Jemma has already heard rumblings that perhaps Latreena's death wasn't just an accident, and that maybe it was the work of some Rottimoldovian terrorists. Although, how a Swiss diva in sequins had managed to piss off some kind of terrorist was beyond Jemma's comprehension. Maybe she was a spy on the side or something. God, Jemma hoped the contest wouldn't be binned... she'd waited years for this opportunity. Surely all of those hours she and Char had spent soaking up every hypnotic moment on YouTube of decades of *Eurovision* contests wouldn't all be crushed in a moment. Just like Latreena had.

Jemma could feel her sympathy wobbling slightly. How typical would that be if the death of some patronizing prima donna from the land of the cuckoo clock put pay to Jemma's dreams. She wouldn't wish such an accident (if that's what it was – apparently the local police were coming in to investigate) on anybody but really... Latreena was a grade A cow. Beautiful face but, really, you'd have to put a bag over that vile personality to find her even vaguely bearable.

Why couldn't everyone be a little more fabulous and adorable like Jemma's *Euro* heroine? She was talented, young, fresh, beautiful and sang her way to the top. All at the tender age of 13. She was legend.

Standing in front of her hotel room mirror, Jemma slid her hand down her ample cleavage and fiddled around inside her bra until she found what she was looking for. Not easy considering the rather fulsome size of her breasts. She'd lost all sorts down there before now. Everything from make-up sponges and chip forks through to pork scratchings and Scampi Fries.

There it was, neatly folded up inside her straining underwear, a photo that Jemma took everywhere with her. Especially during her time in Rottimoldovia. It was more important than ever. It was her good luck omen and would carry her to success, just as her heroine had done in her contest many years before.

She unfolded it and read the words on the photo. "To Jemma, all my love, Sandra Kim xx". A smile instantly painted itself across Jemma's face. Sandra Kim, the 13-year-old Belgian winner of the 1986 *Eurovision Song Contest* with her three-minute slice of pure pop perfection, "J'Aime La Vie". Pop music like that could never be bettered. It was the ultimate *Euro* nugget of feel-good euphoria.

Jemma remembered the day she'd discovered the song. Mon-u-mental! She'd immediately fallen in poppy love with it. Watching a clip of Sandra's performance on YouTube was even better. She was captivated by Sandra's shoulder-padded white jacket and matching fuchsia bowtie/leggings combo. Sparkly and joyous. Sandra's voice was loud, clear and contained a lust for life that Jemma wanted to grab with both hands and emulate in her own singing. She played the song constantly, learning the lyrics in French and singing them with Sandra's Flemish force. While all of her mates (except Char) were raving it up to some banging dance tune or having it large with Oasis, Jemma would be in her bedroom at number 42 Love City Grove, Whittlesey, twirling around in front of the mirror, a vision in wondrous white and rose-coloured fuchsia, pretending to be Sandra Kim.

She googled her constantly, finding out as much as possible about her, pouring over anything she could find. She was still performing and belting out "J'Aime La Vie" to adoring *Euro* masses. Jemma had found her pop idol. Not that Jemma was called Jemma at the time though. Oh no, far from it.

She'd been born Tonya Babbidge, first and only daughter of Ron and Shirley Babbidge. Not too bright at school, but popular with her classmates as she always used to have the best packed lunches and was very liberal with her prawn cocktail Skips and Iced Gems. Plus the boys at Mary Hopkin Comprehensive were big fans of Tonya when she reached an age where Mother Puberty was as liberal in handing out boobs to Tonya as she herself was with her lunchbox treats. You weren't one of the lads at Hopkin's until you'd copped a feel of Tonya's prize assets behind the bike sheds. Not that Tonya would take it any further. Below boobs was off limits despite the protestations of some of the more persistent lads in her year.

But Tonya didn't feel complete. There was something missing in her life. That little spark that would make her feel special. She hated her name. Tonya... rhymes with Sonia (another *Euro* fave, she discovered) but not anywhere as glamorous as the Scouse redhead. In fact, Tonya, as a name, was not at all glamorous. It was beyond unglamorous. Especially as a larger lass. On certain days she felt like Ten-Tonne Tonya. She wasn't, but sometimes every roll of muffin top or flap of baggy belly seemed to scream porker. And Babbidge rhymed with cabbage. Even worse. One of the most hated foods on earth.

She needed something showbiz and worthy of being spelt out in capital letters with multi-hued marker pens on banners outside the local pub, The Pig and Pickle, where she dreamed of singing one day. "Tonight on stage it's Tonya Babbidge!" was not exactly a crowd puller. She needed something alluring and aspirational even if she would be singing on sticky floors and stopping halfway through her set to announce who'd won a jar of pickled pears in the pub raffle. Plus, if she was ever to fulfil her ultimate desire of performing at a massive song contest then Tonya Babbidge as the UK entrant would not exactly trip off the tongue of your genial hosts. It was hard enough to say in an English accent without forming a snigger, so how Monsieur Le Francais or Frau German would manage was not even worth contemplating. She needed something pithy, punchy and *Euro*-tastic. Something to make her nameworthy of her dream to emulate Sandra.

Then it happened. The wind machine of fate blew in her direction. One day, just after her 16th birthday, as she stood in front of her bedroom mirror, this time wrapped in her duvet, twirling around pretending to be Sandra, singing as loud as her lungs would allow. There was a loud banging on the bedroom door. Tonya paused her CD player and opened the door. It was her mother.

'Tonya Babbidge, will you please keep a lid on that racket. Your Aunty Pam is downstairs all upset because she thinks your Uncle Tony is having it off with that brassy stylist with the Chihuahua at Sheri Trims and all I can hear is you and bloody *jemmalavie*.'

It was the way she said it, all together as one word in her Fenland accent, as if *jemmalavie* were a real person. Jemma La Vie? Tonya liked it. It had panache; it had a touch of the exotic and was the ultimate homage to Sandra's "J'Aime La Vie". Jemma La Vie it was.

Six weeks later, Tonya Babbidge was no more. She had changed her name by deed poll to Jemma La Vie. And Uncle Tony was living in a static caravan in Hunstanton with a hairstylist and a pampered pooch called Demiwave. Neither of these facts were pleasing to Jemma's mother Shirley at all.

Back in Rottimoldovia, there was another knock on the hotel room door, this time jolting Jemma from her thoughts as she stared at the prized photo of Sandra. Had she ordered room service? No. For a change. One of the many joys of being housed in a swanky hotel for a week at someone else's expense was her and Char working their way through the entire room service menu. Even when they weren't hungry.

She went to open the door and Daniel was standing there. 'Hi, it's me. Poor Latreena's death has been dealt with. Seems the disco ball was faulty and had a screw loose – bit like her, eh? – the police are investigating with the builders and apparently they won't need to speak to any witnesses like us at the moment, but the contest organisers say that it's business as usual and that the show must go on. They won't let anything spoil the first one. Word is that it will take a lot more than a broken disco ball to force their debut attempt off air. Plus, I'm not sure Rottimoldovia could cope with the loss of income from what I hear if the show got binned.

The powers that be are saying the contest has to happen at all costs. So, Jemma, your sound check is in about 40 minutes. At least poor diva Latreena will be a *Euro* legend for an eternity now.' Daniel paused before continuing, staring at Jemma. 'Are you okay, you seem pretty vacant...'

He waggled his finger towards her face where Jemma could feel that her mouth was hanging open. She shut it with a clatter of teeth. 'Sorry, I was just deep in thought about how doing a contest like this is all I ever wanted and how I used to dream about it when I spinning around in front of the mirror pretending to be my beloved Sandra...' She waved the photo under Daniel's nose. 'All wrapped up in a duvet – I'd tie it around me and turn it into a makeshift dress. I was always the height of bedding department glamour. Sandra, Kylie, Diana Ross... I'd sing them all.'

Daniel loved the story. He'd hung many a magazine article and radio interview on the hook of Jemma, the artist formally known as Tonya Babbidge, performing in front of the mirror dreaming of contest glory. It was pure dreams come true.

'You as Kylie in a duvet. I love that idea. What number did you do?'

'I think it was a 10.5 tog.'

Daniel's mouth fell open. That wasn't exactly what he meant. Thank God she could sing so incredibly well because Jemma wasn't always the sharpest of tools. But she was always adorable, he had to give her that. Wrapped up in a duvet or not.

'I'll come for you in about half an hour,' said Daniel, before walking off.

Jemma closed the door and could feel her brain clicking into overdrive. She hadn't just been thinking about her days in a duvet in front of the mirror. She had been mulling over Latreena's death too. A little niggle in her brain, call it a wily Whittlesey hunch, told her that there might be more to her demise than just a faulty disco ball.

She parked the thought to the back of her mind and readied herself for the rehearsal.

Chapter 5

"…drip drop drip drop…"

Despite the deeply sombre proceedings of the afternoon, the contest organisers were determined to try and yank everyone out of a potential slump and decided to pep everyone up with a hastily arranged evening cruise down Ermpit's River Krudd by filling the free bar with enough booze to float every boat on the river. If anything was inclined to make a wannabe winner forget about the rather messy and squishy death of a fellow contestant, then organisers thought that a bottomless cocktail glass on an "alcohol is free" night out might do the trick.

The aim of the cruise was to booze 'n' schmooze as many people as possible. And even though she didn't realise it, Jemma had somehow pushed all thoughts of Latreena's demise and any suspicions she had out of her head by the time she had finished her second fruity alcoholic concoction.

Having lost Daniel and Char – she suspected she was up on deck having a crafty ciggie – Jemma sashayed her way to the dance floor. In her mind she was sissying her walk with the prowess of a *Drag Race* finalist but in reality her movements were definitely more drunken sway than dazzling sashay.

Blimey, the drinks here are a bit strong, she mused as she squeezed her way onto the neon-lit dance floor, already packed out with many other contestants from the competition, all of them gyrating happily to a selection box of *Euro* songs. If Sandra came on, then Jemma's excitement would doubtless pop the buttons on her already straining silver mesh blouse. The see-through, bra-revealing top (look closely and you'd see the folded fan club photo of Sandra) was a touch daring for the evening maybe, and had certainly raised eyebrows from Daniel when he'd met her earlier.

His words of, 'Hello, Miss *Heat, What Was She Thinking* Fashion Column,' were probably spot on, but Jemma didn't care. This top was a tried-and-trusted and had seen her pull her way to under-the-duvet glory on many an occasion on a drunken night out in East Anglia down at FagButts. Maybe its charm would not be lost on a few of the men onboard tonight. She hoped so as she had packed enough of them to last the entire week.

If Daniel had no qualms in getting his end away, then maybe a little bit of horizontal *boom-bang-a-bang* was a good idea for Jemma too. Now, who to hit on... *Choices, choices*. Scanning the floor, Jemma let her hips gyrate from side to side to the music in an attempt to be sexy. With the rocking of the boat and her semi-blurred brain, the result was more Shrek than Shakira. The Irish contestants for this year, the identical twins, Donnie and Ronnie?

Collectively known as DonRon, the two 18-year-olds were bouncing around the dance floor like a couple of adolescent jumping beans. Completely identical apart from the fact that Ronnie's gravity-defying quiff, sprayed into place with enough lacquer to fill a hole in the ozone layer, was dyed green, in honour of his homeland, whereas Donnie has left his equally quaffed hair in its *natural* peroxide blond with dirty dark roots combination. They'd both been telling *Euro* journalists about their hair-dying decision all week. 'It's so people can tell us apart, so it is. Back home, not even our mam knows who's who. She couldn't even tell the difference when we first popped out. She said we both looked like little pink new potatoes, so we did.'

In fact they'd talked more about their hair than they had about their song, a frantically-performed pop creation called "The Smile High Club" about how a smile can lift your spirits even in a world gone mad. The lyrics, written by the brothers themselves, were worthy of a Nobel-prize-winning author.

'When life has you snoring
Then just move your jaw and...
Head to The Smile High Club
To smash any virus
Just come on and hire us
And head to The Smile High Club.'

They were tipped to place highly and even the legendary Johnny Logan himself had been raving about how the boys were going to "bring it home" for Ireland. Not that they actually knew who Johnny was, as had become embarrassingly apparent at a photo shoot of the three of them together earlier that week when both Donnie and Ronnie had mistaken him for a fan's grandad.

But the twins were beyond endearing and lovable and their cheeky, grinning, hyperactive ways were going down incredibly well with everyone associated with the show. But a potential hook-up for Jemma? No way, Jemma probably had lipsticks older than them.

Dancing rather sexily, if somehow a little awkwardly, next to DonRon was the contest's host, Szymon Rybak. He and Weronika had introduced the evening in their usual trying-to-be-jolly-given-that-someone-has-been-smashed-to-death kind of way. They were all faux-smiles and rhyming couplets, something that had thankfully come to an end when they briefly paid tribute to Latreena. Not too many things rhymed with "flattened" after all. "Patterned". "Fattened". "Grattans". Even the best of poets would have struggled with that one. Mind you, Jemma did think they'd missed a gift horse of an opportunity by not rhyming "death" with "last breath" or indeed "glitter" with "shitter". But each to their own.

Szymon was definitely a knockout in the looks department that was for sure. Mid-20s, taut, toned, tanned. T-shirt stretched over a sizable pair of biceps, jet-black hair floppy at the front, shaved at the side. Yes, Jemma had certainly copped off with worse, in fact she'd rarely had better if she was brutally honest.

But just as Jemma primed herself ready for action by pulling down the open neck of her blouse a few inches and hoiking up her boobs ready to stun Szymon into submission, her plans were thwarted as the other show host, Weronika, darted across the dance floor and threw herself around him. Scarily thin, she was like a heat-seeking Twiglet wrapped around her co-host in seconds. The last time Jemma had seen anyone quite so limpet-like on a fella was watching that film, *Alien,* late night on the telly a few weeks back, when the creature latched itself onto one of the actors. Before Szymon had even had a chance to react, Weronika had attempted to ram her tongue down his throat.

Okay, who else, thought Jemma. Her eyes scanned across to Sweden's Bjorn Bjork. Now he was handsome. The permanent wearing of yellow and blue neckerchief à la Fred from *Scooby Doo* was a touch naff but a gimmick's a gimmick, mused Jemma. Everyone loved a gimmick. And that blond fringe was adorable. 20 years old. Too young? *Hell no*, reckoned Jemma. His age started with a "2" so that made it okay in her cocktail-soaked eyes. She was hardly cradle-snatching like Madonna, was she? There were only a few years between them. And at that second, Bjorn's state was "dance alone". So that meant "come on over and touch my fire" in Jemma's eyes. She checked him out as he timidly watched those around him. Yes, Bjorn was to be Jemma's for the evening... she had already made her mind up. Now all she had to do was convince him.

Daniel was up on deck. He was also feeling the effects of the cocktails but was already being cautious and taking things a little easier than he had the night before. At least there was no Igor tonight to tempt him with that firm, hard Pandora's Box of a body of his. Which was a good thing seeing as its sculpted delights were no doubt an elixir that could guarantee Daniel caving into temptation and pointing his toes skywards and opening his very own box in a heartbeat.

He was launching into a heated debate with two of the journalists Jemma had been made to face during the press event before. Journalists had actually not been invited to the event on board the boat after the news about Latreena had broken for fear that every contestant would be asked their opinion and garner even more doom and gloom column inches. The word on the street – or rue, strasse, strada, depending on which country you were talking too – was that Latreena wasn't exactly the most popular of the contestants so her demise, shocking though it was, was not exactly causing a river of tears to challenge the Danube, Seine or indeed the Krudd. But two of the press gathered for *Eurowide* had managed to slip though the wire and be on board, one at Daniel's very own doing.

UK journalist Lucie Rave was bubblier than a Jacuzzi. And just as inviting. With a permanent smile so big that her face had a job to actually fit itself around it, she was like human poppers. If you wanted cheering up, then effervescent Lucie was the girl to hang with. At four-foot-eleven small she was easy to visually miss with a passing glance but with a giggle shriller than a checkout beeping system and a voice louder than the front row of a Harry Styles concert, she was impossible to ignore. She was also one of Daniel's best friends and the woman reporting on the contest for *Palaver! magazine*, one of the UK's top celeb-filled reads and website.

The readers of *Palaver!* had already decided that Jemma was "one of them" due to her "realness". In a celebrity ocean of *Housewives*-style perfection and *Love Island* pumped-up physiques, Jemma's earthy, girthy ways were a welcome revelation. And as someone who was as wide as she was tall, Lucie loved Jemma and would not hear a bad word against her. Which was why, in her own bubbly way, she was ready to rip the head off her fellow reporter, the scrawny Rottimoldovian weasel standing with her and Daniel. As the reporter from one of the home nation's biggest rags, he too had managed to slip onto the boat. What he hadn't planned for was Daniel and Lucie firing their opinion of him directly at him with such great gusto.

'So, you're the journalist who laid into our Jemma and basically called her fat and unlovable?' stated Daniel.

'Harsh and untrue!' boomed Lucie.

The Rottimoldovian hack may not have planned for the conversation but he was sticking to his guns. Strangely a few of his copious arm tattoos were guns, a fact not unnoticed by a rather horrified Lucie, as she was at the perfect height to see them in all their graphic glory.

'She iz big, she not zing about love. It's no zurprise really.' His air was dismissive in the extreme. 'Men like their women to not be so... what iz ze word... mammoth? Zey like zem a... *regular* size.' As he said the word "regular", he gazed down at Lucie, the top of her head a good foot below his and smiled mockingly.

Despite wanting to wipe the deck of the boat with him, and ignoring the fact that his slightly alcohol-tinted mind was telling him to insert his fingers into the man's earlobe holes and yank sharply, Daniel knew that he had to remain at least some degree of professional in order to placate the man from running a damning story about Jemma in the pre-show press. If the UK were to have any chance of stacking up a few douze points at *Eurowide* then the last thing Jemma needed was troublesome press in the host nation. But Daniel could understand why she'd exploded. The man was the dictionary definition of vile.

Daniel faux-smiled as best as his reluctant lips would allow. 'Look, I'd offer to buy you a drink, but seeing as it's all free, that seems a bit pointless. Is there no way we can keep this misunderstanding between you and Jemma out of the press? Jemma's been under a lot of stress and naturally she's not that adept at handling the press given her newness to all of this. She really is a lovely girl and meant no harm.'

'Lovely girl, totally likable. Totally,' echoed Lucie, also trying to keep a pint-sized lid on her dislike of the man.

'I do not know.' A pause. 'She waz rude, people *should* know...' His attitude and the short delay in completing his sentence hinted that maybe there was hope.

Daniel continued the fight the urge to bitch slap him. Lucie did the same, tempted to jam her knee into his crotch. Even though she wasn't actually convinced that she'd be able to reach. The journalist continued to spout.

'Maybe with Latreena's death I have better zings to write about. I make no promizzes, but I like that you zay zorry.'

'Never did,' coughed Lucie, but this time keeping her booming voice to a minimum. She bit her lip apologetically as Daniel shot her a glance that could curdle milk.

'We do...' said Daniel, crossing his fingers behind his back. 'Now, let me get you a free drink, nevertheless. What's your name by the way?'

'Zandor. I'll have beer. I come wiz you.'

The knot of angst that had been balling within Daniel's stomach during the conversation started to untie itself and Daniel knew that his job was seemingly done. For now.

Just as he was about to escort Zandor to the bar, a rather drunken Char appeared and, with an unsteady tumble, knocked straight into Daniel and Lucie. Char let out a belly laugh as she tried to straighten herself. 'Hi Sweet'N Low, I didn't see you down there, Lucie... sorry.' It was a nickname that Char hadn't tired of using ever since they'd first met. Luckily, Lucie was just as fond of Char as she was of Jemma. 'Have you seen Jemma, Daniel? I've been chatting for ages with...' Char stopped as her eyes fell upon Zandor. Disgust painted itself evidently across her face. She turned to Daniel. 'What are you doing with this dick splat? You're not planning on shagging him too, are you?'

The knot in Daniel's stomach slammed back into play with the force of a medieval battering ram.

Jemma's attempts at wooing Bjorn Bjork into some kind of after-party action back at her hotel room were not really going to plan. She'd attempted her tried and trusted three-pronged man-attack and so far, not a dicky bird of potential. The blond vision, hopping from one foot to the other in front of her to the plinky plonky disco sounds of hits from days gone by, was perfectly pleasant, attentive to her conversation and beautiful to look at. But that was all. So far the only hint of tongue action she'd seen was when Bjorn licked the edge of his cocktail glass to mop up a dribble of refreshment.

Her three-pronged attack was normally foolproof. It never failed back home with the lads in the closing moments of the "erection section" at FagButts. But then, to be honest, most of the lads at that late stage of the evening would have copped off with sexagenarian Mabel behind the bar if she had suggested even the merest whiff of a bunk-up or a hand shandy round the back of the club. Quite an achievement given that

Mabel was the spit of evil Ursula from *The Little Mermaid*, except instead of eight tentacles, she had at least as many chins.

Step one was "Show Interest". This would be Jemma's attempt to show an interest in something she was definitely sure her prey would relate to. A bit like a lion sitting a zebra down and asking it how it loved working the monochrome look before ripping its heart out and feasting on its flesh. Jemma's summation of Bjorn was that she could talk about the subjects Sweden (given his homeland), *Eurovision* (given that they were at a song contest) and fashion (given his outfit). Shit, maybe he was gay? He did sport his neckerchief rather nattily. She'd have to fathom that out as she went along.

She started with Sweden. 'Your country is amazing. I've never been but I'd love to. Me and Char, my best mate, want to go to the ABBA Museum and see that. Have you been?'

'No, never.'

Oh. 'I love ABBA. My mum Shirley had all of their LPs. Char and me... we used to try and do our eyeshadow all retro like Agnetha sometimes. Mind you, the frosty blue smudge is very big in the UK right now. And I once crimped my hair like Frida in the *"Take A Chance On Me"* video too, but it didn't take and I scarred my forehead with the hot crimpers and looked like an oversize Harry Potter.' Jemma belly-laughed. Bjorn didn't. She was rambling.

'ABBA were incredibly good. We Swedes adore them,' stated Bjorn.

This is not going to plan, thought Jemma. And saying ABBA were good was understatement of the century. They were pop perfection. She'd seen the

Mamma Mia films enough times to know every word. But she'd evidently have to pull out all of the stops if she was going to manage any kind of "Honey Honey" action on board with Bjorn this evening.

Next try. 'So, what do you think of the competition? It's crazy isn't it? Who's your tip to win on Saturday, other than me of course...' Another guffaw and a playful slap to Bjorn's chest. Blimey, he was firm. Hard. Frighteningly solid.

Bjorn winced and let out a rather high-pitched shriek. Maybe Jemma's slap had been a bit more Dick Emery than dick tease. Sometimes she forgot how powerful a girl she was, and Bjorn wasn't exactly built like the back end of a Volvo, was he? Ignoring his somewhat obvious look of terror, she moved on with the conversation. 'I think you could win... your song is so catchy it's ridiculous.'

Maybe flattery would win him over. His song, "24 Hours of Sunshine", was among the frontrunners and had *Euro*-winner written all over it with its upbeat poppy lyrics and swinging salsa-like rhythms. Jemma had seen Bjorn perform his sound check and that boy could strut in his platform heels.

'I love your song so much. In fact, I just can't get you out of my head,' she gushed, placing her hands to her face and imitating Kylie as she did so. No reaction or hint of a smile. Not gay then, guessed Jemma. He'd have clocked that reference in a camp nanosecond.

'I hope to win. Many great contest winners have come from Sweden. I hope to be the next.'

Jemma let the conversation hang in the air, hoping that Bjorn would complement her on "Beep the World (Hear my Horn)". He didn't. She clocked that he was still rubbing his chest where she'd thwacked him playfully. Oops.

Time to move on again. 'Your outfits are wonderful. The platform heels, tight trousers, necktie… is it chiffon?' Jemma went to touch Bjorn's neckerchief, hoping to feel some spark of electricity between them as she did so. As she leant in to try and touch the fabric, Bjorn leapt backwards. The poor boy looked petrified.

'Don't touch that!' he yelled, a little more excessively than Jemma deemed necessary.

Jemma volleyed back. 'Okay, sunshine, don't get your fringe in a twist… I was just thinking how fabulous it looked. It wasn't like I was going to wallop you again.'

All hope of any kind of cross-border leg-over drained from her mind. The man was obviously a prissy lunatic when it came to flirtation or a complete novice at the art of the chat-up. Yet somehow, she still found him strangely endearing.

Bjorn realised that maybe he had overreacted and rushed to make amends. 'It's just… this neckerchief belonged to my late grandma and it's very dear to me. Very precious.'

'Fair enough,' harrumphed Jemma, giving up on her three-pronged attack. Following "Show Interest" she still had "Show More Cleavage" and "Show Willing" to work through (the Fenland boys back home never required anything beyond "Show More Cleavage") but any hope of a sliver of passion with Bjorn was already dead in the water.

'I am going to eat something,' stated Bjorn, attempting his escape. 'I will see you later.' Not that he looked in any hurry to do so. 'I have heard the tripe meatballs are a delicacy here.'

Jemma watched as Bjorn disappeared out of sight in search of tripe. Vile. Jemma wouldn't touch it. One of the few things she wouldn't. She'd heard some TV chef describe it as a food with, 'No integrity, no character... the Paris Hilton of meat cuts.' Why would you eat that? Plus tripe Winalot was responsible for her Aunty Pam's Chihuahua billowing out the worst flatulence ever... like, toxic clouds of it.

Scanning around the dance floor, Jemma contemplated her next move. She was still feeling flirtation overload due to the excess of cocktails. The Irish twins seemed to have disappeared. As had dishy Szymon and that Rottimoldovian stick insect. Who looked... what was the word... vulnerable?

Suddenly a scream sounded from up on deck. Not a joyful one, but a proper "I'm a hapless teenager running through the woods in a negligee in the dead of night and I've just stumbled across a masked killer with a whacking great knife" kind of scream.

'What the...?' Jemma couldn't finish the sentence before a wave of people pushed against her from behind, carrying her towards the stairs leading to the upper deck where the scream had come from. A mass of languages mixed in Jemma's ears, doubtless all saying the same thing. 'What, in the name of Mans Zelmerlöw, is going on?'

Deciding she needed to see for herself, Jemma took action, lifted up her elbows and started to barge her way through the crowd. Given her ample proportions and her skill at elbowing shoppers out of the way on the first day of the Peterborough Primark knockdown sale, a nation of equally curious people metaphorically fell either side of her as she worked her way upstairs and out onto the deck.

The deck was chaos, with people running everywhere yet nowhere at the same time. She spotted Daniel's cute ass and the portly rump of the fabulous Lucie as they both strained to look over the side of the boat and made a beeline for them. Lucie's head was pretty much just level with the boat's railings, whereas Daniel was almost hanging over. Jemma resisted an urge to pinch his bum as she squeezed in alongside them.

'What the heck is going on?' I was contemplating getting my groove on to "Ding-a-Dong" down there and then all hell breaks loose. Has somebody jumped ship?'

Neither Daniel nor Lucie had to give her the answer. As Lucie stared through the railings like a dinky birdwatcher and Daniel pointed out into the bobbing waves of the River Krudd, Jemma could see what the partygoers were screaming about. There, face down in the Krudd, was a body. A pool of blood stained outwards from around its head. A green quiffed head.

It seemed that it wasn't just Jemma's chances with Bjorn that were dead in the water.

Chapter 6

"...my secret combination, it's a mystery
for you..."

Bjorn Bjork had not had the best of evenings. What
with the unwanted advances of a fellow *Eurowide*
contestant and the second fatal accident in virtually as
many hours, his nerves were in shreds. No matter how
hard he tried, the vision of the dead body of the formerly
perky Irish teenager floating face down in the Krudd
clung to his mind like arctic moss. How had he slipped
overboard and banged his head so badly before falling
below the waterline, poor thing? Hardly the luck of the
Irish. What would the EWU say about this accident?
Once is unfortunate, but two is a little coincidental.

Bjorn needed to escape the madness as soon as the
boat had docked. Despite the police turning up to
try and interview as many people as possible, Bjorn
had slipped off unseen and headed back to his hotel.
He needed space. Needed sanctuary. Needed privacy.
He needed to get undressed.

Standing in front of his hotel room mirror, Bjorn
raised his hands behind his head, untied his neckerchief
and then unbuckled the back of the blue chemise he'd
spent the evening wearing. Bringing his arms back
round to the front he slipped the material from around

his shoulders and let it drop to the floor. He surveyed himself in the mirror.

Most 20-year-old men would have been staring at a defined chest, maybe a few chest hairs here and there, a flat stomach, some abs and maybe that trail of hair that leads downwards from the belly button. But not Bjorn. Oh no, what greeted him was something quite different.

Wrapped around his upper body was a swathe of white fabric, virtually mummifying the chest area. To the side of the fabric, neatly tucked away under his hairless armpit was a safety pin about the size of a cocktail sausage. Lifting his arm up, Bjorn unhooked the pin and removed it from the material. As he did so, he let out an audible gasp of satisfaction and relief. It was bordering on the orgasmic. Immediately the material started to unravel from his body, tumbling around his frame like one of those ribbons on the end of a stick waggled by Olympic gymnasts. As the last piece of bandage fell to the floor, two flattened yet obviously quite sizable breasts rose up and inflated themselves back into position like a couple of memory foam molehills.

Bjorn brought his hands to his boobs and jiggled them back into place, letting them part slightly from each other and rest into their natural place with a necessary and satisfying slurping noise as the sweatiness where they'd been bound together gave way. Bjorn winced as they did so, the delight of seeing the prize possessions in full glory again mixing with a stab of discomfort from where Jemma has clouted them on the boat. The skin around the chest was sore and a tad red and angry. He placated himself with the fact that in five minutes hopefully the normally healthy glow of his body would return. God Bjorn missed it.

Yep, Bjorn Bjork did not exactly have the body of your average 20-year-old Swedish male. But then that was exactly what he wasn't – 20-years-old. Or male. Swedish, yes, but that was where the similarities between Bjorn and his real existence ended.

Bjorn was in fact Bella. Bella, not a fella. A mercifully youthful-looking 32-year-old woman. Bella with no Adam's apple, a fact concealed by an array of neckerchiefs. Bella with no real manly pecs, just squished down bouncy Swedish boobs. And Bella with no meatballs, a fact revealed as she peeled down her underwear. Meatballs. Such a Swedish thing, and yet anatomically the very thing that Bella needed to enter this year's *Eurowide*. She breathed out a sigh of exasperation. How had it come to this?

Bjorn had been bjorn... sorry, born... a woman. Bella Nielsen. And like many a Swede, she had grown up worshipping the goddesses of her home country's *Eurovision* entries. Sweden was where it was at when it came to *Eurovision* – the crème de la crème, the bee's knees, the *hund's testiklar*. Her sauna-loving countrymen knew how to create a musical winner and Bella had feasted on them all – Charlotte Nilsson, Loreen, Carola, the deities of Frida and Agnetha from ABBA... beautiful women, beautiful voices. One day she longed to join their ranks. Like many a *Euro* contestant, in her opinion, she was put on earth to one day sashay her way into the glittery spotlight of *Euro* glory.

But when you're a young Swedish girl growing up in the backstreets of a tiny, rundown and deeply depressing, long forgotten rustic corner of northern Sweden, most of the time the chances of finding any kind of light, let alone a fame-soaked glamorous one were slimmer than

Greta Garbo's eyebrows. Which was why, as soon as Bella was of an age to escape and had scraped together enough krona for a one-way train ticket to Stockholm, she had packed her bags, told her parents she was gone for good and hit the road with an ambitious spring in her step and a *Lordi Lordi (Hard Rock) Hallelujah* in her heart in search of a singing career to rival her heroes.

But fast forward over a decade later and the quest for international singing fame and glory had not exactly gone to plan. It fact it had fallen flat. Flat on her back. With her legs up in the air. Mainly in hotel rooms. With tourists. Or businessmen. Or mostly husbands behind their wives' backs. To be honest, anyone with enough krona to pay that month's rent and bills.

Bella hadn't planned it that way. It was just that, like many dreamers before her, the yellow brick road she'd hoped to tread had taken her on a rather more pornographic detour than she'd planned.

She'd started singing in clubs and bars. She'd even bagged a regular weekly slot in one of them, but knocking out a few tunes in front of sozzled Swedes did not keep the howling wolf from her door. She'd mentioned her lack of money to the bar owner who suggested that she contact a friend of his who ran an "agency". An agency that traded in pleasures of the flesh.

At first, she vetoed the idea. But then, curiosity got the better of her and before she knew it Bella was leaving a rather ritzy hotel suite a few hundred krona better off having "entertained" a Brit cardiac physiologist passing through the city for work. Feedback on Bella was good and before she knew it, she was being booked regularly, and rising up the agency ranks. Her youthful appearance, cantaloupe breasts and accommodating loins were much more beneficial to her bank balance than endless nights of singing Roxette ever were. She had "The Look"... and for a while singing was forgotten.

But then earlier that year, one of her professional rendezvous' had reignited her fire to sing again. It was just after she'd been finishing her tried and tested tongue technique on yet another happy client's lower portions that Bella's life hit a curveball. The man she'd been servicing was in Sweden's capital with a friend who was part of the *Eurowide* search for potential contestants. His pal was one of a team of scouts being used to find the first Swedish singer for the new contest. In a flash, all of Bella's childhood dreams and desires came flooding back. The chance to represent your country. Some *Euro*-God on high had sent this six-degrees-of-Kevin-Bacon-man to her. If she could prove that her voice was as good as her head then maybe this was her moment. If opportunity knocks, don't blow it. Ironic given her actions for the last 25 minutes.

But then... crash and burn. The client disclosed what his friend was looking for. 'The only criteria is that he's been told to find a young man. Someone wholesome, cherubic, sweeter than Princess Cake and as clean as the Swedish fjords.'

So a 30-something female whore is not fitting the Euro-bill then? thought Bella with a wave of dejection.

'You don't know anyone, do you? He's kinda bored of looking,' he asked.

In a flash, Bella had formulated a plan. A weird and wonderful one. One that would take some doing. But definitely one that she felt she could make work. 'Indeed I do...'

Just 24 hours later, it was a freshly cut and coiffed and boobily disguised Bjorn who walked into a Swedish bar to meet up with the man whose friend she'd been bouncing around on the day before. Having taken six inches off her haircut, industrially taped down her boobs and removed a dozen years off her age it was a look that was suddenly so much more *Euro*-suitable for what was required. Within a month she'd sung, auditioned and impressed and before she knew it she was singing "24 Hours of Sunshine" in every Swedish town square in the land and boarding a plane to head to Rottimoldovia. Her childhood dreams had come true. But now, she just had to deal with the nightmare of trying to keep her real identity a secret. And also hoping that her rather sore boobs could survive a few more weeks of being squished into her carefully picked gender-blurring outfits.

A naked "Bjorn" moved away from the mirror and headed to the bathroom. A good long soak in a tub full of jojoba and chamomile would help sooth those aching titties.

Chapter 7

"...love is just like a merry-go-round,
with all the fun of the fair..."

'So, is it you killing off the competition then, Jemma? It's all a bit Agatha Christie isn't it? People dropping dead all over the shop. That Poirot fella with the crinkly moustache and the waxy tips will turn up soon.' Despite the seriousness of the subject matter, an ever-fizzy Lucie Rave couldn't help but let out a loud squeal of girlish laughter as she spoke.

'It's not funny, Lucie,' snipped Jemma. 'That poor Irish lad just bobbing up and down in the water all lifeless. I won't ever be able to see the colour green without picturing him in my head from now on. I'll never eat peas again, I swear. Or spinach... thankfully.'

'The organisers say it was just another hideous accident. He'd had a bit too much to drink and must have toppled overboard, hitting his head on the way down. He was leaping around that boat like a toddler after too much pick 'n' mix. He must have jumped straight overboard.' Again, an inappropriate giggle.

'Thank God the contest is still happening. After Latreena's death and now this I was beginning to think it might be canned. It's getting like a *Euro*-morgue around here.'

'No chance, the police who came to the boat seem to think that it was another horrible accident. You were questioned like the rest of us. Nobody seemed to see the poor lad go overboard. And Daniel says that the contest is the biggest thing to happen in Rottimoldovia since… well, like ever. It's bringing a lot of attention to the country and the government are determined for it to still shine brightly. Despite the body count. And let's face facts, this country doesn't have a lot else going for it, does it? I tried to go shopping yesterday and couldn't even find a Mango or a TK Maxx. Talk about dark ages.'

'I know. I couldn't find a Greggs either. I sent Char out to find one but no joy.'

Jemma thought about her brief conversation with the Rottimoldovian police officer who had turned up as the boat docked after the accident. She wanted to tell him that she thought it was highly suspicious that there were two deaths of two contestants in one day. That the Nancy Drew inside her said that maybe there was something fishier than Rottimoldovian crabsticks going on. But she didn't. She merely said she'd seen nothing. Which was true. She had no evidence and nothing more than a hunch in her gut to go on. She shelved the thought away again. And to be honest, the police officer she'd spoke to hadn't seemed that bothered anyway.

'So, what are we doing here?' Jemma scanned around their surroundings – a fairground on the outskirts of Ermpit. Well, if a fairground could consist of a busted old mechanical fortuneteller and one clapped-out carousel where the horses were so devoid of paint it was impossible to read their names anymore. Jemma was currently parking her peach on one called blank-R-blank-E.

The other letters had peeled off completely. She guessed it was probably called Prue or Bree but she had named it Arse. Alongside her, Lucie, looking even more ridiculously tiny than usual perched on top of her wooden beast, was riding blank-O-blank-A-blank. Jemma had called that one Gonad. Maybe it was Tomaz back in the day but to Jemma the equine ride was much more suited to Gonad.

'Well, believe it or not, this is one of Ermpit's most popular attractions, the Dicken Platz. Not exactly Thorpe Park is it, but families flock here to ride this carousel, apparently.' Lucie was unable to hide the layers of questioning as to why in her voice. 'We're here as *Palaver!* thought it would make a nice article for our website. You having a bit of fun in the run up to the semi-finals despite the current sombre mood. Daniel's on his way here with the photographer now. It'll be a few fun snaps of you enjoying the ride. We can stick you in front of the fake mechanical fortuneteller and have your future told – see if you're going to win! I love those things, they're always called Gypsy Serhat or something like that aren't they and look like Ming The Merciless from *Flash Gordon*. I can ask you a few questions, write up the copy and we can have it on the website and socials by this evening. And no talk of death, divas, disco balls or drownings, okay!'

'Sounds perfect, now where's Daniel?'

Right on cue, the Hollywood-handsome face of Daniel Spirit appeared from the other side of the carousel. He was accompanied by a goofy-looking man wearing a raincoat, despite the warmth of the springtime air, and dangling a camera around his neck.

'Hi, ladies, this is Klaus, our photographer for the day,' said Daniel, motioning. Klaus didn't react.

Are there no decent-looking men in this country? mused Jemma. She was still somewhat frustrated after her action-free night, but sour-Klaus was definitely not an option.

'Right, shall we crack on?' shouted Lucie. She dismounted her horse and joined Daniel and Klaus. 'Photos first and then I can ask the questions over lunch later. Are you ready, Jemma?'

'Tally-ho!' screamed Jemma. 'Let's ride, Arse! Mind you, isn't that more your cup of tea, Daniel!'

A cavernous laugh from both Jemma and Lucie fused together as the ride creaked into life. Daniel was as stony-faced as Klaus.

Just as the horses started to rotate, at the entrance of the Dicken Platz two more figures appeared. One was Wiktoria, the modelesque Rottimoldovian beauty representing her country and the other was Zandor the tattooed hack. Their moods could not have been more dissimilar. Wiktoria was relishing every moment of her time in the spotlight. At the age of 21, she was already a huge star in her home country, but this year's contest could be her platform to spread her wings somewhat further and fly to even greater glory. Fame should not stop at the Rottimoldovian borders. Wiktoria was very much of the opinion that ambition could take her anywhere. Especially with the song she was singing, an overly daft ditty called "Love Safari". Her nation had chosen it and she loved it, despite such clunky lines as, 'love as strong as an ox, as cunning as a fox, as brutal as a beast, on my love you can feast, but when I come to eat ya, you know I ain't no cheetah...'.

Wiktoria was not exactly a deeply intelligent young woman but she was adored by everyone and one of

Rottimoldovia's most cherished media stars. Because she was genuinely nice. And also genuinely a little naïve. Some would say dim, but naïve was much nicer.

But the great thing about being a celebrity was that she didn't really need to be savvy all the time anyway, if at all. She had people around her to be intelligent for her. Fending for herself was not something she really had to do so engaging her brain all the time was not really a requirement of life. She'd once spent hours staring at her supermarket pizza trying to work out why all of the topping had disappeared, only to realise later that she'd taken it out of the box upside down. Mensa were not exactly unlocking their doors for her. Which is why singing trite lyrics like, 'I loved like a hyena, from the first moment I seen ya,' suited her down to the ground to be fair.

Zandor was his usual miserable self. He sported an ill-fitting black singlet bearing the name of some Eastern European rock combo from the 1980s and showed his tattooed arms in all their skull-laden glory. Unshaven and beyond grubby, he was the antithesis to the beauty of Wiktoria's shift dress which clung to what curves she had with perfection. Not that Zandor cared, he wasn't the one in front of the camera. He'd merely be the one asking questions and taking snaps of Wiktoria in Ermpit's Dicken Platz. Just another day in *Euro*-hell as far as he was concerned. But money was money and he was getting paid well to be there.

Zandor's already black mood seemed to plummet to the levels of a *Euro*-non-qualifier when he spotted Daniel, Lucie and a revolving Jemma by the carousel. It would seem that both countries had the same idea when it came to stories for entertaining their readers.

'I hope zat horse has been strengzenned. Horse riders are normally smaller zan zat, are zey not?' He laughed, his rudeness lifting his black mood.

'There is no need for that, Zandor,' countered Daniel, outwardly pleasant but seething within.

'Awkward,' barked Lucie. 'And highly rude.'

Wiktoria just smiled, stared blankly into space and raised her hand in an attempt of a wave as Jemma circled into view and came to a stop in front of them. Jemma was just about to launch into attack when a raised eyebrow and stern glance from Daniel forced her to bite her tongue. She waved back at Wiktoria, deliberately ignoring Zandor.

'Have you finished now, zen? It is time for Rottimoldovian beauty to ride ze horses instead of... zat.' He gestured to Jemma, who was still sitting astride her horse, teeth gritted in an almost clenching agony. Her cheeks were reddening, a fact not lost on Daniel or Lucie. Zandor still held the threat of running the story of how the UK entry had slagged off his nation so keeping on his good side, if he actually had one, was imperative.

'We can busy ourselves elsewhere, can't we, Jemma? Maybe some shots over by the fortuneteller. Maybe even some with Wiktoria, if Zandor doesn't mind. It would be great to show the UK and the host country entry getting on so well together. Don't you think, Zandor?' Daniel was extending an olive branch as much as his professionalism would allow, despite wanting to punch the tattooed tosser with enough force to challenge Anthony Joshua.

Zandor shrugged in a couldn't-give-a-stuff kind of way but a clapping of Wiktoria's hands in speedy joy proved that she loved the idea. 'Oh yes. We should… the UK are great friends of ours.' *And a much needed country to conquer*, she pondered. Plus Jemma's rather abundant figure would make Wiktoria look fabulous. Didn't they say if you wanted to look thin, get a larger mate?

Another shrug from Zandor.

'I think it's a fabulous idea,' said Lucie, bustling over to Wiktoria, linking her arm and guiding her towards the carousel. 'No time like the present. Chop-chop.'

Lucie did her best to try and help Wiktoria as the singer stepped up onto the carousel and scanned the ride to try and find the perfect horse to drape her slender frame across for the press photos. The fact that Lucie was as wide as Wiktoria was slender was not particularly helpful as she attempted to push the singer up from behind. 'Excuse fingers,' she giggled nervously, worried that her sausage thumbs might easily plough through the flimsy wafers of fabrics that formed Wiktoria's shift dress.

Wiktoria was oblivious and merely nodded her thanks as she weaved in and out of the horses, scanning their names. 'I'm riding this one,' piped Wiktoria. 'Big and strong and just how I like them, nice and easy for me to get my leg over.' She winked at Jemma as she effortlessly lifted her stick-thin leg into the air and landed without a sniff of a wobble on the horse.

Jemma guffawed and snorted as she did so, amused at the leg over gag. A little fleck of liquid escaped her nostrils and landed on the horse she was riding. 'Oh you've made me snot all over my Arse!' she cried, referencing the nag she had renamed.

Zandor looked directly at Jemma, his face like granite. Wiktoria seemed a little bemused. 'Arse? What is Arse?'

'It's the name of my horse,' offered Jemma. 'The letters have rubbed away. It's probably something else but I've decided to call the horse Arse. It's a Brit slang term for your backside, your bottom, your ass, your posterior, your peach, your derriere… you get me, Wiktoria?' Jemma slapped her own fulsome arse as she asked.

She obviously did. The loudest laugh erupted from inside Wiktoria's diminutive frame. Literal shrieks. Her laughter was infectious, immediately causing both Jemma and Lucie, watching on from the side of the carousel, to erupt into peels of laughter too. 'That's a great name, Jemma. *Arse*. I love it. But I must remove my *arse* from this horse. It's not comfortable. My *arse* is very sore. This is not a comfortable ride. My *arse* does not like.'

Jemma loved the way that Wiktoria emphasised the word arse every time she said it. Like a five-year-old hearing a swear word for the first time. *Who knew that she was so much fun*, thought Jemma.

As Wiktoria dismounted the horse, she rubbed her backside. She was still laughing. 'I don't like my horse, Igor is not a good boy, he gives me painful arse.'

A howl of laughter spewed loudly from Jemma. So loud it could be heard across the other side of the Dicken Platz. 'Shut the front door!' she cried. 'Your horse is called Igor and he gives out sore arses. This is too good.' As Wiktoria mounted the horse next to her, still rubbing her backside, Jemma turned to Daniel, his face already as red as a Turkish flag, and winked. 'What are the chances of that, Danny Boy? It's obviously all in the name. Remind me never to get off with someone called Igor. I wouldn't be able to sit down at spin class for weeks.'

Daniel's red turned to purple as he simply stared at Jemma. For once he remained silent, a raising of his eyebrows his only reaction. Photographer Klaus, still a vision of severity and cragginess, continued devoid of emotion.

Jemma leant towards Wiktoria and put her arm across her shoulder, pulling her towards her. 'I like you, why didn't we get to be friends in the run up to the contest. We could have had a fabulous time at those pre-parties in Tel Aviv and Amsterdam. Got royally smashed.' She looked back to Klaus. 'Right then, smiler, I think we're ready for our close-ups, aren't we Wikky?'

Wiktoria winced slightly. No one had ever called her that before. Her name was not for shortening normally. Not that she minded though. As Klaus started to click away, all she could think about was just how petite and supermodel waif-like she'd look alongside the highly likable Jemma. And within a matter of hours those photos would all over the UK press. Wiktoria turned her wince into a pout and worked her angles. If pouting had been an Olympic sport, then she'd be a gold medal winner all the way. Jemma still grinned at the camera, happy to have made a fabulous new friend.

It was nearly half an hour later that the group found themselves in front of a square golden box on legs on the other side of the Dicken Platz. Well, golden with more than its fair share of rust on every corner. The word "Zoltan" was written across the glass window on the front side of the box. Inside the golden cube, a plastic-looking man with a full beard and a fancy headdress stared out at them. He was plastic-looking as he was indeed made entirely of plastic. Funny that. And he looked incredibly old.

'He looks as decrepit as you, Zandor! Except he hasn't got massive holes in his ears,' sneered Jemma. 'Actually he looks like the love child of Conchita Wurst and Chucky!'

She was more than happy to slag off Zandor, despite the death stare Daniel delivered to her as she spoke. She was never going to be a fan of the skanky hack, even if *Eurowide* protocol and a ruddy-faced press officer deigned otherwise. Besides, Zandor was obviously having to be all colours of nice to Wiktoria, and seeing as she and Jemma had walked all of the way from the carousel to the mechanical fortuneteller hand in hand and giggling wildly together he would find it more than a tad awks to try and throw shade at Jemma.

'This is so exciting,' chirruped Wiktoria. 'I've never had my fortune told before. I've never had to. A manager has always told me what to do. I've never needed to ask someone else. A manager is a lot easier than making your own decisions. Sometimes thinking for yourself is really such a pain.'

'Yep, a pain in the *arse*!' boomed Jemma, eager to throw in her new best friend's new favourite word.

'But now I can ask Zoltan exactly what I want and see what the future holds.'

Lucie reached into her pocket and flicked a coin into a hole at the base of the golden cube. An excited Wiktoria went to press the buttons on the machine but Lucie stopped her from completing the action.

'Not just yet, Wiktoria. I need to ask you both some questions for the piece,' stated Lucie. 'So, what are you both going to wish for, what would you like Zoltan to grant you? What are your dreams? Anything you like. Think big!'

The girls both gave their answers. Jemma wished for her cousin Harvey to pass his GCSEs that were coming up that summer, for Orlando Bloom's telephone number, and for Snickers bars to be bigger again. Hardly thinking on a global scale. Unlike Wiktoria. She wished for world peace, worldwide success, to be chosen as the main catwalk star at Victoria Beckham's next fashion show and for a massive *Eurowide* win in the final.'

Daniel, who had remained tight-lipped since the Igor the horse scenario, broke his silence. 'Lucie, can we add that to Jemma's answers as well please. Slightly more on brand than Harvey's GCSEs.'

'Done,' yapped Lucie.

It was now Jemma's turn to raise her eyebrows. 'Really? I don't even like Victoria Beckham's fashion that much. One of her t-shirts would just about stretch itself around my thigh.'

'Sorted, Daniel, sorted,' thundered Lucie, alleviating his fears. 'Okay, ladies, who's going to press the button first?'

'I will,' said Jemma. 'It might be the only time I'm first this week after all!' She laughed. No one else did.

Jemma pressed the buttons and the plastic man jerked back and forth inside the box. Some words attempted to spew out from its speakers, but they were unintelligible. A crease of confusion crossed Jemma's face. 'Is that your language or are the batteries running out? Or maybe Zoltan's pissed. Has he drunk some of those cocktails from the boat last night? He's definitely slurring.'

Surprisingly, it was Zandor who answered. 'It's zee batteriez. Our language iz a beautiful von. Now take ze card.' He reached out as an oblong-shaped card shot from a slot on the front of the golden box. He handed it to Jemma. 'Read your fortune. Maybe I bring you ze luck.' Zandor attempted what appeared to be a smile. It was completely ill at ease on his features.

Jemma excitedly read the card. 'Your wish is granted. A good life is yours. Health and happiness are yours in abundance. Love is in the air.' Jemma burst into song while reading the last sentence. She ended the song with, 'Well that's utter claptrap.'

'What is claptrap?' asked Wiktoria.

'A load of arse if you like. All rubbish. But I'll take it if it means Orlando will be in touch.' Jemma swooned. 'Your turn, Wikky.'

Lucie placed another coin into the slot and Wiktoria pressed the button. Zoltan jerked into action once more and spoke again, no less slurred gibberish than his first attempt. Another card. Zandor coughed loudly and again reached forward to grab it.

A visibly excited Wiktoria took the card and read it. Her face fell as she did. 'Your joyous time will not come. Make the most of the present as the future is unclear, a vision of black bringing bad luck and ending in the ultimate sin of death. Your wish is not granted.'

Wiktoria's lips wobbled as she finished reading. She turned to face Jemma, the dribble of a tear threatening from one of her eyes. The other quickly joined it. 'Death. I'm only 21, Jemma. That's not on my life plan. I've got a song contest to win and world fame to achieve. I can't do that from a stinky old coffin. It's not an option.'

Not knowing what to say in such omen-tinged circumstances, Jemma merely put her arms around Wiktoria and bear-hugged her as deeply as she could. Normally she'd laugh it off as a load of baloney but seeing as this week was hardly going without incident so far, she wasn't sure that she could be that easily dismissive. Her inner suspicion said otherwise. Everyone obviously felt the same. Nobody said a word and the stillness hung horribly in the air.

Lucie broke the silence with her booming tones. 'I might change that slightly for the online piece. Doesn't really end on the right note.' She paused before adding, her tone a touch jovial trying to break the mood, 'Just like some of the classic *Euro* tunes, eh?'

Still nobody talked. The only sounds filling the air were the sobs of a now totally woeful and panicked Wiktoria.

Chapter 8

"…could act the angel but it wouldn't be true…"

Show host Szymon Rybak was enjoying his *Eurowide* journey immensely. Apart from the totally awkward moments when he was having to paint on the concerned face and explain away how hideously tragic it was that another contestant had someone managed to find themselves a teensy bit dead, squished under a disco ball or face down in the local river, he was having a whale of a time. At least this would be a contest that would be remembered in the annals of *Eurowide*-history for an eternity. The "other" contest had experienced everything from Russian disco grannies and dancing penguins through to puppet turkeys and hard metal rock demons in its time. It had even had the likes of Madonna and Justin Timberlake turn up and strut their funky stuff but it had never had deaths. People actually dying off stage and not just on it.

People would talk about the Eurowide "Ermpit Year" for eons to come, if the show managed to survive beyond its first attempt. As Loreen would say, 'forever, 'til the end of time' and that meant only one thing, that Szymon's notoriety and fame would keep going 'up, up, up, up, up, up, up'. He'd be a song contest icon up there with the likes of Petra Mede, Graham Norton and Alexander Rybak.

Szymon was a natural to host *Eurowide*. Like many a person in Rottimoldovia, he had been obsessed with song contests for as long as he could remember. After football and fish eye gastronomy, *Eurowide* was probably the most famous thing in his beautiful country. Not that he thought it was beautiful at all. Far from it. Which is why he'd moved to Amsterdam five years ago just after his lowly 23rd placing at that year's *Eurovision* contest. Amsterdam gave him everything he needed, whereas Ermpit most definitely didn't. Even if he had crafted it as the most incredible cultural hot spot ever in every interview he'd been grilled at over the past few months. But Szymon was the perfect wholesome home-grown host and had to be seen to be perfect in every *Euro* way.

His love of *Eurovision* had definitely started when he was a little boy. Bouncing on his mother's knee, captivated by the tunes he was watching on the TV. Bright colourful outfits, pretty girls, easy to remember la-la-la tunes. He was hooked. He used to put on concerts in his front room to his friends and family. His voice was good, but not overly tuneful but he was cute and that counted for everything. Immediately he knew what he wanted to do in life. He wanted to be on TV, on a show like that, to sing his heart out and make the world notice him. He liked being cute, he liked being adored and he loved being watched. The spotlight was very much his home. He suited it.

Szymon started singing lessons in his early teens and as his voice improved so did his physique and his sex appeal. By the time he was 18, he was singing nightly in local bars, showing off his muscles in the tightest of T-shirts and allowing many a female fan to see what was under it and more after the show. Either back at theirs or in the back alley or car park around the rear of the gig venue.

He'd never take girls home to his mum's. As far as she was concerned, her precious little Szymon, her only child, was as pure as could be. Wholesome and dedicated to his dream. And Szymon, being very much the mummy's boy (Dad had disappeared shortly after his birth, never to be seen again) would never set out to disappoint her. If she thought he was saintly in his actions and pure to the core then that is how he would portray himself to her. As he did to the world. Even if the truth was totally the opposite.

Szymon Rybak had two obsessions in life, one was singing for an audience and that particular fascination was well and truly being sated. He'd studied it all of his life. Watched countless song contests online. Studied each and every song. Seen what worked and what didn't. He'd changed his name to Rybak just before entering the auditions to participate five years earlier. He figured it would get him noticed if he named himself after the Norwegian *Eurovision* legend. Alongside his gym-honed physique, Hollywood-white smile and pneumatic hip-thrust dancing, it certainly did that. Despite stiffing at a lowly 23rd in the contest with his catchy three minutes of pop fluff, "Party People C'mon" (still a fan favourite half a decade later, thank you for asking, despite what juries may have thought), Szymon had become a national fave overnight. Good looks, boyish charm and a media darling, gracing the covers of magazines and appearing on TV shows across Rottimoldovia.

Five years on he was telly's golden boy and one of the judges on *Rottimoldovia's Got Talent*, the show that had spring-boarded Weronika, his *Euro* co-host, to fame the year before as winner. Even if he had been inwardly rooting for the Margot Robbie lookalike with the performing dog who came second. Not that he'd told Weronika that. When he was asked about a co-host for *Eurowide*, she was his first thought. Firstly as he felt sorry for not voting for her and secondly because she was pretty hot to look at. Just not as hot as the dog lady.

So here he was, five years after his poor placing (maybe he didn't know what worked after all), actually hosting a contest. It had been a whirlwind few months that had taken him across Europe and given him more exposure than ever before. And Szymon loved exposure, especially when it was linked to his other obsession in life. Sex.

Szymon Rybak was a sex addict. Not officially diagnosed. But he loved it. Couldn't get enough. He'd have it all day if he could. Morning noon and a very horny night. It was why he had moved to Amsterdam from Ermpit. The Dutch home of all things sexy. Loose living and the ability to lose yourself in an anonymous world of clubs, bars, parties and fetish. In his home country, he could barely sneeze without it featuring in the press so the chances of his countless carefree bunkups after a gig like back in the day were becoming beyond non-existent. Yet in Amsterdam he was a virtual unknown. So he could freely wander around fetish parties and indulge in his swinging ways as much as he liked. Which was a lot. Like four-or-five-times-a-week-as-a-minimum kind of a lot. The only strings in life he cared for were the Sandie Shaw ones on her puppet

– now there was a classic tune – because when it came to lusty bunk-ups it was definitely a case of no strings attached.

Szymon had no boundaries when it came to the pleasures of the flesh. He would try anything. As long as he wasn't caught doing it and it wasn't career-ending. Something that had become increasingly difficult over the last few months. His face was becoming much more known across Europe thanks to contest hosting duties, so if someone spotted him savouring the salacious delights of some carnal canoodlings in a private backroom S&M bar or experiencing the relish of a voyeuristic blow job in a secluded forest full of doggers, then it would definitely be bye-bye wholesome and hello holy crap! Career suicide. It was a risk he couldn't afford to take, even if the constant pulsing and throbbing of his lower portions said otherwise.

His wholesome image meant that "somehow" he was always being linked to people. Wholesome people of course. His publicity wagon had already leaked to the press the "suggestion" that he and Weronika were a couple. She loved the idea, keen to leap upon him at every given opportunity. His lips were still sore from her constant attachment at the boat party – Irish Ronnie's death had actually worked as the perfect distraction to get her off him in the most macabre of warped ways. He'd also been linked to a saccharin kids' TV presenter and a trendy teen fitness vlogger in recent months, but as good as the publicity was, none of those girls really pushed his buttons sexually. They were way too vanilla. Szymon was getting more and more extreme in his tastes. These days a quick frisson in an alley did not do the trick. And with sexy club nights and fetish fiestas becoming way trickier for him to indulge in incognito, he was having to explore every avenue to try and get his rocks off.

Which is why the online world of female domination had been a rewarding source of pleasure for Szymon over the last few months. Granted there were thousands of hot young willing things out there who would have loved to have crawled into bed with TV's glowing hot shot. But not for Szymon. He was finding that these days he needed his ladies to come with a little added spice, and a delicious portion of pain.

Szymon was in his hotel suite, dressed in one of the hotel's fluffy white towelling robes. He wasn't due at the Johnny Logan Coliseum for another few hours yet. Rehearsals for the first semi wouldn't be starting until later that day and he had a semi of his own that needed tending to. Not that it would be a semi for long. No, as soon as he logged on, it would be *log out…* his personal one, hard and proud.

The host switched on his laptop and typed in the name of his favourite fem dom site. It appeared in his search bar in its entirety as soon as he'd typed the first two letters. He was a frequent visitor. He typed in his membership details and logged into his account. He'd spent a fortune on the mistresses there already, but they were worth every euro. They'd be charging a lot more if they knew who he really was.

He opened a cupboard door underneath the table where his laptop was and pulled out a holdall. From inside it he pulled out a roll of black leather, tied into place with a neat leather bow. He placed it next to his laptop. He yanked at the bow and as it loosened the leather roll unfurled itself across the table. An array of metal shiny sex toys, pegs, clips, clamps and restraints lined up neatly before him. He smiled. It was time to get his kink on.

He reached down into the holdall again and picked out another object. A gimp mask. A mass of studs, poppers and zips. He placed it over his head and positioned the breathing holes in the mask over his mouth and nose. Anonymity was everything. He slipped off the robe and chucked it onto his hotel bed. Underneath the robe, he was naked and obviously in a state of "ready for action". He sat down in front of the laptop and clicked on one of the mistress's webrooms.

He scanned the name on the feed. 'Hello, Mistress Kimberley. I'm ready to please you…'

The sound of leather slapping onto flesh on the screen proved that Mistress Kimberley was more than ready to be pleasured.

Chapter 9

"…sing little birdie, sing your song…"

Jemma was listening to her heroine Sandra Kim and singing very loudly. She'd listened to the same winning song, "J'Aime La Vie", on repeat for the last 40 minutes. It was the one song in life that literally filled her with total euphoria; 100% glee from edge to edge as she wallowed in its words. She knew every line. It was the only foreign language she knew, to be honest, unless you counted "two beers please" in Spanish (gracias to a long weekend in Torremolinos for that one) and the classic "voulez vous coucher avec moi" which she had uttered in various states of inebriation at FagButts at fellas while partying with Char back in the UK.

AirPods in, she was in a world of her own as she waded through the mass of online press about her on her laptop in her hotel room. For once she had some time to herself, such a rarity lately. Char was at the hotel spa indulging in a "peddie" and a seaweed wrap. She figured that covering herself in algae would be a sure-fire way of sweating out the various cocktails she'd enjoyed at the boat party. Jemma wasn't convinced. She'd covered herself in seaweed for a few hours on Hunstanton beach back home once as someone said it would help her shift a few pounds. She'd lay there until the tide had come in.

She'd lost nothing in weight but did end up smelling like a cockle kiosk and picking out bits of cuttlefish from her hair for days afterwards. But if Char thought it was a good idea then go for it, mused Jemma.

Daniel was also busy. He was showing Lucie and a famed flouncy showbiz reporter from early morning UK telly, a camp specimen called Euro Dick, a behind-the-scenes tour of the Johnny Logan Coliseum. The "access all areas" tour, he'd called it. That bigged it up massively in Jemma's opinion. He had asked Jemma if she fancied tagging along. It would be filmed for UK telly, but Jemma said no. She was being interviewed by camp Euro Dick later anyway and she'd prefer to do that in a well-lit room or preferably a bar or restaurant rather than wandering around in the soulless back corridors of some under-construction arena pointing out the toilets and the exits. Euro Dick was fabulous, and she couldn't wait to be questioned, but it had to be done properly.

He was various Dicks depending on what he was reporting on. One day he'd be Soapy Dick talking about *Emmerdale* and *Neighbours* and the next he'd be Sticky Dick talking about crafts and recycling. Jemma thought he was hilarious and couldn't wait to meet him.

No, a moment to herself was just what she needed. Plus, she was gagging to read about what was going on in the outside world. She'd been in the *Euro* bubble for so long she needed to see that there was actually life beyond the world of *douze points* and doing an interview with yet another gushy and giddy contest-obsessed blogger.

She flicked to one of her favourite online gossip websites. She may have wanted to know the news, but she wasn't talking about the postings of some political party or the latest ground-breaking breakthrough in the science sphere. Hell no. She needed to know who was shagging who, who was wearing what and who was falling out of favour. The important things in life after all. Then she'd google herself. That would be an hour well spent.

For the next 20 minutes, Jemma, still singing Sandra at full volume – saving her voice for the jury shows and then Saturday night didn't really seem to occur to her – dived wholeheartedly into her fave glam world of celebrity. Apart from the occasional "OMG" in between her vocals, she continued to sing as she soaked in every word. The WAG sending love letters to a criminal in prison behind her husband's back, the married soap hunk caught with his trousers down in a gay bar, the dance star showing more than just a few samba moves on her Only Fans account. This was the stuff Jemma lived for. Tabloid heaven. It was always much nicer and easier to swallow when you were reading about someone else. But she knew she couldn't resist the temptation to google herself, even if she didn't always like what she read.

She typed her name into the search bar and pressed enter. A long list of options appeared on the screen. Near the top of the list was Lucie's feature on her and Wiktoria together. She clicked on it and scanned over the photo of her and Wiktoria on the horses. *Looking good, girls*, she said to herself. She scrolled down to read the article. There was no mention of the deathly premonition from Zoltan. In fact, Lucie has obviously erased any thoughts of including the fortuneteller copy.

A wave of disappointment washed over Jemma at the omission of her best wishes for Harvey's GCSEs.

Jemma clicked off it and looked over some of the other options. A couple of options from *The Sun*. One slating "yet another cheese fest" of dodgy songs and saying how Jemma didn't stand a chance on Saturday night, especially as her song was "a joke". The other an interview she had done before flying out to Rottimoldovia wishing her "good luck" and telling her to "make her nation proud". 'Make your mind up, tossers,' said Jemma, a little peeved. Unable to stop herself, she sang the line again, this time changing it to, 'You're making your mind up, tossers,' to the tune of the Bucks Fizz winner. Not easy when she still had Sandra blaring on her AirPods, yet somehow she managed to keep it in tune.

There was another piece from the *Mail*. The little thumbnail on the screen gave Jemma all of the info she needed. It was a photo of her hitching her knickers out of her backside, taken when she was with Char at the press junket days earlier. The headline was just as expected. 'Thank you, *Daily Fail*,' sneered Jemma and shut the lid of the laptop. She removed her AirPods and contemplated what to do next. She wasn't due anywhere for a few hours. Maybe she should head to the spa and join Char. Maybe some kind of treatment would set her up to look great for the interview with Euro Dick.

Jemma was gagging to try one of the celebrity methods of looking great. Maybe they did those at the spa. Jemma would try anything if a celeb name was attached to it. She'd already tried sleeping on her back like a corpse because Jennifer Lopez apparently did it. Jemma just ended up snoring a lot, and very loudly too, like a walrus. She contemplated Victoria Beckham's apparent bird poo facials as well, but seeing as Jemma's mum had owned a screeching cockatoo called Wogan when she was younger (Shirley had loved him when he was on Radio 2) and she had spent hours cleaning out Wogan's bird-shitty cage to earn pocket money, the process had traumatised her for life. Any thoughts of whipping something from a bird's backside onto her skin was strictly out of the question, Beckham or not.

Maybe the hotel spa did those vampire facials the Kardashians banged on about or maybe today was the day to have her *foofy* steamed. Wasn't that a thing? Some A-lister did it. She'd contemplated trying it over the kettle once. She'd even started to boil the kettle and begun to strip off. It was only when a man from Amazon turned up and started banging on the door with a package for her that she whipped her clothes back on and gave up the notion. Maybe things like that were better done professionally.

Perhaps today was the day. She'd join Char in the spa and see about getting her parts pampered. If she was going to see any man-action this week then maybe having a good steam down there beforehand was a good idea. Just as she was searching for her room key to head off, a knock sounded at the door. She opened it to find Daniel standing there.

'Hello, handsome. I wasn't expecting you till later. I was just contemplating a steam-clean on my *nunny*. Somebody does it in Hollywood so I thought I might head down to the spa and see if they do it here. Care to join me? You could have your bum bleached or something? Treat Igor to a shiny new one.' Jemma chortled. Daniel didn't. 'I thought it might perk me up for my chat with Euro Dick later.'

'As incredibly stimulating and devilishly life-changing as that sounds, d'you mind if I pass on the bleaching and keeping you company while you have your fanny feng shui-ed or whatever they do. It's Euro Dick that I'm here about. I've come straight from the hospital.' Daniel's face was leaden.

'Not another death. Jesus, what is going on with this bloody week. Poor Euro Dick. Shit, I was really looking forward to that interview with him later. Should we send flowers? What happened?' Jemma's words fired at poor Daniel.

'He's not dead but the interview is definitely off. He's broken his leg in three places. It was during the tour of the Coliseum with Lucie. He nipped into one of the loos for a wee. They've only just been put in and obviously the plumbing was crap as he slipped on a massive puddle of pissy water and went flying. Landed on his leg and...' Daniel placed his hands in front of him and pretended to be snapping a stick. 'Boom! Broken in three places.'

'Poor guy. He must have stunk of wee too. How embarrassing. What a pity.' Jemma bit her bottom lip in sympathy.

'I do have good news about tonight though. The meal with Euro Dick may be off but a group of *Eurowide* superfans are having a huge party tonight. It's the place to be. Lots of the acts are on the bill. I've got you on there too. You'll be performing at midnight roughly so it's going to be a late one, but it's a great one to be seen at. Just don't get shit-faced and lairy.

That hack Zandor is doubtless going to be there as Wiktoria is on the bill too.'

'Excellent. About her, not him. As for getting shit-faced… I won't if you won't,' grinned Jemma. 'Will Igor be coming along?'

'Actually he will,' said Daniel. 'But not with me. Now that he no longer needs to look after the totally dead Latreena, he's been employed by Wiktoria's team to look after her. Let's just hope she has better luck with him than Latreena did.'

Jemma started to twerk and sing, 'Don't cha wish your boyfriend was hot like him, don't cha…' Daniel remained clearly unamused. 'Are you sure I can't tempt you to a bum bleach?'

'Quite sure,' grimaced Daniel. 'Right, I'm off to see Lucie. She's a little beside herself about Euro Dick. They're good mates. I'll text you the details for later, okay?' He made to walk off.

'Oh, Daniel, before you go…' smiled Jemma. 'If Euro Dick is sometimes Soapy Dick or Sticky Dick, now that's he broken his leg in three places is he calling himself Limp Dick?'

Daniel couldn't help but break a smile.

'Because nobody wants that, Daniel, do they? Especially not you and dear Igor.'

Daniel's smile vanished immediately, and he hurried off to the hotel lift.

Chapter 10

"…oh… your breasts are like swallows
a-nestling…"

The guitar slammed to the floor with a crack. It bounced slightly before landing face down, a string surrendering with a ping as it curled itself outwards and useless from the guitar.

'Don't leave that guitar there.'

'Screw you,'

'I'd rather put my manhood in Latreena. After the disco ball had landed on her.'

'You wouldn't get it up in the first place. She'd be the only stiff there.'

'No, dear, it just doesn't work for *you*. One look at your face and it dis-a-fucking-pears.'

'Suck that, twat-mouth.' A middle finger was flicked into the air.

It was safe to say that the air between man and wife duo, Turkish *Eurowide* entrants, Baran and Meli, was as amiable and as Mills & Boon as it usually was. To be honest, it was a miracle that Meli hadn't thrown her guitar directly at her husband's head. She was definitely gripped by a shade of rage that could easily have seen her try to bury her instrument just under his receding hairline. He only had to look at her these days and it would literally explode any patience she had. But an hour or so of snarky comments from a Rottimoldovian telly director and a growing frustration at her own inability to perform to his patronising degree of satisfaction had pushed her over the edge. So even the merest snatch of Baran's ruddy cheeks, tousled beard and follically-challenged head was enough to cause her to erupt.

The pair were re-recording their "postcard" for the televised contest. The little vignette that would introduce their song and show them as the fun contestants the *Eurowide* viewers would want them to be. It was a pain in the *Euro*-ass that both of them could have done without but their previous effort, which had been filmed six weeks earlier on their first visit to the host nation had somehow got ruined in edit at the last moment. According to the director, it had been partially deleted and all of the footage that remained was deemed unusable for a variety of reasons. Which meant a day of trying to look spontaneous and happy as they re-shot everything they had done nearly two months earlier for Baran and Meli. Which also meant a rather long and miserable day filming at a disused quarry outside Ermpit where the two of them would pose artily and rather pointlessly in front of two raging fires, highlighting Rottimoldovia's contribution to Europe's heat industry. It was tenuous to the max.

The director they had worked with first time round had at least been pleasant. The one today was definitely a little pedantic when it came to deciding exactly what he wanted in terms of the duo's performance. One shot would be deemed too moody, another too miserable, another too... how had he described the look on Meli's face for her last shot with the guitar? Er… "old-haggy"…

Which is why Meli had stormed off set and marched back to the poky caravan-ette she was sharing with her annoying husband for the day's shooting. The "ette" was all-important to stress just how small their rest area-cum-dressing room for the day actually was. It couldn't even be called a caravan given that it was barely bigger than a couple of portaloos pushed together. And despite her and her husband now being one of Turkey's most loved couples thanks to their spiky ways critiquing TV shows on telly and now their stint carrying their nation's *Eurowide* hopes on their very middle-aged shoulders, she was finding it increasingly harder to be in any space with her irksome husband. Especially one where she could barely swing a cat. Or a guitar. Directly between her stupid and annoying husband's weasely eyes. God, if it hadn't been for their "overnight" success and popularity she could have been divorced from the vexatious prick by now.

'It's not my fault if the director has put you in a mood by saying you weren't good enough,' sneered Baran. 'I've been telling you the same for years.' He knew she'd been getting grief. He'd experienced the same. Plus, he could hear the director shouting at her from his position in the caravan. Ette.

'He didn't say that, actually,' countered Meli, pushing her poker-straight waist-length jet-black hair off her face as she did so. For style, think Cher in the "Sonny and…" years. 'He said the light in the quarry was wrong and didn't show off my beauty. He also said I was standing too close to the fire so I was sweating like a pug.'

She meant a pig. Baran didn't correct her.

'You always sweat. It's the menopause. It's what makes you so narky. Your "personal summers" run all bloody year long. You get so bloody freakily hot and dripping wet it's a miracle your internal organs don't cook themselves. Or drown.'

Meli could feel herself getting hotter. Baran was right, but she'd be damned if she'd admit that to him. Besides, she may have been at that stage in life where a few extra brushes of foundation were needed and the lip fillers and Botox were becoming almost a monthly occurrence, but Meli was still just on the right side of being able to turn heads. And when she did, her 40-something years on the planet had allowed her to perfect her flirtation game to vertigo-inducing heights of success. Any man who showed even the vaguest interest in her would definitely be centre stage for her toying. She could coax a man into bed just by looking at him. "Hypnotic" was the word she considered herself. Alluring and slightly dangerous. She was convinced she'd been the hissing pet of some Istanbul snake charmer in a former life.

The only man whose head she didn't turn, and indeed had no want to, was her husband Baran. The urge to lure him between the sheets was an emotion long gone. Yes, that ship had sailed so long ago it would have been able to circumnavigate the globe a good 20 times by now.

She blamed him for everything in life. Including the aging process that her body was going through with the dreaded menopause. Today she was dripping wet for all the wrong reasons, a condition that was only enhanced by having to pose with her guitar so close to a raging fire all in the name of 20 seconds of *Eurowide* footage. At one point, she could feel the heat so badly that she was certain the ends of her false eyelashes were beginning to singe and curl up in the intense fieriness. Anywhere else in this country she could have blamed her sodden appearance on "herring sweats" from eating one of the intensely spicy fish dishes Rottimoldovia seemed to specialise in but all she and Baran had been offered on-site today so far had been some Haribos from a passing runner.

Meli slammed herself down onto the dinky sofa of their caravanette and gave Baran daggers. 'That idiot of a director wants you again. Apparently, your earlier shots weren't any good either.' A lie. All he'd said was "tell your husband to come back for more shots" – hardly a damning critique. But Baran wasn't to know. If she was getting a hard time, then she was certainly going to give her husband one too. 'So, get back out there.'

Baran stood up and headed out of the door without even glancing at Meli. As soon as he disappeared from sight, Meli began to smile. She was smiling at the thought of the handsome young runner who had been so liberal with his Haribos earlier. Early 20s, if that. Floppy hair, unshaven, slightly geeky. Had a dick and a pulse. Meli's type then. Had he given Meli slightly more than a lingering glance as she helped herself to his confectionary? Were his words of "I love the way a sour cherry makes my tongue fizz" laced with more than just a passing interest in his oral reactions to the jelly treat. Meli was convinced that his words were pure green-light material and that he wanted her to share more than just his bag of sweets. She'd eaten four or five just to keep him near her. And if she had her way, she'd be nibbling on more than just his sour cherry as soon as possible. Who could resist her after all?

She wiped away a streak of sweat that looped itself across her forehead. She'd just need to keep Baran out of the picture for a while in order to get the ball in motion. As she watched him stroll back to the fiery set to film again, it occurred to her that time might be now. He'd be filming his solo shots for a while yet.

Now all she had to do was locate the runner. She scanned the set from the caravanette door looking for a floppy-haired victim potentially still carrying a bag of sweets. She licked her lips with anticipatory delight as she spotted him.

Baran tried to make his face look as effortlessly moody as he could. Not that easy considering the crackle of the heat behind him on set from the turbulent fires. Or the fact that he was not a grimacing, brooding rock star. It was all right for that smelly bunch of oiks representing Germany to be all moody and rocky when they were singing and posing, but Baran was a folk star. There was a softness to his performance, a melodic sway, singing about nature and daisy chains and seedlings popping into view in the sunshine. Their "postcard" would have been much more suited to him and Meli had it been a gentle stroll through a local poppy field, skipping in and out of trees in an orchard or paddling in some local lake. Not sweating their bits off in front of a blaze akin to the towering inferno. The only upside to this scenario is that Meli would be even more uncomfortable than he was. The intensity of the fire and the blaze of her own personal bodily heating were a recipe hot enough to open every pore. And if there was anything that Meli hated, it was an inability to look anything less than perfect. Hence her constant jabs, fillers and general pampering. But menopause was a mistress that not even Meli could control. And that pleased her husband.

Baran had fallen out of love with Meli many years ago. They had been happy for many too, touring around Turkey in their little camper van, playing in bars and dingy dives to make just enough money to pay for petrol to the next venue. Their life had been a simple one. One without the complications of fame, interviews, keeping up appearances. One without showbiz. Even though the last 12 months had been a whirlwind of fame, Baran was not born for the spotlight, whereas Meli had obviously decided that she was. She loved the limelight. She just hated sharing it with Baran. She would have much preferred to be a lone star. Did anybody really enjoy splitting riches? Baran was sure Meli didn't. Especially with him.

No, Baran, could have happily walked out of the quarry right now, taken the next plane home to Istanbul and spent his next few decades living in a camper van with the right person. And Meli had ceased to be the right person on every level an eternity ago. He'd always have a soft spot for her, they'd shared many happy times. He guessed his love for her would always be fluid in some shape or form. But that love was running spectacularly dry and had pretty much turned to bitterness and dislike. They would be so much better apart, but a mud-slinging divorce would hardly fit their celeb profile right now. Divorces aren't the best point-of-sale for a folky, happy, hippy, dippy *Eurowide* duo spouting peace, love and understanding. Plus, Baran really didn't fancy the aggro, to be honest. Life would be simpler if she just disappeared. A momentary vision of Meli performing underneath a faulty disco ball shot into Baran's mind. He smiled before he had a chance to push the image away, a smidge horrified by his wicked thoughts. No, he was a lover, not a fighter. Even if he could give Meli just as acidic an argument as she did if needed.

Sex had dried up with Meli too. He knew that she was sampling it elsewhere. He recognised every lie she told, every moment she sneaked around. Meli was a still a beautiful lady and she deserved a lover. He suspected she had several. Rich. Young. Or both. He'd seen the way she flirted with the journalists, batted her eyes at male fans, always insisted on the most handsome of staff at their newly-acquired house back in Turkey. The buff pool boy, the ruggedly charming gardener, the tempestuous chef. She'd tried to seduce them all no doubt, well the ones that she could. A few of her attempts at flirtation on the *Eurowide* circuit over the last few months had definitely fallen on ground stonier than today's quarry. Most *Eurowide* fans seemed to love Meli's fierce attitude, her teetering-on-the-edge-of-auditioning-for-*Botched* obsession with surgery and folky-cool style, but had no interest in any kind of sexual advances. *Eurowide* was unsurprisingly a rainbow delight, which nicely worked out in Baran's favour.

Yes, there was a very good reason why the sex between Meli and Baran had stopped a long time ago. It wasn't just the fact they had fallen out of love with each other, it wasn't even the fact that they had grown to almost loathe each other – wasn't angry sex still a thing with some couples – it was the fact that they both fancied fellas. And it would seem that they both had the same taste when it came to men as well.

Turning gay was not something that Baran had planned. He guessed it had always been there but hadn't really popped up to say hi until his love for Meli started to wane. His second act, if you will. He'd find himself looking at attributes on people that Meli didn't have – hairy chest, well-kept beard, tidy bulge in their jeans. These attributes turned him on. At first, he quashed the idea, thinking that maybe he was having some kind of mid-life crisis, unable to work out his own true identity, but then, after a discrete and drunken night of naked-bum-fun with a waiter from one of the kebab emporiums he and Meli had played at in a dingy corner of Bodrum, Baran realised what he had been missing for an entire lifetime. Namely penis. It felt right. Hell, it felt good. Hell, it felt bloody fantastic.

After that there had been no stopping Baran. He got his leg over (or both in the air) wherever he could. And Meli never noticed a thing. She wouldn't. On two fronts. Firstly, it didn't involve her and everything in her world had to revolve around her. She was the epicentre of all existence. And secondly, she was incredibly stupid.

Baran had honour at the beginning. When they'd been touring the bars and clubs. Even at first when they made it big. There were guys that she had flirted with – the buff pool boy for example – who were definitely not swimming up Meli's end of the sexual pool, and Baran would have happily dived in headfirst and splashed around until completion. But he didn't. That felt like rubbing salt into a wound that Meli didn't even realise was there. But in time, Baran realised that there was no point in having any kind of moral pendulum swinging away inside him. If he fancied one of Meli's potential shags then so be it. If he could bed him first (or second) then he happily would. He'd recently concluded that there comes a time when you have to stop crossing oceans for people who wouldn't even jump puddles for you.

Now where was that cute little runner that had been on his knees most ravenously for Baran in the caravanette for a pleasingly long time while Meli had been shooting her solo shots? Yes, Baran had been doing some shooting of his own. There was so much more to that boy than free sweeties.

'Can you try and be a little harder this time please,' hollered the director.

'Harder, dear man, harder? Yes, I think I can manage that.' He tried his best rock star pout and whispered, 'I certainly had no problem in that department earlier, did I?'

Baran caught sight of Meli approaching the runner across the set. She was in full torpedo flirtation mode. Baran's lips creased into a wide smile. He knew his wife very well. It appeared that yet again they had the same taste when it came to body shopping.

'For Christ's sake, ditch the smile, give me pout again!' yelled the director, beyond agitated.

Baran pictured the German rockers Die Bolzen in his mind and tried his best.

Meli may not have had a clue about Baran's sexual leanings but she certainly knew exactly what she wanted to do sexually with the cute young runner. In short – anything he damn well fancied! As Baran tried to strike a pose on set, Meli made a beeline for her prey.

'Not been to the sweetshop again?' she cooed seductively. As an opener it was as sickening as too many sour cherries.

The runner seemed a little taken aback but grinned. 'Er... no, but I can get you some more if you'd like some. If there is anything you want in particular, then just let me know.' His words were friendly but not at all come-on. It was one of his jobs to look after the "talent" after all.

Meli purred. 'No, I'm very satisfied in that department, plus I can't eat too many of those if I want to keep this body in order.' She gave a hair flick and ran her hands down either side of her body. The effect was semi sexy and a whole lot of awkward. The runner shifted a little uneasily, brushing his Converse high-tops across the quarry floor and staring down at them, not knowing how to reply. He'd had no such trouble with Baran earlier. He was much more at home with the aging daddy than the femme fatale.

'Er, you look fine,' he stumbled.

'I was wondering if you could help me with a few things at the *Winnebago*.' She pointed at the caravan, her words irony-free yet somehow drenched in a much-intentioned seduction as gloopy as treacle.

'Sure, what can I help you with? I just need to finish something off for the director then I could come on over. What do you need?' He was perkily eager to please, but to Meli his offer of help was definitely a chat-up line. He was hers. She knew it. She'd had this feeling before. A lot. And sometimes she'd even been right.

Meli added an upper lip tongue lick to her hair-flicking and guessed that she oozed seduction. Douze points for effort. She pushed her breasts towards him, hoping the forced swelling would be the divine temptation he would need to maybe drop his current chore for her own particular needs.

Was that a sweat patch under her breasts? Her favourite *Eurovision* lyric ran through her mind as she did so. *Oh… your breasts are like swallows a-nestling.* Nova for Sweden, 1973. Her and Baran had covered it for a fansite tribute concert. The men singing it were hot in that '70s kind of way. It had been an entry the year she was born and it talked about titties. Meli thought it was the best *Eurovision* song ever. Apart from Celine Dion of course. Celine was a goddess to Meli. Nothing touched Celine. And one of the few things that was getting Meli through the uncomfortable grind of her day re-recording the postcard was the thought that Celine had recorded her *Eurovision* one in a muddy field on a tractor. Sometimes glamour had to shine in the most unspectacular of surroundings.

She jiggled her breasts a little more. The runner stared at his Converse once again. His face reddened to a shade of beetroot as Meli listed her needs. 'There's something in the bedroom that needs lifting up and I just can't do it myself. I need somebody big and strong and willing to give a poor woman like me a hand.'

The runner knew exactly where this was going. The accent was Turkish but it was drizzled with pure lust. Maybe it was a Turkish thing. Maybe the air in Istanbul was laced with aphrodisiac. Something seemed to make the Turks horny. Well, the two he'd met so far. The only two he'd ever met as far as he could recall. But he was there to please and to help out, so he'd have to show willing even if he had no intention whatsoever of showing anything else. Not unless "daddy" wanted another go.

'Okay, give me ten minutes and I'll be over. Is that okay?' A vein of worry ran through his words.

'Perfect,' said Meli. 'Thank you so much.'

Meli started to run back to the caravanette. Was there time for a surreptitious bunk-up behind Baran's back? She had no idea, but she was praying that the gods of all things sexy and sordid were looking down on her. She stared across at Baran. He was still posing away on set. Touch wood he would be a little longer yet. But, just to make sure…

Meli made her way over to the director. Baran stopped posing as she did so.

'What do you want?' sneered Baran. 'It's not your turn again yet. Is it…?' He turned to the director, who was obviously more than annoyed that filming had been interrupted.

'No, I'd like to get some more shots of you with the fires. We're going to create some explosions to add more drama. Solo at first, then we'll need you.' He swivelled to Meli.

'I'm feeling faint. I need a lie down. No interruptions. The heat and your demands have pushed me too far. If I am to be looking beautiful for the remaining shots, I shall need rest for at least an hour.' She stared directly at Baran. 'Completely uninterrupted rest, okay?'

'I won't miss you for an hour, dear,' sneered Baran, knowing full well that sleep was the last thing on her mind. It was banging on the menu, not beauty sleep; that much was clear. *Good luck though. You'll need it seeing as you're a little cock-light for his tastes as far as I know,* thought Baran. He loved the smug power of knowing what she was up to and the notion that she had no idea that he knew. She was as easy to read as the chorus to Massiel's "La La La", Baran's own particular *Eurovision* fave and the other cover they'd attempted for a tribute online.

'That lovely runner man can come and knock me up in an hour,' stated Meli, pointing across to where the young man was still beavering with his chores.

There was a joke there about Meli's chances of being knocked up landing at minimal to non-existent due to her age and her choice of partner's sexuality, but Baran resisted the temptation. 'Sleep well.' Baran watched as Meli ran off to the caravan. Ette.

Entering the door, Meli figured she had five minutes until the runner arrived at her boudoir. Well, when she said boudoir, that might have oversold it somewhat. She basically needed to pull the sofa area apart to make some semblance of bed on which she and the runner could possibly get horizontal.

It was a tight space, but doable. She'd heard that before.

Meli began to pull at the cushions and rearrange the area. A few minutes and it was done. Now she just needed to get herself into something more seductive. Her stomach rumbled loudly and somewhat uncomfortably as she undid the buttons on her outfit and began to slip it off. Having discarded that outfit she slipped on something a little flimsier and more transparent that she always had with her from her bag. The great thing about little lacy negligees was that they could be screwed into the tiniest of balls and taken anywhere. You never knew when the need for it would strike. And it often did with Meli. Her stomach churned over again and rumbled even more loudly as she lay back on the cushions. It was bordering on the volcanic. Maybe she had eaten too many sour cherries.

Baran was stood as close to the fire as he could for both comfort and insurance reasons when the explosion behind him filled the air with its fury. As instructed by the director, he was to broodingly stare into the camera and, as the explosion burst forth, swagger confidently towards the lens. The director was just calling "cut", for once happy with the shot, when a second boom of explosion filled Baran's ears. And possibly everyone within a 20-kilometre radius.

But this explosion didn't come from behind Baran on set. And it was clear from the director's reaction that this one was not expected. And that it had not been detonated by one of the crew. A billow of jet-black cloud filled the air.

All eyes turned to the origin of the explosion. What greeted them was the crackling flames raging where the caravan had once been. Sorry, the caravan*ette* had once been.

'Jesus,' stammered Baran. 'Meli did get her bang after all.'

Chapter 11

"...I want the world to know I'm happy
as can be..."

'If I angle myself properly, I can fix it so that the bubbles jet right up my backside,' giggled Jemma as she manoeuvred her swimsuit-clad ass accordingly.

'It's like your own little colonic,' tittered Char.

The two friends were enjoying the health-inducing properties of their hotel's spa. Having both been pummelled rather thoroughly head to toe by two of the spa's recommended masseurs, the girls were now relaxing their still-tender bodies in the spa Jacuzzi. The sign on the wall above the swirling waters called it "The Superjet" due to its rather forceful underwater jet system. Jemma was thoroughly enjoying pressing her backside against it as it worked its way up to "full jet" mode.

Jemma smiled. 'I'm not sure which is better. The pummelling I'm receiving from the water or the one I've just had from *Oddbod*. Talk about deep tissue massage. If he'd have gone any deeper, he'd have been massaging my stomach lining. I'm contemplating another mesh top for tonight's concert, something right classy in gold this time, but I might have to rethink if Oddbod's bruised me with his hairy man hands.'

The girls had nicknamed Jemma's masseur Oddbod after his rather scary likeness to the hairy man-monster created in *Carry on Screaming*. It was one of their favourite hangover movies. A hefty dose of double entendres and a party pack of Wotsits in front of the telly could cure any tequila hangover.

And they had a point about the masseur. It was like being massaged by King Kong. If King Kong had been a good masseur and not just a massive angry ape ranting about his island being invaded. There was hirsute and then there was a hair-suit, because that's what Jemma's massage man had looked like he was wearing. He was full on fur!

'At least Oddbod was giving you a decent massage,' replied Char. 'My masseur was hard but not exactly hitting the spot.'

'Like many a bunk-up back home, hey?' scoffed Jemma, a deep laugh erupting from her mouth. 'When was the last time one of the men you copped off with actually managed to find your giggle pin and *take you to your heaven*.' She'd chosen her words perfectly to include the song. 'The chances of us having to finish the job in hand ourselves is as likely as Cyprus giving twelve points to Greece on Saturday night, should they both make it through the semis. Mind you, I'm happy for as many hotties as you like to give it a go. Most of them would need a fancy Sat Nav to find it though...'

'A Twat Nav,' deadpanned Char. A howl of laughter followed, drawing looks of annoyance from a few of the spa guests reclining on loungers around the pool alongside the Jacuzzi. If they had come for tranquillity, they were unlikely to get it with Char and Jemma in the same room.

'Turn right at the first flap.' Jemma added to the howling, which in turn added to the disgruntled looks of annoyance.

A shush sounded from a stick-thin specimen stretched out like a fresh corpse on a lounger. Jemma was about to give her a mouthful but stopped when she recognised her as one of the international journalists she'd been interviewed by at the press junket a few days earlier. She'd already pissed off one major country thanks to her beef with Zandor, and she was sure Daniel would not want her to do it to another. Points were going to be hard enough to come by on Saturday as it was without more bad press. Jemma bit her bottom lip, raised her eyebrows, and mouthed sorry at the woman. The woman scowled and closed her eyes again. She now looked like an angry fresh corpse.

Jemma turned back to Char, who was busy splashing bubbles across her ample chest. *Silly cow*, she mouthed silently.

'Too right,' said Char. 'And definitely say yes to the dress for this evening. What time are we going?'

'Daniel said we're on at midnight. I don't know whether you'll be needed for backing vocals, but I definitely want you by my side all night for cocktails and manhunting. I'm beginning to think the only man that I get to touch me these days is hairy old Oddbod so I'm hoping that maybe a glass of something fruity tonight might lead to something else fruity, if you get my drift. Mind you, Daniel said we're not to get drunk. *Like sure, Daniel!*' Her words were coated in a layer of thick sarcasm. 'It'll be a good night. Wiktoria is going to be there as she's performing. You'll really like her. She's a lot of fun when she's not worrying about that death threat from the fortuneteller. Honestly, surely nothing else can happen, it's not an episode of *Murder She Wrote,* is it? I've not seen Jessica Fletcher taking in the many varied delights of Ermpit, have you? Searching for the killer behind the shiny disco ball, or the murderer of the bouncy Irish popstar.' The sarcasm was still thick. 'Accidents happen. As long as you and I don't get caught up in one, eh, Char? It would take more than a glitterball the size of the moon to stop us... right?'

Jemma's bravado wobbled slightly and it showed in her voice. Char was still splashing her boobs and just nodded. Jemma was keen to change the subject all of a sudden.

'So you think the gold mesh top is a good idea? The silver one went down well at the boat party. I was getting all kinds of glances from fellas.' *Just maybe not the right ones*, she contemplated.

'Are you kidding me?' said Char, finally bringing her splashing to an end. 'The silver mesh was lush, but gold would bring a whole new level of class to it. Like really dead classy. It'll look great on stage too with the lights I'm sure. Gold mesh all the way. You so suit mesh. I'll have to find something to compliment it. I'm sure I've packed some mesh somewhere. Now, I don't know about you, Jem, but I'm getting a little peckish. How about a little bite to eat? Something thick and creamy?'

'Are we talking men again? I like them thick, and I'm not talking intelligence levels, and the creamier the better, if you know what I mean.' Jemma snorted again, any worry about being crushed by a rogue disco ball or something equally tragic now being shoved from her thoughts. Man-talk tended to do that.

'Well, we've been good and healthy being here at the spa, so how about a spot of cake and maybe a cocktail to chomp down on poolside?' suggested Char. 'There's a café off the reception that has the most incredible pastries and stuff. I'll go grab us two of those and bring them back here. You see if you can grab Oddbod or one of his mates who work here to order us some cocktails to stick on the room bill. I'll see you on the loungers in about ten minutes. What d'you fancy? Something chocolatey or creamy or one of those posh macaroon things they always serve up on *Bake Off*?'

'Something creamy, deffo. Oh my God, Char, could you imagine? Now I'm a celebrity of sorts I could end up going on the star version of *Bake Off*? I'd let Paul Hollywood give me more than just a handshake I tell you.' Jemma snorted again.

The corpse on the lounger shushed her once again, this time even louder than before. Jemma ignored her. Char didn't.

She raised her voice deliberately and stared across at the woman. 'You'd be a whizz on *Bake Off*, Jem. Paul would love you. I've seen the way you get your lips around an éclair. How could any man resist?' Another shush. But Char was in full flow. She stood up in the Jacuzzi, walked up the steps to exit and turned her back to the woman on the lounger as she did so. 'And you, Lady Shushalot over there, to use a *Bake Off* term, can kiss my soggy bottom.' To prove her point, Char slapped her dripping wet ass with a loud crack that resonated across the poolside. The woman stood up, tutted, grabbed her towel and scurried off. 'Job done,' smiled Char. 'Now, Jem, you go and grab that misery's lounger and order two of the biggest cocktails this hotel offers and I'll see you back here with the scrummiest creamiest pleasures I can find.' She walked away from the Jacuzzi, her bum still dripping.

Daniel said not to get drunk, but one won't do any harm, thought Jemma to herself as she got out of the Jacuzzi. *Mind you, he also said not to piss off any other journalists and that boat seemed to have veered into pretty murky waters again. Oh well…*

Jemma placed herself onto the now vacant lounger, grimacing as it creaked a little. She scanned around looking for someone to take her cocktail order. Bingo, she was in luck. A passing towel-collector took her order. She lay back and shut her eyes waiting for her cake and cocktail. *Blimey, it's hard work being a Euro star*, she mused. She smiled at the thought, the sound of the gentle lapping of the pool water filling her head.

Chapter 12

"…even when your lover is gone, gone, gone,
sing ding ding dong…"

A weird concoction of emotions ran through Baran's mind as he looked at the smouldering remains of the caravan. Poor Meli. Killed in her sleep. Well, killed on the job perhaps. The job being her attempt to bed the cute runner. What a way to go. No one had seen the twinky runner since the explosion either. Well, at least they could both say that the earth moved for them. Explosively. And tragically.

The Rottimoldovian fire service had been called right away. They'd been there as quickly as they could. In Rottimoldovia that meant nearly an hour after the phonecall. Yes, the quarry they were filming at was not exactly in the middle of town and overly convenient, but really… nearly an hour? Any slim hope of anyone surviving the intense heat and billowing flames that were spewing out of the caravan were totally burnt to a crisp by the time the alarm of the fire engine registered in Baran's ears. What had they done en route? Stopped for afternoon tea and fishy nibbles or pulled over in a layby to discuss their *Eurowide* faves that year? Either way, Meli and the runner were toast.

Which bizarrely left Baran with a new outlook on life. Of course, he was deeply upset that his partner in crime for so many years, so many long and increasingly miserable years, had met with such an untimely death. Yes, he *was* deeply upset, wasn't he? This was what deeply upset felt like, right? Of course, he was beyond bereft that he would now have to sing alone on Saturday as a touching tribute to his late wife. It's what she would have wanted him to do. He imagined it was, wasn't it? Plus all of those very cute, handsome *Eurowide* fans that he loved meeting would want that too for sure, wouldn't they? He'd be expected to do that. It would make him a *Eurowide* legend. Such heartache for now but yet the chance for Baran to do the ultimate *Eurowide* thing on show night. To "Rise like a Phoenix" and show the world that his country would not be defeated. Even when starring into the fiery jaws of death. The true spirit of Conchita Wurst. On top of that, Baran couldn't help but think that the odds on "La Goes Up La Goes Down" romping to success might be even greater after such a handily-timed tragedy. A star drops dead and suddenly their entire back catalogue of tunes is numero uno on Spotify in a matter of seconds. Plus there would have to be a touching solo tour back home in Turkey as a *Euro* winner. Baran had no doubt that that would be very lucrative, as would the adulation of his nation. Fans would love him. Maybe throw themselves at him. Especially the handsome ones. The daddy-loving ones. Yes. Baran was beyond bereft.

The fire team weren't able to work out what had caused the blast. Maybe a stray spark from the explosion behind Baran on set had found its fateful way and landed onto the caravan. Maybe there was faulty wiring. Maybe Meli had been burning a scented candle that had accidentally fallen over, setting the sheets under her sought-after lovemaking ablaze. What had happened in those brief moments before Meli had taken one last breath? For the moment, nobody was any the wiser. Maybe they never would be. Investigations would take place, no doubt.

The director on set was beyond annoyed of course. Not because one of the stars of his *Euro* postcard had been burnt alive. Not because she had suffered unimaginable pain and popped her Turkish clogs when potentially on the verge of worldwide glory at the newest song contest on earth. Oh no. Merely because, without both Baran and Meli, it was unlikely that the Turkish postcard would be used. And that meant that his wonderful work – because, according to him, it was always beyond wonderful – would never be seen and appreciated. Meli going up in smoke had put pay to that.

The director and Baran stood next to each other starring at the charred remains as the fire people extinguished the last stubborn flickers of flame.

'Such a waste...' said the director, his words enveloped in regret.

'Yes, poor Meli and that beautiful runner,' replied Baran.

'Beautiful?'

'Er... his soul... yes, his soul was so beautiful, you could feel that from the way he, er... shared his cherry sweets,' stammered Baran, attempting to take the spotlight off his words. He chose not to mention the sweet delights of the late runner's mouth.

'Oh, I actually meant what a waste of everything we had done today.' The director realised immediately that his words may have been a little harsh seeing as the poor man stood next to him had just lost his wife. 'And of course, your own poor loss, your dear… erm beloved wife. Such a… dreadful tragedy for you.' His words were filled with awkward pauses and a vacuum of compassion.

'Oh yes. Um… thanks. She'll be missed.' Baran was sure that she would be. He just wasn't sure how much by himself.

The two men stood in silence as the fire service combed the area around the caravan. One of the officers ventured inside the remains to see what grisly secrets lurked within. Baran suspected that they'd find two charred remains locked together in passion. Or, more likely, one poor defenceless male body struggling to get away from the relentless mantis of a female body. It was a few minutes later that the fireman came back out of the caravan. He walked over to where the director and Baran were standing.

'Hello, gentlemen. I understand one of you is the husband of the lady in there.' He pointed at the caravan and removed his fire helmet as he did so.

'That's me,' said Baran, his thoughts more on the fact that the fireman was catwalk-cute and male supermodel fit underneath his helmet than they were on poor Meli.

'I'm sorry to tell you, sir, but there is a body inside the caravan. I'm not able to recognise it for obvious reasons but I can confirm that somebody was inside that caravan and has died at the time of the explosion.'

'Just the one?' asked Baran. 'Just the one body inside? It's just that we were expecting two as a worker from the set has gone missing too and we have reason to believe that he might have been in there with my wife too. Helping her with…' His words petered out. 'Just helping her.'

'I only saw one for sure,' said the fireman.

For a moment, a lightbulb of hope lit itself inside Baran's brain. Maybe the runner hadn't been in the caravan with Meli. The anticipative flash of hope was quickly extinguished by what happened next.

One of the fire people who was searching the area around the caravan began to shout. He was pointing to the floor, to an area of bushy shrubs and hedges a good distance from the caravan. He was gesticulating for some of the other fire officers to join him. A group of them did, including the officer who had just been speaking to Baran and the director. A cloud of frenzied conversation filled the air as the men grouped together by the bushes.

'What the hell is going on?' asked Baran to the director. He didn't reply and gave a shrug.

Neither had to wait long to find out.

The grouping of officers fragmented as one of them started to walk towards Baran and the director. He carried a body in his arms. A body he had found lying unconscious, yet certainly still breathing, behind the bush. One that looked slightly scorched and bruised. One wearing the flimsiest of negligees and not a lot else.

The officer arrived in front of Baran. 'Sir, we've found your wife and she's alive. We'll need to get her to Ermpit's Alpha Beta hospital as soon as possible.'

Baran painted a smile across his face. 'Oh, thank God, she's alive. Meli's alive.' But Baran wasn't really sure how he felt. All of his thoughts about the solo tour, potentially winning on Saturday, rising like the phoenix... they had all suddenly disintegrated. And if Meli wasn't the body inside the caravan then it was obvious who was. Baran was feeling beyond sad.

More sad than glad. His thoughts consumed him. He shook himself back to reality. 'Hospital? Yes. I will need to come too, of course. I want to, I mean. Yes, let's get her there as soon as possible.' He was more than a little flustered.

The director wasn't. 'Oh good. If she's okay then this bloody postcard will get shown after all. Any chance we could do a few extra shots with you before you head off to the hospital? Those last ones you did weren't spot-on enough for my liking.' He motioned to Meli with a nonchalant flick of his hand. 'I know she's in no state to film but you're okay now, right?'

Baran didn't answer…

Chapter 13

"...flyin' high together, on a journey to
the stars..."

Jemma opened her eyes with a jolt. The lapping of the
hotel spa pool still filled her ears. As did the sound of
her own heartbeat. Loud and rhythmic. She lifted her
head groggily, aware that she had obviously been deep
in sleep. The kind of sleep where normally nothing
would wake you. But something had. For a moment she
thought it must have been Char returning with some
creamy treats or the spa worker arriving with
the cocktails, but a confused glance to her left, towards
the entrance of the spa, yielded no signs of Char.

She spun her head to her right, to the lounger lined
up next to her at the pool. A woman lay there, reading a
book. The title was in some language that Jemma didn't
really recognise. That didn't narrow it down. Other
than the fact that she recognised it as not being English.
Blonde hair was visible underneath a wide-brimmed hat
that covered most of the woman's face. A cocktail sat
on the small table alongside the lounger. *At least
somebody is getting their orders delivered*, thought
Jemma to herself. Jemma stared at the drink. A peachy
pink concoction in a tall glass decorated with enough
fruit to keep Carmen Miranda happy. Jemma had no

idea what it was but wished that she had ordered it. She and Char would have to try that next.

As if aware that someone was staring at her drink, the woman turned to face Jemma and removed her hat as she did so, placing it on the floor. She then placed her book alongside it.

'Would you like to try some, Jemma?' she asked.

Suddenly aware that she was being spoken to, Jemma lifted her head from staring at the drink to gaze directly at the woman.

'Shit. A. Brick.'

It was all she could say, every breath in her body seemingly leaking out of her every pore, rendering her incapable of further speech. Her heartbeat, already loud, escalated in its volume, beating at a hi-energy speed worthy of a club dancefloor. It couldn't be, could it? No wonder she had woken up, it had been a sixth sense. Her body telling her that this was a moment that she couldn't miss. A moment she had dreamt of. Lived for. Craved.

Lying alongside her and offering up her very own drink to her in an actual conversation with Jemma was the *Eurovision* legend that was Sandra Kim. Jemma's total hero. Bonnie Tyler had once held out for hers and now Jemma was getting her own perfect moment.

Sandra smiled at Jemma's choice of words, although not really the ones she had expected to hear. 'You're welcome to try,' she said, leaving a miniscule pause before adding the word, 'Jemma'.

It was hearing her idol say her name again that whipped Jemma back to her senses. 'Oh my God, it's you. I swore at you. You're Sandra Kim. You're like the best *Eurovision* legend ever in my books. You're why

I'm at *Eurowide*. You changed my life, 13-year-old you on that stage. Just the best thing ever.' She didn't stop for breath. 'And yes I'd love a swig.'

Jemma picked up the cocktail and took a good gulp, nearly piercing her eye on a cocktail stick spearing a cherry on the top of the glass as she did so. It tasted good.

'And you're the reason I'm here, Jemma. How could I not turn up at a song contest where one of the contestants has changed her own name to sound like my most famous song ever. It's the ultimate homage and I'm deeply touched. I want to wish you all the luck in the world for Saturday. Your song is fabulous too. I love it.'

'You are shitting me?' The words fell out of Jemma's mouth without filter. 'Sorry, didn't mean to swear again.' Sandra didn't appear to mind. 'You're telling me that Sandra Kim, youngest *Eurovision* winner ever, Goddess of all things *Euro* and the singer of the best song to come out of Belgium ever... and you have had some stiff competition now and again, to be fair... actually knows who I am and actually knows my song?'

'Of course,' beamed Sandra. 'I've been singing it ever since I first heard it. I even try to include it in my concerts.'

Jemma's mouth hung open, unable to quite take in what she was hearing. 'No fu... fudging way!' she exclaimed, desperate to stop herself from swearing in front of her heroine again.

As if to prove the point Sandra stood up, gave a slight cough to clear her throat and burst into song.

'Beep the world (hear my horn)
Thank the stars that we were born
To bring the sunshine out in every kind of weather

Beep the world (hear my horn)
Life's so good I could have sworn
That you and I could sing this crazy song forever.'

Jemma couldn't help but squeal. She shifted excitedly in her lounger, keen to hear more. Sandra was pitch perfect and, in her opinion, sang the song much better than she did. She was actually singing words that Jemma had written herself back home in Whittlesey after reading the *Eurowide* ad.

'It's a fantastic entry. Upbeat, joyous, happy, it's what the world needs right now. Even if you do sing it way better than I do.' Sandra obviously disagreed as to who belted it out better.

Jemma clapped her hands like a child on Christmas morning. 'This is the best thing ever. Like, ever! And, FYI, Sandra, your version is way better than mine. Those lungs of yours sounded incredible at 13 and they sound even better now. You're being modest, girl.'

'Let's sing together,' offered Sandra. She held out her hand to Jemma, signalling to her to stand up and join her.

Jemma could feel her brain fizz like a crate of Prosecco. 'Me, sing with you…?'

If she had been standing up already, her knees would have given in and crumbled beneath her. But this was an opportunity that she couldn't miss out on. She looked around the pool. There was no one to be seen. Damn, if ever there should have been an adoring audience then now was the moment. Fans would be pants-wettingly excited about this.

Jemma took Sandra's hand. It felt like heaven and as soft as cotton wool. She lifted herself off the lounger and smiled as Sandra began to sing the chorus again.

Jemma's smile turned into a beam the size of the Johnny Logan Coliseum as she joined in too, singing as if it was final night itself. Hold the front page, people, she was singing a duet with the one and only Sandra Kim. *Eurovision* royalty no less.

The two women sang together, their voices pure harmony as they complimented each other's tones. As they reached the end of the chorus, they both fell effortlessly into one of the verses, the momentum of their glee forbidding them from stopping.

'There's a time when people say

That everything will go your way

When life's a journey that we live and breathe as one

Where we make every moment last

Look to the future from our past

And show our friends that every day is so much fun

We know that everything we do

Let's tell our story, me and you

Have meaning in every single word

Just be triumphant and we're certain to be heard…'

Sandra and Jemma burst into the chorus once more. As they reached the final note, their voices raised, an explosion of happiness at the jubilation of the final note. Smothered in delirium, Jemma pulled Sandra towards her as they finished and hugged her in a bear-like vice grip. It was the best hug she had ever experienced.

'Douze points, Jemma,' stated Sandra, her voice a little muffled within the confines of Jemma's hug. Aware that she may be squashing a legend, Jemma loosened her grip.

'That was incredible,' swooned Jemma. 'You have made my life. Literally all of my dreams have come true in the last five minutes. We need to do that on stage together. I have some *Eurowide* blogger's party tonight at midnight. Loads of the acts for Saturday are singing. Why don't you come along and we could sing together? The press would love it. You're Sandra Kim. The crowd would go wild. You could sing "J'Aime La Vie".'

'I'd like that. But one condition,' grinned Sandra.

'Anything,' said Jemma. She meant it. She'd wrestle a team of bodyguards and security men as hench as Igor to get Sandra on that stage with her. She could have whatever she wanted. Maybe it would be a rider… Sandra was a huge star after all, wasn't she. Maybe she'd insist on a huge box of champagne and a table full of Belgian waffles before going on stage. Sandra could have it. Jemma would pay for it herself if need be. She'd happily max her credit card for her idol.

'You have to sing it with me. I insist.'

Unable to stop herself, Jemma burst into song, singing Sandra's *Euro*-winning entry. She'd been singing it for the last 20 years, so she was word-perfect. Sandra joined in, filling the pool area once again with their harmonies. In her mind, Jemma was onstage at the O2, the spotlight raining down on her and Sandra as they sang, the roar of the crowd deafening in her ears. It didn't matter that in fact they were poolside in Ermpit's only decent hotel. And that the only spotlights to be seen were the LED lights illuminating the pool from under the water, and the only sound accompanying them was the lapping of the water. She was pretty sure that the O2 wouldn't stink of chlorine either but hey… She could have been singing "J'Aime La Vie" with Sandra in a back alley behind FagButts and it would have been magical.

Having experienced another three minutes of vocal delight, Jemma realised that she needed to document the moment. Her ever-growing number of Instagram followers would freaking love this. Sod the fact that she wasn't even in full make-up, the fact that she was alongside her idol beat any amount of Rimmel and Boots No7 she could trowel onto her face. This was a moment that could go au naturel.

'Sandra, would you mind if I took a photo on my phone for Instagram? And Twitter and Facebook and for everybody that I have ever met quite frankly as this is like the most incredible moment ever. Even better than accidentally goosing Mans Zelmerlöw at the *Eurowide* press launch back in London. Well, I told him it was accidental, but that peach needed touching, you know what I mean. You would have done the same, Sandra. Any woman would. And quite a few fellas too, to be honest. It was bubblicious. Tight as anything.' Jemma suddenly realised that she was rambling and that *goosing* and *bubblicious* probably didn't translate that well. She took a breath. 'Can I get a selfie please?'

'Of course,' responded Sandra. 'I'm sure my followers will love it too.'

Jemma reached down into her bag. She wasn't really supposed to be using her phone in the spa, hotel policy apparently, but seeing as the place was empty and also given the fact that she didn't give a stuff what they thought, she grabbed her phone and yanked it out.

Wrapping her arm around Sandra, she pulled her close to her and held the phone above their heads. 'This angle always works better for my chins,' she said, 'now smile…'

Sandra and Jemma beamed into the phone. Jemma pressed the button on screen to take the photo. It made a satisfying clicking noise as it documented the moment.

She took another, and another and another... the clicking repeating itself until it became almost constant.

'This will look magnificent on Insta,' she said. The clicking continued...

'This will look magnificent on Insta. You snoring and dribbling all across your face. You're pulling some right faces. Wake up, will you, I've got the cakes. About three million calories each but who gives a shit.' A hand tapped against Jemma's cheek. The clicking noise sounded again. Jemma opened her eyes to see Char standing over her. She waggled a brown paper bag in her face. 'Cake time. Blimey, you must have been in a deep sleep, you were snoring for England. Dreaming about Paul Hollywood, eh?'

Jemma tried to gather her thoughts. She sat upright and swivelled her head towards the lounger alongside her. It was empty. Sandra was nowhere to be seen. She guessed she never had been. She felt crushed. Not even one of the largest multi-tiered cream cakes she had ever seen being pulled from a paper bag in front of her eyes ready for scoffing could disguise her disappointment.

Chapter 14

"...hey sister, d'you believe in the things
we dreamt we'd discover..."

'Poor Dick,' piped a less-than-usually buoyant and boisterous Lucie Rave as she passed the men's toilets backstage at the Johnny Logan Coliseum where the unfortunate Euro Dick had taken a wet and dangerous slip in a pool of various countries' wee earlier in the day. She hadn't wanted to leave her friend at the hospital, where he currently resided flat on his back with a plaster cast from ankle to groin, but deadlines had to be met and she had an interview lined up with one of this year's *Eurowide* hosts, Weronika Seksi. And seeing as the interview room where she was meeting the 21-year-old presenter was a mere 20 yards away in the same corridor as the loos, she was sadly forced into returning to the scene of poor Dick's urine-soaked misfortune.

Palaver!'s top reporter (actually the only one given magazine and online cut backs these days) attempted to push open the door to the interview room, not easy given her own diminutive height and the fact that it was horribly stiff due to being the wrong size for its own frame. It wasn't just the plumbers of Ermpit's new *Euro*-stadium who were slightly rubbish when it came to the finer details. Apparently, the carpenters were too. It took her three hard shoves before falling into the room.

A panting Lucie was greeted by a red-faced Weronika screaming obviously pissed-off words in her native tongue into her mobile phone. She immediately painted a smile on her face and clicked the phone off mid-sentence on seeing Lucie. She couldn't help but let her gaze run up and down Lucie's dinky appearance. Lucie was everything that Weronika wasn't and hoped she never would be. Ridiculously small, barrel-wide, and possessed a walk like a gluttonous duck in search of its next meal. Weronika had the build of every Rottimoldovian woman – well, at least the famous ones. Above average height, stick-thin in a borderline unhealthy kind of way, Lady Penelope hair in both colour and style, and with a set of pretty yet pinched facial features. Devastatingly darling and fashion-mag-fab in the right light but get the wrong angle and her slightly too angular cheekbones and nose could colour her a touch *Hocus Pocus* witchy. But after months in the spotlight of media fame, Weronika pretty much knew her angles. Her twin sister, Wiktoria, was of the same disposition, no surprise seeing as they were almost identical, but to any onlooker it was clear that Wiktoria was blessed with definitely a more natural degree of beauty. Despite swimming in an identical gene pool, there was a naïve and innocent softness to Wiktoria that Weronika most certainly still had to work at to achieve. In other words, resting bitch face was much more apparent with Weronika than it ever was with her twin sister.

Lucie approached Weronika with her hand outstretched. Weronika shook it. For whatever reason, Lucie had decided that Weronika wasn't an air-kisser. Plus, Lucie didn't actually know how many kisses were appropriate in Rottimoldovia. She inwardly chastised herself for lack of research. Better to be safe with a handshake, though, as opposed to falling short mid-kiss.

'Sorry, very stiff, three shoves to make it work,' she wailed, pointing towards the door. She immediately giggled reminded of a conversation she had been having earlier with Daniel about his encounter with Igor. She banished the image from her mind. 'I'm Lucie from *Palaver!* It's lovely to meet you. I hope I didn't catch you at a bad moment?'

Weronika looked a little perplexed. The penny dropped. 'Oh, the phone call. Just one of the press officers making some crazy requests for me and Szymon. She forgets we have to rehearse like crazy to make sure we're ready to host what will become the greatest show on earth. Millions of viewers. To perform in it is the greatest honour. And it's set to be an incredible first year. One that people will never forget.'

Lucie plonked herself on a chair which disappeared under her width. 'It's not been without incident already, has it? Deaths. Poor people hurt, accidents. Police turning up. I've never known such a thing. It's like an episode of *Luther*. But no Idris of course.'

Weronika creased her forehead as much as her Botox would allow. Even at the tender age of 21, there was no way she was risking even the merest line for her telly stardom. And image insecurities kicked in at an early age in celeb-land. 'I know, isn't it just so awful. Poor Latreena and her faulty disco ball and the Irish boy getting drunk and falling into the Krudd. Surely nothing else can happen before Saturday. That would be just awful. We need to concentrate on the joy and magic of this new event and how it can bring more people together than ever before. Not some poor singer getting crushed by a massive shiny ball.'

Keen to try and force Weronika out of her Snow White autopilot answers, Lucie couldn't resist mentioning the premonition that Weronika's twin sister had received from the mechanical fortuneteller at the Dicken Platz. 'That must be a massive worry for her. She was positively freaked out at the time.'

'Wiktoria gets scared easily. She used to when we were children. She would spend all of Halloween hidden behind the sofa crying her eyes out just because somebody turned up at the door dressed as a vampire or a mummy. She'd cry for days. Wiktoria can be overly sensitive.'

'So what were you two like as kids? Did you hate each other and bite the feet off each other's Wonder Woman dolls?' guffawed Lucie. 'Sorry, that's what my sister used to do to me. She did it to all of my dolls. She only stopped when one got lodged in her stomach lining and she had to have an operation. Silly girl.'

Weronika smiled awkwardly. 'Er. No, she never did that. We argued, I suppose like most children do, but we spent our time playing nurses together or pretending to be Spice Girls in front of the mirror.' Weronika had already given the same answer about 73 times that week. Why was it the press seemed to be so interested in talking so much about her sister too? Weronika was the one hosting the show for heaven's sake. Okay, so her sister was representing the home country blah blah blah, but, really, this was Weronika's moment to shine. Her sister would be on for three minutes during the final, she herself would be on for hours over the course of the semis and the final. Seemingly endless ones if you included the voting. But that was how the press worked of course. So, she etched on the smile and answered. Hopefully, the sibling questioning would end there.

It didn't. 'Wiktoria is lovely isn't she. Lovely girl. Pretty girl. She's been a successful singer here in Rottimoldovia for a few years, hasn't she?'

Weronika tried not to show any disgruntlement on her face as she answered the question. Wasn't this interview supposed to be about her? She was tempted to just walk out but *Euro* rule number one was never piss off the press, 'Yes, she became a star at 16. She was spotted in a shopping mall here in Ermpit by a talent scout. She'd been singing outside a supermarket whilst waiting for our mother to finish buying food. He talked to my mum about her voice and the next thing you know she's appearing on some daytime TV show with her first single.'

'What a lucky girl. I never had any such luck when I used to hang around outside Lidl waiting for my mum to buy our Monster Munch and Turkey Twizzlers. All I got was a cold from being stood out in the rain for too long.' Lucie tutted at her own hardship. 'And now you've followed in her footsteps.'

'I wouldn't say I've followed. I always sang too. Like I said before, we used to think we were two of the Spice Girls when we were very young. And now it's great for the world to see that I can sing *and* present. I'm multi-talented. A double threat.' Weronika was beyond keen to steer Lucie's questioning back onto the most important subject of all. Namely her.

'You won *Rottimoldovia's Got Talent* last year, didn't you? What was that like? You don't have Simon

Cowell here, do you? Or Amanda with her boobs out all the time.'

Weronika wasn't really sure who Lucie was talking about. 'I loved being on that show as it gave me a chance to show people what I could do. That my voice was fabulous. Plus, it was where I met Szymon, of course. He was one of the judges. He told me that he had been rooting for me from the first time I performed.' Although she did have a sneaking suspicion that maybe he had preferred some woman and her dog but, hey, that was history, that bitch wasn't hosting the biggest and newest telly gig on earth now, was she? And neither was the dog.

'You and Szymon seem very close. I did see you both on the boat party. Kissy kissy and all that. Are you an item?'

Weronika smiled, an air of smugness coating her answer. 'As the famous song goes, "Come What May", but for the moment let's just say we are enjoying each other's company both professionally and personally.'

'And after?' yelled a hopeful Lucie. 'Will you still see each other... personally? Does he get your vote as a potential long-term partner? Does he ooze douze points?' Another giggle.

'Who knows what the future holds for us both after Saturday. This is such a massive platform for both of us to profit from.' Once more, Weronika had tired of talking about someone else. Szymon was capable of gaining his own valuable promotion. 'Would you like to hear about how my rehearsals have been going? Some of my solo spots are just incredibly funny and original.'

'Will you be singing? Do you sound like your sister?' asked Lucie.

Weronika was happy to answer the former if not the latter. Enough about Wiktoria. 'Yes, I'm performing a medley of some of my favourite *Euro* songs. It's going to be an amazing. I've picked the tracks especially as they really suit my vocal range. And my costumes, well I call them costumes, they're barely more than pieces of fabric covering the right places if you know what I mean.' She brushed her chest with her fingers just in case Lucie was in any doubt. I'm surrounded by about 30 male dancers. They're all oiled up and bare-chested and wearing rubber shorts. It's quite avant-garde and arty. I'm thinking of wearing a massive ponytail to swing round like Slavko did. D'you remember him? I hope the audience like it.' Weronika had no idea what avant-garde even meant but had heard someone else say it and thought that it made her sound hyper-intelligent.

'Oh, saucy saucy. Of course they'll love it. With gay men galore here, it'll be avant *hard*!' Lucie guffawed and spat a little in appreciation of her own bawdy joke.

Yet again, Weronika unsurprisingly had no notion what the reporter was laughing about.

'And are you tipping your sister to win on Saturday? Wiktoria seems to be loved by everybody, doesn't she, and "Love Safari" is a fantastic song. Total earworm. Hear it once and it's in your brain for days. It's tipped to do very well on the night.'

Weronika sighed inwardly as the conversation steered back to her sister once again. But professionalism came before envy, didn't it? 'I love the song, I'm word-perfect myself.' She gave a quick burst as if to prove her point. 'I think it would be amazing for Rottimoldovia to win on Saturday night. The right song, the right act... it could happen. And that way we'd be right back here next year once more. My country holding the first two *Eurowide* contests ever. I could host it all over again. Maybe even perform for my country. That's such a dream. How lovely would that be?'

'Lovely lovely,' trilled Lucie in agreement. She was just about to dive in with her next question when her phone rang. The room filled with the poppy sound of her ringtone – Sergey Lazarev's "You are the Only One". She'd downloaded it especially for her trip to Ermpit as it was her favourite *Eurovision* song. Normally she would switch it to silent during an interview but for once she must have forgotten. Lucie's cheeks rouged with minor embarrassment. 'Oops. Sorry. Sexy Sergey. Couldn't resist.' She needn't have worried. Simultaneously Weronika's phone sounded too, her ringtone much more conventional.

Weronika looked at her phone. 'I need to get this, it's one of the producers again. Shall we?' She indicated for Lucie to take her call too. Lucie was keen to as it was Daniel.

They both answered their phones. For a good few seconds there was silence as they listened to their calls. As if synced in their actions they both hung up at the same time and faced each other. Their features were both flushed. They both spoke at the same time.

'Oh my, it appears there's been another incident,' purred Weronika, her voice registering alarm yet attempting some semblance of calm.

Lucie was the other end of her spectrum with her explosive outburst. 'Bloody hell, another person's copped it. Nobody's safe, I tell you, nobody! Some poor runner but you can guarantee it was supposed to be the Turkish lady who died. This is getting way too freaky.'

However you said it, there was no denying it. Another death had come to Ermpit. And suddenly the calamity of Latreena and Ronnie DonRon ending up six feet under seemed increasingly sinister and so much horribly more than mere coincidence.

Without either person saying it, both Lucie and Weronika were thinking the identical thing.

Just who was going to be next?

Chapter 15

"…thunder and lightning, it's getting exciting…"

Bjorn Bjork hung up the phone, having just been told about the death of the runner too. Young lad apparently. The news definitely gave chills. An accident they said. A stray spark from a controlled explosion on set. Not that controlled then, was it? Producers were determined to try and keep this death out of the press. It wasn't one of the "talent" after all. Not like the Swiss diva and the Irish teenager. What a tragedy. What were the chances? It appeared pretty high given the last few days.

Bjorn shifted restlessly. No matter how many times it had to be done Bjorn Bjork (or Bella, as we now know) still found it highly uncomfortable to be playing out her *Eurowide* charade with her hefty breasts taped down against her ribcage. But seeing as she wouldn't have even been at *Eurowide* if it wasn't for her kilometres of tit-tackling tape, handily placed neckerchief and age-defying "boyish" good looks, she was more than prepared to put up with it. Even when her six-foot-three frame, aching chest, gangly legs and skyscraper platform heels were squidged and bent rather brutally into the not-particularly-roomy back seat of the taxi taking her through the rain-soaked streets of Ermpit, to the venue for tonight's bloggers' *Eurowide* concert. Bjorn was due to open proceedings with the tropical salsa-tones of "24 Hours of Sunshine" before performing a special Scandi medley of hits from the likes of Carola, Bobbysocks, Emmelie De Forest, Herreys and Charlotte Perrelli, legends one and all. Having already performed it countless times in the run up to *Eurowide,* the singer knew it was a winner. Crowds adored it. Hopefully, in years to come, she, or he, would become one of the legends included in future contestants' medleys. Bjorn Bjork would be another one of those apocryphal song contest names that fans talked about and adored for decades to come.

Quite how Bjorn/Bella would manage that though was beyond his comprehension. Even though it had seemed like the most perfect solution in the world at the time to pretend to be somebody else to gain entry into the contest, the thought that Bjorn would have to keep it up for every future *Eurowide* appearance and potentially for the rest of his career was beyond daunting. Plus, there was the little matter of the fake passport that Bella had had made thanks to a rather dodgy client who enjoyed the delights of Bella's boudoir offerings so much that he was more than happy to furnish her with illegal documentation. If Bella was to continue being Bjorn and if Sweden were to romp home victorious on Saturday, which was the plan after all, then Bella would have to lead a double life. Exist with two identities. And that was a total mindfuck. She already planned to try and move to the most reclusive island she could find in Sweden's famous archipelago as soon as possible to avoid prying eyes. Or if Bjorn lost miserably on Saturday, the plan was to stage his mysterious disappearance and assumed death back in

Sweden. A suicide note of "woe is me, nul points shame, can't cope, national disappointment in my *Eurowide* debut, goodbye cruel world" tucked inside his platform boots and tied with his neckerchief placed on the banks of some raging and dangerous Swedish waterway would do the job nicely. And then Bella could happily go back to her job on the job tout suite.

Bella had been reading about double lives and it wasn't easy. In bed the night before she'd read about Fanny and Stella, two ladies who had been selling *favours* on the streets of London in the 19th century for ages but were actually finally found out to be two "he-she ladies" (as the press oh so deeply wittily called them back then) as they were really two young gentlemen, Ernest Boulton and Frederick Park. They were brought to court on "the abominable crime of buggery" no less and charged accordingly. Needless to say, their illicit world of frilly embroidered hankies and soft kisses with gentleman callers did not end well. Bella prayed that her double life would be easier to manage. And hopefully avoid syphilis, unlike Fanny. Especially as her "work" as Bella was just as rumbunctious and raunchy. And if a little *back door action* was a crime then she was already, no pun intended, "buggered". If Victorian England had taken it so badly then heaven only knew how modern-day Sweden would deal with such dirty deception on such a massive stage.

Bjorn watched the lights of Ermpit flash by the taxi window. Raindrops splattered against the glass. A crack of lightning lit up the black sky over the River Krudd as the car sped along its banks. It was a horribly stormy night and given everything that had been going on over the last few days, Bjorn couldn't help but feel that tonight's storm was merely a taster of the turbulent and murky waters that might still lay ahead.

Bjorn tried to shift his platform heels into a more comfortable position, one that meant that they weren't jammed so dramatically and awkwardly into the foot well of the taxi and his knees weren't deep-tissue massaging the back of the driver's seat. He should have changed at the venue but was fully aware just how much of a danger and an impossibility that would be. A five-minute stage call greeted with "oh excuse me while I just wrap my tits up and flatten them down like knackebrod" (his favourite crispy Swedish bread) before going on to sing his heart out would not be conducive to leading the necessary double life to avoid international scandal. No, dressing in the comfort and, more importantly, the privacy of a hotel room was what was required if Bjorn's knackebrod were to remain a secret.

Chapter 16

"...I'm out of my head, I don't know
what to say..."

On the other side of the River Krudd, at a Ukrainian restaurant called Ruslana's, Jemma was chasing a piece of garlic-drenched pork fat around her plate, unsuccessfully trying to skewer it with her fork. Daniel, Char and Lucie were sat at the table with her. A fifth unoccupied seat belonged to Igor, currently relieving himself in the toilet, before heading off to start a shift protecting Wiktoria at the bloggers' concert.

Having finally hunted her prey, Jemma popped the pork fat into her mouth and chewed loudly, attempting to tear it apart when her teeth. Not easy when it appeared tantamount to trying to eat a kid's bouncy ball. It was that chewy and about as flavoursome. After a few seconds she gave up and, picking up her serviette, spat the half-masticated piece of meat into it. She balled it up and placed it on the table, adding the final flourish of an appreciative decibel-bending burp. As she did, a crack of thunder sounded from outside, luckily disguising her oral explosion from the table next to them, accompanied by a rather dramatic display of lightning.

'I'm glad this concert's not outdoors tonight,' observed Daniel. 'You'd be drenched, and I am not having you risk pneumonia before Saturday.'

'You'd be wetter than a cucumber in a women's prison, Jem,' added Char, rocking herself into a belly laugh. Fuelled by four cocktails already, one poolside at the spa and three during the meal, and in the knowledge that she wouldn't have to sing tonight as Jemma was singing to a backing track, Char was out to enjoy herself.

'Filthy girls, lashings of salad cream,' whooped Lucie, her dinky body also fuelled by cocktails and more than a little tipsy.

Jemma cackled too. 'Jesus, you're not wrong. It's sheeting down out there, tonight.'

'What is *sheeting*?' asked Igor, returning to the table and doing up his flies as he did so.

'Chucking it down, pelting, streaming. We're talking about the rain. It's pissing it down,' replied Jemma. 'Talking of which, you've missed a bit, amigo.' Jemma pointed to his trousers as he went to sit himself down next to Daniel. A dot of shame on his trousers showed where he hadn't quite shaken and dried sufficiently. His face reddened slightly as he noticed it.

'Ignore her, Igor.' Daniel reached under the table and squeezed his leg. It was too wide for his hand to grip around. Like a tree trunk. Daniel felt a stirring between his own legs. Even if Igor wasn't the prettiest fella in *Euro*-town, his musculature was sensational, and Daniel couldn't help but appreciate the joys of a meaty thigh. Even though Igor had invited himself to the meal, Daniel had happily let him join them. Despite the obvious pitfalls of Igor's "neck-up" situation, there was something about Igor that was somehow winning him over. He knew exactly what it was. Oh yes: the massive pecs, washboard abs and weapon of mass seduction. Daniel was nothing if not easy. Show him a total bottom who wasn't happy to roll over, contented puppy-style, for a big-dicked dose of bum fun and Daniel would show you a liar. He'd known he wanted to have a return visit to Igor's lower portions from the first time they'd gotten together, despite his own protestations. And Igor being beyond smitten was definitely a turn on for him. Who didn't love being the object of someone's total adulation?

Char had seen Daniel squeeze Igor's leg. And seen them eye each other up throughout the meal. She knew exactly where this was going (again) – she'd seen enough of her gay mates getting it on to spot the signs. With cocktail number four soaking through her veins, she lifted her hands up to Daniel, shaped one into a ring and the other into a pointy finger and inserted one inside the other. Jemma screamed with laughter as she did so.

'Will you sodding stop it!' mouthed Daniel, only half-annoyed. He shook his head at her.

'C'mon, Jemma, sing up, girl,' yelled Char. 'I'll be Bradley, you be Gaga… let's sing Danny Boy's theme tune. *He's so shallow, shallow…*'

As Jemma joined in, Lucie started to rock with laughter on her chair, giggling so much at the girls' rendition that she almost fell off. Even Daniel couldn't help but let a smile spread across his face. The girls were exasperating but they were a lot of fun. He couldn't imagine the press officers for Die Bolzen or for Baran and Meli were having as much of a laughter-filled time. One dealing with the stench of stale BO and the other with married misery. At least Jemma and Char were a right laugh to hang out with, even if their mouths were a complete liability.

'Oh I love zis song. From *A Star is Porn,*' enthused Igor, jiggling his mammoth shoulders as Char and Jemma sang.

'It's *A Star is Born,*' corrected Daniel.

'No, you were right the first time, Igor,' said Char, breaking off from her singing. She raised her hands and inserted a finger into a makeshift ring again.

Igor blushed and smiled, knowing that something was funny and rude, but not fully understanding what.

Daniel gestured to a passing waiter. 'Can I get the bill please?' The waiter nodded. Daniel looked at his watch. 'I think it's time we headed off to the concert, don't you?'

A fulsome thud sounded as an uncontrollable Lucie rocked with laughter so much that she fell off her chair and landed, still giggling, on the floor.

'Way to go, Sweet'N Low!" howled Char.

'Yeah, it's definitely time,' sighed Daniel. 'I'll order us a taxi.'

Chapter 17

"...like Romeo and Juliet once before..."

The UK party, plus Igor, arrived at the bloggers' concert venue, a disused warehouse on the banks of the Krudd, just as Bjorn Bjork was preparing himself backstage. Although sharing a dressing area with the fragrant foursome that were Germany's rock monsters, Die Bolzen, was strangely not mentioned to him when he agreed to partake in the concert. Thankfully, they were performing after him so at least he wouldn't have to spend too much time enduring them, their deodorant-defying body odour, and a hairspray cloud large enough to not just back-brush every band member's hair into submission but also coat an area the size of the Berlin Wall. On top of that, there was their endless smoking, adding an even more terrifyingly ginormous cloud to the atmosphere. Nuclear mushrooms had nothing on this lot! Bjorn thought that ciggies had been banned pretty much everywhere apart from those hideous glass cubicles at airports now – obviously word hadn't reached Baden Baden or whatever geographical German stone the group had crawled out from under. He was tempted to complain about what it was doing to his vocal chords and that the stench was definitely permeating his sateen. He'd have to get it deep cleaned thoroughly before the next wear. Thankfully, he had a few matching sateen outfits with accompanying accessorised chiffon neckerchiefs to choose from. All in a pleasing mix of Swedish blue and yellow of course. Nobody would ever accuse Bjorn Bjork of not being patriotically on brand when it came to his *Eurowide* fashion.

Bjorn flicked his fringe off his forehead with a gentle sway and stared into the mirror. He smiled, teeth as white as a polar ice cap, pleased in the knowledge that even the hottest sleuth would have a job to crack the gender-busting mysteries of what actually lay beneath the sateen wonderment of his outfit.

His smile disappeared when he spotted one of the members of Die Bolzen, the lead singer, let his fingers do the walking up the tiny pleather skirt of some rather dubious-looking groupie who had managed to find her way backstage. And bring three of her equally attractive mates for the rest of the band too. *Where did they find such delights?* pondered Bjorn. Tesc-ho or Carref-whore or maybe Sweden's very own Old Bikea. They were as rough as a brickie's handshake. But obviously eager to please.

Bjorn's smile returned when show host, Szymon, breezed into the dressing room. Now there was an extremely attractive and sexy man. Bjorn felt his heart flutter a little as Szymon marched towards him. Trying to suppress his inner Bella desire to reach out and kiss Szymon wholeheartedly on the lips, Bjorn simply smiled and gave off his air of wholesome purity despite the deeply impure thoughts coursing through his brain. Szymon was there to help host the evening's entertainment alongside the team of *Euro* bloggers.

He'd also be performing his sensational "Party People C'mon" no doubt. Providing he wasn't doing it at two in the morning, Bjorn would be tempted to hang around a little longer to see him in action. Those hips. That chest. That total package. What a pity he wasn't sharing Szymon's dressing room.

'Hi, Bjorn, having fun, mate?'

Mate? Oh yes, that was him wasn't it. 'Er, yes,' answered Bjorn. 'Not as much as some, it would seem…' Bjorn pointed to the lead singer of Die Bolzen who now seemed to be knuckle-deep in "entertaining".

'Yeah. I'm trying not to see that right now,' offered Szymon, before adding, 'or smell it.'

'I'm only glad you don't think that rather spicy smell is my aftershave,' laughed Bjorn. Was this flirting? If so, it had to stop. Bella was not in the room right now.

'No chance of that! I'm here to mic you up ready to go on. The concert is about to kick off. There's a full house out the front and you're up first. And, strangely, the sound tech due to mic you up seems to have disappeared. He's probably on a cigarette break or something equally as important. So, I thought I'd do it instead. If that's okay with you, Bjorn.'

More than okay, thought the singer.

'I'll need to push the cable up your shirt,' explained Szymon looking directly into Bjorn's face. The Swede felt a flushing spread across his face. Szymon had eyes that felt like they could excavate their way directly to your very soul. Leaving a trail of lusty thoughts and deeply wicked desires in their path.

Lost in thoughts of what Szymon could push anywhere he liked, Bjorn turned his back to the host allowing him access to his shirt. Before he could even think about what he had done, Szymon was bending down and lifting Bjorn's shirt ready to clip the mic pack to Bjorn's waistband and feed the cable up his back to clip onto the sateen flaps of fabric at the shirt's collar. Szymon was a fast mover and his hand was up the back of the sateen shirt before Bjorn had had a chance to contemplate the logistics of what he was doing. Awash on the thought of Szymon's manly hands touching his skin and sending a frisson of electric excitement to his very epicentre, he hadn't actually considered where they were going.

Bjorn froze in horror as Szymon's hands brushed against the fabric wrapped around his body. Would Szymon say something? Ask him why it was there? What would the response be if he did? Countless questions suddenly ricocheted through his head. Bjorn's secret identity and deception couldn't be uncovered so close to the actual contest.

Szymon fed the cable out of the top of Bjorn's shirt and offered the clip to him. 'You'll need to clip that onto your shirt.'

Bjorn span back round to face him and snatched it from him. He looked Szymon directly in the eyes again. What was he thinking? Was there any doubt or intrigue there? Szymon's smile suggested maybe not.

A flood of relief coursed through Bjorn. He made a note not to let it happen again. Nobody must touch him so intimately when he was Bjorn. As Bella, Szymon was welcome to do whatever his red-blooded heart desired. Bella would happily be his sexy flexi shady lady any time he wanted, but as Bjorn... well, that was a whole different ball game... so to speak.

'I'll see you onstage in five minutes,' said Szymon. He smiled at Bjorn and lifted his arm to give Bjorn's shoulder a gentle squeeze. Something stirred inside him. Something sexual. The same had happened when he had been touching the skin on Bjorn's back. He'd ignored it then, considering it was a horny hangover from his session online with Mistress Kimberley. But second time around, as he touched Bjorn's shoulder and looked into his eyes. Well, that was a different matter. There was something about Bjorn's face. He was truly beautiful. Szymon's already hugely liberal sexual appetite was suddenly contemplating the fact that he was finding a 20-year-old man from Sweden deeply horny. The emotion was new to him but he didn't find it displeasing in any way. Surprising but far from unwelcome.

A touch flustered he turned and walked away before the reddening of his cheeks and the potentially obvious eagerness showing in his jeans could be seen. 'Laters.' He waved as he left the dressing area. 'Help yourself to all of the refreshments. Wine, champagne, whatever you fancy…'

Bjorn could feel his own cheeks heating up again too. He was sure that Szymon had not only stuck his hand up his shirt and touched his back, but had also touched his soul as he undressed him with his eyes with every glance. But he was doing that to him as Bjorn. So Szymon must be into guys. But then wasn't he dating the other contest host, Weronika? Or at least sleeping with her. So perhaps he was bi? Bjorn was confused. But if the same had happened between them when she was Bella, then she had no doubt that they would be enjoying some very horizontal refreshments before the night was through.

At least he hadn't noticed the half-mummification when he'd been snaking his way up her body. Or had he? The Swede prayed that her secret identity was still just that.

A squeal of carnal delight sounded from the sofa within the dressing area. Bjorn glanced to see the lead singer of Die Bolzen remove his hand from the groupie's skirt. Despite the inappropriateness of the occasion, Bjorn couldn't help but feel slightly envious by their blatant display of foreplay. At least the stinky rocker and his groupie knew exactly what they were dealing with.

Mind still fizzling with salacious thoughts of Szymon, Bjorn was called to the stage. For now, it was showtime.

Chapter 18

"…I'm your drama queen tonight, everything's
gonna be all right…"

Char put her fingers to her mouth and let out the
loudest wolf-whistle as Bjorn made the all-important
key-change as he segued from one Charlotte Perrelli
song into another, "Take me to your Heaven" into
"Hero", as part of his Scandi medley on stage. His voice
was perfection, and a very drunken Char was keen to
show her appreciation.

'Man, his voice is freaking brilliant. Seriously, this
blond dude could win, Jem. He really could.' She
punched her arms in the air as she spoke, causing herself
to topple sideways into a group of leather-clad young
men about her own age. She steadied herself by grabbing
one of them. They were obviously there for Die Bolzen,
she guessed. She attempted a smile to excuse herself but
was greeted with nothing more than a stoned-looking
stare from all four. 'Well, excusez-bloody-moi' she said,
luckily quietly enough to not be audible over the
tsunami of schlager goodness pouring from the stage.
She turned to face Jemma again. 'Seriously, this Swedish
fella is the bomb.' No reply. She paused before shouting
Jemma's name as loud as she could to try and grab her
attention.

There was no chance. Jemma and Wiktoria, who had squealed excitedly upon seeing Jemma again when she'd arrived at the disused warehouse, were surrounded by a group of hyperventilating fans who were obviously more excited about trying to grab a selfie or a kiss from both Jemma and the host nation's hopeful contestant than they were about watching Bjorn strut his Scandi-stuff on stage. A fact Char couldn't be bothered to comprehend. She shrugged at the lack of response from her best mate and hand-signalled to Daniel, standing with Lucie and a watchful Igor a few yards away from the swarm of fans, that she was heading to the bar. It was her second visit since arriving. She curved her way tipsily across the floor, taking out a fan of two as she did so, unable to control either her direction or her momentum.

Daniel watched on as Jemma and Wiktoria smiled and posed accordingly for the fans scrummed around them. He turned to Igor. 'We may have to take the girls backstage in a minute. They're going to get mobbed if they stay out here.'

'I was thinking the same. Especially as I've only started working with Wiktoria so recently. After Latreena I'm paranoid that something bad is going to happen to Wiktoria too. It's why I'm constantly scowling with worry.' He pointed to his face and attempted a smile.

Daniel smiled back, not really sure that, given Igor's facial arrangements, he was able to read any kind of emotion – scowl, smile or otherwise. The bodyguard's pock-marked skin, lazy eye, scar and crooked nose combo were akin to the severest bout of Botox when it came to trying to decipher Igor's facial expressions and their meanings. Having said that, Daniel was fully aware that he was finding them a lot less jaw-droppingly gagging in their brutality than he had at first. Maybe he was softening up in his feelings for Igor. He certainly knew that he was definitely *hardening* up in all the right places when he looked at anything below Igor's tree trunk-sized neck. He was sure his clubbing friends back home on their nights out to The Man Factory would be horrified about his attraction to Igor as Daniel's conquests' features in the past had always been more *drop dead gorgeous* and much less *dropped as a baby*. But for now, in the confines of the *Eurowide* bubble, that didn't seem to matter. Igor was 100 per cent a worthwhile distraction who was certainly moving up Daniel's leader board.

A voice boomed. 'Can we go backstage *now* please? I saw diddly squat of Bjorn Bjork and I don't want to miss whoever's coming up next.' Both men looked down at Lucie as she bellowed. At four-foot-eleven, seeing over the checkouts at her local Aldi wasn't easy so the chances of her enjoying any kind of action onstage whilst standing behind a throng of star-obsessed fans were a definite nul points.

Daniel was about to answer when a high-pitched scream resonated from about a metre to their left. It was horror film epic in both its pitch and its attention-grabbing volume. All eyes turned to where it had come from. A young man, early 20s at the most, skin the colour of the most delicious dark liquorice, wearing a feather boa around his neck in a shade of vibrant flamingo with accessorising face glitter and wig to match. He had his hands pressed to his face and mouth wide open like Kevin, *Home Alone,* circa 1990. He was jiggling up and down on heels that would need crampons to reach the top they were so high, and his trousers were no more than spray-on latex. He was obviously uber-excited by what he was seeing.

'Sweet Jesus, praise be and beep my horn, I do declare it's Jemma La Vie!' He spotted Wiktoria too. 'And saints preserve us, we also have the delicious delight that is the host nation's Wik-Wik-Wik-Wiktoria.' He waggled his finger outstretched and moved it to the beat of his own words. He then death dropped to the floor, slaying the action in one swift move.

Before he could stand back up, Daniel spoke. 'Yep, if that's an indication of things to come then now would definitely be a great time to move the girls backstage and for us all to sashay away. Let's do it.' He motioned to Igor to grab Wiktoria and Jemma and hurry the situation along.

The fan was in the process of standing himself back up, ready to shoehorn himself into the mass of people surrounding the two singers when he was buffeted back to the floor by the liquored-up stumblings of Char coming back from the bar carrying a neon-coloured cocktail in either hand. Trying to focus her sozzled eyes on the pink-wigged beauty in front of her, she had tripped over her own feet and gone flying into him, sadly tipping one of the cocktails onto his crowning glory as she did so. As he stood himself back up, he stared at Char, his pink locks dripping with sugary alcohol.

'Girrrrrrrl, my weave is drenched!' He ripped it off his head and shook it, dispersing drips in every direction.

'And let's grab her as well, shall we,' stated Daniel, pointing at Char. 'She'll be safer backstage... unless it's a free bar, and then we're all doomed!'

As Igor navigated Wiktoria and Jemma towards the backstage entrance, a gleeful Lucie waddling behind them, Daniel grabbed Char by the arm and attempted to move her in the same direction. She unsuccessfully attempted to swig at the one remaining cocktail as he did so.

As they reached the door, the fan was still wringing out his pink wig onto the floor.

Chapter 19

"...you and me, can't you see, we're playing
with fire..."

Even for a man of his pretty widespread and diverse
sexual tastes, Szymon's stirring in the trouser department
when he had been staring into Bjorn's face had taken
him by total surprise. Sure, there had been many a
moment when he had dabbled with guys in the past, as
part of his joyous fetish scene in Amsterdam, but this
had always been part of a larger group scene or at some
kind of afterparty at a canal-side apartment where,
thanks to a mixture of alcohol and various multi-
coloured pills, one willing and eager body merged rather
beautifully into another. A lusty finger buffet to suit
every carnal taste. One minute you'd be pleasuring a
petite blonde mademoiselle from Marseilles into the
throes of ecstasy and then you'd suddenly find some
hairy-chested Herr from Hanover with his lips wrapped
around your lower portions. It was one of the things
that Szymon loved about the party scene in Amsterdam.
It was international, interacial and into-anything.

But he'd never fully concentrated on a guy before.
The thought didn't irk him in the slightest, but his
attraction to Bjorn Bjork was definitely making him
think that there was something about Bjorn that was

completely different to any other guy he'd met. He just couldn't put his finger on what it was. He knew that he might be playing with fire but had no qualms whatsoever about the notion of getting his fingers burnt.

He'd watched Bjorn as he performed from the wings of the makeshift stage. Stomping around to the beat of his act with such confidence for a man of just 20 years of age. His image was pure butter-wouldn't-melt wholesome, as was Szymon's to the outside world, but Szymon could feel that there was something volcanically delicious and sexy bubbling away just beneath the surface. Most wouldn't see it, but Szymon could. He felt it. A kindred spirit somehow.

As Bjorn left the stage and ran past Szymon he flashed a huge smile in the host's direction. Yep, there it was. He felt it again. A definite stirring. In all the right places.

Szymon adjusted himself as sneakily as he could before running back out onto the stage to introduce the next act.

'OMFG... how good was Bjorn! Such a cutie and what a mover!' screamed the excited puppy dog of a blogger hosting the evening's entertainment with Szymon to the crowd. 'Wasn't he just sensational, Szymon!'

'Er... yes, yes he was. Just incredible. Absolutely phenomenal,' replied Szymon, trying to push the thought of Bjorn from his mind for fear of more stirring. The trousers he was wearing were more than a little snug to say the least and standing on stage in front of hundreds of *Euro* fans in a state of obvious excitement was not the best thing to do to keep his image as wholesome and fresh as people believed. Luckily,

Die Bolzen were up next and they would certainly kill off any inkling of the host's passion in a sweat-smelling nano-second.

Baran and Meli had been given a dressing area of their own backstage. Organisers had felt that it was the best thing they could do seeing as they'd not exactly had the best of days. Both of them were still in shock about the explosion at the quarry and the death of the poor young runner. How could a stray spark cause such devastation and loss?

Brushing her long dark hair from root to tip, Meli gazed into the mirror and sighed. She'd been brushing it religiously for the last 20 minutes, lost in thought. How could life be so cruel? One minute she'd been eagerly awaiting a potential young lover, ready to take him to her bosom and show him the love of a real Turkish delight and the next minute she was waking up behind a piece of scrubland bush wearing nothing but a grubby negligee. At least her once-over at the Rottimoldovian hospital she'd been taken to had revealed that the extent of her injuries were no more than just a few bruises and a couple of light grazes. And she had to admit that the young dishy doc, Doctor Anilorak, who had cast his knowledgeable gaze upon her, was handsome enough to take her mind momentarily off the death of what could have been a most beautiful and tender lover. Meli had been reliving the runner's obvious attraction to her over and over in her mind for the past few hours. How cruel that fate had taken him from her before they could be as one. Her chance of love, or at least a good session between the sheets now so near yet so far. On again, off again… wasn't that always how it seemed to go lately?

At least a strange quirk of fate had saved her from what would have been a definite roasting at the heart of the explosion. If she hadn't eaten so many of those sour cherries then her stomach wouldn't have suddenly started tying itself up in knots a boy scout would be thrilled by as she lay there in the caravan(ette) waiting for the runner. If she hadn't have felt the urge to head to the toilet to placate her gurgling insides then she'd have stayed in the bed. If she hadn't run off to a bush far away enough from the van to ensure that if she did need to go to the toilet rather badly then any bodily explosions would not cause a lingering stench that would quash any potential paramour (and more to the point stink out the bijou bedroom acting as the scene of her love making), then she'd have stayed in the bed. How bizarre that her own vanity and need for a number two had saved her from being body number three when it came to the deaths of this year's *Euro* hopefuls. Selfish though it may seem, for Meli the names of Latreena, Ronnie DonRon and that poor runner were a much better victim list than Latreena, Ronnie DonRon and that poor, beautiful, stunningly young-looking Meli. She was a survivor. Death would not become her. Especially if it was by being blown into a zillion pieces. Meli had daydreamed her own demise before and it involved being laid out beautifully on a sheet of silk, clutching roses to her chest as sobbing mourners trooped past her coffin wailing about the loss of such beauty and talent. Her daydream did not involve scraping her charred remains off the wall of budget accommodation.

She stopped brushing her hair for a moment to turn and look at Baran, who was sitting on a chair strumming idly on his guitar. 'I might sing "I Will Survive" accapella at the end of our set tonight. Get the audience to hold up lighters and the organisers to dim the lights. It will look beautiful and people can give thanks to the fact that I'm still alive after such a near-tragic brush with death. Kind of like a vigil to what might have been. What d'you think?'

Baran didn't even look up from his guitar as he replied, 'I think you'd be better off singing "It Should've Been Me".'

'Pig,' harrumphed Meli, annoyed by his reply.

'Cow,' volleyed back Baran. 'Plus, the idea of a thousand lighters is pretty sick given it was a stray spark that sent that poor runner to meet his maker. One piece of cheap man-made fabric in the audience, which is highly likely, and the whole place could go up in flames.'

Baran's mind flashed back to his encounter with the runner in the caravan. Such a shame he'd been taken before his time. Time for him to sample the joys of Baran's lusting again. Baran had enjoyed it more than many of his recent liaisons. The boy had a talent, that was for sure. Hopefully some angel with a slipped halo was enjoying that talent right now, pondered Baran.

'You'd have been pleased if I'd have been blown to smithereens too, wouldn't you?' Meli attempted to squeeze out a tear. It was a fruitless task. Fillers and Botox wouldn't allow it.

Baran strummed his guitar, looked directly up at his wife and started singing, 'Con-grat-u-la-tions and ju-bi-la-tions. I want the world to know I'm happy as can be.' He finished the words off with a fanfare and a burst of hefty slapping on the edge of his guitar to emphasise his amusement.

'Bastard,' sneered Meli.

'Bitch,' countered Baran.

Meli turned away from her husband, images of him burning like the Wicker Man inside a caravan dancing through her mind. Now that would have been a twist of fate that she could have benefitted from. Her hypnotic charms would have been working their mesmeric ways on some hot young Russian oligarch or buff Milan Fashion Week model before you could say "Dum Tek Tek". They'd know how to treat a lady like her.

She busied herself applying a tarantula-sized set of false eyelashes to her face as Baran continued to pluck away at his guitar. Both of them did so with images of the young runner painting their thoughts. Silence gripped the room for a few minutes until Baran spoke again.

'What time are the dancers getting here? They should have been here by now.'

'We're not onstage for another hour so I suspect they'll be here in a while. It's not like it'll take them ages to get ready, is it?'

'I guess not, seeing as their outfits are minimal in the extreme. I assume it was your idea to spice things up with *male* belly dancers?' He knew darned well it hadn't been as he'd been the one to suggest it to their manager in the first place. Song contests like this loved a bit of flesh onstage and, well, so did Baran, especially if it was a rippling set of abs shaking and gyrating around with an enticingly jingly and sparkly coin belt across their loins. It screamed tradition and titillation all in one beefy package.

'It wasn't actually, it was our manager's and I think it's fabulous. I'm all for flaunting my feminism and having men on the stage belly dancing instead of women. It shows what a modern woman I am.'

'And a thirsty one,' muttered Baran under his breath. He had seen the way that Meli had mentally stripped the dancers from the moment they had turned up for their first rehearsal. Not that she stood a chance with them again. Baran had made sure of that when he first auditioned them behind his wife's back. It was very easy to persuade your manager to let him do the picking and not Meli – especially when you threaten said manager with the push if he lets on to Meli that he's doing it. Four hours in a dance studio watching ten dancers work their jiggly magic and it was a cinch to tell which ones were twirling their harem pants and hip scarves up his end of the dance floor. Baran had picked the four dancers who had caught his eye and given the impression that they would do anything to be part of Turkey's *Eurowide* debut. Anything.

As if on cue, a cackling of laughter sounded in the dressing area as the four male dancers arrived in a strut of satin and silk. They were already dressed in their stage costumes of voluminous trousers and tiny waistcoats. Decorative coin belts draped themselves across their beyond-six-packs. Both Baran and Meli beamed as they came into view. Every one of them had a body chiselled like a God from Turkish mythology.

'Evening, boys,' purred Meli. 'I see you're all dressed and ready to dance for me?' She jiggled her breasts in their direction. Baran rolled his eyes at her desperate actions.

Two of the men rolled their stomachs while the other two burst into a choreographed firework of vogueing. They whooped as they did so, no words needed to show their enthusiasm and excitement.

'We're on in about an hour so there's plenty of time to relax first,' said Baran, staring one of the voguers directly in the eyes. He raised his eyebrows back at Baran and smiled, understanding fully what Baran was saying. 'There's a bar around the corner and it's free. I'm heading there now if anyone cares to join me,' added Baran.

'Fetch me a champagne,' barked Meli. 'I need to apply the rest of my face.' She lifted the lid on a make-up box the size of a shopping trolley. The names of at least six top brands were easily visible. Three of the male dancers squealed and sashayed over to where Meli was seated. They immediately started cooing and oohing over the make-up. As Baran left to go to the bar, the other dancer by his side, he couldn't help but smile to himself.

'They're literally frothing at the mouth about the L'Oreal and Mac and whatever else she's got in that trunk of hers and she still thinks she's got a chance with them. How misguided can one woman be?'

Sure that Meli wasn't spying on him, Baran patted the dancer on his hard bubble backside and the two of them left the dressing area together. 'We'll fetch her champagne in a bit,' grinned Baran, squeezing his own crotch. 'But I think something else needs de-corking too first, don't you? There must be an empty room around here somewhere.'

The dancer raised his eyebrows expectantly.

As Meli entertained the trio of dancers with her copious mascaras and lipsticks, Baran headed off to search for somewhere suitable. Neither of them were giving a second thought to the poor dear departed runner any longer.

Chapter 20

"…stop, don't say that it's impossible,
'cause I know that it's possible…"

Daniel had wangled it so that Jemma and Wiktoria were sharing a dressing area backstage at the concert. The satisfactory sound of a cork popping split the air as Jemma opened a complimentary bottle of champagne left there. She wasn't sure if it was for her or for the host nation's entry but either way, it was getting opened as quickly as possible.

Jemma couldn't work out whether it was the afternoon of pampering or the vision she'd had about performing with her *Eurovision* heroine Sandra poolside that had put her in such a good mood but she was living her best life right now. Despite the deaths and the police questionings, she was surprisingly chilled about everything, and couldn't wait to be on stage. She wasn't wearing her best gold mesh top just to chase a piece of pork fat around a plate in a foreign eatery after all. She was ready to shine with both her fashion and her performance. Plus, she was loving her newfound friendship with Wiktoria. She was fun, silly, laughed at pretty much anything Jemma said even if she didn't understand it and she loved both *Euro* tunes and a glass of bubbles or six. In short, she was a very easy and appreciative audience. Plus tonight she was becoming a rather fabulous partner in crime as poor Char seemed to be not just three sheets to the wind but a whole bedding department at Dunelm's-worth. There were nights when booze had a habit of creeping up behind you and wrestling you to the floor in submission without you realising it was actually approaching in the first place. And seeing as Char was now lying face down on the dressing room area's only sofa, a glistening string of spit dangling from her mouth and a soft but audible ripple of snoring emanating from her, it was clear that Char was not going to last the distance as far as tonight was concerned.

'Char, d'you want some champagne?' boomed Jemma, bending down to be on a level with Char's ear. 'Free booze. And that means...' She paused for a few seconds before continuing, her voice becoming much louder, *'party for everybody...'* As she said the words she glanced across at Wiktoria, some shade of sixth sense telling her that her new friend would understand the reference too. She did. Throwing her hands in the air she burst into the chorus of the Russian grannies' *Euro* hit. Jemma sang along too, whooping with glee that Wiktoria and her were definitely on the same wavelength when it came to their taste in music from contest days gone by.

Daniel and Lucie also swayed in time to the girls' singing, the infamous tune obviously known to them both as well. They looped their arms together and circled around each other. Igor too attempted an awkward shuffle, keen to join in even if he was oblivious to what they were talking about. The only one who didn't react was a virtually unconscious Char.

Wiktoria was frothing with happiness. 'That is one of my first memories. I loved the Russian grannies! I was quite young but I thought they were fabulous. I used to wrap a tea towel around my head and pretend it was a headscarf and dance around my bedroom to that song. Such a fantastic song.'

'Oh my God, Wikky, it's one of those songs that just makes you so bloody happy!' enthused Jemma. 'Char and I used to sing it when I was working in the fish and chip shop back home. There are only a few things in life that make serving up yet another jumbo sausage and large chips to some jumbo arsehole and his large ego bearable, believe you me. Ain't that right, Char?'

Char didn't respond, unless a louder snore and a line of dribble hitting the floor counted as an answer.

'Jesus, she must be wasted if she's not reacting to the Russian grannies. She sings it better than I do.'

'Have you always loved *Eurovision* too, Jemma? It's been my dream for so long to be in a contest like this. I long to win on Saturday, but even if I don't it's still like all of my Christmases at once just to be here. I'd do anything to win though, anything.'

'Wikky, I hear you, girl. I have always loved it, ever since discovering Sandra Kim.' Jemma picked up a collection of plastic cups that were sitting next to the ice bucket she'd pulled the champagne from and poured a hefty measure of fizz into each. She handed them around to those present. Igor refused, seeing as he was on the clock.

'There have been so many great songs and I always knew that one day I'd be doing something like this. I could feel it in my gut.' Jemma looked down at her stomach. 'And that's a big enough gut to know what it wants, you get me?' Jemma laughed and wobbled her belly in Wiktoria's direction. 'Char and I used to discuss the song contest at great length all the time at Chips Ahoy. That was the name of the chip shop I worked in. Char worked down the road at The Pig And Pickle pub as a barmaid in Whittlesey, the village where we live back in England, and would come to the chippy after her shift finished. She used to help me clear up after closing. Drain the fat fryers and stuff like that. We'd stick the *Euro* tunes on Spotify and be singing and dancing around to God knows what having the most incredible singalong. We fantasised about being on stage one day, we really did. I reckon we manifested it. This was meant to be, Wikky, even though I pinch myself daily to make sure it's not a dream. It only seems like two minutes ago that I was sieving out the scraps from the fat vat at the end of another greasy shift. That's the most mind-numbing job ever. Can you imagine…?'

A completely captivated Wiktoria just nodded, not really sure what she was nodding about but loving every second of her time with Jemma.

'Honestly, Wikky, those fat vats were bloody horrible…'

'Pissing hell, there's enough scraps in this fat to fill a wheelie bin,' moaned Jemma.

'There always is, Jem. You must know that by now,' replied Char. 'What time is it, Jem?'

Jemma turned her wrist to look at her watch, momentarily forgetting that she still had the vat sieve in her hand full of the gnarly deep brown scraps of batter piled up like the most calorific of molehills. It was just after midnight in the Whittlesey chip shop. All of the scraps fell back into the warm oil, the liquid still simmering from where she had turned the temperature of the chip range back down to make it easier to clean.

'Oh arse!' Jemma watched as the scraps sunk back below the mucky brown surface.

Such were the joys of another Saturday late night shift at Chips Ahoy, which according to the dog-eared faded poster in the window was one of East Anglia's premiere fish "bars". Jemma, who had worked there for the best part of two years, begged to differ. It was no more a premiere fish bar than she was Holly Willoughby. It was a typical rough-as-arse fish and chip shop whose main clientele were those customers turfed out, barred or too drunk to actually stand any more at The Pig And Pickle pub down the road. The place where Char worked. Char who was now sitting in the window of Chips Ahoy under the poster, ploughing her way through a bag of scraps, a spare fish cake and a can of cream soda that Jemma had given her minutes earlier. Char's pub shift had finished 30 minutes ago and, as ever on a Saturday night, she would head straight to the chippy after work to see her best mate and help her clear up (after finishing any spare food on offer) and talk men, make-up and *Eurovision* music. The three best things in life, right?

'What's the matter?' asked Char, picking out a morsel of fish cake from between her teeth with a wooden chip fork.

'Nothing, I've dropped the scraps back in the oil. It's like panning for gold trying to get them all out. I wish they were gold. I wouldn't have to work here anymore and wear this.' She pointed to the trilby hat and disposable hair net combo that she was wearing as normal for her shift. Fashion it was not. 'I'd be decked out in head-to-toe Burberry. Swanking it up and down some Parisian fancy boulevard instead of Peterborough high street with some fabulous *Euro*-hunk on my arm.'

'Classy AF,' agreed Char. 'So, question…'

'All ears, even underneath the hairnet,' said Jemma. It was their usual post-shift game. Pick a *Eurovision* song and act and critique accordingly. Rate, date or slate.

'So, Michael Ball, UK 1992, "One Step Out of Time".'

'A worthy second place. Strong performance. Good vocals. Liked by the nation. 90s fashion on point – black roll neck and white jacket combo. A crowd-pleaser.' Jemma knew her stuff inside out. She'd spent years pouring over performances on YouTube.

'But would you have done him?'

'Hell yeah,' said Jemma without a second thought, sifting another batch of overbaked scraps from the reservoir of oil. 'He was pure *Eurovision* crumpet. Butter-wouldn't-melt face but with a cheeky grin that you know hides a multitude of smutty thoughts. That's one Ball I'd go to anytime.'

Char snorted at the thought. 'Yeah, me too.' She fiddled with her phone and in a matter of seconds the opening bars of "One Step Out of Time" burst through the speaker the girls had set up in the corner of Chips Ahoy. They both sang along, Char doing her best with a mouthful of scraps. Jemma spent the three minutes tipping as many sieves full of scraps as she could into the bin in time to the music. They both punched a fist into the air as the song finished, as Michael had done on the night. Although he hadn't splatted a flick of warm oil up the wall as he did so, but then he didn't have the worry of holding a chip sieve at the time, did he? Unlike Jemma.

'Tuneage to the max!' said Jemma, loving every last moment of the music.

Char swallowed her scraps and wiped her lips on the back of her hand, leaving a greasy smear. 'Right next up, I give you Eric Saade, Sweden, 2011, "Popular".'

'Third place, well deserved even if he did rhyme the word *possible* with *impossible*. That's not exactly *University Challenge* boffin heights of genius, is it.'

'You'd give him a starter for ten, though, eh?' leered Char.

'Seeing as he was wearing a single black leather glove and a set of buckles on his shirt and was obviously trying to work the fetish look even though he looked about 14, I'd say yes. But only cos he was really 20 and the fact that his moves were pure sexy boyband. You could hear the giddy heartbeats of a million teenage girls across the land. And it wasn't just their hearts that were beating, eh? Plus, great use of prop-forward-slash-gimmick. A massive glass box which of course has to be smashed to buggery on the key change. It's up there with hamster wheels, double-ended pianos and Moldova's astronaut. And it certainly beats a quick trip to Moss Bros and a horse's head or being carried on stage by someone who's 12-foot tall. And "Popular" is a top tune though. As if to emphasise the fact, Jemma burst into song as she wiped down the shiny silver surface of the chip range with a dishcloth. 'I will be popular, I will be popular...' She continued singing, with Char harmonising on BVs in the window, until she could see her own reflection in the metal surface. It was amazing how a bit of Europop could work up the most prolific of elbow grease.

'I reckon you'd be popular if you ever managed to represent the UK, Jem. People would love you, I reckon. Real salt of the earth.'

'As long as people liked their salt stinking of chip fat,' laughed Jemma, smelling the sleeve of her work uniform. 'That wants washing when I get home.' Jemma paused from her cleaning. 'I'd be perfect for it though. I've been obsessed for the longest time. We both have. It's all I've ever dreamed of. Even when I've watched the old contests from way back in black and white times online, I just love so many of the songs. Even if I don't understand what's being sung half the time. One of my faves is the winner from 1960, like even before Shirley and Ron's time,' she said, referencing her parents. 'Jacqueline Boyer singing "Tom Pillibi". She was only 18 and sings in this beautiful crystal-clear voice. Not like we sound after a night at FagButts, especially if I've had a crafty B&H, not all hoarse like that, she sounds so beautiful. I googled the lyrics. She's singing about his bloke she likes but even though she thinks she's his girlfriend he's lying to her cos there's all these other women he's getting it on with too behind her back. It's a bit like when you dated Shaun The Brawn from Ring's End and thought that you and him were going to be like, "Ding Dong Marry Me", and in fact he was having it off with Lacey, that girl with the lazy eye who works in the 99p shop off the market square. You had no idea until you wondered why he had so many plastic bags from that store jammed under his kitchen sink. It's a really beautiful song.'

'Unlike Lacey – she was far from beautiful,' stated Char, ramming more scraps into her mouth.

Jemma continued. 'There have been so many amazing songs that have won and actually some even better ones that came last for God's sake. Take "Mata Hari", Norway, 1976, sung by Anne-Karine Strom. She looks like one of *Charlie's Angels*, not the Drew Barrymore lot or the girl from *Twilight* one, but the campy original Farrah Fawcett one back in the 1970s. She's got these huge glasses on and the most wonderful gold shiny catsuit that both of us would literally die for and she's just slaying it. She looks hot as hell and she's singing this disco number that just gives you all the thrills. I'd give her douze points any day. But it came last. Ridiculous. But it's still *Eurovision* legend decades later. There are so many great songs out there. I reckon I could write a winner, I really do. Maybe I should give it a go.'

Char let out a burp, the possibly-past-its-best fish cake repeating on her. 'You'd be ace, Jemma, I swear it. You write the song, get us on that international stage and I'll do backing vocals for you. Your voice is amazing and you know your stuff. In the words of the UK entry that we're always singing, "*No Dream Impossible*".'

'A classic. Lindsay Dracass, UK, 2001, a criminal 15th given the power of her voice but a criminal choice in tracksuit chic for the night that will never be forgiven by many a *Eurovision* fan, but I've worn way worse so I'll always overlook that. Massive tune though, even despite the now dated dodgy rap section. And Lindsay landed that end note perfectly. Vocally sensational.' To prove the point, Jemma sang it herself. '*No dream imposs... iiiii... bullllllllllll!*'

'Wow!' nodded Char, impressed as ever by the deep-seated power of Jem's lungs. 'Well, that's what I reckon about you, Jem, no dream impossible. One day you'll think about our nights here at the chippy and our nights drunkenly singing at FagButts getting trollied and throwing up on the bus on the way home and you'll be there, ready to represent your country. And I'll be there with you singing backing vocals if you let me. You'd better let me, you cheeky mare.' Char stood up, drained the last of her cream soda and walked towards the chip range, which was now a lot cleaner and sparklier than it had been an hour ago when it was full of fish, scampi and steak and kidney pies. 'So, do we have a deal?' She held out her hand for Jemma to take.

She shook it. The two friends kept their hands locked together. 'I'll write the song,' said Jemma. 'I promise. Now just let me sort out the mucky batter buckets and we can get out of here.'

Backstage at the concert, Jemma had her hand tightly grasped in Char's as she recollected about that night. Char had been right. It had happened. She had made it happen. Here she was, about to represent her country. That girl who had been cleaning out the batter buckets. No dream impossible indeed. Spotting that magazine ad and being brave enough to submit a song had changed everything.

'We did it Char, we did it!' Char never answered. She was still face down on the sofa. Well, she was until a rather forceful spasm caused her to throw up the technicolour delights of what she'd been drinking all over the dressing area floor.

Jemma couldn't help but smile. They'd come such a long way yet somehow, some things stayed exactly the same. And that was how it should always be.

Chapter 21

"…you gotta be sure that it's something
everybody's gonna talk about…"

Jemma had to admit that her performance at the bloggers' party was definitely her best so far. Even though she had been singing "Beep the World" for months already, there was something in the air tonight that had risen her vocals and stage show to stratospheric quarters high enough to bump into Venus. Her vocals were effortless, the crowd were crackling with electricity and lapping it up and even her choreographed dancing, which left a little to be desired on many an occasion and often turned from more of a slick routine into a slack botch job, was worthy of a *Strictly* champ with its rhythm and timing. Plus her gold mesh top had behaved itself beautifully – a fashion miracle seeing as Jemma had expected it to split mid-song due to the fact that an already tight fit was made even more precarious by the mammoth feast at the Ukrainian restaurant earlier. With her ever-present signed photo of Sandra Kim tucked neatly away in her bra (on view for an entire audience given the sheer abundance of holes that made up her mesh top) Jemma had no intention of leaving the stage having finished her song. The spotlight was on her and she wanted to wow, wow, wow, wow!

'Give it up for the UK's Jemma La Vie!' shouted Szymon as the crowd went wild. Jemma rushed over to hug the host, clinging to him as if her life depended upon it. *Gosh, he is solid*, mused Jemma as she clung onto him a little too long for his own comfort. Receptive at first, Szymon tried unsuccessfully to shake her off. Jemma was aware that she was probably outstaying her welcome as far as body contact was concerned and that maybe she should let go.

Her mind flashed back to her visits to her Uncle Tony back home downing a bottle of Pinot Grigio while trying to persuade her libertine uncle to quit the frilly chintz of his hair-stylist affair's caravan and return to Jemma's devasted Aunty Pam. She'd conduct the entire conversation with Demiwave, the equally randy Chihuahua clung to her cork wedges humping them as if they were the Marilyn Monroe of the dog world. Stupid animal. Tony never listened, stating that the stylist could do things in the bedroom that Pam had not even heard of let alone performed, and more often than not, Jemma would return to her family home half-sozzled on wine and with the stickiest of gloopy trails splattered across her shoes.

Aware that she might be "doing a Demiwave" she let go of Szymon but knew that that would mean leaving the stage and the end of her singing. And she knew she had way more to give.

Jemma spotted Wiktoria and a towering Igor flanking her stood at the side of the stage. Wiktoria was next on the bill and had obviously loved Jemma's performance from the way she was beaming from ear to ear and clapping her hands excitedly like an eight-year-old that had found a kitten under the tree on Christmas morning.

Jemma made a snap decision. It was clear from their conversation backstage about the Russian grannies that the Rottimoldovian singer was a massive fan and knew her tunes. The grannies were from 2012. Jemma rifled through the encyclopaedic contest knowledge stacked up in her mind. One of her fave tracks from that year was "Aphrodisiac" by Greece's Eleftheria Eleftheriou. Now there was a woman who could shake her tushy in the shortest of dresses and flick her flowing mane with enough hairography to challenge Beyonce. Jemma remembered watching her and endeavouring to copy her in her bedroom mirror afterwards. Sadly, the resemblance was not strong. She'd flicked her bouff so much that she gave herself whiplash and had to rub Deep Heat into her aching neck for about a fortnight afterwards. Also, in the hope of replicating the Greek Goddess's look, she'd hitched her own skirt so high up her legs that it was barely covering her own "downstairs" and when her mother came upstairs to complain about the racket she was making, the sight of her jiggling thighs was greeted with the comment, 'Will you can the din for heaven's sake, but thanks for reminding me that I need to get a decent sized leg of pork in for your father's roast tomorrow.' Jemma was defiant and kept her jiggle on.

Before Szymon could manhandle her off the stage, Jemma burst into song. She beckoned Wiktoria to join her as she did so, praying she would know the song.

'Oh oh oh oh, oh oh oh oh...

You make me dance, dance like a maniac

Oh oh oh oh, oh oh oh oh...

You make me want your aphrodisiac...'

Wiktoria didn't need asking twice and was greeted by an eruption of cheers from the crowd as she appeared from the sidelines singing the song. It was one of her favourites too and, just like Jemma, she too had bounced around in front of the mirror at home pretending to be the singer.

The two women sang the chorus over and over, their voices and hands raised in salutation to the crowd. As they linked their hands and punched them into the air on their final note, the roar from the crowd was deafening. It was a good 90 seconds before it even started to subside, both Jemma and Wiktoria drinking in the love. It erupted again as the speakers in the venue burst into the song's intro once more, the house DJ for the night playing it for the crowd. As the lyrics kicked in both Jemma and Wiktoria sang over the top of them. Szymon joined in too, albeit a little sketchily as he obviously didn't know the words as well as the others. He did, however, hold his arms outstretched at shoulder level and shimmy his rather mountainous pecs in time to the Greek beats as if he were working the cabaret bar at a five-star Athens hotel. The crowd wolf-whistled his every gyration. He linked arms with Wiktoria and Jemma and the three of them crabbed across the stage to the music. Jemma flicked her hair back and forth with nostalgic recollection and more than a hefty dollop of dizzy hysteria. If she had told the young girl dancing to the song in front of the mirror that this would actually happen in her life then she wouldn't have believed it. This was a *Euro*-gasm of the most nerve-tingling, body-jerking jubilation. *Euro*-elation at its best. She whipped her hair back and forth, lost in the music. She only stopped when the final burst of the song sounded from the speakers. It coincided with a rather painful cracking in her neck. Perhaps that was one last snap of hairography too many. She chose to ignore it as she, Wiktoria and Szymon group-hugged each other and bounced up and down at the front of the stage.

Jemma could see Daniel in the crowd giving her a massive thumbs up, obviously thrilled by both Jemma's popularity and also her teaming up with the host nation. Lucie's mop of hair was just visible alongside him. Jemma was glad that she had returned from taking a drunken Char back to the hotel in time to see her perform. Alongside her was the unwelcome tattooed sight of Rottimoldovian hack Zandor, overly sweaty in the party's extreme heat and not really looking like he was enjoying himself. In fact he looked like he'd rather be anywhere else, but doubtless he was obliged to be there to check out Wiktoria's appearance up next. At least he had seen Jemma at her best. He could shove that right up his hole, and she didn't mean the ones distending his earlobes to brutal lengths.

'Smile you grumpy tattooed bugger,' she mouthed, a ginormous Joker-like grin on her own face. She was fully aware than Zandor would neither understand her or indeed be able to hear her above the glee of the crowd but it satisfied her hugely to say it nevertheless. He didn't respond or even appear to see her, seeming more occupied with a glitter-covered, pink-wigged man next to him screaming at a level of decibels somehow louder than anyone else at the party. Jemma couldn't help but think that the wig looked like it had definitely seen better days. It could do with Uncle Tony's bit on the side giving it a serving of TLC and a style that didn't make it look like it had been thrown in the nearest canal.

'Give it up one more time for the UK's fantastic Jemma La Vie!' Jemma's thoughts were dragged away from the pink wig by Szymon's words. She knew that now it really was time for her to exit stage left. She waved to the crowd, again ignoring the throbbing ache from her neck as she did so and hugged Szymon once more. Copping a feel of that chest was definitely worth a second pop. Shame he was supposedly getting it on with Wiktoria's sister, Weronika. She'd have to ask Wiktoria if her sibling had shared any dick pics with her of her current squeeze. She'd be more than happy to check that out.

She hugged Wiktoria too and chirped happily in her ear. 'That was in-cred-i-ble – I knew you'd know that song. Bell me when you get back to the hotel and join me for a nightcap. All this Greek has put me in the mood for some Ouzo. I'll order room service to send up a bottle and some nibbly Greek bits. What do Greeks eat? I'll google it. See you back at the hotel.'

Wiktoria said she would and watched her newfound friend, smiling hugely, as Jemma left the stage. She loved Jemma's effervescence and if she could ditch Igor back the hotel, she would be more than happy to join her for a goodnight drink. She'd be buzzing so sleeping straight away was pretty much impossible. She was giddy already and she hadn't even performed her own set yet.

Szymon shouted to the crowd. 'Which of you sexy beasts want to go on a "Love Safari"?' The roar that ricocheted back at him was worthy of the huge lion that popped up on a screen behind Wiktoria, part of a montage that looked like it had been cobbled together from a few episodes of some old David Attenborough shows. Giraffes, rhinos, monkeys, hippos and strangely a rogue donkey seemed to feature.

The opening beats of Wiktoria's song began to play as a still jubilant Jemma arrived back at her dressing area. Daniel and Lucie were there waiting for her.

'Respect, girl, that was amazing!' said Daniel, high-fiving Jemma.

'Such a big bag of fun. Loved it sooooo much!' screamed Lucie.

'Thanks, guys, I loved it,' cooed Jemma, rubbing her neck. 'How's Char?'

Lucie put her fingers to her mouth, opened it, and pretended to shove them down her own throat.

'Oh dear, she'll sleep it off and be as right as rain in the morning. She never gets hangovers, lucky cow. I get stonkers that feel like someone has literally decided to use my head as a human litter tray.'

'Not nice, kitty poo head,' giggled Lucie.

'Shall we head back to the hotel?' suggested Daniel, checking his phone. 'It's almost 1am and you have a lot of things to deal with tomorrow with rehearsals and stuff.'

'Yeah sure, but can we try and stop on the way at a Superdrug or something – do they have them here or some chemist that's 24/7?'

'There's no Superdrug but there's one on the way called Janus. I stopped there to get some painkillers for Char, just in case,' offered Lucie.

Stretching her neck from side to side, Jemma kneaded the palm of her hand into the flesh there. The rigours of her attempted hairography had certainly touch-lit some kind of muscle twanging under her skin.

'Oh terrific, Janus it is. You didn't see if they sell Deep Heat did you? Oh yeah, and do either of you know what Greek people eat by the way?'

Chapter 22

"...on the day of Rockening, it's who
dares, wins..."

Gunter Hoop was told off and sent to bed without any
abendessen (usually his fave snack of sausage and
gherkins) at least once a week when he was a child.
His mother, a stern Teutonic woman of rather ample
proportions, was a stickler for tidiness and deeply
fastidious and if young Gunter hadn't ordered his
bedroom into a level of cleanliness that she saw fit then
abendessen would be off the menu.

This taught Gunter three important lessons in life.
That sneaking food into his bedroom from the fridge
when he had no intention of tidying it was a wise way
to beat the system. That if he decided not to clean his
room on a Wednesday and was sent to bed before half
past eight he could sit and watch his favourite TV show
with his earphones in without his mother knowing. And
lastly that his mother was a bit of an old *forelle* (trout to
you and I) and even at a tender age he was counting the
days until he could quit homelife and not have to listen
to her constant nagging anymore.

He also learnt that forgetting about a plate of
gherkins that you had concealed in your bedside table
drawer and finding them six months later covered in

black dusty spores of rot was not the most pleasant of discoveries, but that was another story.

Gunter's favourite TV show was *Rock Explosion*, a music show which featured the best heavy metal, rock and grungy musical acts across Europe. If a studio full of leather outfits, hair that went down to your shoulders and tunes that didn't so much sing to you but shout you into a frazzled heap were your thing then *Rock Explosion* was your weekly number one telly destination. And a nine-year-old Gunter loved it. It was his way of escaping the nagging world of his family the other side of the bedroom door.

But that was 25 years ago. Gunter Hoop's mother was now in a care home in the middle of the Bavarian forest unable to do little more than attempt the odd jigsaw and listen to the radio as she stared out of the window. And Gunter was the famous drummer with one of Germany's most popular rock bands, Die Bolzen. He had been for the last ten years, ever since four rock fans had first come together after Gunter had advertised for a singer and a couple of guitarists to join him for jamming sessions in his garage. The results of the ad had been finding Walter on rhythm guitar, Jurgen on bass and finally Fritz on vocals. It had also resulted in his neighbours moving out due to the horrendous noises that boomed from the garage on a nightly basis. Four consecutive sets of neighbours.

But Gunter couldn't have given a damn. He had found his place, doing what his nine-year-old self had always dreamt of. And that was producing music that was just as raucous, just as loud, and just as anarchic as the songs he'd witnessed and devoured with relish on *Rock Explosion*. He dreamt of becoming a Rock God and that was just what he and Jurgen, Walter and Fritz had done. In a decade of being together they had released four albums, their latest *Schlachthaus Der Lust* (literal translation *Slaughterhouse of Lust*) was currently sitting atop the German charts at near-platinum status, toured sell-out arenas across Europe and sold millions of records. They'd also probably had no more than a handful of haircuts between them since they had signed their first record deal. Some would say that showers had been pretty few and far between too.

Sitting in the band's massive hotel suite, Gunter finished chopping the lines of coke on the table in front of him and leant over to hoover it up in one swift sniff using the rolled 100 euro note in his hand. He turned and offered it to the woman sat next to him. He didn't know her name, he never did. None of the guys in Die Bolzen did. All they knew is that wherever they went there would always be an inexhaustible supply of beer, drugs and groupies ready to please their rock star heroes in any way possible.

The woman snatched the note and snorted the fat line on the table, ending with a satisfying sigh. She leant over towards Gunter in an attempt to kiss him fully on the lips. She was in the mood for some loving, the immediate effect of the drug taking hold of her, and she was keen to show Gunter just what she could do. Gunter already knew. He'd sampled her delights no more than 20 minutes earlier when the band had first headed back to their hotel suite after playing at the bloggers' party. There was already a good dozen or so women in the suite on their arrival. Their manager always succeeded in finding them and providing them no matter where the band were playing.

Die Bolzen's fan base was massive and certainly far-flung enough to have no problems finding fans ready to "sexplore" with their favourite rockers. Their many fan clubs and fan-sites online boasted tales of those who had managed to find themselves backstage with the filthy foursome. Anyone who had done the dirty with one of the band had officially "been Bolzened". There were also tiers of fandom for those who had showed willing. Sex with one member of the band made you a Bronze Bolzen, two a Silver, three a Gold and four was a Platinum. For happily married female fans who just liked the music and wouldn't have found getting up close and very personal with the unhygienic four piece in any way pleasurable, the tag was merely a Basic Bolzen. Given that the band were famed for their rather ripe body odours, many fans were happy to boast their pride at being a Basic Bolzen. It was an honourable and odour-free badge to wear. At the other extreme, one famous duo of identical sisters who had experienced the carnal joys of all four members on multiple occasions and were happy to tell the world about it were now millionaires thanks to their online Only Fans account offering full frontal nudes of themselves and tales of the group's antics. The Bolzen Twins, as they were called, were two of Germany's most popular online stars. Their speciality was to ask eager horny long-haired Die Bolzen lookalike fans to join them online for sex. Their price tag was massive, the waiting list even more so.

Gunter pushed the woman away. She was good, but not worth a second go, not just yet. Certainly not when he looked around the hotel suite at the rock star carnage that surrounded him. The air was heavy with smoke, a constant cloud hung over the band wherever they were.

Virtually every surface was decorated with chunky white lines of coke and bags of pills. The other three members of the band and a few crew members were spread around the room, nearly all of them enjoying the company of a groupie or two. The door to the bedroom on the far side of the suite was wide open and inside Gunter could see bassist Jurgen lying on the bed surrounded by what appeared to be at least three groupies. Jurgen was always the most in demand of the four of them for sex. When your nickname amongst the fans was Jurgen the Organ due to the fact that his tight leather trousers could barely conceal the fact that he was packing a tubulous nine-and-a-half inches at least, it was casy to comprehend why any horny Bolzen fan would make a beeline for Jurgen immediately. The only problem was that after being pleasured by Jurgen, any fan trying to earn their Silver status with one of the other group members couldn't help but feel slightly disappointed when sizing up.

Gunter spotted a fan he hadn't seen or been with before sitting on a chair just outside the bedroom door. He caught her eye and she smiled. It was all he needed to know. As he passed the stereo system in the suite, he turned up the volume of the music playing, heavy metal of course, until the room literally vibrated to the pulsating bassline of the sound. He lit a cigarette and weaved his way across the mass of clothes, empty bottles and fag packets that littered the floor.

His mother would have undeniably sent him to bed without any German sausage and gherkins had she seen such chaos.

Not that Gunter had to worry about that anymore.

Chapter 23

"…it's been a long time since they had a
teenage life…"

'What is that racket going on? I can't even make out a tune. Is it that German lot partying in their room? Still, two can play that game. This is real German music.'

Jemma turned up the volume of the *Euro* playlist she was playing in her hotel room although given that the current tune was Nicole's "A Little Peace" its tinkly gentle melodies were hardly going to drown out the heavy rock coming from Die Bolzen's hotel suite down the corridor from Jemma's.

'Germany, 1982, first place, absolute beauty of a voice, love that when she sung it back as the winner she performed it in English, Dutch and French as well as the original German. That's sheer talent. I might try that on Saturday if I win. Mind you I'll have to look up "Horn" in all those languages. That should be interesting, eh, Wikky?' Jemma let out a laugh.

Wiktoria was sat on the big soft red sofa in the middle of Jemma's room. She had been there for the last 30 minutes, ever since she had managed to persuade Igor that she was going to bed and that she would see him again in the morning. Mind you, it was already heading towards 2:30am so just how much of the morning Wiktoria would see remained to be seen.

Wiktoria had changed into her zebra-print onesie and skipped her way as quietly as she could to Jemma's hotel room. It felt good to be "off the clock" for once and not under the watchful eye of Igor or indeed immersed in the hectic world of the contest bubble. Being with Jemma was fun and now that both of the girls were slobbed out in their casuals and having a giggle it felt like a classic slumber party like the one that Sandy and the Pink Ladies had in *Grease*. The only difference is that she and Jemma were hopelessly devoted to *Eurovision*, not Elvis and the 1950s, and Wiktoria didn't remember Olivia Newton-John attempting to drink ouzo.

'I could have sung "Love Safari" in Rottimoldovian but it's a horribly harsh language and would just sound like I was trying to clear my throat after a bad infection.'

'That'll be *Flemish* then,' howled Jemma, her belly wobbling with laughter. 'Get it… phlegm… flemish?' Wiktoria didn't.

'You're funny, Jemma,' said Wiktoria. She thought she was, even if she didn't always understand why. 'I like hanging out with you. This is like a slumber party, like the one in *Grease*,' she said, vocalising her thoughts.

'Now that's a movie. Let's drink to Olivia Newton-John. UK *Eurovision* singer, 1974, at Brighton Dome with "Long Live Love". She didn't stand a chance, poor bugger, as she was up against ABBA, but fourth place ain't bad. I'd be happy with a *Eurowide* placing like that on Saturday.'

'You know everything,' half-joked Wiktoria.

'I know a lot of stuff. But I love that song contest. It is the best. It's my life.' She resisted the temptation to go Cezar falsetto. 'I've watched that '74 show back on YouTube countless times. It's got more drama than *EastEnders*, or whatever you have over here. *Rottioaks? Mouldynation Street?*'

Wiktoria looked on blankly.

'Honestly, so much went on. France withdrew, so did Malta, the previous year's winner couldn't turn up to dish out the prize to ABBA, and apparently Portugal's song was used to start a revolution. Plus, most scandalous of all, and one of my favourite *Eurovision* facts of all time is that host Katie Boyle presented the show with no knickers on as her underwear had to be cut out from underneath her satin dress cos of VPL. Yep, she had visible panty line, and Katie was right posh so you couldn't have that. I might try that on Saturday too, but I suspect it might all get a tad sweaty under the Coliseum lights, so best not, eh? Might be a bit beefy by the end of the night. Let's drink to legend Katie and her no knickers. Cheers. Long Live no VPL.'

Jemma handed a glass over to Wiktoria. In it were two ice cubes and the cloudiest of white liquids. It was the ouzo. She took a glug of the liquid, as did Jemma.

'It's so strange,' cooed Wiktoria staring at the drink. It was clear when you poured it in the glass, but it touches the ice and goes all frosty and white. I've never had it before, but it tastes nice.' It was their second.

'That's the Greeks for you. Never a dull moment and always tasty. Look at Sakis Rouvas, Greece's singer at *Eurovision* in 2004 and 2009. Back flips, ripping people's clothes off, shaking and shimmying like a pneumatic drill, levitating light boxes and wiggling those incredible granite buttocks of his like a couple of snooker balls in a gym sock. He used to be a pole vaulter too, you know, before singing. Christ, I'd vault his pole any day. Hello daddy Sakis! Hashtag DILF. He co-hosted one year too and was voted the most beautiful man on earth at one point as well. Douze points across the boards for Sakis. Let's drink to Sakis.'

The two women took another gulp.

'Help yourself to nibbles, Wikky,' offered Jemma. 'According to Daniel, Greek people eat a lot of octopus and vine leaves. I think he found that out on a boys' holiday to Mykonos, although I'm sure that wasn't the only thing he put in his mouth while he was there, if you ask me.' A snort of laughter erupted from Jemma, spraying a little arc of ouzo into the air. 'But they didn't have either of those things at Janus the chemists, so I bought us the nearest I could – a bag of jelly wiggly worms and a packet of wine gums. Oh, and excuse the smell coming from my neck, it's the cream I had to buy to put on it. I wanted Deep Heat but, again, I had to settle for some other tube of stuff as they don't have it here. It smells like I've plastered my neck with a pint of lager to be honest, but I think it's working. I gave myself whiplash shaking my head around to our "Aphrodisiac" earlier, but it feels a little less painful now. Either that stuff is working, or the ouzo is making me care less. Either way I'm happy if it stops the pain.'

'That was a lot of fun. I loved singing with you. We should record it for my next album,' said Wiktoria, chewing her way through a wiggly worm as she spoke. 'I'd like that.'

'Are you kidding me? I would like, die, to do that. We could be icons in Greece. I could be bigger than the Acropolis. Is that what the ruined bit on the hill is called? Mind you, if I eat many more of these worms,

I'll be bigger than it anyway. Or at least the same size.' She popped another one in her mouth despite her apparent worry.

'Let's do it. To our future duet.' Wiktoria raised her glass and drank again.

Jemma glugged too.

'So, Miss Wikky, you have got to tell me all about your sister's thing with Szymon. He is totes gorgeous, isn't he? Are they getting jiggy? Has she shared any pics with you, you know… of his… of his, er… you know. *Something to suck on for landing, sir?*' Jemma dangled a wiggly worm in front of Wiktoria to get her meaning across and giggled. 'Although I hope it's a bit longer and not as soft as that! I'm sure it will be if the size of his other muscles are anything to go by. C'mon spill…'

Wiktoria's cheeks reddened at the tone of the conversation. Or that may have been the ouzo too. She giggled nevertheless. 'I don't know. Believe it or not, she hasn't actually sent me any pictures of his *ding dong* and I've not asked her to. Me and Weronika don't have that kind of relationship. Would you show Char photos of your boyfriend's thing?'

'No, of course not,' lied Jemma, crossing her fingers around the ouzo glass as she drained the last drops from it, trying to count up the number of times she and Char had sat down together on barstools at FagButts and compared body part pics that had been sent to them via Tinder and Bumble. It was always part of their night out. They called it their very own comparethemarket. com section of any night out. Most times it ended in howls of screaming laughter as the girls discussed girth, flabbiness, sack size and manscaping. Once it had ended in total horror when Jemma realised that one of the men who had sent a particularly porny and graphic full-frontal to Char was in fact one of her sweetest regular customers at Chips Ahoy, a timid and shy chap who would come in for food at least twice a week. Jemma had struggled to serve him a saveloy ever since without blushing the colour of a London bus. 'I bet he's big though,' continued Jemma, her mind formulating a rather pleasing image of Szymon. 'You'll have to ask her.'

'I'm not really sure what state their relationship is in, or if, in fact, there is a relationship in the first place. They might have been put together to gain some press for *Eurowide*.'

Jemma raised her eyebrows at Wiktoria. 'Er, sure... three deaths in, this new contest is not exactly struggling for press is it? It's the most talked about event at a song contest since Katie and her no-knickers. If they were put together though, maybe Weronika's a beard and Szymon's really gay. He is Zac Efron-pumped and has a real flare with his outfits, after all. He's all meat, no moob. A million *Euro* fans would be on their knees quicker than you could say bien-bleeding-venue.'

'I don't think he's gay but that would certainly make a lot of people around here very happy. I think Daniel and Igor would be very happy about that. Another drink?' Wiktoria held up her empty glass.

'Absolutely. A little OFTR is called for at least – one for the road. So, you've worked it out with Daniel and Igor, then? Daniel was mortified when they first slept with each other, but he does seem to be warming to him now. He's an acquired taste, I imagine, given what's going on.' Jemma circled her face with her fingers and grimaced in regard to Igor's unique look. 'But the body is obviously incredible and he seems like a really nice guy and he pleases Daniel so that's all well and good. And now he's looking after you too.'

'I knew Igor liked Daniel and guessed he was gay. You can see from the way he looks at Daniel. He goes all misty eyed and gooey. Igor is sweet. After that horrible accident with Latreena it's good that the firm he works for placed him with me. My guard had to go back to his wife as she's just had a baby. So I had a hole and Igor filled it.'

'That's what's Daniel said, Wikky,' eyeballed Jemma with a wink, holding a now replenished glass of ouzo.

'Thanks,' she replied. 'To the road.'

'Eh?'

'You said one for the road, we drink to the road, yes?' Wiktoria turned to the window in the hotel room that looked out onto the Ermpit street below and raised her glass into the air. 'To the road.' Her words were beginning to slur a little.

'To the road!' joined Jemma, not bothering to explain either the meaning of the phrase or attempting to understand why Wiktoria would think it totally normal to drink to a piece of tarmac.

'So do you and Weronika get on with each other? I imagine you're like those two Russian twins who did *Eurovision* a while back, the Tolmachevy Sisters, the ones on the seesaw with their hair tied together. Very strange. If I had a seesaw on Saturday I'd have to have Char on the other end plus a couple of other backing singers to even stand a chance of balancing it out. Plus there's no way I'd tie my hair to hers. Not since she caught nits from her little niece last year. So were you and Weronika always singing together and playing dress-up and being girly?'

'We did until I was about 16, but then I suddenly ended up on TV and recording songs in the studio. I was incredibly busy so any chance to have fun together disappeared. We used to play together all the time when we were little. Our mum had some Spice Girls songs and video tapes and we loved pulling them out and playing them. We really thought we were two of the Spice Girls and Weronika used to put make-up on me and style my hair and we'd sing. I was like a little doll to her. She loved dressing me up. She loved playing the big sister to me even though we're the same age. Well, she's ten minutes older. She popped out first.'

'You're so lucky having a sister. I'd love one. Char is the nearest thing I've got to one, so I'm chuffed she's here with me to share all of this. You must be thrilled for Weronika too. Hosting and all?'

'I'm so proud of her. And I know she is of me too. I can't wait to see what she does on Saturday for the final as she has the most unbelievable performance planned. You'll love it, Jem. She's doing a disco medley surrounded by male dancers. And they're not wearing many clothes. Neither is she either. She's always loved being the centre of attention so being in the middle of the stage on Saturday surrounded by hot guys with millions of people watching will be a dream come true. It will be for both of us.'

'That sounds amaze-balls. So which Spice Girl were you? I reckon you were Posh as I know you love Victoria Beckham cos you said so to Lucie when we did that interview. Were you Vicky, Wikky?' She tittered at her wordplay.

'No, I was Baby. I always loved her most as she was so cute and had pigtails. I would do my hair in the same way.'

'Who was Weronika?'

'She was Scary, as she was just like her. Not to look at but she was really loud and a bit bossy about our dance routines to be honest. She'd always moan if I got it wrong. Which I did. Sometimes I just couldn't work out which foot went where. Luckily I've got a lot better at that, but heaven help her dancers on Saturday if they get it wrong! I remember she had a little leopard-print t-shirt and tried to make her hair all curly when we sang together. She'd do my hair too. Once she tried to make mine curly cos Baby had done hers like that for a video for one of their songs. I'd tried but couldn't get it right so Weronika said she'd help by making it bigger with hair gum. But she accidentally used chewing gum instead and I had to have my hair virtually all cut off as it was stuck everywhere. I was so upset but she was only trying to help. Mum went crazy at her as she loved my hair. She always has done. Weronika was sent to her room for a week. I still can't have a piece of chewing gum as it gives me awful flashbacks.'

'Blimey. If those Russian twins had gotten chewing gum in their hair, they'd have never got off that seesaw, would they? They'd have been yanking each other back and forth,' pondered Jemma. 'Ah, it sounds like you and your sister had a great time together when you were kids. Do you still hang out now?'

'When we can, although we've both been so busy, especially since she won the TV show last year. And who knows what will happen after the contest. For either of us.'

Jemma was just about to inform Wiktoria that she could envisage her being a massive star back home in the UK when she was distracted by a commotion outside their hotel door. Even with Jemma's own choice of music playing, her playlist currently dishing out Bardo's 1982 UK song "One Step Further" – a drunken Jemma and Char had often writhed around on the floor on a night out in unsuccessful imitation of the dance routine – and the heavy metal racket still throbbing through the air from the German contingent just down the corridor, she could hear panicked voices outside the door.

Wiktoria must have heard it too as she pointed towards the door and held her hands out as if to say, *what's that noise?* Both of them stood up and moved, a little wobbly, towards the door.

Jemma pulled the door open a little and she and Wiktoria gazed out into the hotel corridor. Wiktoria, who was pressed up against Jemma, was shaking a little.

'Jees, Wikky, you're shaking like Sakis's butt cheeks. What's the matter?'

'I scare easily anyway, always have, but ever since that prediction from the fortuneteller I've been nervous about everything. Something bad has happened. I can feel it. And *this* is not a good sign.' She indicated into the corridor.

The *this* in question was a team of about half a dozen paramedics running up the corridor like Olympic sprinters and another group of people, mostly long-haired men and very busty women from what they could see, running around like headless chickens screaming crazily at no one in particular. Most of them, the non-medical ones, were only half-dressed, and nearly all of them seemed to be wearing at least two items of leather.

Chapter 24

"...give me something I can feel, 'cause love
kills over and over..."

Half an hour before any kind of mayhem had started to
occur in the hotel corridor outside the Die Bolzen suite
– tonight definitely earning its Checkpoint Charlie
nickname – Gunter Hoop zipped the flies back up on his
leather trousers and lit a cigarette as he walked out of
one of the bedrooms and back into the main area of the
suite itself. He was a happy man. Happy. Contented.
Spent.

Another groupie had just managed to climb up yet
another nerve-tingling, orgasm-making rung of the Die
Bolzen ladder of *sex-sess*. Well, Gunter had reached his
climax, he assumed she might have done too. He never
asked. He never did. All he knew was that another fan
could now say they had tasted the fruits of Rock God
desire thanks to Gunter. No doubt she would watch him
onstage on Saturday banging his drum and be turned
on. She'd be at home or in the crowd, or wherever,
saying, 'Yep, he banged me too,' her status now risen
to Bronze Bolzen at least, or maybe now to Platinum.
It was an additional thing that, again, he never asked.

Could you imagine...? '*Entschuldigen Sie, bitte, am
I the first, second, third or fourth member of this band*

to climb on top of you and slip you a length. Nah, he didn't need to know that. Or indeed care about it. All that he cared about was getting his rocks off, having his very own *Rock Explosion.*

He wished some suited TV exec would bring that TV show back. It was so incredible. Maybe he and the Die Bolzen lads could suggest it. They could front it. Maybe it could be a competition to search for a rock band to support them on their next tour. The band could take an indecent percentage of their support act's profits. Act like a manager but not actually have to do anything other than clean up the cash. Yeah, that could work. A TV show would be something different to try and do. They'd not attempted that before. They'd done most things by now. Gunter and the rest of the group were always looking for the next challenge. Reaching for the next high.

That's how *Eurowide* had come about. An act of their degree of success would never normally contemplate a gig like this, but after Gunter joked in an interview on German telly that they should do *Eurowide* to put real rock music on the map, the German contest organisers approached the band's management company about them taking part. At first they were totally against it, many of their fans saying that it would kill the band's career, but to Gunter, that was like a red rag to a bull. Being told that they shouldn't do something meant that they most definitely had to prove that they could. Nobody got the better of him or the band. It was just like being back with his mother again. She said no, go to bed without supper, he said screw you, my supper's already sorted. When the fans said don't do *Eurowide,* he was, *bugger that, let's give it a go.* Nothing could kill his career off. Die Bolzen were bigger than this.

Even though their song, "The Sweet Smell of Europe", was not as rock heavy as some of their back catalogue it was still dark enough and sufficiently shouty to blast previous German song contest highlights into oblivion. Having never watched any kind of contest like this before he'd checked out a few previous entries from his homeland online. Some had caught his eye more than others. The group kitted out in fancy dress singing about a Mongol warrior. The year that burlesque queen Dita Von Teese strutted around with a riding crop in her hand looking as fit as. Germany had tried a lot of different things but they'd never had an entry as mammoth as Die Bolzen. Gunter reckoned they were in another league. "The Sweet Smell of Europe" was tipped to do well on Saturday. They'd win, of that he had no doubt, but they wouldn't return next year to hand over the trophy. No, far too cool for that. They'd go down as the coolest rock act ever. Even their lyrics were anthemic. People thought the song was about uniting Europe. Yeah, sure, it was really about shagging. Any fool could see that. That's what rock stars did for Christ's sake.

'Rock Gods from a mountain high
Lighting up the demon sky
And rising to bring new-born to the fold
Spreading seed from coast to coast
Take it where you want it most
Come together, come together, let's just come
Tattooed devils on our chest
One foot east and one foot west
The swelling of the world between our legs

Bring your daughters to the town

Give it up as we go down

Let's breathe in the sweet smell of Europe now.'

Subtle is was not, shouty and a fan favourite it most definitely was. If you were looking for a poppy pick 'n' mix of *Euro* hearts and flowers, then you were decidedly sniffing in the totally wrong place.

Gunter sat down on the sofa, next to lead singer Fritz who was attempting to eat some poor fan's face off. Fritz may have been famed for his vocal chords in the rock world, his range and technique better than most singers could dream of, but he was also famed amongst the fans online as being the worst kisser imaginable. But luckily he made up for it elsewhere being just a couple of inches behind Jurgen the Organ in the trouser department.

As Gunter seated himself. Fritz stopped spin-cycling the fan's face, now a rather angry shade of plum, and gave a stoned sideways smile in Gunter's direction.

'All right, man,' he drawled, his words slow and not particularly clear. It was evident that he was wasted, his eyes rolling upwards in their own sockets.

'Jesus, Fritz, you need a pick me up, man.'

'Yeah, reckon so,' slurred Fritz.

Gunter pulled out a bag of white powder from his pocket. 'Fresh supplies, always good...' He'd finished the last one before his coupling with the groupie. He opened the new bag and poured a molehill of the powder onto the table in front of him. He turned back to Fritz who was badly kissing the fan again.

'You want some, Fritz? Powder to all our friends and all that.'

Fritz didn't answer, deep in lip service once again.

'Suit yourself then, man,' said Gunter, shaping a fat line for himself. He leant over and took it in deeply. It stung a little. And then a lot. And then even more.

He lay his head back against the sofa and tried to work out the fizzing in his head as the line took effect. It wasn't long before he started coughing and then foaming at the mouth.

Eurowide wouldn't kill off his career. But something else sure would. Quite dramatically. In a matter of minutes.

Chapter 25

"…kisses for me, save all your kisses for me…"

The following morning, word of Gunter's death spread quickly. Despite the paramedics doing their best to try and revive a frothing Gunter, he was dead by the time the ambulance had taken his sweaty leather-clad body to Alpha Beta Hospital. Die Bolzen were now officially a threesome.

A panicked Weronika was desperate to discuss the latest news with co-host Szymon. 'Apparently whatever he was taking was not exactly what he thought it was. He was snorting rat poison or something equally as ridiculous up his nose.'

Weronika moved her position slightly to place her hand on Szymon's pert backside as the photographer in front of them both clicked away. Another day, another promo shoot.

'As long as it doesn't stop the contest from happening,' she added dramatically, more concerned about that than the fact that three deaths had now occurred in as many days. She and Szymon, as hosts, had already been informed that in the interest of entertainment, and more importantly the economy of Rottimoldovia, it would indeed be "willkommen, bienvenue and welcome" as normal on Saturday night.

The first ever *Eurowide* could down go down in a blaze of deathly goings-on. But even though she knew that, Weronika as ever was determined to ramp up the melodrama.

'It was his own fault, surely,' said Szymon, subtlety angling his pack-a-punch peach away from Weronika's grasp. 'That band were famed for their...' He searched for the right words before continuing. 'Colourful lifestyle, so it's no wonder that sooner or later something like this would happen. It's pretty rock 'n' roll to be honest, isn't it? I just wish it hadn't happened this week. It's beginning to resemble a morgue around here lately.' Even if Szymon was loving the fact that the contest was gaining major notoriety and enlarging his legend-potential by the nano-second, the phone calls informing him that yet other contestant had popped their clogs were becoming a trifle tiresome and horribly dime-a-dozen. There'd be nobody left for the semis at this rate.

'At least this death is a little easier to explain than a faulty disco ball crushing diva Latreena and that Irish kid falling into the Krudd. This one is druggie does drugs and dies after taking bad shit. Case closed. Even the police don't seem too anxious about this one.' Weronika angled her head, a little awkward as it tilted, to rest it in the crook of Symon's neck. Her lips skimmed the stubble on the skin there. She focussed her eyes towards the camera, her lips retaining contact with Szymon's neck. The photographer, Klaus, the same craggy baggy photographer who had snapped Wiktoria and Jemma at Dicken Platz earlier in the week, captured the shot. He nodded his approval.

'Nice. I zink zat could be ze main image of ze piece.' It was Zandor now giving his approval to the shot, his skeletal frame dressed in a pair of overly tight plastic trousers and a grubby "The Scorpions" vest top. His pipe-cleaner arms, the skin barely visible under the mass of tattoos scribbled there, hung limply by his side.

Zandor was writing a final piece on the contest's hosts for one of the host country's largest publications. Pictures by Klaus, words by Zandor and loving coupled-up photos of the two hosts all over each other fuelling the fires of their supposed romance would be just what his country would need to divert away from the chronic ongoing saga of death after death. And Weronika was certainly making sure that she and Szymon were looking as together forever as possible. Even if it didn't take a body language expert to realise that she was far more into the intimate posing than Szymon was.

'Do you have to pick one where Weronika is kissing my neck?' asked Szymon. 'It's a little crass isn't it. I want to come across as wholesome and not some cheap Lothario trying to get my end away.'

Weronika giggled and, ignoring his evident wishes, pulled him towards her for another photo. The bodies touched together, her arm wrapped around his waist, as Klaus grabbed the shot.

Szymon tutted and sighed. He knew that he was fighting a losing battle. His thoughts returned to the deaths. 'And it's not just the contestants who have been dying. What about that poor runner who frazzled to death filming the Turkish postcard? One stray spark and boom! End of play.'

'That might not have been an accident,' replied Weronika, adjusting her breasts underneath the lime-green plunging-neckline dress she was wearing for the shoot. 'That could have happened to Baran and Meli. Maybe it was meant to be them who went up in flames.'

Zandor's ears pricked up. 'You reckon? Zat would make an amazing story if somebody was actually killing off ze contestants. I'd write zat story up in a heartbeat.'

'*Dying To Win. There's something murderous going on at Eurowide and it's not just the songs they're killing.* I could see the headlines now,' cooed Weronika, happy that her breasts were now positioned for maximum wow factor. She took Szymon's hand in hers and gave her best attempt at a Hollywood smile directly into Klaus's lens. Still not having mastered the finer nuances of working her angles, the result was not so much Hollywood as made-of-wood. Or perhaps inflatable plastic.

Szymon had obviously observed. 'Let's not use that one either, eh Zandor, it's a little... er... sex doll.'

Weronika blushed at his words. 'Oh, Szymon, I would have thought a wholesome boy like you wouldn't even know what one of those is.'

Szymon blushed back. *If only she knew*, he thought to himself, before adding, *but thank heavens she doesn't.*

He returned to the grisly subject of the deaths. 'Do you two really believe that somebody could be behind these deaths? That they're not just horribly tragic accidents? The police don't seem to be getting anywhere do they?'

'Probably not,' countered Weronika. 'Although that would be far juicier. You and I would be forever known as the hosts of the murder contest. That'll be pretty cool, wouldn't it?'

Zandor interjected before Szymon could answer. 'Yes, as long as you both survive until Zaturday night.

If somebody is killing people zen what's to say zat one of you isn't next on zer list?'

The sex-doll smile immediately dropped from Weronika's face. Her face read *I could be next*. Her career plans for the future had not included an early trip to the nearest coffin.

Szymon wasn't smiling either. 'No, I'm sure they're just horrible accidents that just happened to have come at the most unfortunate of times, right?' He wasn't overly convinced. None of them were.

Both hosts stood there a little dumbstruck as they considered what the rest of the week could potentially bring to the table. Fame, fortune and fabulous frocks were one thing (well, actually it was three), but their own fatality was quite another. The sound of silence hung in the air.

'Can you both try and look a little happier please? This pose is not working for me.' It was a normally mute Klaus who broke the silence.

Chapter 26

"...rock bottom, rub it out and start it again..."

'Why did she have to pick this morning of all mornings to be throwing up ouzo?'

Daniel placed his phone back onto his bedside table and huffed his annoyance. He pulled the bedsheet he was lying under up across his bare chest, screwing it into a tight ball as he did so. With a host of back-to-back radio interviews all lined up for Jemma starting at 10am, the last thing he needed was a phonecall from his star at just after nine saying that she could barely string two words together due to bingeing on ouzo and wiggly worms until the early hours of the morning. Who the hell drank ouzo for heaven's sake?

'I knew she was up to something when she started banging on about what Greek people eat at the concert last night. She said Wiktoria was with her in her room too. Have you heard from her this morning?'

Daniel turned to the body in bed beside him and prodded it with his finger. 'Er... hello? I'm talking to you.'

He pulled back the sheets to reveal Igor's naked torso, face down, his overly wide back and plenteous bubble butt filling his side of the bed quite stupendously. A grunt emanated from his mouth as the finger connected with his body for the second time.

'Jemma's hungover and she and Wiktoria were drinking all night in her room. Have you heard from Wiktoria this morning? She might be wrecked too. I bet nobody ever had this kind of trouble with Engelbert Humperdinck. Or had to make excuses to Radio 2 because Cheryl Baker was ripped to the tits on tequila.'

No response. The finger prodded again. This time Daniel aimed it at the bubble butt. Despite his annoyance he couldn't help but admire its domed beauty.

'All right, I hear you...' stirred Igor, reaching up for his own phone on the table on his side of the bed. There was a message on the screen. He lifted his head to read it. It was from Wiktoria.

'Yes, she's up and headed to the spa. I don't have to be with her until midday. She seems fine. Obviously she can take her drink more than Jemma. Jemma must take after her friend, Char. She was completely drunk too.' He returned the phone to the table and lay his head back down, unwilling to move.

'Char's the one holding Jemma's hair out of the way as she throws her hoop up in the toilet. Apparently, she's fine this morning.' Jemma had said she would be. 'I'm going to have to sort her out with paracetamol and gallons of water. There's no way that I'm telling every buggering radio station from Scottish-bloody-Borders FM or whatever it is through to Rainbow Radio: The Throbbing Beat of Gay UK that they have to reschedule because Jemma's feeling unwell. There's no time to pigging reschedule.'

'Oh...' It was all Igor could manage.

'Oh? Oh? Is that all you have to say.' Daniel could feel his rant brewing. Even if Igor wasn't particularly receptive to his blustering, Daniel needed an audience.

And seeing as they had been spending a lot of time together over the last 72 hours, both professionally and personally, Daniel felt that he now knew Igor well enough to let rip good and proper. 'It's all right for you, your fabulous act is up and ready for her day ahead, all sweetness and light and ready to shine. Mine has her head down the pissing toilet right now. How do I explain that to Ken Bruce? I can't have her being halfway through explaining her favourite ever *Euro* songs to some local DJ in the middle of Cornwall or darkest Wales live on air and then having to excuse herself to go and throw up enough wiggly worms to fill a damn Halloween trick or treat bucket. It's not professional. Do you think Latreena, may she rest in peace, would have informed the Swiss version of Rylan or Claudia Winkleman that she'd have to stop the interview as, and I quote Miss Jemma La Vie here, "her guts were as rough as rats". I think not. But I'll stay calm, I'll sort this, and everything will be okay... I have dealt with much worse.'

Daniel's eyes were still on Igor's rump as he finished his quickfire diatribe.

Igor certainly hadn't understood every word that Daniel had just yapped in his direction, but he did understand enough to get the gist and know that (a) Daniel needed to go and see Jemma and that (b) Daniel was lightyears away from calm.

'Why don't you go and get Jemma ready for her interviews. I am sure it will be fine. I will let myself out in a while if that's okay.'

He turned over in bed to lie on his back and look at Daniel. Igor's early morning pleasure was clear to see between his legs. Daniel's eyes widened and for a millisecond all thoughts of an ouzo-soaked Jemma were banished into thin air. Daniel had no idea why but the sight of Igor's morning glory made him suddenly think of the other news Jemma had told him on the phone, the workings of his own thought process totally bizarre and unfathomable.

'One of the German rock band has overdosed on drugs and died apparently. I'm not sure which one.'

The news seemed somehow oddly unimportant when faced with such a glorious pleasure in front of him. He reached out to grab Igor's prize. As he did so, Igor opened his eyes fully and smiled. Daniel moved to Igor's side of the bed and straddled his legs over the bodyguard's torso. He checked the time on Igor's phone. It was 9:20am. He'd sort Jemma out and have her interview-ready for 10am. He could do it. He could do anything. He'd been in charge of the press for a snotty reality diva once who had recorded a tropical workout DVD in the summer ready for Christmas release and had only bothered to tell him in November when it came to a round of press opps that she'd put three stone back on wolfing delivery pizzas. If he'd coped with that, he could certainly cope with too many ouzos and an overdose on Haribo.

Daniel would sort it, but right now other things closer to hand needed sorting first.

Chapter 27

"…look at me, I'm climbing up a ladder…"

In a previous life, Bjorn Bjork had posed for all kinds of photos. Ones that had hopefully stayed off the internet. As Bella, she had positioned her body into more contorted, comfort-defying, beyond-graphic, splayed displays of erotism that most people would even contemplate – and all for a good price. She had certainly been many a client's flexible friend, happy to pose accordingly as long as the krona were free flowing.

But that was then…

And this was now…

Bjorn's current position was one that was certainly causing him all sorts of issues. In fact, he'd say that it was the hardest photoshoot that he'd ever undertaken. Well, at least the most uncomfortable. And there weren't even any krona up for grabs with this shoot. This was all in the name of *Eurowide* and the rather amusing if slightly bemusing idea of bubbly boombox UK reporter Lucie Rave.

'Right, Bjorn, if you could just throw your arms further back over your head and stretch right the way across the wheel that would be awesome. It'll make the most incredible photo, especially with the dancers either side. Your performance on Saturday is going to be in-cred-i-ble.' Lucie split the word into four to layer her thoughts on with a trowel. 'Eat your heart out, ABBA! Water-who? They didn't have a hamster's wheel, did they? Waterloo-sers.'

Lucie guffawed. Bjorn didn't. ABBA were Gods, they didn't need a hamster's wheel. Did Anna Bergendahl ever have a hamster's wheel? Mans? Loreen? Carola? Or did Greta Thunberg's mum have one when she did her opera thing for Sweden at *Eurovision*? No, they didn't. Sweden had quite capably managed without one so far so why had the Swedish *Eurowide* bigwigs decided that Sweden's "hamster wheel moment" had to come now.

Yes, the famed and much derided hamster wheel. Spun into the *Euro*-spotlight for the glamtastic Mariya Yaremchuk's 2014 Ukraine banger "Tick-Tock". The song may not have won but somehow it had rotated its way into every fan's heart because of the wheel. And doubtless the hottie spinning around in it.

And somehow, much to Bjorn's annoyance, if he was honest, his tropical stage performance of "24 Hours of Sunshine" featured a wheel. Thankfully he was spared the indignation of trying to spin around in it himself – that joy went to the two scantily clad backing dancers joining him on stage. It was they who added the visual burst of "tropicana" to Bjorn's salsa-based tune. A guy dressed in tight-fighting swim shorts and pec-hugging crop top in a fetching hibiscus and parrot combo design and a young woman with matching design and equally tight bikini were flanking Bjorn on stage as he jumped around in his now renowned blue and yellow outfit. Neckerchief always in place of course.

Sweden had tried many a gimmick at song contests – treadmills, stickmen cartoons as a backdrop, Napoleon conducting... yep, they'd pulled a lot out of their Scandi hats, but they'd never done the hamster wheel. So why, *Eurowide*, why?

And right now, as Bjorn stretched himself across the top of the wheel, as instructed by Lucie Rave, his two dancers holding either side of it in full stage costume, he was hating every last inch of every last rung. Because trying to lie flat on your back across a circular object when you have your breasts taped down under your armpits was pain on another dizzying level. Not that he was trying to let Lucie see that in his face as he posed. Sweden were tipped to place highly on the night and every bit of press helped, especially in the UK where everyone seemed to love this kind of thing.

'The readers of the *Palaver!* website will adore this!' chirped Lucie. 'You look so cool up there, Bjorn. Is there any chance you could kick your platform heel up in the air as well? Just to give it extra pizazz!'

Bjorn wasn't even sure what pizazz was and knew precisely where he'd like to stick his platform heel right now – even if he had to confess that Lucie was all sorts of adorable despite being wholly responsible for his current predicament – but he altered his position accordingly and served teeth as he smiled through the pain.

'Did you ever dream you'd be doing something like this when you were a little boy back home in Sweden?' asked Lucie.

I never dreamt I'd be doing this six months ago when I was a high-class hooker, thought Bjorn internally. He voiced his real response. 'Gosh, no, I never thought I'd be lucky enough to represent my country and be here at *Eurowide*. And to have a wheel as part of my stage show is incredible. It's so iconic.'

'Spin, spin, tick tock!' shouted Lucie excitedly. 'Your song is so catchy and it's like being on a tropical island isn't it. It's proper calypso music. Very happy. Fizzier than a can of Lilt. Even if I'm in a right old bad mood about something, I cheer up immediately when I hear your song. You must love singing it.'

To be fair, even after a good few months of pretty much singing it at every major city in Europe, Bjorn did still enjoy the upbeat feel to the song. Good job, really. If it did do well on the night of the contest, he would doubtless be singing it for decades to come.

'It's a fun song, Lucie, one for everyone to enjoy. We live in such troubled times that it's nice to switch off the outside world for three minutes and have a burst of tropical joy. It's like a three-minute vacation to your favourite beach with your hunky boyfriend by your side. Or girlfriend...' Bjorn was keen to be as PC as possible.

'Hunky boyfriend. I wish!' roared Lucie. 'No such luck!'

It was true, "24 Hours of Sunshine", had all the makings of a winner from its first opening steel drum beat.

'The sound of the waves on the shore
The cry of laughter makes my heart soar
You and I together walking hand in hand
You and I together footprints on the sand
Yes there's music in the air tonight
And still the sky's so bright tonight
With people moving to the sway of happy vibes

Never let your life be dark

Always shine and leave your mark

Feel the heat of all life's goodness on your skin

Live life in the here and now

But spread the joy and make it last the whole day through

Cos I know that there's a place, with a smile on its face

And waiting there's…

24 hours of sunshine for me and you.'

'Have you always been a song contest fan?' asked Lucie. 'Oh and any chance you can swing your platform heels over the front of the wheel now? Just let them dangle down.'

Bjorn manoeuvred himself to do as instructed. It was a much more pleasurable position than lying on his back even if his posterior was now pretty much wedged between two of the wheel's rungs.

'I've loved *Eurovision* for the longest time, this really has been a lifetime's ambition for me. I remember watching Charlotte Nilsson sing in 1999 with "Take Me to Your Heaven" and thinking that was inspirational. I was praying she would win and was so glad when she did. I wanted to be just like her. Those sparkly pink trousers and that pink clingy top – too fabulous!'

Quite how Bjorn would look in Charlotte's ultra-sparkly feminine attire was a bit of a conundrum to Lucie, but she let his somewhat gender-fluid answer pass. She was a little perturbed though about his love of the 1999 winner. 'Wow. You weren't even born in 1999. How did you watch that? Did you have some sort of time machine?'

Bjorn inwardly chided himself for his somewhat overly revealing answer. He had to remember that he was a *Eurovish*-age of 20, and not his real age of 32. Thankfully his thought process in correcting the answer was necessarily swift.

'Oh I watched it on a friend's DVD in Sweden a few years after the actual competition. My friend, Joakim, he had seen one of the *Eurovisions* because his parents loved it and they had a few DVDs of different contests. He said I should watch it as me and him used to sing pop songs together and he knew I'd love Charlotte's song. I was very, very young when I watched it of course. I sing Charlotte's song in my Scandi medley.'

'Oh I know, I saw you at the bloggers' concert. You were incredible, I have to say. Such a huge voice for a 20-year-old.'

'Thank you, I love singing. It makes me feel free. And I love the fact that singing unites people from so many places. Unite Unite Europe and all that...'

'You have a very mature attitude for one so young,' remarked Lucie.

And a very mature pair of breasts tucked away giving me all sorts of grief sat up here right now, thought the Swede.

'So do you think you'll win on Saturday?' continued Lucie.

Bjorn wasn't sure he wanted to, but he couldn't let that show on his face. So, a painted-on smile floodlit his face as he answered. 'Oh I'm not sure I'll win. There are so many good songs. I was a big fan of the Irish song, "The Smile High Club", with the two lads but, well, I'm not sure what's happening with that now given that...' His reply tailed off, unsure what to say that would sound caring, professional, and *Euro*-friendly. 'I think your song from the UK is very catchy too and I do have a soft spot for the Rottimoldovian song as well, "Love Safari". That could win on home ground. Wiktoria is a great singer.'

'And her sister is hosting the week's shows of course. Have you spent much time with the show's hosts, Weronika and Szymon? They're a very cool pair aren't they. I think they might be... you know.' Lucie made a rather unnecessary gesture with her fingers to convey her meaning. It may have been inappropriate, but it made Bjorn giggle.

It also made the inner Bella a little jealous. She had been thinking about Szymon a lot. She shelved her thoughts of him to the back of her mind.

'They're such great hosts. I think they could be the best double act since Sweden's very own Mans and Petra,' replied Bjorn, always keen to fly the flag for the homeland. Bjorn could feel his butt cheeks going to sleep as they wedged further between the rungs of the wheel. He was keen to move. 'Any chance I could get down from here?'

'Oh my, silly me, of course. I think we're done.' Lucie looked over to her photographer who nodded her approval and turned back to Bjorn. 'Would you like a hand down, although I'm not sure my little dumpling body can reach all the way up there to be honest.'

Keen for as little body contact from others as, possible given what he was hiding underneath his sateen, Bjorn declined the offer and instead pulled his backside out from between the rungs as discretely as he could. He then tried to stand up so that he could position himself in the right direction to climb his way back down the wheel.

Standing up was a bad move. Particularly in platform heels. Bjorn began to wobble and as he did, one of his heels slipped itself around one of the rungs. Bjorn let out a scream. Rather a high-pitched one given that he was supposedly a 20-year-old male and felt himself starting to tumble.

'Javla helvete, jag faller,' he cried. Rough translation, "pissing heck I'm falling".

He tumbled forwards off the wheel and as he did so heard a snap. He was convinced it was his ankle but before he had a chance to register the pain, he felt himself landing in the arms of the male dancer accompanying Bjorn on stage. Luckily the muscled mover had been there to break Bjorn's fall and prevent any further injury. The dancer grinned, hero-like, as he deposited Bjorn safely to terra firma.

Certain that he would be unable to walk, let alone sway his way through three minutes of Swedish salsa on Saturday night, Bjorn yelped as he touched the floor. But there was no pain pulsating from his ankle. In fact it felt fine. As good as new.

So what had the snapping noise been?

'Oh my gosh, Bjorn, are you okay. Should I call an ambulance? The organisers? The king of Sweden? Are you hurt?' Lucie was more than a little hysterical having watched Bjorn tumble from the top of the wheel. It was her fault, after all, that he was up there in the first place. But she was still sure it would make a fabulous photo for the webpages of *Palaver!* Even if trying to cripple Sweden's star turn wasn't part of the total plan.

'I'm fine, thanks to this guy,' replied Bjorn, pointing to the dancer. He was still grinning inanely, absurdly pleased with his quick response. 'But I thought I'd broken my ankle. What was that snapping noise? I didn't imagine it, did I?'

'Er... no, you didn't. Look... oh crikey...' There was a tremble and an unusual timidity in Lucie's voice as she crooked her neck up to look at the top of the wheel. One of the rungs, the one that Bjorn's heel had slipped around, had clean snapped in two. It hung woefully in two separate pieces.

'Oh dear, we'll have to tell the props people to get that fixed,' said Bjorn, thinking how glad he was that that hadn't happened when he'd been sat on it minutes before.

'They'll have my guts for garters, I tell you. Guts for garters,' warbled Lucie. 'But at least you're safe. It must have been those platform boots of yours, Bjorn, they're so high. The heel must have snapped the rung when you fell. I was going to ask you if I could borrow them to wear for a photo for the article as I wanted to see what being so many inches taller would be like, but I won't bother now. I think I've done enough. Oh dear, oh dear...'

Bjorn felt that he had done enough too. His hidden body parts were still a little painful from where he'd been lying across the wheel and the thought of going back to his hotel room and soaking in a long hot bath was serving him major thrills.

'Can I go, are we finished?'

'Yes, thank you so much. Don't worry about the wheel, I'll let the props people know it was... er... dodgy.'

Bjorn thanked Lucie for the interview and walked away from the others to pick up his bag. As he did, a phone sounded inside it. The Swede grabbed it and looked at the name on the screen. A smile spread across his features.

This was a phonecall for Bella. The name on the screen was a blast from the past. A name that Bella knew she shouldn't really answer right now, but she couldn't stop herself. Making sure that the others remained far enough away from her not to hear, she pressed on the screen to answer the call.

She was smiling as she spoke. 'Hello, you, long time no speak. It's been ages. What on earth do you want, my friend? You'll never guess where I am...'

Chapter 28

"…what do you say when words are
not enough…"

'It's what Ronnie would have wanted,' said Donnie DonRon, trying to etch another streak of sorrow across his 18-year-old Irish features for those watching. He was talking to Weronika and Szymon in the Irish sector of the *Eurowide* green room during the live transmission of one of the *Euro* semi-finals.

Weronika nodded as earnestly as she could and made sure to wiggle the diamante black armband she was wearing as a mark of respect for those who had lost their lives this week in the run up to the contest. She was the only one with diamantes, Szymon was wearing a solid black one, as was the entire Irish party, including Donnie. But Weronika was determined that hers would be "fashion" and make her stand out. It did, but as ever, for all the wrong reasons.

Szymon continued the questioning. 'It must have been an incredibly hard decision for you to carry on performing so soon after the death of your dear brother. It's still been such a shock to us all. The entire week has been, but your twin was so incredibly young. Just 18 and such a terrible, terrible accident to fall off the boat.'

'Terrible,' added Weronika before Donnie could answer, checking her features in the monitor placed on the floor in front of her to make sure her concerned face was suitably so. She then stared directly down the barrel of the camera and pulled a highly insincere sad puppy face. Szymon ignored her. Luckily Donnie didn't see.

'We'll never know what happened to Ronnie. We guess he just had one too many on the boat and must have tumbled overboard. But he died partying and that's the true spirit of my brother and I know that he would have wanted me to still perform tonight and to try and reach the final on Saturday and bring the trophy home for Ireland. Plus, our manager, Wally Leish, thought it would be best economically if we carried on and didn't pull out. There's too much riding on it to stop now apparently, plus he's phoned home to speak to our mam to make sure we can put the funeral on hold. The church has got a few spaces in the calendar so it's not too urgent.'

A nervous cough erupted from the camp rotund little gentleman sat next to Donnie and he moved his head swiftly in front of the microphone to interject.

'Er... hi I'm Wally. Can I just say that Ronnie was a true entertainer and had a massive future ahead of him, so it seems only right that we honour him tonight by letting him perform on the *Eurowide* stage from beyond the grave. It's worked for Whitney, Tupac and Elvis so now we can add Ronnie to that incredible list of hall of fame fatalities too. He will be with us this evening through the magic of holograms. It's what the entire family has requested. Isn't that right, Donnie.' His voice cracked slightly. A feast of sorrow or a famine of sincerity? It was hard to tell.

Wally pushed Donnie's head back towards Szymon's microphone. 'We've used footage of Ronnie from past performances to create a hologram. It's pretty amazing, to be honest. It's all done with laser beams and mirrors, it's like something out of some Marvel movie. It's pretty cool.'

'Oh I met Chris Hemsworth once, he was in the dressing room next to mine on some talk show. I think he flirted with me,' beamed Weronika. He hadn't actually even looked at her, but what did details matter to a good story?

Szymon attempted to get things back on track. 'So tonight, for the first time you're going to be performing with your brother again on stage, representing Ireland and hoping that you go through to Saturday's contest. But your departed brother will be a hologram? That's a true *Eurowide* first.' It was now Szymon's turn to barrel the camera and give eye contact to the viewers, but unlike his co-host, his tone hit exactly the right note.

'That's right, we're doing it for Ireland in the true spirit of *Eurowide* to prove that nothing can stop DonRon. Not even Ron not being here anymore. I love you, bro!' Donnie looked towards the heavens and raised one hand into the air.

'You'll be DonGone from now on,' said Weronika without even a soupcon of irony. Before her lack of tact could land fully, Szymon gestured to the crowd gathered inside the Johnny Logan Coliseum.

'What an incredible story. And DonRon will be performing their song "The Smile Mile Club" in the next part of tonight's contest. Let's hear it for Donnie and the entire Irish party.'

A roar erupted from the crowd.

'But right now,' said Weronika. 'It's time for a break. We'll be right back…' She grinned fully at the screen.

There was still five seconds until they were due to cut to a break but had Weronika listened to the count in her earpiece? Of course not.

As the producer in her ear screamed, 'You're still on, fill for a moment!' Weronika just grinned and then turned to Szymon and removed her earpiece assuming they'd already cut to break.

'Don't be jealous. But he did flirt with me, you know, Chris Hemsworth, total babe, he was a fit as f…'

Luckily for the millions of viewers watching the semi around the globe, the adverts cut in just in the nick of time and decency.

'Oh DJ, please don't play, don't play that song again…' Char and Jemma sang in unison and then burst into a fit of laughter sitting in the UK sector of the semi-final green room as a rather dodgy entry from one of the Baltic countries finished on stage. It was a sullen little number performed by four wailing women who looked like they were attending a funeral and had just discovered that the buffet was decidedly below average in both size and flavour. To say it was drenched in misery was an understatement. A lacklustre reaction from the crowd showed that Jemma and Char were not alone in their opinion about its potential as a winner.

Despite his own dislike of the song, Daniel, sitting alongside the girls, was mortified by their singing. He whispered as bitingly to the two friends as he could, 'Will the pair of you just shut up, please. That country's sector is only a couple of booths down from ours and we don't want to start some kind of international incident just because you don't like their admittedly very dull-as-batshit song.'

Jemma let the criticism bounce off her. 'Oh, come on, Daniel, we were just singing a little UK entry from days gone by to show true Brit spirit, and let's be honest, if *Eurovision*-ledge Nicki French was here herself she'd be quite justified in bursting into song about that pile of dirge too. Ah, Nicki, an underrated UK bop from the year 2000.' She paused in contemplation before adding, 'And anyway, you're just still in a mood with me because I was hungover this morning. I'm fine now, and all of the radio interviews went to plan, so you don't need to get your stressy-pants in a twist. Unless you're still infuriated that I dragged you away from lover boy Igor.' She was goading him. She had been all day.

In truth she did feel fine although liquorice-scented burps of ouzo had been repeating on her all day and there had been a moment during a live interview with the female DJ on Waft FM, the Beat of Beautiful Burnley, that Jemma had definitely felt that a sick bucket by her side might have been a wise decision, but she'd made it through and everyone was happy, so Daniel had no reason to moan too much. Unless he was missing his boning bodyguard of course.

'If it were possible to flick you a finger right now, Miss La Vie, I would do. But seeing as there are hundreds of cameras flying about in this arena, I daren't risk it, which is why I'd rather you and Char didn't sing songs to slag off other countries.'

'Yep, he's pissed about leaving Igor,' smirked Char, who was feeling a million times better than she had done 24 hours earlier, face down backstage at the bloggers' concert. She couldn't resist a dig either. *'He was only playing love games, he was only playing love games with your arse...'*

'Oh, seventh place, UK entry, 1984, Belle and the Devotions, "Love Games", added lyrics by Char Grills. Nice choice, sweetie…' She raised her hand to high-five Char. 'A Chips Ahoy fave if ever there was.'

Daniel spoke, his teeth gritted, 'I am not annoyed about you being hungover this morning, and seeing as I did it earlier in the week, I haven't really got a leg to stand on, have I? Not that I was hungover, of course, I was just a little queasy. Yeah that's right…' He stumbled over his words a little, eager to stick to his original story as to why he was absent from the press junket.

Daniel had been decidedly hungover the morning he had first woken up with Igor by his side. Tequila and fish eye canapes didn't mix as he found out first-hand, but he hadn't been required to schmooze Dermot O'Leary on the phone the next morning, had he?

'No, you haven't got a leg to stand on, and that's why we love you, Daniel Spirit, because you're one of us.' Jemma leant over and squeezed his cheek with her fingers. Despite everything he couldn't help but smile.

'He's not got a leg to stand on, but he certainly found something to sit on, didn't he? Where is Sister Steroid tonight?' asked Char, amused with herself as ever.

'Will you stop calling him that. And FYI he's over there.' Daniel pointed two rows back and three booths along where Igor was sitting alongside Wiktoria and the Rottimoldovian team. His face lit up as he spotted Daniel staring in his direction and he waved gleefully to him. Without thinking, Daniel couldn't help but happily wave back.

'He's a good egg is Igor,' said Jemma. 'Wiktoria really likes him already. And I don't think she's the only one, is she?' She winked at Daniel. 'How come he's with her tonight?'

'Because she's doing her little interview with the hosts tonight as well. Wiktoria's been getting freaked out by that premonition from the fortuneteller still, so she wanted Igor with her. Her interview is near the end of the night. Yours is coming up after this next song, so prepare yourself, Szymon will be over after this.'

'He can sit between you and me, Char,' said Jemma. 'I'll have one end, you can have the other. I reckon there's enough of him to go round.' She licked her lips and smiled. And then let out a liquorice burp. Char cracked up into more laughter.

The lights dimmed in the arena.

'What's next?' whispered Jemma.

'It's DonRon, minus Ron,' said Daniel.

'Oh good, I'm gagging to see this.'

For the next three minutes, the three of them watched in silence as the Irish entry played out on stage. Donnie bouncing around on one side of the stage and a hologram Ronnie virtually bouncing up and down on the other side, the two boys identical apart from the green hair. And one being dead of course. It was an impressive performance and the crowd loved it, a tidal wave of applause crashing around the Johnny Logan Coliseum as it ended. Was that a tear in Donnie's eye? It might have been. Or maybe sweat from bouncing around too much.

In the Irish sector, Wally Leash clapped his cupped hands together and grinned. He could smell an Irish win on the horizon. Death was often a good career move. 'Oh, the wee lad gave 110%, he really did,' said Wally to anyone within ear shot.

Back in the UK sector, Jemma, Char and Daniel were all equally impressed.

'Whaddya know. The boy done good. That was amazing,' said Jemma.

'That must have been dead hard, performing with your brother's laser image when the real one's body is barely dry yet from his dip into the river.' Char could feel herself welling up. She cried at anything. She couldn't watch an episode of *The Pimple Popper* without getting through a box of Kleenex crying over some poor soul's misshaped blackhead.

All thoughts of boils, bumps and blisters popped out of Char's mind as stunner host Szymon made his way towards the UK booth and placed his walnut ass between her and Jemma.

'Hi, ladies,' he smiled at them both and then turned to face Jemma. 'Weronika's just doing her link on the other side of the arena and then she's throwing to us. We'll have about two minutes, okay?' He then smiled into the camera in front of him, not moving until the red light came on.

Suddenly he burst into action.

'Thanks, Weronika, I'm here with another of our *Eurowide* stars, it's the UK's Jemma La Vie and her faaaaan-tastic song "Beep the World (Hear My Horn)".' A cheer thundered from the crowd, a sea of Union Jacks greeting Jemma's appearance on screen. 'Great to see you, Jemma. I know that you're a massive fan of shows like this and can't wait to perform on Saturday.'

Jemma burst into life. 'Oh, I love it, Szymon. And your song from a few years back, "Party People C'mon", is still one of our fave tunes of all time. You were robbed. Me and Char,' she pointed at her friend, who waved into the camera, a little stunned to hear her name, 'we're always singing it although we can't do the hip thrusts as well as you do.' She went to jiggle her hips and let out another small and thankfully inaudible burp into Szymon's face.

'Hey that's great,' said Szymon, before moving on swiftly, not wanting to veer off the path of his pre-planned script. 'The UK doesn't always do so well at these types of contests, do you think you can change that on Saturday?'

'Here's hoping.' She crossed her fingers to the camera. 'It's a great song that I'm really proud of writing and performing and people seem to like it so you never know. But you can never tell what's going to happen on the night. Just ask SuRie, eh? Or that Spanish bloke who looked like he was singing in a toy shop. Stage invaders a-go-go.' Again, another slight ouzo-flavoured burp hissed out from between her lips.

'That's right. And what tricks have you got up your sleeve for your stage performance, Jemma?'

It hadn't been officially announced to the *Euro* fans as yet but the backdrop for Jemma's performance was going to be a video wall of UK supporters all beeping their horns. In their cars, on their bikes, in trucks in laybys. Not that you'd be able to hear the horns, but everyone would get the drift. Daniel had given her strict instructions not to give too much away if asked. She hadn't worked out an answer though and for a moment a sense of feeling flummoxed enveloped her. Another slight burp. God, why had the ouzo picked her live *Eurowide*-telly debut to come back with such repetitive vengeance? Jemma picked her words carefully. But sadly not carefully enough. 'It's a surprise, Szymon, but I can tell you that once you've seen me on that stage on Saturday you and everyone else will be feeling really *horny*.'

The duality of the word's meaning hadn't even occurred to her. It obviously had to Char, who shrieked a burst of loud exclamation, and Daniel, who merely chewed his bottom lip in vexation. When it did strike Jemma, she couldn't help but let out another nervous and this time slightly audible ouzo burp.

'Wow,' exclaimed Szymon. 'We can't wait for that, Jemma. Good luck.' He stared directly into the lens once again. 'And now it's time for another incredible song, and it's the entry from Greece.' He held his fingers to his earpiece and corrected himself, obviously prompted by one of telly voices in his head. 'Sorry, it's not Greece, it's Denmark. My mistake.'

The arena lights dimmed again, and the camera went off. The link was over.

'Thanks, Jemma, that was awesome. Can't wait to see your *horny* performance.' He laughed. 'I can't believe I said Greece though, then. I knew it was Denmark, but Greece kept popping into my head when I was talking to you. I have no idea why. Weird.'

Jemma didn't say a word and kept her lips together as the ouzo repeated on her once more.

Chapter 29

"...Miss Kiss Kiss Bang, now let us swing..."

Bjorn Bjork looped his neckerchief around the hook of his coat hanger and placed his entire outfit inside the wardrobe of his hotel bedroom. It lined up neatly against the other half dozen identical blue and yellow costumes hanging in a row. He slid the wardrobe door into place and stared at himself in the mirror.

Or rather herself.

Because tonight Bjorn would be nowhere to be seen. Tonight was full on 100% Bella. And her reflection in the somewhat harsh and unflattering light of the hotel bedroom mirror proved that to erotic perfection. Bella had to admit that even though she'd have preferred better lighting – which woman wouldn't continually wish for that? – she looked irresistible which is just what she needed to be tonight. Irresistible, desirable, tempting to the max and exquisitely expensive. As Bella it was what she was famed for. She took in her full length. Sleek caviar-black bobbed wig a la Zeta Jones in *Chicago* covering her own blonde locks, now safely tucked away in a netted hair cap underneath the wig. Full-on make-up, lashes proud and prominent and lips slicked with the deepest shade of crimson.

Her breasts, more than joyous to not be crushed and hidden away for once, flaunted themselves proudly in the wet-look faux-leather low-cut bodysuit sheathed around them. Flamboyant and flirtatious, they sat perkily invitational, awaiting what the night ahead had to offer.

Bella's legs, more toned than ever due to months of jiggling to the salsa beat of "24 Hours of Sunshine", had never looked better in the fierce energy of her high-shine black vinyl thigh-skimming boots. The long length of the micro-slim heel adding inches to her appearance. She had swapped platforms for power, disco for domination, smiles for smoulders and camp for vamp. It was a miracle she had packed all the things she was wearing for her trip to Rottimoldovia, but she guessed old habits die hard. Mind you, a habit was one of the many outfits in her erotic repertoire that she hadn't packed. But something had told her to pack the latex and rubber. And the phone call earlier from an old and dear friend had proved her hunch right.

Mistress Kimberley and Bella went back a long way. Maybe a decade or so. Back to Bella's first forays into the wonderful world of whoring. Mistress Kimberley was one of the most notorious girls on the Swedish sex worker scene. With a definite love of all things kink. She was famed for being at the top of her game and her game was most definitely domination. Bella adored her, admired her, and looked up to her as a deity of devilish delight. Not easy when Kimberley was famed for the most monumentally dizzy-heighted heels. She was like a mother to Bella. When times had been tough and life on her back (or all fours depending on the individual client's wishes) had not been dishing the dosh as she had hoped it had been, and paying rent was beyond her reach, it was Kimberley who had taken her in, kept her fed and watered and had, ironically for one so kinky, put her back on the straight and narrow.

Moving into Kimberley's apartment-come-dungeon was the best thing that had ever happened to Bella. It was like she had enrolled in a school of seduction, with Kimberley passing clients on to Bella when her own bookings were overflowing and moulding her perfectly in the art of pleasure. It was Kimberley who became Bella's headmistress, with the emphasis on the head. Teaching her all of the tricks of the trade that many years of sexual mayhem had taught her.

The two women had lived together for nearly a year, allowing Bella to build up her bank balance and also build up her skills when it came to the striking art of kink and female domination. And strike she did, with a lip-licking joy that her subservient clients relished with rosy-buttocked gratification. By the time Bella flew the fetish fold of Kimberley's palace of pleasure, she was the ultimate protégé of passion, a princess to Queen Kimberley herself.

Nearly ten years on, the two women were still incredibly close. Even if they didn't speak for months on end, they would always be forever linked in their friendship. A bonding over bondage.

Which was why Bella had been more than overjoyed to receive her mentor's phone call as she was finishing the photoshoot on the hamster wheel with Lucie Rave.

'Hello, you, long time no speak. It's been ages. What on earth do you want, my friend? You'll never guess where I am...' Bella was ecstatic to hear from Kimberley. If ever there was something that could take her mind off the pain her already ache-filled body was in after having to contort itself around a hamster wheel, it was a chinwag and a gossip with one of her oldest friends.

The voice at the other end of the phone purred, her voice a drizzle of sexiness. 'Darling, it's been four months and I know exactly where you are as the last time we spoke you told me about your hairbrained scheme to be a 20-year-old boy. Darling, you've not been 20 since I was in my four—' Kim stopped herself mid-word. 'Early 30s...'

Of course, Kimberley was the *one* person she told everything to. Everything. Bella laughed about her verbal 180. Kimberley's real age was an enigma, but it was safe to say that she had spanked her way around the block for a good few years.

'So how is life as Bjorn at *Eurowide*?' continued Kimberley. 'The odds for you winning on Saturday are looking very good. I assume you want to win?'

'I'm not so sure about that. If I do, then I have to be Bjorn Bjork for the rest of my life, don't I? That is not going to be easy.'

'Well then, girlfriend, you had better pray that you're not the next ABBA or Soreen and that you gain a few nul points on Saturday night. I'll be watching of course. But fear not, my lips are sealed. You know that. The only ones on me that are, of course.'

Soreen? A flash of perplexity grazed Bella's mind before she realised her friend meant Loreen. Thankfully her knowledge of fetish was way better than her know-how of song contests.

'So business is good?' asked Bella, by now wending her way out of the Johnny Logan Coliseum.

'Booming, sweetheart, booming. I'm getting to grips with the whole internet thing nowadays. Chat rooms and Instagram and all of that. It's a whole new FemDom world where my skills seem to be very appreciated. And very well paid for. Which is why I'm ringing you, my lovely. I'm a little pooped and can't be bothered with any kind of action tonight. Plus, I want to watch a show about Swedish antiques on the TV later as a friend of mine is showcasing her chest on it, so I was wondering if you'd do a job for me. The money is very good. It'll keep you in whips and paddles for months. But I really can't be arsed. Do you have time in your schedule, darling?'

'It's online, right?' queried Bella. The thought of some extra money coming her way was highly appealing. And she had packed a few items that would come in handy.

'Well, no, it's a client that I had online the other night. Really lovely man actually. Very sexy and he was loving what I did. Massively. We chatted for ages afterwards, which I never normally let happen, but he was very friendly. He wants to meet again and said how he would love to experience me in the flesh. In the flesh is not possible as I'm here in Sweden and he, as chance would have it, just happens to be on your doorstep right now which is why I thought of you. He's very sexy, as I said, none of your sweating, blobby, middle-aged comb-over brigade. I suspect he's over your way because he's involved in your contest thing. Maybe a dancer? Or he's some crazy fan. A very dirty bugger. Has all the toys. You'd just need to turn up and do your thing. Up to you what you want to give him sexually, but you'll enjoy yourself, I assure you. I enjoyed Domming him hugely. Originally, he wanted a session online with me at about midnight, his time, tonight. Said he was busy earlier. Midnight clashes with my friend and her chest here. So I suggested a face-to-face with a very skilled friend of mine, seeing as I knew you were that way too. He's very keen. Needs total discretion. But don't they all, dear? Probably has a wife who won't go beyond missionary. So, could you?'

Bella considered her night ahead. Bjorn had qualified in the first semi. Tonight was the second. Bjorn wasn't needed. Bella had pretty much a clear night ahead.

'How much is he paying?'

Kimberley told her his minimum. It was sizable. Kimberley also filled her in on what the client was packing downstairs. Sizable too. The deal was sealed.

Bella said she would.

'Thank you, dear girl,' oozed Kimberley elatedly. 'You'll have fun. I'll get back to him and then text you his hotel details. Does that sound good? Show him some of those tricks I taught you, darling.'

Bella smiled, recalling their teacher-time in the apartment together. 'That sounds perfect. So did you see me perform at the semi?'

No answer came as Mistress Kimberley hung up the phone. *Probably not*, thought Bella. Her interest in all things *Euro* was smaller than San Marino. So tiny.

Bella hailed a taxi outside the Coliseum and headed back to her hotel.

Bella looked at the clock on her hotel room wall and read the time –11:45pm. The hotel details Mistress Kimberley had texted through showed an address about 15 minutes from her own. She took an ankle-length coat from the bed and slipped it on. She gave herself one last all over check in the mirror, observed her own sexiness satisfactorily and headed to the door. She opened it slightly and looked out into the corridor to make sure no passing contestant was visible. It was empty. She moved out into the corridor and headed for the lift.

It was just after midnight when she knocked on the hotel room door at her destination. It opened an inch or two. The interior inside was dimly lit as she walked in. A man was sat on the bed. He was wearing a dressing gown from the hotel and a gimp mask.

Even in the dim light and hidden behind the mask, there was something remarkably familiar about him. She was fairly sure she knew who he was.

'Good evening,' she purred, loosening the belt on her coat and letting it fall open.

'Good evening, mistress,' he gasped, pleased to see what lay beneath the coat.

Bella recognised the voice immediately. She now knew exactly who it was. A flicker of doubt crossed her mind. She should leave. Say that the raunchy rendezvous wasn't possible. But she couldn't. She didn't want to. He'd never know who she really was, would he? She walked towards the bed.

Playing with fire? Hell yes, but burn, baby, burn…

Chapter 30

"…show you all it's my time now…"

As Bella slinked her way towards her client's bed and reached for the arrangement of toys lined up alongside him in their leather housing, across the hotels of Ermpit, a million voices (well, a good few dozen) lay in their beds contemplating the day that had passed.

Turkey's Baran and Meli were both in their own beds. In their own separate bedrooms. In their own separate suites. Despite being a much-loved husband-and-wife duo on screen, behind closed doors there was no way that either of them would consider sharing a bad. That ship had not only sailed, but it had also been torpedoed and sunken to the bottomless depths of a loveless marriage a thousand fathoms below.

Baran flicked off the TV he was watching from his bed. Some late-night TV show called *The Housewives of Some American Hellhole* or something like that. Baran had only kept watching as one of them, some ex-Bond girl with silicone boobs was doing a photoshoot with half a dozen male models. All of them steroid-buff and wearing no more than a pair of tight budgie smugglers. It had held Baran's attention long enough to keep him interested, but when the show changed to the story of another Housewife party-planning a bar mitzvah, his interest didn't just wane, it evaporated. The horniness he'd felt watching the male models didn't though.

He threw down the remote control on the bed and picked up his mobile. 'Maybe a little late-night app action might sort you out.' He lifted up the bed sheet and looked down at himself. He was talking to the excitement between his legs.

He scrolled through his apps. He deserved a little treat. Hopefully a big one if he could find it online. He and Meli had qualified for the final today. "La Goes Up La Goes Down" had placed well. The crowd reaction had been good. He was excited about Saturday. Even if it did still mean embossing a smile of matrimonial harmony onto his face yet again.

He found his favourite gay app, Twink-All. Full of young hot men looking for daddies. Eager to please 20-somethings with washboard abs you could bounce your guitar plectrum off and then roger royally. He opened it up, scanned the screen and found those nearby looking for action. *Eurowide* week, it was naturally busier than Verka Serduchka's dance routines – 50 hopefuls mere blocks away.

Within minutes the job was done and a daddy-lovin' hottie was making his way across Ermpit ready to give his votes to Baran's second performance of the night. Except this one would definitely not involve Meli.

Meli was also watching *The Housewives of Wherever* in her bed whilst devouring a box of peppermint cremes and loving every face-fillered, lip-pumping, drama-dripped moment. If ever they cast a *Housewives of Istanbul* back home then she was definitely tossing her name into the ring of consideration.

She mulled the idea over in her head. *Mind you, maybe I could join one of the American ones. New York or Beverly Hills?* she said to herself still staring intently at the TV screen, now showing one of the housewives watching on with a mixture of pet parental pride and utter horror as her prize Pomeranian, Gwendolyne, was administered with a deluxe anal glands draining at some chi-chi pet spa. Even that looked glamorous on *Housewives*.

'Maybe Beverly Hills,' she said, happily talking through her ideas to herself. 'One of them was a singer wasn't she. The one that had the pensioner husband. But she's never won *Eurowide,* has she. America loves this kind of contest, doesn't it? Why else would Madonna turn up being all *Madame X* and eye-patchy. Yes, that's a great idea, Meli, I must try and arrange a casting opportunity once I've won *Eurowide.* Get that in the bag, then I can safely ditch Baran and that dreadful Turkish TV show and become an international sensation. Plus, just think how close I'd be to the best plastic surgeons in the world.'

She only stopped talking to herself when she popped another peppermint crème into her mouth.

Two floors up at the same hotel, Char Grills was lying on her back on top of her bed in her XL panda onesie, phone pressed to her ear. She'd been invited back to Jemma's room where she and Wiktoria were having another late-night drink and gossip ("wine and winge" as Jemma liked to call it) which normally she would have been diving into straight away. Especially after the excitement of the night's semi and the hilarity of Jemma's *horny* confession. But tonight she wanted to let the girls fly solo as she had some horny business of her own to deal with. That business being talking dirty and flirty to Ashley, the totes-drop-dead-gorgeous male dancer she'd met the night before at the bloggers' party before she had managed to fall into the black hole of her own drunkenness.

Ashley was one of the backing dancers for Baran and Meli. Not that Char had known that when she first caught his eye at the bar when ordering drinks the night before. Had he been wearing his harem pants and hip scarf she might have recognised him. She'd seen him strutting his chiselled stuff on stage many times over the last week but had automatically assumed he was gay. Men that looked like that normally were, but something from his eye contact with her at the bar and the cheeky squeeze of her arse as he walked past her and slipped a card with his number on into her hand made her think that perhaps that wasn't the case. When she'd found his number that morning, she texted him just to make sure that she hadn't hallucinated after one too many cocktails.

Lying on the bed talking to him now was 16 hours and perhaps 200 WhatsApp messages later. Messages that had proven that he was openly bi, not gay (Char could happily live with that, she was a modern kinda girl, and let's face it, if she had a body like that then she'd let any gender have a pop too) and that even though he was a backing dancer for the Turkey song, he was actually from Kettering.

'So, how did a total fittie like you from Kettering end up wafting around in a coin belt at a song contest?'

The answer was that he'd been working in Turkey as part of a resident hotel cabaret dance troop when he'd seen an ad for the audition.

'How long have you been bi?'

As long as he could remember, having fiddled with the male cricket team captain at his school and also having a bunk-up with the captain's sister a few weeks later in an alley behind a pub in Kettering. He'd enjoyed both sexes and still did. Char found it "exotic and continental". You didn't get much of that back in Whittlesey. Well not that she knew of.

'Have you finished for the night now?'

He had, having been dancing at the semi with Baran and Meli.

'What are they like?'

He was miserable, she was stupid. Both could be wrapped around a little finger with a come-hither glance.

'Have you shagged either of them?'

A definite no.

'D'you want to come over here now and see me?'

Sadly, he couldn't but how about tomorrow night?

'What can I expect then, Ash, you gorgeous specimen?'

He let her know.

Char spent the next half an hour staring at photos that Ashley sent her of himself in various stages of undress. And arousal. Char guessed that there would be no lonely symphony for her tomorrow night...

In another part of the hotel, Wiktoria and Jemma were jumping up and down on the bed in Jemma's hotel room both singing into hairbrushes. Jemma was on a high despite her embarrassment about her comment to Szymon live on TV earlier in the night. Wiktoria, as ever, was just happy being happy and happy to still be alive when so many people around her seemed to be dropping dead.

'And the category is *Eurovision* duets!' screamed Jemma, aware that the various bits of her body didn't really seem to be bouncing in any kind of coordination as she selected another track on her classic *Eurovision* play list.

'First up, 2017, "Lost in Verona"…'

They were supposed to just be having a quiet drink. After the fun of ouzo night 24 hours earlier, it was supposed to just be a glass of wine back in Jemma's room. Before they knew it, both girls had passed an entire hour and sung their way through "Playing with Fire", "Running Scared", "Goodbye to Yesterday", "Calm After the Storm" and at least another eight or so of their faves. Wiktoria only retired to her own bed when Jemma suggested Jemini's "Cry Baby".

'Oh yes, harder!' Not too far away on another floor of the hotel, Daniel was seeing his favourite part of his bed yet again. The headboard. On all fours gripping onto the wooden headboard a naked Daniel looked over his shoulder. Igor was doing what Igor did best. Looking after bodies. Having finished his duties looking after Wiktoria's body for the night at the semi-final he was now more than admirably looking after Daniel's.

'Oh my God, wow you're big…' Daniel's eye glazed a little with the pleasure of it all as he wallowed in enjoying the moment. Igor was growing on him and right now, it felt like he was growing in him too…

In the room next door, Lucie Rave was oblivious to the protestations of pleasure coming from Daniel about the size of Igor's manhood as she lay in bed. She was fast asleep dreaming about taking part in a *Eurovision* fashion show. She had just been strutting her way down the catwalk flanked by Dana International and Netta in a riot of feathers and bling when she suddenly sat bolt upright in bed, wide awake.

'Oh my God, I forget to tell the props people we broke the hamster wheel.'

Before she gave it another thought she lay back down and immediately dropped off again. Weirdly, her dream returned to the *Euro* catwalk where Donnie and Ronnie DonRon were reunited once more. But Ronnie was still soaking wet with green hair dye all over his shirt.

On the top floor of the hotel Donnie DonRon was sitting upright in bed shooting the cyber crap out of someone on his Xbox Series X. Nothing relaxed him more than an hour or five of *Call of Duty* shooting away at his heart's content. Normally he'd have had Ronnie alongside him, but a certain boat trip and too many drinks had stopped his partner in crime in his tracks. But at least he had still been with him tonight, albeit in hologram form.

'Take that, you little fecker!' he trilled at the screen, having just sent another victim to their virtual grave.

A knock sounded on his bedroom door. He knew who it would be. It was the same every night, both pre- and post-Ronnie. 'C'mon in, Wally.' Why their manager always insisted on sharing their hotel room was beyond him. It was always two bedrooms, one bathroom. Wally Leash was always insistent, but he'd turned DonRon into the biggest Irish song contest stars since Dustin the Turkey so that was all that mattered, right?

Wally Leash sprung his head out from behind the door. 'Can I come in?'

'Sure.' Like Donnie had a choice. If he'd have said no Wally would just shuffle right in anyway.

'It's late, Donnie. Time to go to sleep. You've worked really hard tonight, and you performed really well with the hologram. We sailed through to the final.'

'Thanks, Wally.' Donnie carried on firing as he spoke, not really looking in his manager's direction. Before he knew it, Wally was alongside the bed.

'It's time to put that down and get some shut eye. Unless you want me to play with you?'

He meant the game, right? 'No, I'm fine, Wally.' He turned and smiled at Wally. Was his manager sweating a little bit? He did seem to be glowing somewhat.

Wally reached out and placed his hand on Donnie's. There was a little awkward silence before Wally took the console from his hands. 'Then there you go. That's enough for tonight. We've got a big day of rehearsals tomorrow. You'll need to be all bright and sparkly in the morning as we have lots of press to do.'

Donnie knew not to argue. He never did. Donnie lay down and pulled the bed sheets right up over his pyjama top to his shoulders. He knew what was coming next. It was always the same. He and his brother never liked it, but Wally was always emphatic about it.

'Now turn the light off, Donnie.'

He did. Donnie lay there until his eyes became accustomed to the dark. He could see the short squat silhouette outline of Wally still stood by the bed.

'That's better. Now let's tuck you in nicely. Wally worked his way around the bed, tucking in any stray bits of sheet. He then left the room. Ronnie never shut his eyes until he did. Some nights he seemed to take a lot longer to leave than others.

'He's a funny thing is Wally,' Donnie chirped to himself, finally alone in the dark. But it was true, he had made him into a household name like Ronan Keating, and he'd presented *Eurovision* and done all sorts of fabulous things, so what was a little tucking-in between friends?

Back on the other side of Ermpit, a highly satisfied and spent Szymon Rybak couldn't believe his luck as he sat naked on his hotel room bed. Naked apart from his mask. The last two hours had been amazing. Mistress Kimberley had been right about Mistress Bella. She was sensational and had given him everything he needed and more. After the rush of hosting the semi-final earlier he knew that he would need to unwind, and Bella had made sure of that. His body ached just where it needed to ache. That thin line between pleasure and pain had been one that Bella had walked with tightrope precision. The toys had been used and Bella had finished the evening's fun and (BDSM) games with a nerve-tingling display on her knees with her head between Szymon's legs doing what she did best. As far as Szymon was concerned her technique was absolutely the best he'd ever sampled. And there had been many to compare it to. He was in complete rapture as he watched her little black bob – he guessed it was a wig – bobbing up and down against his thighs.

'I trust I pleased you, Mistress?' he said as Bella stood up in front of him.

'Oh, you did, very much so.'

'I must pay you. I have the cash.'

'Yes, you must, but I must just go to the ladies' room.'

Szymon looked at her face. She reminded him of someone but he couldn't work out who. As she turned to head to the bathroom a massive penny dropped in my mind. A penny big enough to make him question his own sanity. Surely not...

There at the base of Bella's back, just above the line of her faux-leather bodysuit was a small tattoo. But it was an unmistakable one. A small white flower with a date below. He guessed it was a birthdate. He had seen it before. And he knew where. But what kind of crazy coincidence was that? 'Nice tattoo, Mistress', he said.

Bella stopped in her tracks and turned back around to face him. She seemed a little flustered. 'Oh that, I forget it's there. It's a bella flower, it's where my name comes from. Oh, and my date of birth, not that you should ever ask a Mistress her age, you naughty boy.'

'Shouldn't it say Bjorn?' asked Szymon, standing up off the bed. As he spoke, he reached round to unzip his mask and took it off. 'You know it's me, right? And I know it's you.'

Bella's face dropped as she looked Szymon directly in the eyes. Despite being hooked on his deeply handsome features, a wave of terror crashed over her.

'Sorry? I don't know what you mean.'

'You can't lie. Unless this is just the most mixed-up, fucked-up thing ever. I've seen that tattoo before, when I was putting your microphone on at the concert last night. The date is the same and everything. If it's your date of birth, then you're...' He did a swift calculation. 'Thirty-two?'

'Microphone? What microphone?' she bluffed. 'But I don't know what you're... er, even talking about... why is my age a problem?' Bella could hear her voice crackling, a whole heap of trouble whirl winding in her mind.

'It's not. But it is you, isn't it. I recognise your face. I found you sexy as Bjorn. Not as sexy as you are tonight but there was definitely something there even then when I thought you were Bjorn. Now I know why. You're him. He's you.'

Before Bella could formulate an appropriate excuse of an answer, a naked Szymon walked up to her and placed his hand on her wig. He left it there, not moving it until she had reacted. Knowing that she had to, she nodded. She didn't just have to, she wanted to.

Szymon gently removed the wig revealing the netted cap underneath housing a mass of blonde hair. Bella lifted her own hands to her head and removed the net cap, letting the yellow-coloured locks underneath tumble free. She felt she might cry; she wasn't sure.

Before she could decide, Szymon reached his arms around her and pulled her tight towards him. His hug was both comforting and sexually charged in equal measures. She felt safe yet every nerve ending inside her fizzed with excitement.

They remained clinched for what seemed like minutes, in reality maybe no more than ten seconds. Szymon kissed her fully on the lips as they parted from each other. She let him happily.

'I think I need to tell you a few things, Szymon,' said Bella.

Szymon sat himself down on the bed. Bella sat beside him and began to talk. The words flowed freely and without hesitation. Maybe it wasn't just Mistress Kimberley that Bella could share everything with.

Chapter 31

"...give a little love back to the world..."

30 hours until *Eurowide*.

There were a mass of bleary foam-filled heads the next morning as a group of *Euro* hopefuls gathered at the *Eurowide* fan village. It was the day before the contest final itself and everyone needed to be at the top of their game. They all had a big day ahead of them. The dress rehearsal for the contest was happening that evening and a jam-packed day of press, photo opps and general *Euro* bonhomie was on the cards for all of them. Starting with an hour or two of pressing the flesh and posing for selfies for lucky fan club competition winners across Europe who were gagging to meet their *Euro* heroes. Yep, the fan meet 'n' greet. And those gathered at the *Euro* village, a cordoned off fan area two streets away from the Dicken Platz, were greeting the prospect with various degrees of excitement ranging from gleeful to woeful, gratitude to attitude.

Bjorn Bjork's head was all over the place as he stood in the line-up, hand outstretched, ready to face the public. By the time Bella had finished her night and allowed Bjorn to head to bed, it must have been about 5am. The après-kink confessional to Szymon had taken a while and was, to use a well-coined but totally valid phrase, an "emotional rollercoaster". But Szymon had listened. And loved. He totally understood. Something that had shocked Bella to her very foundation.

As they had hugged goodbye as the first rays of morning light raised their sprightly heads over the Ermpit horizon, Szymon held her in his arms and simply said, 'Your secret is safe with me.'

It had genuinely been that easy. The host of the show knew her secret but had promised not to say a word. It made Bella wonder what other scandalous *Euro* secrets had been kept over the years, but that didn't matter now. A weight had been lifted from Bella's shoulders, and whatever happened over the next day and a half, at least she had one particular personal jury voting in her direction.

Sadly for Bjorn, the weight that had lifted off Bella's shoulders had now landed squarely and firmly on his brain. That what's two hours of sleep and an hour taping your beautifully man-handled breasts (Szymon was ticking all the right boxes last night) into position did for you. As Bjorn lined up on the makeshift red carpet (actually it was woven into the muddy colours of the Rottimoldovian flag) waiting for the next fan to come his way, he could feel his brain becoming dangerously heavy and jaded. But the show must go on. It was all about the theatre and just like Katja Epstein's backing clowns way back in 1980 – "Theatre" was definitely one of Bjorn's favourite retro *Eurovish* tunes – it was time to paint on the face and not let anyone know just how he was feeling underneath. So when the next fan arrived in front of him, a rather annoyingly bubbly guy in full glitter make-up and a pink wig who proceeded to death drop to the floor with a shrill and needless scream, Bjorn merely smiled and plastered on his smile. Theatre indeed.

Further up the muddy-coloured carpet, Jemma turned to Wiktoria, both somewhat fatigued from their singing the night before, and commented on the candyfloss-coiffed fan. 'Here, Wikky, have you seen who's on his way. Our mad fan from the bloggers' concert. Seems he likes Bjorn too judging from the way he's just landed flat on his back.' Jemma coughed a little, aware she was still sounding a little hoarse from her vocal gymnastics the night before. Even though every sensible thought in her head had said, *save your voice for the shows,* any sense and reason had been drowned out by fun and alcohol. 'God, I sound like Darth Vader this morning. I'd better find a Fisherman's Friend to suck on or else I'll be sounding like those Icelandic bondage boys, Hatari. God, they scared me a little... give me Brotherhood Of Man any day. You didn't see them all wrapped up in buckles and studs, did you?' She giggled before screeching "Save All Your Kisses for Me" in the raspiest voice she could muster. Another thought of *save your voice* meandered through her mind but was ignored once more.

Once again, Wiktoria didn't really have a clue what Jemma's warehouse of *Eurovision* knowledge was talking about, but as normal she nodded sweetly and smiled at her friend. She merely responded with, 'I like the drag fan with the pink wig, he's cute.' And then, 'My uncle was a fisherman... he used to go and catch herring.'

The buckles and studs at the meet 'n' greet this morning were being provided by Fritz, lead singer of

Die Bolzen, standing mercifully far away enough from Wiktoria and Jemma for them not to experience the rather potent and pungent ping of Fritz's BO. A leather Die Bolzen tour jacket that had never seen so much as a whiff of Febreze, nicotine-impregnated T-shirt with bonus cigarette burns, and a lack of showering for the last 24 hours made for quite an odorous combination. Aromatic in was not. Gag-making it certainly was. When Jemma had caught a nostril full of Fritz's lack of hygiene earlier, she'd turned to Wiktoria, grabbed her own throat, stuck out her tongue and coughed the words, 'Polina Polina Gag-arina!' causing Wiktoria to collapse into giggles.

Not that some of the fans seemed to mind. Die Bolzen fans seemed to fall into two camps, the awkward, shy ones who merely wanted to tell Fritz how much songs like "The Sweet Smell of Europe" meant to them as they hung their head down in front of him and mumbled their adoration, and those fans, all female, who merely wanted to literally press the flesh with their rock God. For the rest of the meet 'n' greet line up, pressing the flesh meant merely shaking a hand or maybe a peck on the cheek. For Fritz and certain female fans, the flesh being pressed was two pairs of lips and about a bucketful of saliva as Fritz badly swirled his way around their faces. With his piss-poor kissing, miasma of smelliness and a semi-heartfelt cry of, 'For Gunter,' as Fritz and yet another fan fist-punched the air for a selfie, it was quite the spectacle.

One which Baran and Meli were watching with total disgust. Neither of them wanted to be on the "muddy" carpet this morning. Baran was beyond beat from his Twink-All hook-up which had lasted until sunrise at least. A little blue pill and an endless offering of butt-cheek from his trade had made for an incredibly satisfying night. If a little draining, in every way. As for Meli, she wasn't good with the public at all. Unless they were rich, famous or useful to her future career. Shaking hands with some unknown Darren from Dagenham or Wolfgang from Warsaw was way beneath her these days. Add that to the fact that Baran and Meli were both definitely close enough to German rocker Fritz to savour every acrid moment of his filthy funk and be within range of the backsplash of his awful snogging technique, it was no wonder that neither of them were happy bunnies this morning.

Meli had already decided that she would have to spend at least a good two hours that afternoon washing her buttock-skimming hair to try and rid it of the stench. But at least she looked immaculate right now. Full glamour-puss hair and make-up was needed, even at this time of the day. Meli flicked her hair over her shoulders and begrudgingly held out her hand to the next passing fan, a small and excitable spiky-haired girl no more than late teens. She was crying profusely, her entire face stained with wetness. Her smile showed that they were tears of happiness. She was serving *Euro*-fanatic realness.

'What on earth is the matter, dear?' asked Meli, faux-concerned.

'I just love you so very much,' she sobbed between gasps of air and deep sorrowful blubbering. 'Meeting *Eurowide* stars is. Like. The. Best. Thing. Ever.' Every word was separate and dotted with another sob. 'Can I have a selfie please?' The fan collapsed into more tears of euphoric hysteria.

'Of course.' Meli and Baran bent down to be on a level with the fan, who then proceeded to jam her face up against Meli's for the photo. She was still crying.

The photo taken, the fan moved her cheek away from Meli's with a small damp squelch. Meli's make-up, pristine seconds before, was now a drenched mess of powder. All semblance of contouring drowned.

'Oh sorry, I've messed up your make-up,' wept the fan, before realising that that meant she probably had some of Meli's face powder now on her own cheeks. A realisation that thrilled her. 'Oh my God, I'll never wash again!' she cried.

'Well then I suggest you shack up with him then,' deadpanned Baran, obviously a little bored, pointing at Fritz. 'You can both save on buying soap.'

Ignoring Baran, or more than likely not hearing him over her sobbing, the fan bawled again to Meli, 'I'm sorry I've ruined your make-up. You. Are. So. Beautiful.'

Meli attempted a smile but was inwardly seething. 'No worries, my dear, it's only teardrops. Only teardrops…'

The fan ran along to the next star in the line-up, leaving Meli to fume inside. She placed her hand to her still-damp cheek and turned to Baran. 'Will you find me a freaking mirror as soon as possible please.' It was greeted by a shrug of disinterest. Meli raged silently, aware of her surroundings and the press gathered. The sooner she managed to get herself on *Housewives of Wherever* the better, as far as she was concerned. They didn't have to deal with this kind of crazy.

Donnie DonRon was as perky fresh as ever and bouncing merrily up and down on his spot on the meet 'n' greet carpet. Fans were the most important thing of all. Without fans, there were no sales, without sales there would be no buying things like Xboxes, and without Xboxes there would be no fun. So fans were all important. Wally always said that. Treat the fans nicely. Which was another reason why he'd carried on in the contest without his brother. The fans loved DonRon and would be upset if they didn't perform. Plus, they were getting Ronnie's hologram on stage so it wasn't that different from the real thing was it? Apart from switching him off at the end of the song, it was pretty much identical to the old living version.

Today at the *Euro* village, the fans were getting Ronnie as a cardboard cutout so that all selfies would still feature his brother. And next to line themselves up with the Irish teenster was the fan with the pink wig. He greeted Donnie with his normal high-pitched shriek. Not to be outdone, Donnie did one back and bounced up and down on the spot. The fan volleyed another shriek back. This game continued for about eight shrieks.

'Stanning you and your song, sis, sick-en-ing! I am feeling the fantasy right now,' said the fan.

'To be sure,' replied Donnie, assuming that was a compliment. 'I like your hair, it's very pretty…'

'No T, no shade, no pink lemonade…'

'Lemonade to match your hair, right?' smiled Donnie.

'My hair is fierce, girl. Now. Now that's you're on your own you gotta step your pussy up for Saturday and turn the party, girl. Mamma wants to see some glory.'

'Er, thanks, yeah I'll… er… step mine up and try to win. I think we're better than some of the other songs.' Donnie gave a cheeky point at the other contestants in the line-up.

'Oh the shade, the shade of it all!' piped the fan. 'I hear you, Donnie, but I got to say that Meli slays, well her face is beat for the Gods, she is dusted, but if the library is open then both him and him look busted.' He wiggled his perfectly manicured nail in the direction of both Baran and Fritz from Die Bolzen.

'Okay...' Donnie wasn't really sure what to say but he was loving the fan's enthusiasm. 'Would you like a selfie with me and... er... Ronnie?'

He obviously did and sashayed his way into position between Donnie and the cutout. He took the photo and then switched his phone to video. 'Come on, girl, tongue pop with me.' He clicked his tongue expertly into the lens.

'Sorry, you what?' queried Donnie.

'Tongue pop.' He did it twice again to show what he meant.

Donnie tried but the end sound was more of a quack than a pop.

'And now a death drop...' The fan fell to the floor with his signature move.

'A what? A death drop? I'm not sure about that.' But Donnie could hear manager Wally Leash in his head as he spoke. Never disappoint a fan. Always try to keep them happy. They make you rich and famous.

So he attempted a death drop as the fan filmed him. It was a clip that would go viral within two hours. Donnie bounced up and down and then tried to fall to the floor with the flare he had seen the fan deliver. Instead, he merely crumpled into a messy heap, legs and arms in no semblance of coordination.

Even the fawning fan couldn't praise it. 'That is not letting them have it. You cannot clock that lack of fierce, girl. Let's be honest, out of the two of you, it's clear that dear departed Ronnie did the best death drop. Right off the side of that boat. Bye Felicia.' And with that the fan was gone.

Donnie stood back up, smothered in bemusement, and aching a little from his inadequate attempt at the death drop. Fans were a little weird. Wonderful. And necessary. But sometimes a lot weird. He bounced around again, jiggling off his pain and smiled as the next fan approached.

It was early afternoon by the time the meet 'n' greet ended. As the contestants contemplated the rehearsals coming up later that day and headed back to their hotels, different things crossed their minds. Bjorn, in Bella mode, was still thinking about Szymon and last night's pivotal conversation. Fritz was contemplating a fan bunk-up back at the hotel with one of the women he had snogged and taken a number from. Baran was still dreaming about a potential life without Meli and life with the twink from last night. Meli was contemplating which of her many lotions and potions to use on her long flowing hair to banish the pong of the German rocker. Wiktoria was still fretting and freaking out over the fact that nobody had died for a while. Jemma was considering where she could buy Fisherman's Friends. And Donnie was wondering who on earth Felicia was.

Chapter 32

"...ladies and gentlemen, your exits are here,
here and here..."

The aeroplane slowed gently to a halt at the one and
only runway at Ermpit's Lysassia Airport, Terminal 3.

The passenger, who had slept for most of the
journey, stretched her arms outwards and clicked her
body into place. Flying was fun but it played havoc
on your body, sitting in one place for so long. At least
this flight had only been, what, five hours. Not too
bad really.

The melodic ting noise telling her that she could
move from her seat sounded overhead. She looked out
of the window and onto the runway and then at the
sky above. It was blue and cloudless. Perfect weather.
She stood up and then opened the locker above her
head taking out her coat, not that she'd be needing
that by the look of it, and her handbag. She'd have to
collect the rest of her luggage at the carousel in the
airport. Not that she'd packed particularly heavily.
Just a couple of outfits for tomorrow. Who knows?
She might end up on the TV so it was always good to
have choices. Plus one for tonight. Something fabulous
to make her shine. It had been a last-minute decision

to come but she was so glad she had plumped to in the end. She'd have definitely felt she was missing out on something special and new had she stayed at home. She would have been busy though no doubt.

'Excuse me, it is you, isn't it? Could I possibly have a selfie please? I thought it was you when we boarded but I was too shy to ask and then you went to sleep and I didn't want to wake you up. But I'm a big fan. I follow you on Instagram and everything. Would you mind?'

The voice came from the seat behind her. Of course she didn't mind. She never did. It came with the territory, these days more so than ever. She posed for the selfie, not sure she'd look her best after five hours in the air but a fan was a fan and that was never taken for granted. The fan was still beaming as he headed off down the aisle of the plane towards the exit.

She opened her handbag and checked inside. Passport still in place. Good. She grabbed her compact from the bag and opened it, staring into the mirror to check her reflection. She looked good. Always nice to know after you've posed for a selfie. Especially as doubtless it would end up on some Insta wall or story within a matter of minutes.

She gave herself a light dusting of powder. More out of habit than necessity and snapped the compact shut before depositing it back into her bag. She draped her coat over her arm and made her way towards the exit.

The fresh early summer air felt good on her face as she stood at the top of the aeroplane stairs. It was certainly warmer here than back home. The heels of her boots clicked against the steps as she descended giving off a metallic sound. The tone only changed when she stepped onto the tarmac. She walked into the terminal and stood in line for passport control. Arriving at the front of the queue, she flashed her passport to the man behind the glass and smiled. He smiled back. A smile of recognition? Maybe. It happened.

Thankfully, her luggage was one of the first to arrive on the carousel. It meandered its way over to where she was standing and she lifted it happily onto the floor. It was always good to know that the luggage was here too. At least she wouldn't have to beg, steal and borrow an outfit for tonight.

Through customs, she stopped to buy a coffee at a shop in the main area of the small airport. She couldn't help but think that they must have seen a real increase in business this week. The entire country probably had. She'd not been there before. Even though she wasn't going to be there for long, she hoped she'd have a chance to look around and see something. She'd visited many countries and it was always good to try and soak up at least some of the local culture.

Now, where was her cab picking her up? Out by the taxi rank at the front of the airport, she'd been told. She was blowing her coffee to cool it down as the warm comfort of the air embraced her face. She took in the blue sky again. Cloudless. It was her favourite time of the year. It had been for the longest time. For as long as she could remember. It made her love life. It was what she was famed for.

Her driver had a sign with her name on it and was easy to spot. They both smiled upon noticing each other. He opened the car door and she sank into the comfort of the back seat as he placed her luggage in the boot.

He then sat himself in the driver's seat and looked at her in the rear-view mirror. 'Welcome to Rottimoldovia, Miss Sandra Kim. It's wonderful to have a song contest legend in town.'

'Thank you,' she smiled. Her first *Eurowide* appearance was happening.

Chapter 33

"…let the love light carry, let the
love light carry…"

Bjorn Bjork strutted off stage at the Johnny Logan
Coliseum after his dress rehearsal performance with a
smile painted from ear to ear. Unlike everyone else in
the Swedish camp, he was ecstatic that the Swedish song
had been drawn to perform last on the night and even
though the joyous salsa fun of "24 Hours of Sunshine"
was a happy enough way to end the show he had a
sneaking suspicious that after the 25 songs before him,
the viewing audience at home and the juries themselves
might just be a teensy bit bored by the time he and the
hamster wheel were rolled out to play and, as a result,
his chances of winning could slip under the radar.
Sweden would not be happy but he would be. Because
he had already decided that after the contest, he was
hoping that Bjorn could quietly disappear into a big
black hole and vanish for good.

The reason for the decision. Szymon Rybak. The
host, who had done a sterling job on tonight's dress
rehearsal, even if he'd had to prop Weronika up for
most of it due to her misreading autocues, not hearing
counts and generally not quite understanding the
importance of getting everyone's names right. Basically

the basics. Although Bjorn had to admit that her disco medley was all kinds of fabulous. Sexily so. Who said baby oil and hot pants didn't mix? Not the *Eurowide* stage, that was for sure.

But enough about Weronika. Bjorn, or, indeed, Bella's head, was full of Szymon. They had been smiling at each other all evening. And not just that placatory kind of smile that says, *yeah I enjoyed last night but woke up feeling kind of meh about it.* This was a smile that penetrated right to the soul. A joyous shaft of light that literally knocked you off your feet and made you already be counting the minutes until they could be reconnected again. And Bella never felt like that after meeting a client. Normally any emotional connection, should there be any, would be gone faster than the stains on her work toys as she sterilised them immediately after the rendezvous. But not with Szymon. Their meeting of both bodies and minds was a strong one. And Bella was sure that he felt it as much as she did.

So when Bjorn was placed to perform in 26th position, the Swedish singer had been more than elated. If the song won on Saturday or did incredibly well, then Bjorn would be performing at every Eurofest from Sarajevo to Seville for the rest of his days. And both of the singer's breasts had decided that that couldn't possibly happen. As had his brain. The lesser chance that Sweden had of romping home to victory in 24 hours' time the better as far as Bjorn, Bella and her boobs were concerned.

Szymon and Weronika passed Bjorn as he strutted off stage. Weronika didn't give the singer a second glance – why would you when nobody was watching – but

Szymon still made time to look up into the Swede's eyes. At six-foot-three he had no choice. Bjorn towered above him, especially in his platform heels. As their eyes met, the spark between them fired off again – fuego hot – it was undeniable. This was a song that had only just played its opening notes.

The Swede was still smiling from ear to ear when an unwrapped Bjorn, now a very contented Bella, climbed into bed an hour or so later back at the hotel. She had just been texting Szymon and it indeed seemed that he too felt the connection between them. Bella placed her hands on her breasts and squeezed them slightly. They were, as ever, overjoyed to be freed from their bindings. Bjorn Free? The thought made Bella laugh.

'Fear not, boys, hopefully this won't be for much longer.' She hoped not. It looked like love was shining a light on her from the most unexpected of sources. And Bella loved that idea.

Jemma, Char, Lucie and Daniel were sitting together in the UK press area at the Coliseum, debriefing after the dress rehearsal. The UK song had been picked to perform in the second half of the final and judging from the reaction at the dress rehearsal tonight, the crowd had loved it. And that was with Jemma feeling that she was performing it at about 70% of her capabilities. Daniel had been worried after he had discovered that she was feeling a little hoarse after the hotel room concert the night before – the smell of Fisherman's Friends on her breath all afternoon had caused him to ask what was going on – and he was panicked she had peaked too early. Jemma was under strict orders to do everything she could to make sure she impressed the juries but still make sure she saved her voice for tomorrow. But the "horny" video wall had gone down a treat and the crowd had loved the song. Maybe the UK had a good chance of finishing in a decent position. Maybe.

'So what do we think of Sweden going last then?' asked Daniel. 'Their camp isn't happy about it but at least it means the props guys don't have to bring that hamster wheel on until the last moment. Not that Bjorn's dancers were able to use it tonight of course...' Daniel smirked, raised his eyebrows and looked over at Lucie's ever-reddening cheeks. 'Could they, Lucie?'

'Shut it, Daniel!' she wailed, only annoyed at herself. 'I didn't mean for it to get broken when we did the photo shoot, and I didn't mean to forget to tell the props guys to fix it before tonight. I'm just forgetful. It's not my fault I only remembered just before tonight's show. Well, I know it truly is. Totally. Silly me. I know. Daft Little Lucie. I think I might be approaching my "personal summer", I was talking to Meli from Turkey about it and she gets flushes, she said. And forgets things.'

'Did she forget to mention she is virtually twice your age, Lucie Rave?' sneered Jemma. 'You're no more having a "personal summer" than I am. You just forgot. At least you remembered before the final itself. They'll have it fixed by tomorrow. And Bjorn's dancers can spin around in it to their Swedish hearts' content.'

Char couldn't wait to chip in. 'They might not be Swedish. Look at delicious Ashley. He's dancing for Turkey and yet he's from Kettering. It's hardly, er... hardly... where's a city in Turkey?' she floundered.

'Istanbul?' offered Jemma. 'That's where Turkey's winner, Sertab, came from. Winning song, *Eurovision* 2003, "Everyway That I Can". Tune.'

'Well, if I have my way tonight Ashley can have me every way that *he* can,' added Char, air rolling her body in anticipation. Char had spent a lot of the day telling Jemma all about her latest object of lust. And showing her.

Jemma winked her approval at Char. Her thoughts returned to Daniel's question. 'There's nothing wrong with going near the end or even last. Lots of songs have been successful even though they're performed late on in the *Contest*. Riva from Yugoslavia with "Rock Me" back in *Eurovision* 1989 won the whole thing and they went on last so it can be done. As did Corinne Hermes with "Si La Vie Est Cadeau" for Luxembourg back in 1983. Depends on the song. Mind you, there weren't about three million extra countries back then, were there? It might be a little easier for juries to get bored stiff these days by the time the final song comes on. But Bjorn's song is great and I think he'll do well. It could be Stockholm or Malmo next year, you never know.'

'It could be Whittlesey if you sing your little heart out tomorrow night, Jem,' joked Char. 'We could have next year in the front bar at The Pig And Pickle. I'll do *Eurowide* bar snacks – you know, stick a German flag in some sauerkraut and an Italian one in the pizza. It might be a bit of a squeeze but we could do it.'

'French fries. Paella. Swiss cheese cubes!' squawked Lucie, loving the idea.

Daniel did too. 'That I'd love to see. It can't be any more bizarre than this year's contest, could it? At least people wouldn't be dropping down dead left right and centre.'

'Not so sure about that, Danny Boy,' said Jemma. 'There was a fight last time we had a *Eurovish* night there. D'you remember Jemma. It was Shaun the Brawn again. When he found out that Lacey, the girl with the lazy eye from the 99p shop that he'd been banging, was two-timing him with his best mate, Coke Can Colin. Served him right really after what he did to you. They might not have killed each other but they certainly had a right good old go at each other. There was definitely teeth found on the dance floor when we tidied up later.'

Daniel was aghast. This did not happen amid the rainbow-coloured joy of The Man Factory back home. 'So you girls held a *Eurovision* night in your local pub? That's pretty cool. And I have to ask, why was Coke Can Colin called that?'

Jemma held up her two hands in the air as if she was holding a rolling pin in them. 'You'd have loved him Daniel, but he preferred lazy eyes to lazy arse. Sorry, love. But yeah, we held a *Eurovision* night in The Pig And Pickle. We all watched the final in the pub and then the karaoke came out. Me and Char had a fabulous time, didn't we? D'you remember...?'

'I see forever in your smile, this woman is a child again, when I look in your eyes...'

As usual, Jemma's voice bought the house down at The Pig And Pickle. Well, those who had stayed around long enough to see her take to the karaoke machine to perform her rather rousing rendition of Ireland's 1993 *Eurovision* winning song. Most of the punters had either gone on to FagButts where it was BOGOF night on pints – two pints for the price of one – (no contest really for 75% of those gathered earlier, hence why they left as soon as the nightclub's doors opened) or home to their beds. *Eurovision* night at the pub was only popular really because of the free food the girls made and brought in. A themed dish for every nation, and that meant a lot of food. Pizzas and French fries disappeared before the opening song whereas some of the more unusual delights the girls had attempted to showcase from various other nations had been hardly touched.

'Nobody's touched your pastizzi have they?' commented Char as she pushed a plate of rather unappetizing greasy-looking pastries under her friend's nose as she rejoined her at the pub bar. 'Well, someone's tried half of one,' she remarked, spotting some teeth marks, 'but obviously thought better of it. I guess Maltese street food stuffed with pea paste is not everybody's cup of tea, eh?'

Jemma picked up the plate to smell them. 'Can't say I blame them. If they taste as good as they smell then they taste like dog poop. Mind you, I'm surprised Shaun the Brawn hasn't eaten them. He'll have anything in his gob, won't he?' She pointed across the karaoke dance floor to where muscly Shaun was currently chewing the face off Lacey, the skinny girl from the 99p shop with his hand down the side of her skirt. 'Poor cow. How could he give you up for her? There's nothing to her, she's like a streaky piece of bacon. He obviously likes his woman calorie-free.'

'And moral-free too by the looks of it,' said Char as he watched Shaun's hand move round to the front of the skirt, their lips still locked tightly together. 'Another Malibu and lime?'

'Don't mind if I do. If this party is to get anywhere near swinging then we're gonna need all the drinks we can get our hands on. No ice in mine, ta.'

To be fair, the *Eurovision* night was never a massive puller for the locals. Not once the contest had gone off the telly and the (desired) free food had been eaten. Only a handful of people tended to stay for the girls' late-evening karaoke afterwards. A few of the local oldies loved it. Char's grandparents, Edie and Dave, were always there, just so that they could have a pop at Pearl Carr and Teddy Johnson's 1959 entry "Sing Little Birdie". Providing that she'd not had one schooner of sherry too many, Edie always gave her all and gave good Pearl. One schooner too many and she'd usually stagger across the karaoke floor falling into the nearest speaker earning bruises for herself and £250 for someone on *You've Been Framed* if they caught it on their phone. Edie's bestie, Mavis, would always tag along for the night too and would happily sing her own special and unique version of Clodagh Rodgers' "Jack in the Box". Special in the fact that one too many sherries for Mavis would result in a change of lyrics and Mave, as she was known to one and all, writhing around suggestively on younger male villagers' laps, wailing tunelessly that she'd like to *"be your Jack in the box, take off your pants and your socks, and bounce up and down on your thing"*. This would normally continue until Mave's false teeth fell out and landed on the beer-stained carpet.

Shaun the Brawn would stay for a while, as would his mates, Nipples Norman (he had four apparently) and Coke Can Colin. All three stayed on in the hope of a leg over in the car park after kicking out. It was Colin who was now doing his best rendition of ABBA's "Waterloo" on the karaoke. Best being terribly bad.

'He's literally murdering that,' steamed Jemma, throwing visual daggers in his direction. 'No one sings ABBA like ABBA. You just don't do it.'

'What about STEPS. They did "Dancing Queen",' said Char.

'Given,' concurred Jemma with a nod.

'And "Lay All your Love on Me".'

'Another winner.'

'And "Story of a Heart" was written by one of ABBA, wasn't it?'

Jemma caved. 'Okay, okay, STEPS are the one exception who prove the rule. Other than them, no one should touch ABBA. Ever.'

'Cher... entire *Dancing Queen* album. Saved *Mamma Mia 2*. You said it yourself.' Char knew she had the upper hand and was proving Jemma wrong.

Jemma did too. 'Yeah, all right then. Cher smashed it too. But there is no one else. End of.' Jemma's words were dripping with stroppiness.

'Bit touchy aren't we, Jem? Who pissed on your Corn Flakes this morning? Another Malibu, love?'

'Please.' She passed Char her glass. 'Sorry. It's just you understand more than anybody how much I love *Eurovision*. Because you do too. I don't just want to sing *Eurovision*, I want to win *Eurovision*. It's my fantasy. What about my dreams? It's such a joyous thing and here we are trying to convince a bunch of boy racers and some pensioners that it's the best thing ever. We've loved it for as long as I can remember, and I want to experience something more than this.' She gazed around the bar. 'I want both of us to. I'm sure you do too.'

'I'll drink to that,' said Char, pouring a heftier measure than before of Malibu into the glass. With a smaller splash of lime. 'And listening to Coke Can Colin killing every note doesn't help. And besides, there is more to *Eurovision* for you than this. I feel it. You have...' She paused before continuing. '*That special something*. That certain *je ne sais quoi*... you know where I'm going with this, don't you?'

Jemma did. 'Hera Bjork, Iceland 2010, "Je Ne Sais Quoi". Total and utter Euro banger. Bring it, Char, bring it.'

As soon as Coke Can Colin had brutally strangled the life out of Agnetha and Frida's last note, the girls hit the karaoke machine and put on the tune. Within seconds, the entire bar was tapping their toes and swinging along to the pair of them in action. Even Mave bounced up and down for the right reasons this time.

The joyous revelry only came to an abrupt halt halfway through the final verse when an extremely pissed off Shaun the Brawn piled in to stop Coke Can Colin snogging the face off an ever increasingly racy Lacey up against the fruit machine. They indeed stopped. They had no choice when both a drunken punch and an uneaten plate of pastizzi came flying in their direction.

Char looked across at Jemma as Lacey ran from the pub screaming. 'Yeah, soon, Jem, your dreams will happen soon, Jem. There definitely has to be so much more than this for you and I when it comes to *Eurovision*.'

'So this week's been pretty tame in comparison,' joked Daniel, as Jemma and Char stopped reminiscing. 'But how amazing would it be for you to actually make your dreams come true and win tomorrow. Stranger things have happened. They have this week, to be fair.'

Jemma thought it over. 'Well if I do, Danny boy, I'll be buying so much Malibu and lime you'll be able to take a bath in it. Roll on tomorrow night.'

Chapter 34

"...you are the one, you're my number one..."

Jemma felt a burst of sudsy bubbles of excitement explode inside her belly as she scrolled down the latest *Eurowide* news on her phone back in her hotel room.

'You are kidding me...' Jemma's words were accompanied by a spray of white wine spritzer shooting from her mouth as she spoke. It landed with a pitiful shower on her cleavage. Even though Daniel had demanded that she and Char have an early night to rest their voices before the big day tomorrow, both of them had decided that a quick nightcap in Jemma's hotel room was still a good idea. Vital in fact. There was still loads to discuss about tonight's jury show dress rehearsal and, more importantly, Jemma's critiquing of the back catalogue of flesh-flashing photos sent to her best friend from Ashley, Baran and Meli's backing dancer and Char's potential new squeeze. They'd have done it in FagButts, so they would certainly be doing it here.

But Jemma's scrolling through the latest news while Char sexted Ashley, might be changing everything.

'Whassup?' asked Char, looking up from her phone as she lay on the bed.

'You'll never guess who's doing a club appearance tonight down by the Euro village. It's just been announced.'

'Not Queen Celine of Dion?'

'No.' Jemma's eyes widened, and she smiled, prompting another guess.

'Dana International? Conchita? KEiiNO? Cliff Richard? Duncan Laurence?' Char fired the names in rapid succession, pulling out the first names she could be bothered to think of. Her thoughts were purely on the latest explicit offering Ashley had just sent her. His keenness to hook up with Char as soon as possible was growing quite considerably.

'No to all of those. Cliff Richard? Really? No, it's only the ultimate legend. The star that is... Sandra "J'Aime La Vie" Kim. She's flown in for a show tonight.'

'Oh my God, really... you've got to go, right? Despite what Daniel will say.'

Jemma downed what was left of her white wine spritzer and checked the time. It was just after 11pm. 'Daniel's an old fart. Age blunts any kind of joy for life, doesn't it? And besides, we don't tell him.'

'An old fart? He's how many months older than you and I?' Char's phone pinged again as she spoke. It was another offering from Ashley.

'He'll be with Igor anyway. Plus we have to go, this is one night only.' Jemma leapt up and starting singing the chorus of "One Night Only" from *Dreamgirls* as she checked her face in the mirror. 'C'mon, Char, let's get a face on and get out of here. She's not on until 1am so we can get ready and head out for a few cheeky liveners before she takes to the stage. I'll try and blag us backstage. I'd phone Daniel to organise it but, as I said, he'll be all Dolly Downbeat and ultra-sensible about it and say we're to stay here. And it's one night only...'

She started singing again and made for the bedroom to choose the perfect Sandra-stanning outfit.

Char didn't move from the bed, a fact not unnoticed by Jemma.

'Oi, Grills, shift your ass. This is a matter of life or death, lady. I have to meet Sandra. Or maybe that should be *vie* or death.'

Char gave a cheeky frown. 'Sorry, hun, but to quote another *Dreamgirls* classic, "And I'm Telling You I'm Not Going".' Char didn't sing it. Neither did an obviously vexed Jemma.

'You're not coming? This is Sandra Kim we're talking about here. Have you taken leave of your senses, girl?' The thin line between Jemma's jollity and disbelief was blurring.

'I do have a very good reason,' offered Char. 'A very big and satisfactory one, to be honest.' She turned her phone around to flash it at Jemma. The screen was full with Ashley's latest temptation for them to hook-up.

'Bloody hell, Char. He's been packing a punch under that coin belt, hasn't he?' She rushed over to join Char on the bed and grabbed the phone.

'He wants me to go to his room. I'm not going to be able to see him tomorrow night, am I? Small matter of you trying to win the final and all that. And I'm not sure when he's back in Kettering, if at all, in the near future, so tonight might be my only opportunity to give my votes on...' She pointed at the phone. 'That.'

'"One Night Only" for you as well then, eh?' grinned Jemma. She could fully appreciate Char's desire to sample the dish on offer. Especially when it was such a large portion. 'It's ginormous, Char. Has he sent you more?' Jemma already knew he had and started scrolling through Char's phone. The gallery of girthy offerings on show proved that the first photo she looked at was not just a fluke or a lucky angle. Ashley was definitely a whopper of a catch.

'And he seems like a really sweet guy too, Jem. In every department. That is definitely one of the biggest I've seen though. Even Coke Can Colin would have a job comparing to that. It's definitely top five.' Laughter burst from them both.

'One of the Big Five, eh? Seems kinda apt given where we are. Europe will be united tonight.' The laughter became dirtier.

'Er... hardly, he's from Kettering, remember...' sniggered Char. She paused her laughter. 'You don't mind me not coming to see Sandra though, do you? I'll come if you really want. Mates before dates and all that.'

'No, it's not a problem. I *completely* understand it,' winked Jemma, placing her hands in the air a good 12 inches apart. Maybe 15. As long as they conveyed a massive length then the job was done.

'Thanks, Jem. I'll report back with every inch of detail though of course.'

'I'll text Wiktoria and see if she wants to come. Hopefully if Igor is satisfying our horny little press officer right now, then she might be off the hook and free to come party for a few hours. I'll persuade her.'

Jemma typed out a message to Wiktoria on her phone and pressed send. It was only a matter of seconds before it beeped back at her. 'Sorted, Wiktoria's up for it as long as we don't mention anything to Igor. Not an issue.'

Char's phone pinged again too. She checked the screen. 'And we have a hotel room number. Result.

Thunder-thighs Are Go!' She slapped her legs panto-style and leapt off the bed. 'Right, I need an outfit too. Something that screams class and that falls to the floor in the jingling of a coin belt.'

'Oh my God, I've got just the thing you can borrow, Char. And you've got to try out my bottle of glittery cleavage powder. A quick dusting across your puppies and the men can't resist you. Mind you, given what Ashley's already sent you, I hardly think resistance is a word that'll be on the tip of his tongue tonight, will it?'

Char jiggled her boobs. 'No, but these bad boys might, so if you can make them sparkle like snow globes then bring it on. It's always good to advertise.'

It was less than half an hour later when the two women knocked on the door of Wiktoria's hotel room. Char was wearing one of Jemma's shift dresses, a deep tone of blood-orange, which clung to her every voluptuous curve like an ex who won't take no for an answer. The plunging neckline revealed a misting of silvery glitter across her chest, except for one sticky solid clump of silver on one boob where the nozzle of the spray had blocked itself momentarily before miraculously unclogging itself with gusto, spitting a splat of silver goo onto Char's flesh. By the time she'd tried to wipe it off with a wet wipe it had dried rock hard. Jemma vowed never to buy beauty products from the 99p shop again, even if Lacey with the lazy eye had been rather convincing with her sales pitch. Jemma knew she wasn't to be trusted.

Jemma had plumped for another of her classic mesh tops. This time in a shadowy hue of gunmetal. The black bra underneath housed both her ample bosom and her prized signed photo of Sandra Kim as ever. She'd need to be whipping that out to show her heroine. The photo, not one of her boobs. Although frankly she'd consider anything for Sandra.

Wiktoria opened the door. A crisscross halter sequined in aquatic shades of blue and green wrapped her tiny frame. The result was dynamic.

'Channelling a horny mermaid tonight then, Wikky?' nodded Jemma. 'You look as fit as f—' She stopped before adding a final word, fully aware of the F bomb she was about to drop.

'You are serving! Serving party girl Ariel Disney realness,' echoed Char, snapping her fingers with sass. 'You girls are going to have a brilliant night. I can feel it.'

Wiktoria smiled at the girls' compliments and gave a twirl in the doorway, revealing an added dose of sexiness as the dress was backless. Her smile was replaced by puzzlement. 'Are you not coming with us? I thought you were a fan of Sandra Kim's too.'

'Oh, I am, she's a massive legend, but I'm also a fan of a massive one of these.' Char looked at her phone and pressed on camera roll. Jemma stopped her before she could offer up a slice of graphic evidence to Wiktoria as to why she was not heading off to see the *Euro* winner in action.

'She's on a promise with one of Baran and Meli's backing dancers. His room's on the next floor up, so Char's on her way now.'

'I just thought I'd come say hi seeing as it's on my way,' added Char.

Wiktoria nodded her approval. 'So it's just you and me, Jemma?'

'Two's company,' said Jemma.

Wiktoria held up a piece of paper in her hands. 'Can we just make a quick detour to the Coliseum on the way there though. Igor must have just slipped this note under my door telling me that I've left something there earlier during the dress rehearsal and organisers have said that we have to pick it up. Not sure what it is. Igor didn't say. It's probably an earring or my purse or one of my coats or something. He's asked me to meet him there. I texted him to say midnight. Is that okay? It'll give us enough time to get to the club afterwards for Sandra, and I'll tell Igor not to say a word to Daniel. I've no idea what it could be. I'm always leaving my things everywhere. Mind you, Weronika's just as bad. She actually left me in a toy shop when we were about four. She went to look at a huge teddy bear and never came back. Told my mother she couldn't remember where she'd left me. I was so afraid.' She lost herself in recollection for a moment. 'So is it okay if we just go and collect whatever it is? We're meeting him on the main stage. Where we'll all perform tomorrow night in front of the world. I am so excited.'

Wiktoria's excited jiggling made her sequins fizz with extra sparkle.

'I'm surprised Igor's not putting on his own performance with Daniel right now to be honest,' sniggered Jemma. 'But as long as he doesn't grass to Daniel about where we're going then everything is hunky dory.'

'Hunky whaty?' asked a confused Wiktoria.

'It means everything is good,' smiled Jemma. She pointed at Wiktoria. 'Okay. Let's get going then.

Taxi to the Coliseum to meet Igor and then you and I have a date with Sandra.'

'And I have a date to make my eyes water,' grinned Char. 'Let's skedaddle.'

Wiktoria had no idea what that meant but grabbed her hotel room key, slipped it in her bag and shut the door behind her. The three women headed for the lift and pressed the buttons for both up and down. The up arrow flashed first as it arrived and the door opened. Char stepped in. 'See ya, ladies. I'm going up. You're going down. But given where I'm off to I'm sure you both understand the irony in that. Cos I'll be going down in just a matter of—' The lift door closed stemming her words mid-flow.

Jemma certainly understood the irony and smiled. Wiktoria certainly didn't.

A minute later, having deposited Char on the floor above for her rendezvous with Ashley, the lift door opened again.

'Right then, Wikky.' They stepped into the lift. 'Let's go meet Igor and then we party.'

On the other side of the hotel, a deliriously happy Igor was just spooning his massive tree-trunk arm around an exhausted Daniel as they dozed off to sleep, all energies spent having passed the last hour or so indulging in some rather spectacular duvet gymnastics. Igor's phone, turned to silent since they started their romping, sat on the bedside table. He should have charged it earlier but given Daniel's eagerness to sex up the evening and his own inability to say no to his handsome young stud, Igor had forgotten. A solitary one per cent of battery pitifully remained.

Igor drifted off to sleep, darkness enveloping him. He fell into a deep slumber, a happy Igor. It had been quite a week. Change of job. New lover. The loss of diva Latreena had definitely been his very own gain. As a smiling Igor's mind tumbled into a dream featuring a ghostly Latreena and a massive disco ball chasing him *Indiana Jones*-style into the naked embrace of a horny Daniel, the percentage on the phone went from one to zero and the screen slammed to black.

Chapter 35

"...in dreams we're untouchable,
forever invincible..."

Igor's wasn't the only *Euro*-filled dream that night. With less than 24 hours until a winner was crowned, a lot of hopefuls let their minds run riot as their inner thoughts bubbled with prospects of what might be.

Meli had opted for a solid eight hours sleep if possible and switched off her bedside table lamp just before midnight. She'd considered a clandestine booty call with one of her dancers. There was one called Ashley who had so far managed to resist her advances. How on earth, she couldn't fathom. He possessed eyes, didn't he? But one look in her harshly-lit bathroom mirror had pushed any notions of that aside tonight. Ashley and his deeply hidden desires would have to wait. The needs of her greyish and tired skin were much greater than the needs of her booty. And anyway, Ashley must be gay if he'd not fallen for her charms by now. His loss. So Meli had plumped for a night of pampering her skin to look beyond delectable for the millions who'd be watching tomorrow. Indulgence was key. Especially at her age. The last thing she wanted was to find herself in any kind of menopausal state come showtime. Personal summers should be just that. Personal. Not to be shared on the

Euro stage. You never saw Katrina telling her Waves that she couldn't shine a light again because she was having a hot flush with rivulets of sweat dripping down the back of her neck, did you?

So any kind of steaminess in the bedroom was not an option tonight for Meli, despite what the constant carnal beating of her lower portions was telling her. It was replaced with a much more relaxing steaminess of the facial kind. And a gelatinous elixir of grapeseed and almond oil slathered onto her T-zone. By the time Meli switched off the light her face had been smoothed, smothered, teased, and treated into a heavenly state and any slight laughter line or wrinkle that dared to show itself on the main stage tomorrow would be booked in for a blitzing pull and lift at Istanbul's finest plastic surgeon before she'd even touched down on the flight home.

Meli drifted into slumber with the smell of almond still circulating her nostrils. Her dream consisted of her singing the winning song, "La Goes Up La Goes Down" on her own, Baran strangely nowhere to be seen in her fantasy, as the four male dancers swirled around her, all of them mouthing words of lusty adulation to her as she sang. As the song finished, the crowd rose to their feet and began chanting her name. The front row consisted of every *Housewife of Beverly Hills* there had ever been throwing bouquets of roses at her and Meli's ultimate Goddess, Celine Dion, was so thrilled with Meli's performance that she placed two of her fingers to her lips and wolf-whistled piercingly, standing on her chair and holding up a banner with the words "I don't need to Think Twice, you're my Number One, Meli!" scribbled in crayon. Then, in the splintered way dreams do, her next image was of her and Celine sharing a table in a glitzy bar, *Eurowide* trophy nestled between them, discussing the finer details of men's bedroom habits. Celine seemed aghast but was hanging off her every word as Meli shared some of her most desirous dealings.

It wasn't so much just another dream; this was an idyllic vision of what Meli really wanted life to be like. She'd be more than sorry to wake up from this one. And to find out that she was still singing with Baran.

Baran had also decided that, for once, hook-ups were out of the question. So for a few hours, his favourite Twink-All app remained unfingered. His hours, post-dress rehearsal, had been put to good use strumming out potential new tunes on his guitar. And he'd also decided for good that he couldn't care less if he never sang with the annoying Meli again once *Eurowide* was done and dusted. He knew that whatever happened tomorrow night, he and Meli would go their separate ways. It was long overdue. What they both wanted. Both needed. Would anybody really cry themselves to sleep if their union was snapped in half? Did people stop loving Cher after Sonny, or Simon after Garfunkle? Or even Milli after Vanilli? No, they didn't. And Baran and Meli would be exactly the same. He'd just have to make sure that he employed the best lawyer possible. He trusted her as far as he could throw her butt-lifted ass-cheeks. Yet again he found himself wishing that life would be easier if she would just disappear but, as yet, that hadn't happened. So divorce it would have to be. And, doubtless, a vampiric Meli would try and bleed him dry in the courts.

When Baran plunged into sleep, his dream was of him and Meli in a court, their bickering presided over by Moldova's epic sax guy in one of those curly white judicial wigs, and a jury of 12 twinks who obviously had become bored of the officiality of the proceedings and decided to spice things up by removing their clothes. Within seconds, Baran's dream had become less divorce and much more debauched as he joined the twinks for some jurisdiction of his own. Epic sax guy played on. Talk about a *son-stroke project*. Meli just faded away.

It was about an hour before a highly aroused Baran woke up and had to rush to the bathroom fearing a rather sticky situation was imminent.

There was nothing sticky or in any way erotic about Donnie DonRon's *Euro* dream that night. But it definitely did contain all kinds of everything strange and most definitely had more than a flavour of all things Irish about it. Donnie found himself lifting the *Eurowide* trophy, his brother circling around him mid-air in a shamrock green angel's outfit complete with massive feathery wings and halo. A long line of Riverdancers gaily kicked their way around them, leaping into the air with a cheery cry. Wally Leash, dressed as a leprechaun, stood in front of them all, handing out Donnie and Ronnie plastic dolls to a long line of DonRon fans, taking their money gleefully and shoving it deeply into his already over-filled leprechaun pockets.

Donnie woke up with a start when Wally attempted to sixty-nine the two dolls and made them play-kiss each other. He uttered the words, 'Dirty fecker,' half-awake to himself before sloping back off into sleep and thankfully another completely different and doll-free dream.

There were dolls in Die Bolzen singer Fritz's victorious *Euro* dream that night as well. Of the blow-up variety. As he punched his trophy-holding fist into the air at the climatic note of "The Sweet Smell of Europe", a mass of groupies invaded the stage ready to shower their love upon the German foursome – it appeared that Gunter Hoop had not yet banged his final beat in Fritz's dream – but instead of the rather unique-looking fans that Fritz and his band members were normally used to sampling after a gig, these groupies were all blow up dolls. Like the frontline of some plastic inflatable army marching towards them, arms outstretched and mouths permanently open and ready for action. Fritz and the boys, not exactly famed for either their flawless taste or their ability to say when any groupie would be less than suitable for a ball-emptying bunk-up, were all soon indulged in a variety of awkward squeaky penetrative love games with the air-filled audience as *Euro* hosts Weronika and Szymon tried pointlessly to interview them about their win. Fritz enjoyed this dream, badly tongue-swirling a dozen or so blow-up dolls until dawn broke.

Char had revelled in the dreamiest of times with Ashley. His photos had not false-advertised. But after an hour or so of getting to know the dancer a *whole* lot better, both whole with a "w" and without, she said goodnight and made her way, walk-of-shame-style, back to her own hotel room. Her make-up was smudged, slashes of deep red lippie streaked across her face and mascara punching her eyes, her hair looking like she'd been through a bushtucker trial, and her glittering cleavage enhancer was beyond patchy as most of it now found itself on a satisfied Ashley's face. The lone dry, hard, silver blob still glued itself snail-like to her breast.

She was walking down her hotel corridor to her room when she bumped into a shuffling Igor. He was wearing a hotel towel wrapped around his waist and nothing else. He had his phone in his hand.

Char's attention couldn't help but direct itself immediately at his ninja-like body. His body, her first time seeing it in the bare flesh, put Ashley's to shame, even if she was almost certain that he probably wasn't packing what the exquisite XXL Ashley had swinging away beneath the hotel towel.

'Bloody hell, Igor, how many abs can one man have?'

A bleary-eyed Igor didn't reply and merely smiled, a little dazed and confused by Char's appearance. Char picked up on the fact.

'Oh, ignore this,' she exclaimed, pointing at the confusion of colours on her face. 'I've been... er... seeing a friend.' It was the politest way she could think of to actually say what she'd been up to. For a moment she found herself flying back in time to those Whittlesey moments when she'd have to justify to her parents why she was stumbling home so late and unkempt after a rather successful night out at FagButts. But unlike her parents, thankfully Igor didn't grill her for answers. 'So why are you wandering the corridors of *Euro*-land in nothing but a towel at this time of the night? Daniel not worn you out, then? You looking for another peach to play with?'

'I need to collect my phone charger from my room. I woke up and it had finished so I must charge it for the morning. Tomorrow will be a massive day for Wiktoria.'

'Oh...' Char had been hoping for a much meatier answer than that. 'Did you catch up with the girls? What was it that Wiktoria had left at the Coliseum? And you're not going to tell Daniel that they've gone off to see Sandra Kim, are you? He'll go radio rental ballistic.'

Igor's already befuddled features fogged over with even more bewilderment at Char's questions. 'I do not understand what you are saying. Did Wiktoria need me to collect something from the Coliseum?'

Char explained about Wiktoria telling her and Jemma about the note that Igor had slipped under her hotel room door requesting to meet her at the Coliseum. Igor's face screwed up even more than its normal natural screwiness as she spoke.

'She messaged you on your phone to say she'd meet you there,' offered Char.

'I didn't see it. But then I see nothing on my phone right now.' Igor held his phone up to prove the point.

'I'll phone Jemma now, see what it was.' Char dialled the number. There was no reply, instead the other end gave the "this phone is unavailable" message.

'Can you phone Wiktoria too? I know the number. I always learn my clients' numbers. It is the sign of a good bodyguard.' He fed Char the number and she dialled. Again, no response.

Char was about to comment that Igor having Latreena's number hadn't stopped viva la diva being squished by a massive mirror ball, but checked herself, given the sense of unease that was brewing ominously in the air. 'You didn't go to the Coliseum, then?' queried Char again, now more confused than ever.

'No, I have no need to.'

'But you shoved the note under Wiktoria's door telling her to go there.' The penny hadn't dropped with Char yet.

'But that's it. I didn't leave her a note. I didn't need to meet her at the Coliseum. I haven't put anything underneath her door. I would telephone her if I needed her.'

Now the penny dropped. With a hefty force of a sack full of loose change.

'Well, if you didn't put the note there, Igor, then who the fuckery did? And why aren't either of them answering their phones?'

Char's initial thought was that they'd probably be gyrating around in some sweaty nightclub to *Euro* bangers or fan-girling Sandra Kim. But given the rather gruesome events of the week so far and an on/off police presence, that notion was swiftly replaced with a much more panicked one thinking that both Wiktoria and her best friend in the world might be in all sorts of double trouble.

Chapter 36

"…got her lipstick on, here I come, da da dum…"

The security guard standing at the main entrance to the Johnny Logan Coliseum was not exactly overly friendly to either Jemma or Wiktoria when the two women exited their taxi and scampered their way over to where he was standing.

Even when they explained that they were there at the request of Wiktoria's bodyguard, Igor, a man that Jemma told him "was not to be messed with seeing as he's built like three Jason Stathams", the tall, thin, moustachioed jobsworth with a main of dark hair framing his features all the way down to his shoulders was still reticent to let them into the venue. His caginess even extended to doubting that they were even who they said they were. If they were "two of ze favourites in ze contest tomorrow", as they said they were, then what were they doing at the Coliseum at such a late hour? It was only when Wiktoria gave the official a rushed verse of "Love Safari" and Jemma jiggled her Mount Rushmore-sized breasts along to the beat, a fact he seemed to appreciate favourably considering her rather exposing mesh top, that he finally deigned to let them in for their pre-arranged engagement.

'Thank you, you're so sweet,' quavered Wiktoria as they finally escaped him and headed towards the main stage.

'Sweet?' questioned Jemma. 'Only if they made candy assholes. He was a right wanker, Wikky.' Jemma laughed at how the words sounded. 'Now, let's find Igor and then we can head to the club. I am not missing Sandra for anything.'

It felt totally alien to them both being in the Coliseum without either a huge gaggle of screaming *Euro* fans and hysterical bloggers trying to grab them for a selfie and a chat or masses of pass-wearing "Access All Areas" crew rushing by barking into walkie talkies and dealing with the latest crisis. Or, for this week, the latest death. The place had an eerie, empty quality and an inexplicable feeling of icy chill came over them both as they took in both the enormity and the vacuum of the space around them. Only the main stage was still fully lit, the rest of the Coliseum a tapestry of darkness, camouflaging its normal exuberant delirium.

'It scares me when it's like this,' whispered Wiktoria. 'It's so quiet and like something from a horror film. Two helpless women. It's like we're totally alone. It's kinda scary.'

'To be fair, Wikky, you're scared of your own shadow and have been ever since that gloomy prediction that we're all going to die in the Dicken Platz, but you've got nothing to worry about. I'm here and I'm anything but helpless.' She placed her hands on her hips, superhero-style, despite the fact that she too was feeling a little spooked out. 'And so is Igor, somewhere. Nobody would mess with the size of him. Where is the big friendly giant?'

The two of them climbed up the small staircase at one side of the main stage and walked to the centre. The hamster wheel was still placed there, a lone sentinel to the next day's songfest, in the middle of the stage. The two women stood underneath it and Jemma called out into the twilight of the Johnny Logan Coliseum.

'Igor, where are you, matey? We have a date with a legend to get to so can we crack on?'

Nobody answered, but a lone figure walked out onto the stage from the shadows. Dressed in black tracksuit bottoms, trainers and a hooded, rather oversized sweat top. It wasn't Igor, but it was a very familiar face. Both women smiled. It was Wiktoria who spoke first.

'Oh wow. What are you doing here at this time? Did you leave something here too?'

With a definite air of smug swagger, the hooded figure walked over to join them.

Daniel had just been in the midst of a disturbingly vivid and x-rated dream involving three Turkish backing dancers and a bucket of butterscotch Angel Delight when a cacophony of pummelling woke him from his own lurid thoughts. It was the violent sound of a somewhat urgent fist banging at his hotel bedroom door.

'What the hell just happened? Who the heck is that waking us up at this time of the night?' he asked, swivelling his somewhat confused body around to face Igor before finding that the space alongside him was glaringly vacant. Finding his bodyguard beau absent, he automatically assumed that his lover must have locked himself out of the room for some reason. It hadn't been that many days after all since he'd struggled to find the right door out of it. Swinging his legs off the edge of the bed he shuffled, still bleary-eyed and naked, to the door. He swung it open to face Igor. Except it wasn't. Instead, he was greeted by a highly expressive and red-faced Char. Daniel immediately became aware of his own nudity and went to push the door closed to stem any embarrassment. Before he could, Char pushed the door open with a bang and charged into the room. Despite the urgency of her situation, Char was unable to stop herself from scanning down the length of Daniel's naked body. She couldn't help but be impressed by what she took in.

'Bloody hell, Daniel, talk about *la det swinge…*'

Daniel clamped his hands across his groin immediately and ran back to the bed to cover himself with a sheet.

'Christ alive, Char, what are you doing here? And where the hell is Igor?' The second question wasn't especially aimed at the backing singer, so Daniel was more than surprised when she supplied the answer.

'He's gone to grab his mobile charger. His phone died and Wiktoria sent him a message about going to meet him because of the note he shoved under her hotel room door but he didn't even send the note in the first place and now her and Jemma have gone to the Coliseum to collect something that she left there even though she probably hasn't left anything there in the first place so it's just someone trying to get her there for whatever reason and given that loads of people have dropped dead this week I'm really worried about what has happened to the two of them and now neither of them are answering their phones.'

The words rattled from Char's lips, spraying like rogue fireworks across the room. Daniel was unable to take in most of them but heard enough to gather that something was seriously wrong.

'And then they were going to see Sandra Kim at some club, but Jem didn't want you to know that cos she knew you'd be pissed off as it's the night before the final,' added Char needlessly.

'What the...?' Daniel tried to place all of Char's ramblings in some semblance of order but they still teetered Jenga-like in his brain ready to collapse into nonsense at any moment. 'Run that by me again? Jemma and Wiktoria are where? And why?'

'There's no time. I'll tell you on the way. Igor wants to go to the Coliseum now to see if they're okay. He said he'd meet you in the hotel lobby as soon as possible. So put some clothes on, man. It's a matter of life or death... and I'm coming too. Jem's my best mate and if anything has happened to her then they'll have me to deal with.'

Char stood there motionless, her cheeks raged and flushed, as Daniel still sat on the bed. He raised his hands in a questioning manner at her lack of movement. 'Okay, well turn around and I can get my kit on.'

Char couldn't help herself. 'Flipping 'eck, it's impressive, Daniel, but I've seen bigger tonight, believe you me.' She turned around anyway as Daniel leapt from the bed and hurriedly dressed himself.

It was five minutes later when Daniel and Char reached the lobby. Char had tried to explain the evening's events to Daniel as clearly and as chronologically as she could as they descended in the lift. His face embossed deeper with worry as each detail became clearer.

A fluster-consumed Igor was already in reception. The pint-sized Lucie Rave stood alongside him.

'Oh, Daniel, this is terribly worrying,' she boomed as her friend approached them with Char. 'I was just sitting down here finishing off some copy for *Palaver!'s* website ready to get it online for first thing in the morning. Deadline deadline. *Eurowide* day. Hurrah! And then I saw Igor all stressy and worried and he's explained, and I must come with you. I hope Jemma and Wiktoria are okay. So many deaths this week. Gosh. You never know. Oh my word. What a worry.' Lucie's words were as emphatic and random as ever.

'I've asked for a taxi,' smiled Igor, moon-facing his pleasure at seeing Daniel with a twisted contortion of his lips. 'The woman at reception said it should be—' Igor didn't finish his sentence as he spied the woman he'd been speaking to behind the reception counter wave over at him and then point outside. 'It's here. Let's go.'

The four of them ran, the most awkward-looking of school sports teams, to the taxi rank situated outside the hotel. The taxi was pulling up. Igor had the door pulled open before it had even come to a total halt. He piled into the front seat as the other three squeezed into the back, Daniel sandwiched somewhat firmly between Lucie and Char.

Igor barked instructions for the driver to hotfoot it to the Coliseum as quickly as possible. He turned to face the others in the back seat as the car whizzed into action with a satisfyingly speedy screech of the tyres. 'I hope everything is good. Wiktoria might be in trouble. I can't have a second client die on me this week.'

'No, that's not going to be particularly good for your CV, is it? I probably wouldn't employ you,' remarked Char. Her words were flippant but still threaded with huge knots of worry about what might have happened to Wiktoria and her *Euro*-loving best friend.

Chapter 37

"…shady lady, I'm gonna strike like thunder…"

Wiktoria's thoughts had been a cocktail of happiness and bafflement when she had seen the figure walk onto the stage at the Coliseum. Why were they there? Unless they'd been called there too. It was the natural first question.

'So did you leave something here too? Apparently, I did. Igor has it. You've not seen him, have you?'

The figure remained silent and lifted their hands up to the hood of their sweat top before lowering it and shaking their shoulder length head of hair into place. It never fell perfectly like it did for every model out there doing those TV ads for shampoos, which the figure had always found annoying. But at least the reveal was good.

But then Weronika Seksi was never totally satisfied about anything in life. She never had been.

'Hello, sis…' There was a pause before Weronika looked across at Jemma too. 'Hello to you both.'

'Bit dressed down aren't you?' commented Jemma, taking in Weronika's shapeless outfit. 'You're definitely not off to see Sandra Kim with us then? Your sister's outfit is dazzlingly on point. Stun-to-the-ning! As is mine, to be fair.' Jemma gave a little wiggle of self-appreciation.

'Unless you've got something designer on underneath that massive hoodie.' It was a fair critique seeing as Jemma had never seen the *Euro* host in anything less than high fashion.

'Do you think I give a shit about what you think about my outfit?' snapped Weronika back at her. 'And just why are *you* here anyway? You're not supposed to be. Only she is.' She pointed at a confused Wiktoria.

It was her sister who answered. 'She's here with me as we're meeting Igor. Then we're going out.'

'But you're not.' Weronika seemed adamant. 'You're not going anywhere.'

Jemma didn't care for the stroppy sass she was witnessing. 'What? Not going out? I think you'll find that nothing is stopping me from seeing the legendary Sandra Kim, thank you very much. Especially not you, you streaky vile stick insect of rudeness. What are you going to do to stop us?'

'Shut up will you? You're not even part of the plan until now. And yes I will stop you. Or at least this will.' Weronika reached into a large pocket on the front of the hooded sweat top and pulled out a small gun.

She pointed it straight at Jemma, whose immediate reaction was to scream loudly, the sound seemingly bouncing off the walls of the cavernous arena as she did so. A feeling of terror immediately gripped her. She automatically placed her hands to her chest, directly over the spot where the photo of Sandra rested beneath her bra. She could feel the ever-increasing "haba haba" of her heart beating fretfully under the photo. Weronika had a gun. And stroppy sass. And a short temper. And that wasn't a winning combination in Jemma's eyes. She thought it best to remain silent – perhaps less antagonistic given the situation – but couldn't help herself.

'Er, what plan?' She was going to add "you psycho" but bit her tongue.

A visibly-shaking Wiktoria had to ask too. 'Yes, what plan? And where is Igor? And why have you got a gun?' Maybe she should have put that question first.

'Igor's not here, you idiot. He was never going to be, was he?'

'But the note under the door.' Wiktoria wasn't quite grasping the situation as yet.

'Which I put there, you fool. I was the one who wanted you here. I just didn't plan on *her* being here with you, though.' She sneered in Jemma's direction.

'Charmed, I'm sure. Oh I'd rather be anywhere else right now, believe you me, Weronika,' snapped Jemma before adding, 'no offence, Wikky.'

'None taken,' smiled Wiktoria at her friend. Despite fear bubbling away inside her, Wiktoria was still not really understanding what was going on as the three women stood in the shadow of the hamster wheel.

Weronika was keen to explain. 'Just one more tragic accident in the last few hours before the final. Or maybe it will have to be two now. After the sad demise of diva Latreena, little Ronnie DonRon, that poor innocent runner – that was unfortunate to be fair – and a drug-addicted German rocker, what is one more tragic accident where the host country's singing hopeful is found dead too?'

The severity of the situation finally seemed to be really sinking in for Wiktoria. 'Found dead? What me? But I'm singing tomorrow?'

'Not if everything works out as planned you won't be. It will be my moment to shine, finally. I'll be singing. I know every word to "Love Safari", every action, every dance move.'

Jemma felt her mouth fall open as she listened to Weronika's revelations. She knew that there had been a very valid reason she had never warmed to her. Something had always put her off. And she figured that massive murderous tendencies was valid reason enough.

'Oh I'll be mourning you, of course, dear sister, but for once I'd finally be free of your shadow. No longer feeling like the number two sister. I'd be a hero. Stepping into your dear departed shoes to sing for Rottimoldovia and host the contest at the same time. A double threat. I'd be invincible. A national treasure. A *Eurowide* Goddess. And more importantly, the number one.'

Jemma wasn't sure that *Euro* rules would actually allow that in the first place but again bit her tongue. She reckoned it wise not to attempt to piddle on the chips of a complete and utter lunatic when she was in full maniacal flow.

'You actually want to kill me? Why, what have I done?' Wiktoria's bottom lip was wobbling as she spoke, tears pricking her eyes. 'I'm just your sister.'

Weronika's voice was becoming more demonic as she spoke. 'But that's just it, you're never just *my* sister. It's me that's always just *yours*. It's always been that way. Back home you were always favoured. I had the spotlight for ten minutes before you were born and then that was it, the moment you came along, I was second best.'

'That's not true. Mum has always loved us both.'

'Well then how come she never made me feel like a star. You've always been the preferred one. You had the best toys, you had the best smile, you had the best hair. It even grew back better after I deliberately ruined it with chewing gum.'

'Oh my God, you actually did that on purpose, you weren't just Scary Spice, you were Totally-Off-Your-Trolley Spice.' Jemma had to interject. She stopped herself from going further when a scary Weronika continued to waggle the gun in her direction.

'You did that deliberately?' echoed Wiktoria.

'Sure, I wanted your hair gone. I was better than you at dancing yet you always received the most praise from Mum. It was like I didn't exist. I was better than you at singing yet you're the one who was discovered outside the supermarket with Mum and then ended up on television and became loved by the entire nation. Ever since that moment the world has only ever seen me as your sister. The other one. The one with the not so good hair.'

'But you won a national TV show last year. You are a star. You won *Rottimoldovia's Got Talent*. The public voted for you.' Wiktoria was struggling to understand her sister's bitter jealousy of her. Although she did know that she did indeed have better hair. Maybe now wasn't the best time to mention to her sister that she'd just been offered a nationwide campaign for Pantene.

'Yes I won it and deservedly so. But every interview always called me your sister, talked about your success, talked about me following in your footsteps. Like some stupid puppy dog following its master, unable to think for itself. I don't want to follow in your footsteps,

I want to be creating my own. And doing this show was finally going to be my chance. I should be the one singing "Love Safari", not you. But no, you were picked to sing, and not me. Yet again I feel like second best. That you are taking the spotlight away from me.'

'But you're hosting the entire thing. That's incredible. I'm so proud of you. You're going to be incredible. I was telling Jemma how good you will be. Wasn't I, Jemma?'

Jemma just nodded unable to take her eyes away from the gun still wobbling in her direction.

'Who remembers the hosts? Hardly anybody. A few exceptions maybe but most of the time they're just pretty faceless people in a pretty-looking dress or wannabe male models in tight-fitting tuxedos. To be remembered you've got to be the one singing. That's what I wanted.'

'But you're hosting because you won the TV show. You. All on your own. Not me.'

'I bagged this because of Szymon being picked to be the other host. He felt sorry for me because deep down I know that he didn't even want me to win the talent show. That hot-looking girl with the dog that balanced on beach balls was his choice. He thinks I don't know but I do. I know everything. Plus he told me at our first show meeting that, and I quote, "you being my sister was brilliant press". Not me winning a national TV show, not my own incredible talent at singing, but you being my incredibly talented much loved sister. D'you think that I don't know that I'm not the best host in the world. I know I'm not. I'm pretty crap but that's what people will expect from the less talented sister, won't they? Even here on one of the biggest stages in the world I'm in your shadow. But not for much longer. Not after tomorrow. Christ I really wish I had been able to lose you in that shop years ago. That would have made life a lot simpler. And less angry. And then none of this would even have to happen.'

Wiktoria could feel her emotions bubbling, on the cusp of tears, a childhood full of scary moments suddenly filling her head. 'Sing it. Sing the song. I'll say I'm ill, that I have stage fright, that I can't do it as I'm too scared. You know that I scare easily. I can make something up. You don't have to...' Wiktoria gulped, a large swallow sounding in her own throat at the thought of what she was about to say. 'Kill me.'

'Oh tell that to my therapist. She says the only way I can ever feel happy about who I am is to eliminate all thoughts of you from my mind. How am I supposed to do that when every website I look at, every podcast I listen to, every newspaper article I read, has your name written all over it. I only have to look at you now and my stomach contracts with all of these horrible feelings of envy and anger. It's classic sibling rivalry and I don't like it. You think I want that for forever? No I don't. So that's why I had to run with this week's plan. It's been amazing. And no one has had a clue that it had anything to do with me.'

Jemma's heart was beating faster than a 132 BPM Matt Pop hi-NRG disco remix as she considered her options. The fact that she was staring down the barrel of a gun was one thing, the fact that she was risking missing her icon Sandra Kim in the flesh was quite another. Something needed to be done. And fast. Why wasn't Char with her? She'd know what to do. She always did. She always had done.

For a brief moment, Jemma's thoughts filled with the joyous times that she and Char had spent together back in Whittlesey. Nearly all of them featuring their joint passion and adulation of *Eurovision*. They'd spent days in front of the telly dissecting old *Contests*, studying the finer nuances and moments from decades of different shows. They may not have always been considered the coolest, but they were always the poppiest. Pretending they were Cheryl and Jay from Bucks Fizz in the playground at school and ripping their PE skirts off or recreating the Sweet Dreams' "I'm Never Giving Up" stool slide in Jemma's mum's kitchen back at 42 Love City Grove. The nights when they'd bounce around Jemma's bedroom getting ready for yet another belly-laugh-filled night at FagButts, doing their make-up to the frenzied notes of Jedward's "Lipstick". Great song, bouncy dance routine, but not always easy when trying to apply a raven-coloured slick of lipliner or not wearing an appropriately supportive bra for the larger than average rack. Fun times. Brilliant times. Messy times. And if Jemma was to have more of them with her best mate Char, and she was determined that she would be, she would have to find a way out of her current perilous and more than potentially fatal situation.

Which is why she was desperately trying to grab the attention, without alerting the obviously two-bangers-short-of-a-mixed-grill Weronika, of the security guard who was walking towards the stage from out of the shroud of the Coliseum shadows. It was the awkward one with the moustache and long hair who had not been particularly pleasant about letting her and Wiktoria into the Coliseum moments earlier. Maybe given her current view, it might have been better had they not been allowed in and forced to head directly to see Sandra belting out "J'Aime La Vie". If only she and Wikky hadn't been so bloody persuasive. They'd made the wrong choice. What with imminent death from a crazed *Eurowide* host being a very high possibility right now.

Jemma knew that she had the guard's curious attention. She could see he was staring at her. He was aware that something was going on upon the stage and thankfully his jobsworth busybody nature was making him want to come and investigate. Jemma was keen that his arrival should not be spotted by Weronika though.

As Weronika continued to fill her sister in on a lifetime of sibling dislike, Jemma attempted to inform the approaching security guard to be as silent as possible. A shaping of her lips into a cursory shush was all she would dare try, given that she suspected Weronika's fermenting rage could go stratospheric any minute to a height that would suit Lena's "Satellite". He nodded back at Jemma, signalling his understanding, and gingerly made his way towards the stage.

Her momentary hope set in action, Jemma continued to listen to what the two sisters were saying. And keeping her focus on the wobbling figure of eight being made by the weapon still pointed at her. It appeared that Weronika might be shaking just as much as she and Wiktoria were. Mind you, nobody seemed to shake as much as Wiktoria did. Jemma wasn't sure it was humanly possible.

'So, all of the deaths this week were because of you?' Wiktoria couldn't believe she was asking the question to her very own sister.

'It was the only way. If yours was the only death then all the emphasis would be on you – yet again – and people would be looking a little too close to home for my liking as to why you'd died. This way you're just one of many, not so much the centre of attention. It just seems better. More practical. And beneficial. As I'll be remembered as both the host and the singer for the year when people at *Eurowide* were literally dying to win. The legacy of this first year will live on forever. It'll set me up for life.'

'Unless you get caught. Somebody might actually think about a murder investigation after five people actually die in less than a week. Six if you kill Jemma too.' Wiktoria pointed at her friend. 'No offence.'

It was now Jemma's turn to reply, 'None taken.'

'You underestimate me,' said Weronika. 'I've already thought about all that.'

As Weronika was speaking, the security guard had gently tip-toed his way around to the side of the stage and was working his way up the stairs as silently as possible. Weronika had her back to that side of the stage and was unable to see him. From his position it was clear that he could see Weronika had a gun.

Jemma was praying that the guard had a weapon of his own. She willed him to reach inside his pockets and pull out something that could do some damage – a truncheon, a taser gun, a Japanese ninja star, a bloody ancient blunderbuss or a schoolboy pea-shooter for all she cared, just something to stop wacky Weronika in her stride. She was bitterly disappointed that he hadn't done so by the time Weronika turned around and saw him on the corner of the stage.

'You don't think I was doing this on my own, do you? Every girl needs a willing partner in crime. And mine was more than willing when I allowed him to sample what's under here.' She stroked her body through the large shapeless outfit she was wearing. The most non-descript one she could find for the night. And the only one with a pocket big enough for a gun. Most of her dresses didn't even have pockets. For guns. Or for anything to be honest.

'And he's just arrived,' she added, winking at the security guard.

The guard reached up with his hand and pulled the moustache from his face with a harsh yank. He then took off his hat and removed the wig he was wearing. The one that virtually covered his face and hid most of his neck. It also covered both of his ears, and the large holes that they both contained.

Weronika walked over to him, keeping her gun pointed in Jemma's direction. Wiktoria continued to shake, unable to move from the spot she was on.

'Good evening, Zandor,' she cooed, and leant in to kiss him fully on the lips.

Jemma felt sick. With worry. With rage. With disappointment at herself for not recognising him at the Coliseum entrance. And with disbelief that anybody could actually bring themselves to pucker up for that rodent-like piece of trash.

Chapter 38

"…and I'm running scared 'cause I adore you…"

Luck was not on Team Igor's side. They had been sat in the same traffic jam for the last 20 minutes. And seeing as the traffic around them was nose-to-nipple the chances of them actually going anywhere soon were supermodel thin. A fact that was frustrating all five of the people sitting in the taxi that was heading (just not right at that moment) to the Coliseum.

'I'm sorry but I've never seen the traffic like this before. There must be something wrong,' bemoaned the driver of the vehicle who was already regretting the fact that he'd chosen a route that had taken him down this particular road. Why couldn't he have had a nice juicy airport run going in the opposite direction? At least there would be plenty of those after tomorrow night when the final was done and the *Eurowide* revellers of countless different nations packed up their feather boas, national flags and banging hangovers and headed back to whichever country they had come from.

'It was all right until we hit this street,' said Daniel, his body still squished from Lucie to his left and Char to his right on the back seat of the cab. He imagined this was how people felt when they were sat upon. Didn't some people pay top dollar for that? From his disad-vantage point in the back seat, he couldn't see any appeal whatsoever in playing human cushion.

'Is everybody out in Ermpit partying tonight?' asked Lucie, scratching her head. 'There ain't no party like a *Euro*-party! And everyone seems to be beeping their horns. Maybe for Jemma!' Lucie's attempt to lighten the funk in the air was not working.

'There have been massive dance parties every night this week, Sweet'N Low, and the traffic has never been like this,' commented Char, trying yet again to phone through to Jemma on her mobile. 'Something must have happened. Hopefully it might have stopped Jemma and Wiktoria getting to the Coliseum too. But then why aren't they answering their bloody phones? Any joy with you, Igor?'

The bodyguard looked like he was on the verge of tears in the front seat as he tried yet again to contact Wiktoria. 'No, nothing. Maybe they don't have their telephones.'

'Jemma never goes anywhere without her phone, Igor. She's in a million WhatsApp groups for one and also it's the best way to check your make-up before entering a club. Plus she'll definitely want to get a selfie with Sandra Kim at the club. There's no way she'd be without it. Don't you know anything about girls. Plus I saw her leave with it at the hotel so, duh...' Char was a little harsh, a fact she swiftly reconsidered when Igor turned round to smile at her and she could see he had puddles of tears pooling in his eyes. 'Sorry, I didn't mean to snap. I'm just worried about Jemma and Wiktoria.'

Daniel squeezed himself as far forward in the back seat as he possibly could given his space restrictions and then squeezed Igor on the shoulder to show his concern too. 'I'm sure the girls will be okay,' he said, but he wasn't overly convinced that they would be. Not when he considered everything that the week in Ermpit had thrown up. 'The reception at the Coliseum is probably awful in the evening probably and the Wi-Fi probably doesn't work.' He was aware of his abundance of probablys. He directed his next questioning at the driver. 'Could there have been an accident up ahead? Is that why we've come to a dead stop? It is a bit strange. There's not been traffic like this at any other time this week.'

'Nothing's been reported as yet at the taxi office. Sorry.' He didn't really seem that apologetic to Daniel, which vexed the PR greatly.

'Is it okay if I get out of the car and have a look?' asked Daniel, ready to get out no matter what reply was given. He wanted to see what was causing the bottleneck for himself and also, the thought of not being squidged into either Lucie's armpit or Char's silver glittery chest was massively enticing.

'Sure,' replied the driver.

Within 30 seconds, all four of them had quit the tight confines of the taxi to try and see what was happening further up the street. The road they were on was a long one, and all they could see for as far as their eyes could take in was a line of rear lights from a seemingly never-ending line of immobile cars snaking off into the distance.

'Igor, you're the tallest. Can you see anything up ahead? Blue lights or anything?' queried Daniel, his patience waning as his worry increased. 'Do police cars have blue lights over here? They do, don't they?'

'Not sure, maybe,' offered Lucie, rather uselessly.

'I can't see anything,' offered Igor. 'Why don't you sit on my shoulders, Daniel, maybe you can see something from higher up.'

'It won't be the first body part of his you've sat on this week, Daniel!' deadpanned Char, causing Lucie to snort with mirth. 'It's a good idea though. Igor's six-foot-plus and you're way taller than me and Sweet'N Low. So you'll be able to see much more.'

'Pot Noodles are taller than I am,' Lucie piped to herself seeing as no one else was loving her attempts at flavouring the mood with some light relief.

Daniel agreed with Char that it was a pretty good idea and, ignoring her first comment, wrapped his leg around Igor's head as Igor bent down in front of him. He secured himself into position on Igor's shoulders and held on with a scissor-like grip as the bodyguard stood upright again.

'Well, this has all gone a bit daddy/son hasn't it?' sneered Char, still fruitlessly speed-dialling Jemma on her phone.

Daniel had to admit she had a point. The last time he could recall going on somebody's shoulders was indeed his own father's years ago on a trip around Chessington World of Adventures.

'FYI, Char Grills, Igor isn't that much older than me,' hissed Daniel, his voice at a whisper. 'It's just that maybe Touché Eclat just isn't so readily available where he's from.'

Daniel attempted to look as far down the road as he could from his view 12 feet up in the air on Igor's shoulders. Despite loving the feeling of his lover's solid body between his legs he was disenchanted not to see any blue lights. Not even any flashing ones.

The taxi driver got out of the car, slammed his door behind him and joined his passengers on the pavement. 'I've just heard on the radio from the office that there's been a burst water main at the top of this road. Apparently water everywhere and the police have cordoned it off as a hazard so they're not letting anything through. They reckon it will be at least an hour to clear away. You'd be quicker walking to the Coliseum to be honest. It'll take you half an hour. Maybe 20 minutes if you jog.' He looked directly at Char and then at Lucie. 'Or maybe not?'

'What is it with men is this country? Why are so many them such pigs? Why don't you just undo your chauvinist self?' Char took a step towards the taxi driver, who was immediately regretting his comment. 'And let it be known I bet I can run way quicker than you can so unless you want to feel the force of my boot up your sorry excuse for a backside, I suggest you start running now, matey.'

As the taxi driver scuttled around to the other side of the car, climbed into the driver's seat and locked the door behind him, Char returned her attention to her phone, this time clicking on her Maps app. She typed in the street name for the Johnny Logan Coliseum and pressed the directions button – 28 minutes by foot. At least the cab driver had been right about that. She informed the others. 'Shall we go then?'

'Daniel Spirit, are you getting down or what?' asked Lucie. He was still perched on Igor's shoulders. 'Oh I say, Daniel "Spirit in the Sky", all the way up there. How funny.' She gave a makeshift joik and stomped across the pavement as she imagined a Nordic warrior would.

Finally the others laughed. Even Igor. He must have known the KEiiNO song too. Lucie felt pleased with herself and grinned from ear to ear.

'This way to Johnny Logan!' hollered Char as she pointed up the street and the group began to jog away from the taxi in the direction of the Coliseum.

Lucie wasn't grinning for long as she attempted to keep up with the others.

Char led the way, wishing she was wearing a more supportive bra. She was immediately reminded of good times back home dancing around to *Euro* hits in Jemma's bedroom getting ready for nights out at FagButts. Jedward's "Lipstick" was particularly painful in the wrong bra, she seemed to remember. She'd happily have bounced around to it topless in the middle of the Rottimoldovian streets right now if it guaranteed that her mate Jemma was not in any kind of danger. Hopefully, luck would be on their side this time and they'd find Jemma and Wiktoria safe and sound. She held onto her chest with one of her arms and kept running as fast as she could.

Chapter 39

"…we are the heroes of our time…"

Weronika was positively giving herself douze points for effort and ingenuity as she paced up and down the stage in front of Jemma, Wiktoria and a now much more recognisable Zandor. The hack was looking puppy dog pathetic (providing this particular puppy dog was the runt of any litter) having been kissed by the object of his dreams, Weronika Seksi.

'I might have guessed that he would have to be involved somewhere. I've never liked him from the moment he interviewed me in the press room. And that day at the Dicken Platz with me and Wikky you were a right arse too.'

'Ze feeling iz very much two vay,' scoffed Zandor. 'If I'd have had my vay, you'd have been dead about zree days ago. You're lucky you're still able to shift that blob you call a body around anywhere.'

Had it not been for the fact that Weronika was still waving her gun around like a televangelist in front of her, Jemma would have launched herself at full speed at the scrawny excuse of a man straight away. She made a mental note to herself that should she survive the next 20 minutes, she'd be sure to drum up some kind of revenge that would hit him where it hurts.

Her immediate thought was to hang something very large and heavy (maybe herself given his dislike of her fuller figure) from his ridiculous earlobes until the holes literally tore apart. Try hiding that with a cheap wig, mister.

Jemma was never one to remain silent though. She took a step towards Zandor. 'Screw you, needle dick!' She flicked a middle finger in his direction and wagged it at him.

'Ok, I think we need to sort this one out, don't you?' said Weronika, pointing the gun directly at Jemma once again. 'She's getting itchy feet.'

Jemma took a sharp intake of breath and was immediately wrapped in the feeling that she might be about to wee herself with fright on the *Eurowide* stage. For a millisecond, the thought diverted her mind away from the fact that wacky Weronika was holding a gun a metre away from her face. Had anyone ever weed themselves a song contest stage? She'd like to think not, but maybe it was one of those facts that you'd never find in a textbook. Despite her situation Jemma couldn't help but let her mind wander to whether a nervous Serbian dancer or an over-excited Spanish backing vocalist had ever been caught short. Surely the Russian grannies ranked high on the possibility list. Or that Italian in the monkey suit a few years back? It could definitely happen.

The feeling of the cold metal of the gun suddenly pressed against her left cheek made all thoughts of inappropriate urinary mishaps vanish. This was one hundred per cent a concentrate-on-the-job-in-hand moment. Or in this case, gun in hand.

'Can you sort it, Zandor? I'd say blow her brains out now but I think she'd like to hear what all of this has been in aid of first, don't you?' Weronika was enjoying her moment in the spotlight. Not even Wiktoria could outshine her on this one. Even with her much better hair.

Zandor reached into his pocket and pulled out a pair of handcuffs. He approached Jemma, grabbed her wrists and roughly pulled them above her head. He snapped one of the cuffs onto her wrist, pinching the skin a little as he did so, causing Jemma to squeal. He then placed the other cuff over the top of a rung on the hamster wheel and snapped it into place on her other wrist. The result left Jemma, hands over her head, gunmetal mesh top straining to a point of almost indecency as her body elongated on tiptoe with her hands firmly shackled onto the hamster wheel. Despite her discomfort she was well aware that the alternative of a bullet between her threaded eyebrows was a much darker and less desirable option.

Wiktoria, still shaking like a four-year-old needing a wee, could feel the prick of tears welling up in her eyes as she watched her sister's delight at seeing her new friend suffer.

'How did you do all of this? Did you and Zandor plan it all?' she asked. Despite not really wanting to, she needed to know.

'We've been planning it ever since I was given the gig hosting. I want to sing, to represent Rottimoldovia and to become world famous, so what better way to do that than to get rid of you. It's what my therapist meant, surely? But if it was just you being bumped off then all eyes would be on you when it comes to looking for suspects, and enough people look at you for my liking already. The last thing you need is more attention. So what better way to disguise your death than to make it one of many. And that's where my dear friend Zandor here comes in.'

Weronika walked over to where the journalist was standing in front of Jemma and backed her body onto him, writhing her backside against his groin. A lecherous grin spread across his face like bacteria in a petri dish as she did so and he placed his hands on either side of her hips. She swivelled her neck to face him over her shoulder and smiled, licking her lips as she did so. Jemma couldn't help pull a disgusted face at their actions. This wasn't just love is blind, this was a case of love needing an army of guide dogs and enough white sticks to build the Eiffel Tower. But each to their own, eh?

'I met Zandor when he interviewed me after I won *Rottimoldovia's Got Talent*. He wrote the most wonderful story about me and for once it wasn't all about *you*.' She pointed the gun at Wiktoria as she spat the word. Wiktoria yelped like a pup who'd just had her paw stepped on. 'It was about me, my talent, my voice, my looks.'

'Needy cow,' breathed Jemma before she could stop herself. She was thankfully quiet enough for Weronika not to hear.

'It was clear he liked me for who I really am so when I got this job I was determined to make sure that he was on the official journalist list for the contest. I knew he'd write *beautiful* things about me. And more to the point, *not* about anyone else. But Zandor doesn't really have any interest in shows like this do you, my dear? So at first he didn't want to do it but I can be very persuasive and I managed to wrap him around my finger, shall we say.'

'Not just your finger, I bet, you thirsty crackpot.' This time Jemma was loud enough to be heard. Mercifully Weronika ignored her, enjoying the sound of her own voice unravelling her genius.

'We were together one night, planning another fabulous feature about me, and I was telling Zandor just how much I would have really loved to sing in the first ever *Eurowide Song Contest* and not just host it and also how my therapist says I need to eliminate all thoughts of my sibling rivalry. And I just happened to mention how magnificent it would be if somebody could help me find true happiness and be the one to help me realise my dreams. And how grateful I'd be.'

'And you showed your gratitude in every position you could, I bet. Pillow talk is at a whole other level in this country, isn't it?' interrupted Jemma again. If she was going to pop her clogs tonight, then Jemma was at least going to have her say and not head six feet under silently. Silence had never been her forte. Ever.

'But you didn't have to kill people?' offered Wiktoria, rapidly realising that her opinion would make diddly-squat difference. In fact, she was beginning to understand that possibly her own opinion had never mattered to Weronika. She was blinkered by her own deep insecurities.

'Collateral damage. Just to paint an easier picture. Zandor had free rein. It was a case of kill who you like and make it all look like a series of tragic, horribly coincidental accidents.'

'It vos eazy. People are stupid. I did it for you,' bragged Zandor punching his own chest with pride.

Jemma would have happily right-hooked his shrew-like features into outer space. You couldn't just go around murdering people, no matter how good the sex on offer was. Just because you were being taken to heaven between the sheets by some pompous pillow princess didn't mean you had the right to send others on their way to the pearly gates.

Weronika blew him a kiss. Sycophantic toad Zandor caught it in his hand with a playful catch.

Jemma could feel the bile rising in her throat. 'Gag. Get a room, preferably a prison one,' she mumbled to herself.

'It was so incredibly easy. I kept people out of the way while Zandor made a few adjustments to Latreena's disco ball with his tool box. A few loose nuts here and there and down it came. That was pretty impressive, wasn't it? The perfect death for that stuck-up diva. I was pleased Zandor suggested her. Plus she stood a good chance of winning tomorrow and we didn't want that, did we? Then there was poor little Ronnie from Ireland. Sweet lad but when Zandor found him coming out of the toilets on the boat trip looking all drunk and wobbly, it was easy to just tip him over the edge of the boat when no one was looking. Shame. Oh so young, but needs must and all that. Wrong place wrong time that's all. Plus who dyes their hair green, I ask you. That's a crime in itself!' Weronika banged her hand to her forehead obviously perturbed by DonRon Ronnie's lack of coiffured taste. She turned to Jemma. 'It could just have easily been you.'

'Except that scrag-end of a man would never have been able to flip this piece of bootylicious overboard.'

It was now Zandor's turn to flip Jemma the finger.

'Next up was that poor unfortunate runner. It should have been that silly Turkish cow, Meli. She was the one who was supposed to have been blown sky high. Plant an explosive under her caravan, wait until she's in there, blame a stray spark or an electrical fault and boom! Bye bye bye to another potential threat. Taking out the competition to make it easier for me on the big night. But she got lucky. The runner didn't. Nobody cares about a poor lowly runner though, do they? Did anyone talk about that death as much as the others? No, they didn't. And menopausal Meli suddenly became centre of attention. No, that one didn't quite go to plan, did it, Zandor? And after you'd sabotaged the edit of their previous postcard and everything. What a cock-up...'

He was oblivious to the annoyance in her voice, a grin coating his face.

'Then we have Gunter Hoop. He drew the short straw, or should I say he obviously used it to snort the rat poison or whatever it was that Zandor sold him. That was the easiest one of all. Zandor befriends the German band who love their partying, gets himself invited to an afterparty back at the band's hotel suite after the blogger's concert and simply throws a bag of anonymous white powder into the mix. It just happened to be Gunter who sampled it first. I didn't mind which one copped it. It would have been easier had it been the singer as they'd have had to withdraw but hey, a death's a death.'

'We've all been living in fear because of you,' said a disbelieving Wiktoria. 'I thought I was going to die.'

'You were meant to be petrified. I needed you to be. That's why I had Zandor give you the fake forecast of doom at the Dicken Platz. That was so easy to print up off the internet and freak you out with it. You've been scared of everything for your entire life. I was worried you might have quit the contest yourself from fright, but I'm glad you didn't as then you would have had a heap of sympathy from the press. Poor little Wiktoria. They've shown you enough kindness don't you think? Oh… and as for thinking that you're going to die, well you are.'

Wiktoria screamed, the thought of her imminent doom at the hands of her own flesh and blood terrifying her. 'When did you become this horrible person?' she asked.

'I reckon about ten minutes after I was born. When you first made an appearance. You made me this way. It's all your fault.' Her words were ribboned with madness.

'You can't go shooting people. That's never going to look like an accident, is it? I can tell the world it was you, you total loon.' Jemma had reached the stage where she was going to say exactly what she felt. The forecast of her future was not exactly sunny days so she might as well throw as many insults in Weronika's direction as she could while she still had breath in her lungs. She stared down at the photo of Sandra Kim tucked away in her bra and prayed that the presence of her icon, albeit in photographic form, had to be a good omen. It may have been the Danes who were famed for their bacon, but she was praying that the presence of the Belgian star would be saving hers and Wiktoria's.

'Not if you're dead you can't.' Weronika was waggling the gun at her again. 'You're lucky you're not dead already.'

'I only never killed you before as ze UK never wins this kind of show anyvay. You are hardly a threat to dear Weronika, are you?' chipped in Zandor.

'You wait until tomorrow night, mister. I'll show you!' volleyed Jemma back at him, even though she realised the futility of her words.

'Just shut up, all of you!' hollered Weronika. 'This is how it's going to go, right. I won't be blamed for anything. I've got it all worked out. I'm the hero in this story. My poor sister shot to death and you too now you're here, Jemma La Vie. Another two unfortunate deaths to add to the list at the inaugural and destined ever-to-be-famous *Eurowide Song Contest*. The host nation won't be able to believe that poor "Love Safari" singer Wiktoria is gone so, even though I'm grieving for my poor departed sister, I will offer to step in and sing it as well as hosting. Or instead of hosting if that's what's chosen. I don't care. But I will get to sing. And given the sympathy vote, I suspect. So I will win. I'll be the greatest winner for Rottimoldovia. I will become a national treasure and people will realise that I am a star in my own right. Not just because I'm related to you, Wiktoria.'

'Can I ask a question?' Jemma was more than confused. No surprise given that she never guessed whodunnit on *Miss Marple* or even on the re-runs of *Columbo*. 'Who's shooting me and Wikky? There's all sorts of fingernail tests and stuff you can do these days to see who fired a gun isn't there? The cops are bound to test everyone. Even a national treasure like you.'

Jemma shifted her position on tiptoe to try and alleviate the pain in her wrists from hanging off the hamster wheel.

'Oh that won't be me. That'll be Zandor. My knight in shining armour. His final act of love for me. Well the final one and the last but final one given that there's two of you rather awkwardly now that need shooting.' As she spoke, she reached into the large pocket of her sweat top again and pulled out a pair of black leather gloves. She slipped them over her hands.

Zandor grinned with pride again and then stopped mid-thought, all notion of any fairytale happy ever after ending suddenly draining from his face.

'But Weronika, ze police will test my fingernailz zurely?' He took a step towards Jemma as he spoke.

As he was running through potential police procedure in his mind and questioning Weronika's words, Weronika moved over to her sister and grabbed her hand. Wiktoria shrieked again, tears bursting forth in fear. Weronika placed Wiktoria's hand around the gun, forcing one of her fingers into the hole by the trigger. Manhandling a shaking Wiktoria into position, she aimed the gun towards Zandor, a sudden look of what-the-fuck plastered across his face.

'Yes they will, and they'll blame you for everything. That was the plan. It always was. D'you really think I was shagging you for your looks? Dream on.' She squeezed Wiktoria's finger and the sound of the gun echoed through the empty Coliseum, spreading a cankerous air of doom as it did do. The bullet landed squarely in the top of Zandor's chest and he fell to the floor.

'Jesus, you've killed him you crazy nutjob.' Jemma was approaching hysterical, tugging at the wheel to try and free herself. 'Wiktoria's shaking like a shitting dog. Any closer and that could've been me.'

Letting a sobbing Wiktoria drop to the floor, Weronika walked over towards Zandor's motionless body. 'Your turn's next, Jemma. So this is how it works, right.'

Weronika reached inside her sweat top pocket again and this time pulled out a small knife. The kind fishermen used to gut big catches. Jemma recognised the type from weekend trips to Great Yarmouth when she was a kid.

Weronika unfurled her ultimate plan. 'So Zandor is actually just a crazy killer, right. And he wants to cause death and destruction at something he really dislikes in life, the *Eurowide Song Contest*. So what better way to be able to do that than by going on a rampage and killing off the contestants and hosts. That's why the police will find a note under my hotel room door too, telling me to come here tonight to meet my dear sister as she is desperate to see me before the big day tomorrow. Then when we are here, Zandor tells us of his evil plan and tries to kill us both. Obviously, he didn't know that Wiktoria was going to bring you along as well, Jemma, so unfortunately you have to die too. Just hard luck, I'm afraid. Zandor has a gun and starts waving it around in our direction. I see him shoot you dead. Then he aims the gun at poor Wiktoria and I can't have that, my poor sister dying, so I rush at him and start to struggle. The gun falls to the floor and a hysterical Wiktoria picks it up and says she'll shoot him. But she's too scared to isn't she at first, and Zandor pulls a knife, grabs me and says that he'll kill me unless Wiktoria drops the gun. He's got it pressed to my throat. It leaves a horrible mark.'

Weronika took the knife and pressed it to her own throat, pushing it hard enough to leave a red mark but not enough to break the skin. A horrified Jemma, still struggling with her wrists around the hamster wheel, looked on.

Weronika rubbed her neck. 'Make-up will cover that up tomorrow night. The viewing audience won't see a thing. Where was I? Oh yes, so I tell her to shoot, selflessly saying not to worry even if she hits me, that she must save herself, but she can't. So I find some incredible inner strength from somewhere, try to struggle with Zandor and somehow manage to move myself away from him. I tell my dear sister to shoot but she can't and rushes towards him. They struggle and somehow, in a cruel twist of fate, she's stabbed, and he is shot. They both die.'

'What the actual...? You are totally three members short of a full voting jury aren't you? You are completely barking! So they both die. And then you phone the police, right? And poor defenceless you is sitting there shaking like a weak innocent victim as the boys in blue charge in.'

'It's genius, isn't it?' Weronika couldn't help herself and gave a little smug shimmy of joy, the revelation that her plan was coming together so beautifully rushing through her veins like a delicious high.

'But that means stabbing your own sister...' Wiktoria was still a slow-poured cocktail of confusion, disbelief and horror.

'Oh yeah, I guess I should get on with that...' Weronika looked down at the short sharp blade still in her hands.

Just as the crazed host started to move towards a nervous and quivering Wiktoria, the attention of all three women on the stage was distracted by a thundering of feet entering into the Coliseum from the far end of the cavernous and shadowy hall.

Weronika placed her hand to her eyes and endeavoured to stare out into the darkness. Silhouetted forms dotted her vision, but recognition was impossible.

Or at least it was until a billowing voice boomed out filling the echoey void. 'Don't worry, Jemma, we're coming, girl. We're here!'

It was the unmistakable voice of Char. As she came into vision she was followed by a worried-looking Igor – if that was indeed the look his face was trying to make – a sweaty-browed Daniel and a berry-red-faced Lucie, who looked like she had pushed herself way too hard at a HIIT class and was about to burst. As cavalries went, it was an odd but totally welcome grouping.

Jemma felt a corkscrew of joyousness twisting its way through her as she saw her friends approach the stage. She continued to yank at the hamster wheel bar she was handcuffed to and watched desperately as Weronika, realising that perhaps her cunning plot was potentially not even making it past the semi, raised her hand in the air, knife glistening in the stage lights, and ran towards her blubbering sister.

For the next few seconds, everything seemed to happen in slow motion. Jemma yanked one more time at the bar trapping her on the hamster wheel and with a satisfying crack it split at the point between the two cuffs, setting her free. Seizing her opportunity, she ran towards Weronika, who was now screaming banshee-like hunched over her sister like some possessed Nosferatu, the knife waggling perilously close to her sister.

Her hands still attached with the cuffs, Jemma screamed as she reached Weronika too. The host turned to face her holler and as she did so Jemma fisted her cuffed hands together and swung them as solidly as she could across Weronika's face.

'Nobody else dies tonight, you crazy bitch! Not on my watch.'

Jemma, and all those gathered, watched as the knife flew from Weronika's hands and circled through the air before landing with a disarming clank on the far side of the stage. Weronika's screaming stopped as she fell to the floor. She was out cold before her miniscule frame hit the ground.

As Char, Igor, Daniel and Lucie mounted the stairs to the stage, Jemma bent down to wrap her arms around Wiktoria. Well as much as possible given her cuffing. Her face was wet with tears. In a heartbeat Igor was by their side.

Char enveloped herself around Jemma. 'What the shitting heck has been going on?' she bellowed, squeezing Jemma so hard in her arms that Jemma could feel the underwiring in her bra digging into her flesh.

'She...' Jemma pointed at the inert figure of Weronika on the floor. 'She is behind it all. All of the deaths this week. She... and that odious little snot rag over there.' This time she pointed at the equally inert figure of Zandor.

'What, that stuck up little twiglet?' asked Char, words slathered with disbelief.

'Yep, she's full on wacko. Like *herrrrrrre's Wronnie* crazy. She wanted poor Wikky dead so she had all the others killed to cover her tracks.'

'She killed my Latreena?' asked Igor.

'And poor little Ronnie DonRon?' added Daniel.

'And the smelly German bugger?' remarked Char.

'And the other fella?' snapped Lucie, in between pants.

'All of them. And she was going to kill me too. And then poor Wiktoria.'

'I'm so sorry,' sobbed Wiktoria from the sanctuary of Igor's arms.

'What for? Having a nut job for a sister. It's not your fault, Wiktoria.' Char's words were harsh but true, but aware that blood may still be thicker than water she followed them with a cursory, 'No offence, love.'

'That was quite some punch you knocked her out with,' said Lucie, her breathing returning to some trace of normality. 'I wouldn't want to mess with you. Mean girl!'

'That's FagButts training for you, Lucie,' replied Jemma. 'I can't tell you the number of overly-handsy blokes I've had to knock back in FagButts car park trying to get past first base. Always comes in handy. I've got to say though, Lucie, you're the hero of the hour, my friend, thank God you and Bjorn broke the hamster wheel and forget to get it repaired until the last minute. Luckily Zandor must have cuffed me to the dodgy rung you broke and the glue hadn't quite set hard yet from where it had been fixed by the props team. It took a few yanks but luckily I was able to break it off and then clobber the crazy cow before she could stab Wikky. You, and the power of Sandra Kim, of course, have saved the day.' Jemma patted her cuffed hands against her chest where the photo of her icon still nestled in her bra, mentally bemoaning the fact that she had also missed the chance to see her hero perform tonight. 'Now, can somebody get me out of these bloody cuffs please? I think the stiff over there must have the keys in his pocket.'

Char went over to Zandor and started to root around in his pockets. She found the key. As she did, the weasely journalist began to stir, a moan emanating from his thin lips and he tried to lift his head off the floor. It was now Char's turn to scream.

'Oh my God, he's not dead!' Char's reflex action kicked in and she involuntarily pushed his head back to the ground with a clonk and scuttled over to Jemma again with the key to free her wrists.

'I'm phoning the police. They need to get here now.' It was Daniel who spoke. 'These two need to be arrested before they can wake up and run off.'

'They're going nowhere,' said Jemma. 'Char and I can sit on them if need be until the police turn up. And they won't mess with Igor will they? I can't believe the scrawny bugger Zandor is still alive. I was stood right next to him when he was shot. Right next to him. Like a foot away. Honestly, Char, *one step further* and I could have been there…'

There was a tiny pause before Jemma and Char both smiled, looked into each other's eyes and said in unison, their wonderful friendship still tied in its unique *Euro*-loving bow despite the nightmare of the scenario.

'Tune!'

Chapter 40

"...unite unite Europe..."

Eurowide night.

The opening and fanfare musical notes of the *Eurowide Song Contest* music sounded throughout the Johnny Logan Coliseum in Ermpit, Rottimoldovia. Despite everything that had happened throughout the week, including the revelations to those in the know of what had occurred less than 24 hours earlier on the very stage where countless countries would sing their hearts out tonight to try and secure victorious honour for their nation, the newest song contest on earth was going ahead. Police may have said they preferred it didn't, but the Rottimoldovian government pulled rank and power and deemed otherwise. Like the burst of poppy, feelgood, smile-spreading wondrous joy that it was, millions around the world tuned in to watch.

Eurowide officials had suggested to the police that perhaps the fact that one of the show's famous hosts and a journalist from the first ever *Eurowide* home nation had gone on a murderous week-long killing rampage should remain hidden for now. At least until the contest was over and all of the competing nations had safely returned home. Panic had been through the Coliseum roof as it was with people thinking the deaths were a series of random unfortunate accidents so if they actually had found out that two familiar faces were the evil masterminds behind them, the show itself might spun into a world of jeopardy before its very first airing.

Jemma was standing backstage in the competitor line-up. She was wearing another of her famed, figure-hugging mesh tops, this time a virginal white, and gold glittery leggings with matching gold heels. As ever, a photo of her beloved Sandra was tucked into her bra. She was looking and feeling fabulous. She'd chosen white for the night as she believed that more *Eurovision* winners had been victorious wearing white than any other colour and the combo of that fact and her treasured photo had to be good omens, right, for her attempt to bring the *Eurowide* crown home?

All of the contestants were required to walk onto the stage after Szymon, now the show's sole host, had finished his opening song and dance number and introduction. Weronika's absence had been blamed on a mysterious and highly contagious illness that has knocked her senseless overnight and meant that she couldn't present anything unless it was from the confines of her bed at the infectious diseases ward at Ermpit's Alpha Beta Hospital. And that couldn't happen.

'Are you sure you're okay to perform tonight?' asked a supportive Daniel, who was keen to be by Jemma's side for as much as he possibly could before having to take his seat in the UK area in the Coliseum green room. 'You've had quite a week. Especially last night. Most people would be allowed to be a gibbering wreck right now. I'm astonished you can even talk let alone go out there later and sing.'

It was true, the hours since last night had been a whirlwind she wouldn't ever care to repeat. Four hours in a stuffy room at Ermpit's police headquarters explaining all of the underhand dealings that Weronika and Zandor had managed to achieve throughout the week. Then a few last-minute telly appearances where she had to be all smiley and chirpy even though she hadn't slept for over a day and was so exhausted her words made about as much sense as some of the undecipherable *Eurowide* songs. Plus she was still spitting about the fact she had lost her chance of seeing Sandra Kim perform in the flesh. Word on the *Euro* grapevine was that she had been nothing short of sensational. But a few hours of shut eye later and with enough make-up on to cover any saggy pocket of knackered flesh, Jemma was ready to go. To go and win. To do it for her country.

'To quote past *Eurovision* winners Herreys, Daniel. *Life is goin' my way, when I'm walking in my golden shoes.*' She pointed to her heels and gave them a wiggle. I'm as ready as I'll ever be. This is my dream, Daniel, it always has been, you now that. Back from the days when I was… you know, *Tonya*.' She mouthed the last word and whispered it, not ashamed of who she was, but more exhilarated about who she had become. 'Ever since I first saw Sandra belting out "J'Aime La Vie", I knew that this was my destiny, to be in a contest like this. To be just like her and to go out there and give it my all. I want to show every person back home and every little girl out there that dreams can come true. That if you believe in yourself and follow your heart that you can do anything. Tonight is my moment and even though this week has been the weirdest week ever

I wouldn't swap any of it for the world... except the deaths, of course, and maybe the bit where I was handcuffed to a hamster wheel. That wasn't brilliant. But apart from that, it's what I have always dreamed of. My best mate Char's been here with me and that just means everything to me. The fact that she will be on that stage with me tonight belting out "Beep the World (Hear My Horn)" alongside me is incredible. It makes every pigging moment where I had to clean out another batter bucket at Chips Ahoy or Char had to rinse out another fag-filled ashtray at The Pig And Pickle worth it, because we never stopped dreaming.'

'Get ready everybody, you're on in two minutes.' A frantic backstage crew member hurried past, a clipboard soldered to their hands and worry branded onto their face.

Jemma continued. 'I've made some brilliant friends doing this.' She looked at the line-up ahead of her and saw Wiktoria, who, despite everything she had gone through in the past few hours, had also decided that she would take to the sanctuary of the stage and try to forget about what her sister had attempted to do. She had considered pulling out. But had then decided against it. There would be enough column inches written about her family after tomorrow as it was. It would be nice if some of them could be about a *Eurowide* win or high placing and not just focus on the gorier lethal bits of her sister's jealousy and psychotic side.

'Wiktoria is amazing. A friend for life. I've enjoyed meeting so many people. Some more than others, admittedly.' Her gaze focussed on Fritz from Die Bolzen who was again terribly tongue-swirling some adoring hanger-on towards the end of the line-up and a miserable Meli and Baran who were silently waiting for the evening to begin, neither of them looking at the other. It was only on stage that they would need to coat on their smiley faces and portray a united front. Both of them were currently staring at a hot and hench Hungarian singer further up the line-up that they had both been fruitlessly trying to flirt with all week. 'But there's been some awesome people here. Like the lads from DonRon and Bjorn.'

Little Irish Donnie DonRon was bouncing like a sugared-up jumping-bean in the line-up, the cardboard cut-out of his late brother horribly evident in its motionless state alongside him. Meanwhile the Swede was stood at the end of the long line-up seeing as he would be performing last. He stood fiddling with his neckerchief, lost in his own thoughts. There was an air of serenity and calm across his wholesome features. A knowledge that whatever the evening brought with it, that life après-*Euro* would be glorious and that there was no reason to fear the future.

'Thank the Lordi for his platform boots breaking that hamster wheel, eh?' mused Jemma. She lifted her hand and placed it on Daniel's chin, cupping his defined jaw. 'And you, my little Ryan Gosling, have been an absolute joy. I know you've been a bit of a task master with me at times, making me do three million interviews in a row, but I couldn't have done this without you. You get me. And I get you. And you'll be my friend for life I hope too. You're welcome down at FagButts anytime you like. It might not be your cup of tea, Daniel, but we'll force the DJ to play some Tay Tay and Britney for you to camp it up. Bring Igor. I've gained such a soft spot for him and his big, lovely lumbering ways. And I think you have too deep down. He's bound to be over in the UK with Wiktoria at some point. I told her she's got to come to Whittlesey. We can do a gig together in the market square.'

'Fifteen seconds!' the hyper crew member shouted at a pitch normally reserved for dogs.

'I think you and Wiktoria might be a little bigger than gigs in Fenland market squares after tonight,' smiled Daniel. 'This is the first ever *Eurowide Song Contest.*'

'We'll see.' Jemma leant forward and kissed Daniel on the lips, holding his face between her hands as she did so. 'Right then, kiddo, let's do this.' A tremor of excitement and anticipatory delight sparkled through her.

The crew member's voice was jubilant, her moment finally arrived. 'And start walking onstage please…'

Jemma clapped her hands. 'Time to fly the flag. Wish me luck.' Sandra's in position.' She felt for the photo, her good luck talisman, to make sure it was still safely housed in her bra. 'It's my time tonight, Daniel. Let's try and bring this home.' She gave a little jiggle on the spot, waiting for her turn to walk forward. Wiktoria turned, smiled and waved at her as her own turn came.

'I'll see you at the voting room seats,' said Daniel, his nose curling as he spoke. There was a smell in the air he couldn't quite fathom. And it wasn't overly pleasant.

Jemma knew exactly what it was. 'Sorry, love. It's nerves I guess, and I couldn't help but have a nibble at the fish canapes buffet out the back. I don't think they agree with me. But they taste so good. I've been loving them all week.'

It was Jemma's turn to move forward and head to the stage. 'Right, here I go. Let the show begin. Here's to douze points all round. No dream impossible and all that...'

Daniel watched the one-in-a-million Jemma disappear out of sight, waving her hands in the air to the capacity crowd inside the Coliseum and the gazillions of new *Eurowide* fans glued to their TV screens in different time zones around the globe. And despite the lingering nasty fishy niff in the air backstage, he couldn't help but wish the singer the hugest slice of sweet-smelling success. She deserved it, she really did...

Chapter 41

"...the history book on the shelf is always
repeating itself..."

The streets of Ermpit were full to the brim the next
morning as people headed to the airport ready to fly back
to the normality of life after the party that was this year's
debut *Eurowide*. The air was pendulous, as it would be
the morning after, with the heady mix of disappointment,
jubilant elation, and resigned expectation.

But after the week that fate had delivered in
Rottimoldovia, normality would not be a dish served on
the afterparty menu for many of those heading back to
their homelands.

Bjorn Bjork, overjoyed that this could possibly be the
last journey for the foreseeable where a neckerchief
and platform heel combo would be necessary folded his
six-foot-three frame into the back seat of his taxi and
smiled as his Ermpit hotel disappeared from view.

Baran and Meli sat at opposite ends of their taxi's
back seat as they headed towards Lysassia Airport. Meli
flicked at her long black hair and licked her lips,
relishing the taste of the ridiculously expensive lipstick
she was wearing. It was called A Divine Taste of
Hollywood and was worth every Turkish lira that she
had paid for it. Which was a lot. She deserved the best,

and as she watched a plane leave its gaseous trail in the sky overhead, she knew she would get it. Somehow.

Baran shifted a little uncomfortably in his seat and stared out of his side window. A warm glow of satisfaction defrosted across his core. His discomfort was worth it. The rest of his evening after last night's contest had most definitely been worthwhile. The hot and hench Hungarian singer had finally proved to Baran that he was definitely swimming up his end of the pleasure pool. Maybe it had been the penetrating gazing in the line-up that had finally done it. But when the two of them had found themselves in the same hotel bar later that night one thing had led to another and before he knew it, Baran was biting his pillow with delight. Hence his downstairs discomfort this morning. But it had been worth every inch.

Donnie DonRon was playing yet another computer game in the back of his taxi as he headed to the airport. This one also involved shooting as many people as possible, but these were zombies, so they were already dead to begin with. He was killing the undead. It helped take his mind off what had been going on this week at the contest. Death. Manager Wally Leash sat alongside him, his hand rested on Donnie's knee. It often was. Donnie chose to ignore it.

'I have a huge gig lined up for you in one of Ireland's biggest gay nightclubs, The Good Craic, when we arrive back home, Donnie,' said Wally. 'It's a fabulous place, so I hear. Never been there myself of course, acting the maggot. But I've heard it's good, like. Have you ever been there, Donnie? You or your young friends? D'you know the gay scene well at all?'

Donnie was too busy beheading a zombie and ignored him again. He ignored a lot of the things that Wally said and did. He found that best.

The three remaining members of Die Bolzen were not flying home. They were on their tour bus driving past the airport heading back to Germany. This meant the security checks weren't so necessary, a wise move given the abundant narcotic cargo of their vehicle, and also so that as many groupies as possible could travel with them. Fritz, Walter and Jurgen were sitting in the main area of the tour bus, a photo of departed Gunter staring down at them from the wall. They had ripped his photo from their latest tour programme and pinned it into the padded sides of the vehicle. The effect was like the laziest of shrines.

'To Gunter. Good man. Great drummer. Bad judge of drugs,' toasted Fritz, raising his beer bottle to the photo. Walter and Jurgen raised theirs too and all of them swigged back the liquid within. For a second there was silence and contemplation. It felt awkward and unnecessary. 'Gunter would want us to party, right?' said Fritz. The others didn't need to answer as within seconds Walter was chopping out another fat line of white powder and Jurgen the Organ was letting the latest doting fraulein sample his nine-and-a-half inches. As Fritz let his slug of a tongue invade yet more uncharted territories, Gunter Hoop stared down from his postery grave on the tour bus wall.

Had any of our returning *Eurowide* hopefuls stopped off on route at the Dicken Platz to see what Zoltan the ancient mechanical fortuneteller would predict for them for the months ahead, they would have heard what the future had in store for them. Well, providing his prediction was a whole lot more genuine than the one that conniving Weronika had printed off to freak the life out of her sister when she had given it to Zandor to give to poor gullible Wiktoria.

EPILOGUE

"…we're going up, up, up, up, up, up, up…"

Bjorn Bjork was not really heard of much again when he returned to Sweden after the contest. Not overly surprising seeing as one of the nations who took song contests like *Eurowide* the most seriously had to contend with Bjorn's song "24 Hours of Sunshine" not living up to hopeful expectations and barely scraping enough points to warrant Bjorn's return air fare to Rottimoldovia. In fact, he finished 23rd on the night. It was blamed on the fact he was drawn to sing last at the end of a long night of competition and also on the fact that his hamster wheel could no longer be used as it was seized as police evidence in the case against Weronika and Zandor. No hamster wheel meant no backing dancers writhing around on it to the tropicana beat, so they merely limboed behind Bjorn while he did his thing. In a world of high-pyrotechnics and fancy gimmicks, Bjorn's song, despite a great performance, failed to capture the *Euro* vote.

A fact which Bella, after a week of interviews as Bjorn lamenting Sweden's loss, couldn't have been happier about. There was no way an act in 23rd place would ever be asked to appear at next year's contest or indeed at pretty much any *Eurowide* gathering from now on. Bjorn could just simply disappear. Be forgotten about to leave the song contest glory days of Sweden to the evergreen likes of Loreen, Carola, Mans and ABBA.

Plus, the fact that Bjorn placed 23rd in particular pleased Bella hugely as that put her on an even footing with Szymon and his contest showing years earlier. As far as Bella was concerned it was another sign that they were meant to be together.

Szymon spent a few days in Ermpit after the final but then flew home to Amsterdam. He had loved presenting the show solo with no Weronika to carry, either professionally or faux-personally, and critics and *Euro* fan clubs across the borders had lapped him up, saying that he was the perfect mix of funny, sexy and cool for the first show. He was besieged with offers of presenting work but for now he turned them down.

Back in Amsterdam, he took the first flight he could to join Bella at her home in Sweden. The two of them were a perfect match, especially sexually. Bella loved Szymon's dark side and he, hers. Within weeks they had both left Sweden for good and returned to Amsterdam, the pair of them setting up home in a swanky new apartment together. One with a custom-built dungeon in the basement. That they both used. Within six months there was talk of marriage and within nine the couple were indeed spliced together as one. Countless magazines featured the happy couple on the cover with guests including Wiktoria Seksi and Mistress Kimberley. It was a surprising collection of guests for a very surprising coupling but it was definitely a coupling that worked.

But back before Bella and Szymon left Sweden, they had one last thing to do. Bjorn needed to be laid to rest for good. As she had planned, Bella left Bjorn's *Euro* clothes on the side of a busy Swedish waterway along with a suicide note saying that 23rd place was a disgrace and he'd bought shame to the nation. The plan worked a treat. The nation mourned and despite a massive search, a body was unsurprisingly never found. The only difference to the plan that originally went through Bella's mind was that she decided to leave only one of Bjorn's platform heels on the riverbank alongside his clothes. She kept the other. It was the one that had broken the hamster wheel. The one that had helped her come 23rd in her opinion. The one that had put an end to the torture of tit-taping for good. And for that she would be forever grateful. The platform boot hung pride of place behind glass on the wall of Bella and Szymon's dungeon. If anyone ever asked Szymon he just said that he had kept it after Bjorn left it backstage at the Johnny Logan Coliseum.

Donnie DonRon returned to Ireland as a bit of a hero. Having finished 7th on the night with "The Smile High Club", Donnie and a hologram of Ronnie were featured on nearly every Irish talk show from Lifford to Limerick. The workload was massive and hugely busy, but a few spare hours for Ronnie's funeral were put aside by Wally Leash providing they could make sure Ronnie's interment didn't clash with a hopeful performance on Ireland's most watched entertainment show where Donnie would sing a medley of old Irish *Eurovision* hits with Johnny Logan. Luckily, Donnie was able to leave halfway through the serving of the vol-au-vents at his brother's funeral back at his ma's home after the service to hotfoot to the studio in time for the opening bars of "Hold Me Now".

Once the furore of DonRon's success had died down, Wally was keen for Donnie to record a follow-up single, but something about the stale atmosphere of trying to lay down vocals solo without his bro in the studio told Donnie that his heart wasn't in it anymore. The recording was scrapped before it could be completed and much to Wally Leash's fat-cheeked annoyance, Donnie said he was quitting showbusiness and left a crestfallen Wally for good. Leaving showbiz was not strictly true as two months later Donnie became the face of a computer gaming company, having mentioned in his countless interviews his obsession with them, who turned him into a lean, mean mechanical-zombie killing machine in his own action computer game. For Donnie this was a dream come true. The game, *Zomboids*, was optioned as a feature film before the end of the year and before he knew it Donnie was learning his lines for his first action flick about undead robots on the rampage. When it was released, the only person in the whole of Ireland not to rush out and buy a ticket to go and see it was an acidly bitter Wally Leash. Donnie dedicated the film to his late brother.

Die Bolzen's life after their 11th placing at Ermpit didn't go to plan either. In fact it went very much off the rails. Or maybe that should be off the roads. High mountainous, treacherous roads in the middle of Germany. In unseasonably snowy conditions. With a tour bus driver who had drunk a little bit more than someone in charge of the Bolzen Party Bus really should have done after an appearance by the smelly rockers at one of the country's annual beer fests.

Thankfully there were no fatalities in the 1am crash but the two-hundred-foot drop off the mountain road, that only came to an abrupt halt when the bus hurtled headfirst into a gathering of spruce trees was enough to send the three remaining members of the group into rock meltdown. Walter became terrified of ever travelling again and quit the group to teach rhythm guitar to wannabe rockers near his home in Stuttgart. Jurgen the Organ decided that he had experienced enough of life on the road too and moved into online porn by teaming up with The Bolzen Twins. Their three-ways and group online offerings raked them in a sizable fortune. And, as Jurgen knew, size always mattered.

Fritz seemed to have an epiphany in the near fatal crash and, convinced that he had seen the lights of divine salvation as he watched the barks of the fir trees smashing into the tour bus, turned his back on rock music and indeed his entire rock 'n' roll lifestyle to record a religious album called *The Sweet Sacred Smell of Success*. His album tanked and he was last heard of trying to convince any passing worshipper to burn copies of Die Bolzen's *Slaughterhouse of Lust* for its sacrilegious content.

Baran and Meli's life after *Eurowide* couldn't have placed them further apart. Literally time zones. Baran returned to his native Turkey and informed the press that despite the duo's very impressive 3rd placing in the first ever *Eurowide,* they would no longer be performing together and that they would be "uncoupling". Baran had read about big Hollywood stars who did it. It seemed to be the new way of saying we can't actually bear each other but the delivery was wrapped up in a grown up, neatly tied bow of politeness. He figured that telling the world that they were both shagging around with any passing piece of hot male flesh could be omitted for now.

The news came as a shock to Meli as Baran hadn't so much as mentioned the word "uncoupling" to her. But, as his last words to her when she told him that she was taking a flight to Los Angeles as soon as possible to start a career there were, 'I don't care if I actually never see you again until hell freezes over' she had a pretty good idea that something might be bubbling as far as the end of their union was concerned. And that suited Meli down to the ground. She had plans. And none of them involved Baran. So while he started playing solo gigs across Turkey and successfully managed to DILF his way through every up-for-it option on Twink-All, Meli put her own plans into operation.

Coming top three at *Eurowide* was perfect for Meli's vision and no sooner had she touched down in LA than she had bagged herself a celebrity agent. She'd wanted one who dealt with the Kidmans and the Witherspoons of Tinseltown. They were unavailable apparently. So she eventually bagged one who dealt with a couple of actresses who once had a small part on *The Bold and the Beautiful* and played "second corpse in the morgue" on an episode of *General Hospital*. But everyone had to start somewhere, right?

Splitting with Baran whilst on top gave Meli a Beyonce-post-Destiny's-Child spirit of invincibility (with added hot flushes of menopause though) and she was determined to succeed. She waited for her big break by playing her guitar and singing tunes at small yet trendy bars around Hollywood and by sleeping with as many wannabe actors (AKA waiters) as she could. Which was many. After six months of no telly work other than playing an alien with prosthetic green skin and no lines on season 32 of *American Horror Story*, a little slice of luck finally came her way. One of the waiters she was sleeping with was just about to serve amuse-bouches at a private party for one of the *Housewives of Beverly Hills* and he'd heard on the grapevine they were looking for somebody to sing at the party. Meli knew that if the stars aligned in her favour, she could make it happen and that would be the springboard to her bagging a regular slot on the show and marrying a filthy rich and famous plastic surgeon. Her dreams would come true. If she didn't then she'd be off to the law courts to brutally divorce Baran for every dime he had. Luckily for her (and Baran) the surgery Gods were on her side and before long she was staring into the eyes of her new beloved and undergoing a full Hollywood face lift which was being streamed live onto the net for the adoring fans of the latest "Housewife" on the LA glamour block.

Baran watched it at home in Istanbul in bed with his latest piece of trade.

Wiktoria Seksi was sitting in her manager's office in Ermpit a week after *Eurowide*. An ever-present Igor was at her side.

The manager was in full flow. 'Well, there's already talk about you being the face of tourism in Rottimoldovia and I have at least a dozen clothes shops who would like fashion ranges from you. Plus there's a massive chance of you being offered a publishing deal for an autobiography. Publishers are already bidding. And for your next single, Wiktoria, there are a couple of choices but one I'm thinking about is a cover of "Rollercoaster" by the Swedish girl group Dolly Style. They tried to get it into *Eurovision* a few years back at *Melodifestivalen* and failed. It's the perfect song for you seeing as your *Eurowide* journey this year has been such a rollercoaster. It's not every singer who has a family member try to kill them and wins *Eurowide* in the same week.'

Wiktoria listened to his diatribe but she was still a little numb. She had been all week. But her manager was right. She had indeed won the contest. "Love Safari" had romped home in first place and placed highly in nearly every online chart across Europe. She was a sensation. A *Eurowide* legend overnight in the strangest and most morbidly macabre of circumstances.

When the news had broken about Weronika and Zandor and the plot to kill her, every news outlet and TV show had wanted her side of the story, but she had kept silent. It was the best way of dealing with it for now. She'd avoided logging onto Instagram and Twitter too as doubtless there would be a million trolling comments there that she wouldn't want to read. For now she was happiest staying in her bubble of safety and just speaking to those she knew she could trust.

And that included the incredible Jemma. The two women had spoken constantly since the final and had already planned for Wiktoria to come and visit Jemma in the UK when, as Jemma put it, 'All the fuss about your fruit loop sister has died down.'

Wiktoria would never really understand why Weronika had felt as she did about her, but then she guessed that you could never truly place yourself in somebody else's mind, could you? Even as twins. In time she would come to understand it a little more, no doubt, but for now she was numb.

The months ahead would be hard for Wiktoria but with friends around her, those who cared, she could deal with anything. Hey, she was a winner, after all.

'Sure, I could record that for the follow-up if you think that's a good choice. I know the song. I like it.' Wiktoria attempted a smile but it wasn't easy. Even as a winner she was going through a patch of post-contest-blues. Apparently, that was a thing. Even for fans. Jemma said she and Char experienced it every year back in the day, especially if the UK crashed out in last place.

There had been a moment when Wiktoria was singing her winning song at the end of the contest, glittery tickertape raining down around her and for a brief moment, just for a few seconds, she had forgotten about everything that had happened. Her sister, her fear, her confusion. She had spotted Jemma and Char in the UK area of the voting room and they were dancing along to her winning song. Cheering her on. Smiles covering their faces. Her new friends. A friendship that could temporarily erase her worry and her stress. Temporarily erase the worry lines that suddenly attempted to be ever-present. A bit like one of those cheap facial creams you could buy on Rottimoldovian shopping telly channels.

Friends you could choose, family you couldn't. Never a truer word. No, Wiktoria would surround herself with good people for the next few months. People to give her the support she needed and deserved. People who understood her. They're the only ones who counted.

Her manager placed his hands together as in mock prayer and spoke. 'Well, I have had another idea about the follow-up single too and I know it's a bit out there, but I thought I'd run it by you. Given what's happened with Weronika I was thinking that maybe your next single could be a cover of "I Am (I'm Me)" by the '80s heavy metal band… er, Twisted Sister. I'm going kind of ironic, here. We could make it much more dancey and less rock, but it would be a massive talking point given their name. You taking ownership of the dreadful situation you've been in.' There was a brief silence that parcelled the room. 'You like the idea? Yes? No?'

Wiktoria didn't. Who would? Evidently neither did Igor as he reached out and placed a placatory hand on Wiktoria's shoulder. Igor was certainly in her bubble of friends. He made her feel safe and that was everything right now.

'I'll get back to you on that,' said Wiktoria.

She did, two days later, when she fired her manager. With comments like that he would definitely not be in her bubble as she looked to the future.

Except for the Debbie Downer of possibly being killed, Jemma's *Eurowide* experience had been everything she had ever dreamt of growing up loving *Eurovision*, which she had gleefully told everybody from *Lorraine* and *BBC Breakfast* through to Scott Mills on the radio when she landed back in the UK.

Okay she hadn't won, in fact she'd finished 13th, but that was on the all-important left-hand side of the scoreboard. She had returned to the UK a hero and somewhat of a national treasure. Which she found odd seeing as she was still in her 20s. Although maybe saying to Lorraine Kelly that national treasure status was normally given to "someone of your age, Lorraine" was not the most tactful of responses mid-live interview.

Daniel had been wincing inwardly as he listened to Jemma from the studio side-lines.

Performing on the *Eurowide* stage with her best mate Char sharing it with her was an experience that neither of them would ever forget. And for once, she was not experiencing any kind of emotional post-show doldrums, which she had always done as a fan. How could she? Life had changed forever and Jemma La Vie was loving her life. Plus the countdown was already on for next year.

If a young *Eurovision*-obsessed Tonya Babbidge had been told that one day she would be centre stage on a huge singing show singing for her country and even gaining a 12 points (way to go, Malta!) maximum along the way then she would never have believed it. She would have thought that there was more chance of her bumping into Sandra Kim at Peterborough Dog Track. And that was never going to happen!

But *Eurowide* had been launched and her dreams had materialised and so had finally meeting her heroine. It had happened backstage after Jemma had performed her best ever vocals on "Beep the World (Hear My Horn)". Strange how she had managed to save her finest vocals for the night itself. Maybe she should stare into the face of a crazed loony and have hardly any sleep more often. It obviously did wonders for her lung capacity.

She was having her microphone removed backstage when Sandra Kim approached.

'That was incredible. I loved your vocals and the video wall was terrific.'

'Oh my God... Sandra Kim. You're my utter hero. I have a photo of you stuffed down my bra. You're the reason I am Jemma La Vie.' Jemma was aware that she was already gibbering. She scooped Sandra into her arms and hugged her tightly. She didn't really give her any choice but thankfully Sandra didn't seem to mind.

'I know, I have followed your story from the beginning. I'm honoured,' she said, slightly muffled by the embrace.

'I'm so glad you're here. I wanted to come and see you last night at the club but then I couldn't because of all of the stuff that was going on. And seeing you perform is like my ultimate *Euro* fantasy. If it was you or Celine, I'd be watching you. No offence to her, mind, she has a voice of an angel too.'

Sandra laughed. Perhaps a little uneasily. Jemma wasn't sure.

'You can see me perform tonight. Seeing as Weronika can't be here because of... well, she can't, can she?' offered Sandra.

How much did the youngest *Eurovision* winner ever actually know? Jemma wasn't sure and for once decided to keep schtum. It was a police matter after all.

Sandra carried on the conversation. 'The organisers have asked me to perform the disco medley that Weronika was going to do. The dancers have been practicing all week, so it didn't seem right to not let them perform, did it? Not just because Weronika is... er... ill.'

'You've learnt her entire medley in less than day? You are legend. When is it on?'

'Just before the voting. To be fair I knew the songs she'd chosen inside out and we may have added "J'Aime La Vie" to it to make it more personal.'

'You have made me and a lot of baby-oiled dancers incredibly happy. I seriously can't wait.'

'You're welcome. And I must thank you for being such a fan. It's such a thrill. And I hope you win.'

'Really, Sandra, I'm not sure I have a chance, but we'll see. But I've won just by meeting you. Life. Made.'

'I have to go and start getting ready for my performance,' said Sandra, but whatever happens tonight, let's stay in touch. I'd love to record with you if you'd consider it. Your voice is incredible.'

Jemma's law dropped. 'Can you pinch me?'

'Sorry?'

'No seriously, pinch me, because I kind of had a bit of a dream about you earlier this week and this is kind of what happened and then I woke up. And you were gone.'

Jemma held out her arm to a bemused Sandra. 'Pinch me please. As hard as you like.'

Sandra did, but not too hard. Jemma closed her eyes as she did. When she opened them, Sandra was still standing in front of her.

'Thank the f... – sorry, heck – for that,' she cooed, biting her tongue to stop any potential swearing. 'If that bruises, I'm getting a tattoo line put around it. Badge of honour.' Jemma was laughing as there was no way it would bruise.

Sandra handed her a small business card. 'My management number is on there. Let's sort something out.'

This time it was Sandra who leant in for a hug. To Jemma it was the best hug in the world.

'So, is it happening?' asked Daniel, sliding into the backseat of the taxi as he and Jemma left the *Lorraine* studios. 'You and Sandra? Are you recording together?'

'Are you and Igor ever getting butt-jiggy again? What a silly question, Daniel Spirit, of course it's going to happen. We just have to sort out dates. As do you and Igor. There is no way I am not going to make this happen. Sandra Kim is the reason I have always wanted to represent my country at a song contest in the first place. And look at me now. I did it. I came... er, 13th. That's not too shoddy right?'

'Not too shoddy at all,' said Daniel.

Jemma looked out of the window and smiled. Life was good. The sun was shining, she'd just been interviewed by a national treasure and she'd finally met her heroine in the flesh.

'J'aime j'aime ma vie...' sang Jemma to herself as the taxi pulled off, wondering just what lay ahead. She was loving life and ready for a new tomorrow.

Sandra and Jemma did record together, and their duet was featured on Jemma's first album which came out just before Christmas that year. It also featured a duet with Wiktoria who had visited Jemma on several occasions since winning the contest. She had insisted to her new manager that she and Jemma were to record together. This pleased Igor hugely as it meant he got to spend more time with Daniel and even though Igor wasn't his normal type, the two of them caused quite a sensation at The Man Factory when Daniel took Igor there to show him off. Daniel's gay posse may have been a little dubious re Igor's face to begin with but there was no denying that his body and his personality were adorable. He soon won them all over. It looked like Daniel and Igor would be seeing a whole lot more of each other when their schedules allowed.

Jemma's debut album, *Chip Chip Hooray*, also featured a duet with Char. It was their cover of the UK 1980 *Eurovision* entry "Love Enough For Two", which Char was dedicating to her recent engagement to Ashley, the dancer from Kettering. The two of them had been inseparable since Ermpit and were now buying a first home together near Milton Keynes. Jemma had moved to London. They would be residents of Whittlesey no more, although their hearts would doubtless always be there in their Fenland origins. In fact, when Jemma and Char were asked to cut the ribbon on Whittlesey's newest fish bar, The Whittlesey Batter Bucket (formerly Chips Ahoy but a lick of fresh paint and new sign gave it a totally modern makeover), they were more than honoured to do so. They even helped out dishing up battered cod and singing tunes on opening night.

Jemma hadn't stopped since she'd arrived back from *Eurowide* and had been asked to appear on countless telly shows. She'd turned a few down but there was one that she was very keen to try out. In fact, the week before her soon-to-be-chart-topping album was released she was crowned queen of the Aussie jungle by Ant and Dec having won the nation over yet again by drinking blended kangaroo anus on *I'm A Celeb*. It had played havoc with her guts but what the heck, her campmates needed feeding. They'd just have to suffer her flatulence as a result.

The newspaper headline on her return said it all. 'EURO QUEEN JEMMA'S WHIRL-WIND SUCCESS CONTINUES AS SHE MAKES A ROO-D SPLASH DOWN UNDER'.

Some things would never change.

One year on…

Szymon Rybak took to the stage at the Johnny Logan Coliseum for that year's *Eurowide Song Contest*. Only the second ever. He was on hosting duties again following his country's victory the year before. This time he had a shiny new co-host with him, current champion Wiktoria Seksi.

Jemma La Vie was sitting in the VIP area at the side of the arena. She'd been in Ermpit all week making appearances in packed out Euroclubs and catching up with Wiktoria. Jemma and Sandra Kim had performed together at one club night. They'd bought the house down. Char would have been there too had she not been six months pregnant with Char Junior and already the size of Free Willy. She'd threatened to come over and serve Katie Price *Making Your Mind Up* telly show vibes in a pink PVC catsuit but Char's mum had mercifully persuaded her otherwise. Char had already decided on a name for her baby. It would be the ultimate song contest tribute seeing as that was where she and dad-to-be Ashley had met. Her baby would be called Sandie Lulu Agnetha Grills. Winning names one and all. Jemma adored the idea and had already decided she was going to crochet a set of monogrammed initial blankets to present Char and Ash with the moment the offspring popped out. That'd be dead classy. She'd seen someone try something similar on *Sewing Bee*, except that was sewing not crochet but surely that didn't matter. It couldn't be that hard could it?

Sitting a row in front of Jemma was Szymon's new wife, Bella, proudly watching her husband onstage.

At one point she stood up, turned around, smiled from ear to ear and waved at Jemma. It seemed strange as they had never really met. She was massively tall. And there was something deeply familiar about her. Jemma just couldn't put her finger on what it was. She seemed dead friendly though. And that was all that mattered.

The atmosphere inside the Coliseum was electric. Anticipation hung in the air like the most welcome of friends. Szymon and Wiktoria walked together to the front of the stage and as a huge spotlight found them, they raised their arms aloft.

'Ladies and gentlemen, let the second *Eurowide Song Contest* begin...'